LATE NIGHTS & LOVE LINES

SINGLE DAD HOTLINE

AVERY MAXWELL

That's What She Said Publishing, Inc.

LATE NIGHTS
and *Love Lines*

ISBN: 979-8-88643-958-8 (ebook)

ISBN: 979-8-88643-959-5 (paperback)

091224

*This book is for everyone getting through life by their todays and
their tomorrows. You will find your place, your space, and your
own merry fucking meddlers.*

I promise.

*It's also for my very first pet, a black cat named Tux. Thank you
for being my inspiration for Lucky the cat, even if you did like to
crap in my bed every day when I was little.*

PLAYLIST

https://geni.us/LateNightsPlaylist

Music came to me for this story well before I wrote it.

Harmonies I couldn't place, lyrics that had soul, and songs that had a story, they were all at the heart of these characters, this town, this love story.

Each song in this playlist pulled an emotional reaction from me as I was creating these characters. It's in their soul, and now, it's for you.

Rowan went to school for music therapy, and it was therapy for these characters when they were at their lowest. I hope you enjoy this playlist as much as I loved creating it for Sebastian, Rowan, and especially little Seren.

AUTHOR NOTE

Dear Reader,

Families can be tough, and no one knows that better than Rowan Ellis. This is her story of learning to live after the trauma her dysfunctional, indifferent family caused, and learning that sometimes the best family is truly the one that you choose.

This is a story of surviving, thriving, redemption, life-long loves, and a celebration of family that chooses you.

Chosen family is the family some of us need, and I'm proud of the fictional people in Sailport Bay who gave Rowan the stability she never had, but desperately needed.

Life is all about choices, my friends, so choose love, choose kindness, choose to surround yourself with people who love you especially when your ugly is showing.

Kindness & Luvs,

Avery

1

HELLO, AGAIN

SEBASTIAN

"**M**y fart smells like fish," Kade squeals from his car seat in the back. My six-year-old has one speed—his. "I wanna fish. Can I, Daddy? Can I fish?"

Thank fuck I chose to drive from Boston to the Outer Banks overnight. I can't imagine the kinds of questions or the number of bathroom breaks we would have had to make if all three of my children were awake for the majority of the drive. And that's not even factoring in my grandfather.

My daughter groans and rolls down her window. "You can't do that in the car, Kade. It's gross."

"I can't help it, Ser. My butt likes to say wallop, wallop, toot." He laughs. "Can I fish, Daddy?"

"I'm not sure," I say steering the Range Rover over a gravel drive that's seen better days. Boston's potholes have their own zip codes, but this driveway is worse than outer space—one wrong turn and we'll be lost to a black hole.

"These places are made for fishin', kid."

I give my grandfather some side-eye even as I laugh. Unwillingly. Despite the clusterfuck my life has become,

I

he's been the one constant in every uncertain time in my life.

A weathered sign for Shoreline Adventures sits in the gravel lot at an odd angle.

"We're here," I say quietly as I park in front of the office.

A sudden rush of nostalgia washes over me as I take in the well-groomed paths to the right of the main building. Old bunkhouses line one side of the trail. At least those appear to have received a fresh coat of paint.

Tilting my head toward my grandfather, I take in his expression, but he simply smiles at the view before him.

"You never would have allowed your camp to end up like this."

When he finally faces me, his soft brown eyes twinkle with mischief and so many stories I can't begin to fathom them all.

"Spaces are a lot like people, Seb," he says gently.

"How so?" My brow furrows, so I smooth it out with my fingertips.

"They can both fall apart without a little love and care. This place will be good as new in no time though."

"You sure about that?" I chuckle, and he nods his head.

"I am. That's what we're here for, right? A little love and care will go a long way for this camp—and for your family."

Oof. His words pack a punch today.

Leaning forward, I scan the tall trees and inhale deeply. With Seren's window down, the scent of the forest melds with the salty air of the ocean I know is down one of the paths ahead of me, and an ounce of tension uncoils in my shoulders.

At least until I glance at the faces of my children in the back seat.

Kade's too young to truly understand why we've

suddenly left Massachusetts—it's a blessing and a curse, I suppose. Miles sits in the middle, his plastic smile a permanent fixture on his face these days. Seren's stoic expression burns in my gut like acid.

She's worn that impenetrable mask for months now. Gone is my shyly inquisitive girl with the soul of a musician. In her place sits a shell of a person holding a violent storm beneath her surface.

"Seren?" She lifts vacant green eyes to mine in the rearview mirror. "I hear they have an entire music room. There's even a brand new piano and a huge selection of guitars."

It only cost me a small fortune to get them all here before we arrived.

When Elijah, one of my new business partners, introduced me to his sister six months ago, I never could have envisioned we'd be on this path. Lottie Sinclair owns The Single Dad Hotline, a phone-based support team for single dads who are out of their element. But I was born to be a dad, so I never needed it—until now.

No matter how hard I try, I can't be everything to everyone. I need help. I need a nanny, and now Lottie has the best service in the country. I have no idea how Elijah roped her into helping me, but I'm thankful since her waitlist is already over a year long.

Catching my wife fucking around with my ex-best friend slash soon-to-be ex-VP of sales at Walker Meridian during Seren's middle school recital has turned our lives upside down.

My generally mild-mannered kids have been...acting out. Well, Seren has. We went through six nannies before I gave up and called in my grandfather.

Seren shrugs, then opens her door. "Thanks, Dad, but I told you." She points to her forehead. "The music died."

"It's not dead, Ser. It's sleeping," Miles says, following her from the car. "Music can't really die, it bends. Like a fishing pole. Right, Dad?"

I swear I must have swallowed razor blades—they slice my throat with each of my wife's indiscretions.

If only I could agree with Miles. But I know the heartache of having the music stop, and when it does, the silence screams with the worst kind of pain.

"Music never dies," my grandfather replies for me. "The chorus just changes is all. You'll see, Seren. It lives in you, it's a piece of you."

She nods then slams her door. Her hair flies on the breeze as she heads toward the door marked 'Office' with a green hand-painted sign.

Closing my eyes and lowering my chin to my chest, I inhale deeply, listening to the noisy silence that happens in the forest—branches rustling, birds chirping, and if I strain, I swear the ocean waves whisper to me.

I hope I've made the right decision by bringing them here for the summer. Boston was slowly killing my little girl's spirit, and in turn, killing me too. My ex-wife vanished immediately after the scandal, so she's no help. Not that she was ever overly involved in their lives, but a girl needs her mom.

"Go get things settled in there. I've got the little fisherman," my grandfather says softly, while I suck in air as though I've forgotten how to breathe. There's an ache in my chest that's been slowly gathering speed as a runaway ball of emotion threatens to decimate me. "And give her time. She's got a lot to work through. I know you're feeling all the guilt and fear of what's to come, but she's got something you never had growin' up."

Pinching the bridge of my nose, I keep my face lowered. I'm afraid to ask, but I do it anyway. "What's that?"

When he doesn't immediately respond, I lift my gaze.

"A father who will burn the world to the ground to give her a fresh start."

I'll do more than burn the world down, but I think he understands that.

———

"I THOUGHT I had another week to get everything ready," Leo says from my left as we sit on the tired front porch of the office building.

I purchased the house from him and got the kids down here as quickly as possible. As the co-owner of Shoreline Adventures, he's been working to get the camp ready for the season, and our arrival has probably thrown off his schedule. Somehow in all of this, I bought a house that shares Shoreline's beach and became a silent partner in a kiddie camp.

That's not something I ever thought I'd say, but Beck Hayes and Elijah Sinclair, the new partners in my actual business, are very convincing.

Beck said it behooved him to have me close. Who the hell says *behooved* anymore? But I get what he's saying. When Covid shut down the world, our luxury businesses— mine in corporate leasing, and his a luxury brand— suffered. The best way for us to recover is by joining our ventures. Once we do, we'll be an unstoppable team, one that will skyrocket us back to the top of the market.

But Beck seems to have trust issues, even worse than I

do, so he wants us all to be in person to prevent any chance of our merger going public to our competitors before we're ready.

I take a look around the property while Leo taps something into his phone. Everything about this place has seen better days, especially the stairs that creak with age every time I shift my weight. I've already explained that, as far as I'm concerned, this was a land deal and he can do whatever the hell he wants with the camp.

It helps that Leo's a good guy. I met him at his baby shower, of all things, when I came to meet with Beck and Elijah during my divorce.

"Sorry about this," I say for the fourth time, silently cursing the Sinclairs for not giving him the heads-up that I'd be arriving before the nanny event in a few weeks.

His laughter is easy and loud. "No worries. I've known Beck since we were kids, and he's out of his damn mind with a new baby in his house. Don't get me wrong, fatherhood suits him, but he's a bit of a tyrant when it comes to their care, so if having you here early gets him to calm the fuck down, I'm all for it."

The benefits of coming to North Carolina are twofold for me. It gets my kids out of Boston, away from the fallout over their mother's behavior. It also gets me closer to Beck Hayes and Elijah Sinclair, two people who had the ability to demolish my entire professional career if they had chosen to. Something else I have to thank my ex-friend for. Nick tied up every single one of my properties in this deal. If it goes south, or if Beck pulls out, they'll lose some money, yeah, but I'll lose everything. I never should have trusted Nick so blindly.

The only good thing he did do was introduce me to Beck and Elijah. They could have so easily turned and walked away after the scandal with my ex-wife hit the press, but instead, they chose to stand by me and my family. I'm still coming to terms with that.

I open my mouth to respond to his comment about Beck when the men in question walk around the corner. But I've never seen them like this.

Beck is holding a paint can and is covered in yellow paint. Elijah has his hands full of what appears to be cleaning supplies.

Elijah approaches me first. "I met your boys down at the beach. Kade is rolling around in the tide pools pretending to be a shark."

My chest expands with warmth. At least one of them is happy. "Sounds about right. He's got a lot of energy, but he's a good kid."

Beck drops his paint can on the deck, then approaches us slowly with his hands in his pockets and his head bowed.

Strange. He's always been a hard one to read, but his utter confidence has never been in question.

"The house is all set," Beck says to no one in particular. "We cleared the trail from the house to camp last week so the kids can play at the beach or over here during the day doing...camp things." He frowns as if the idea of a summer camp confounds him. "The crew will be here over the next week getting everything finished for the campers, but there's enough to keep your kids entertained for now. Did Leo show you the house yet?"

"I've never met anyone who dropped four million on a beach house without ever stepping foot in it." Leo chuckles.

"I'd have paid double if it meant getting my kids out of Boston," I mutter without thinking, and my shoulders tense.

Leo simply pats me on the back. "I understand the need for do-overs, and I do appreciate the partnership. You taking that property off my hands while sharing the land is why I can get this camp up and running."

I hadn't intended to start another partnership in this small town, especially not one that makes me a silent owner of a children's camp, but life, and my grandfather, have a funny way of making shit happen.

"I told you I would have bought in," Beck grumbles.

Leo chuckles. "Now you don't have to."

Beck looks at me again. "Anyway, my wife was over at your place for all the furniture deliveries, but she vetoed your linens."

Why would a woman I've never met have an opinion about my sheets and towels?

"Stella said they were too itchy," he continues, "and the kids need something soft. She wanted their rooms to be welcoming or something. Listen, she was a kindergarten teacher in a former life. I just do what she says." He tugs on the back of his neck as if he's uncomfortable with this conversation.

"Thank you?" I appreciate the help, but everyone here— even the people, like Stella, I haven't met yet—has gone above and beyond what I expected for a corporate deal. Making sure kids are comfortable is something you do for friends and family, not a new business partner.

"I'm sorry to hear about your divorce...and all that followed it," he says.

And there it is. Pity. I school my features.

"The divorce was painless," I lie. "We both come from money so the prenups were ironclad."

"I doubt that, but I've lived through deceit," Beck says gruffly. Now he has my attention. The scandals with his family have never been confirmed, but rumors always fly in our circle. "And I have girls at home who understand all too well how to survive. Kids shouldn't have to deal with that kind of shit," he says angrily. "I should tell you I'm not here to get into your personal business, but...well, it happens in small towns. Especially Sailport Bay, but also in this partnership of ours. Walker Meridian and Hayes Sinclair—Crystal Waters are now forever tied together, and we're here to help with whatever you need."

"Why?" Every other recent business transaction I've had has ended with a handshake or unsigned contract, thanks to Nick's machinations. Beck is making this feel personal, pushing my fears to the forefront.

"Because professionally our success is now tied to yours, and personally, I know what it's like to fight for your kids, your company, and an asshole trying to take it all away from you."

Okay, so they're not only my partners but the welcome wagon—got it.

Meridian Waters, the combining of two powerhouse companies, pushes the boundaries of luxury investments. That's what the PR release will say, if I can get our investors back.

And once again, my mood takes a nosedive.

"Nick won't be with my company much longer," I say.

Beck's brows raise. "I'd question your decision-making abilities if he were."

Thank fuck he wasn't the factor that sold them. My shoulders drop about three inches.

"Listen, Sebastian. Nick may have brought us this deal, but we agreed because of you—it was your name on that letterhead, your reputation we were interested in. But we need assurances that Nick isn't going to fuck us," Elijah says.

"You have my word." It must be the nostalgia of summer camp that has me twisting my fingers behind my back as though I'm ten years old again, and I silently send up a prayer that I can follow through with this particular promise.

Elijah grins, and Beck holds out his hand. "Welcome to Sailport Bay, then. We'll work out of my home office once you've got your kids settled. I've had personal experience with internal sabotage. I think it's best if we keep the details on lockdown until we've closed the deal."

I should be pissed that he believes I've lost control of my company, but I'd be just as careful if I were him.

Dropping our handshake, I say, "My CFO, Alexei Stepanov, will be my only contact on this deal."

Beck's jaw twitches, displaying his hesitancy.

"I've known Alexei since I was in diapers. If anything were to happen to me, he'll be my children's guardian, so when I say I trust him with my life, believe it."

Something similar to respect sparks in Beck's eyes.

"Understood," he says.

The rumble of a sputtering engine cuts the silence, and we all watch as dust kicks up behind a beat-up light blue Jeep blasting music my daughter would love.

"She does like to make an entrance." Elijah chuckles.

"Who?" I ask.

The Jeep lurches to a stop, and a plume of smoke billows from the hood.

I don't move as the driver's door opens and tiny pink Chuck Taylors hit the ground followed by long, tanned legs that disappear into denim cutoff shorts as she bends over, out of view, and my body pitches forward as if her actions are tied directly to my reactions.

When she stands up to scan her surroundings, familiarity knocks the air from my lungs. A sudden surge of sweat trickles down my forehead, while my chest expands and falls as though I've lost the ability to take a full breath at the sight of dirty blond hair whipping in the wind.

Then she smiles with a shrug and a wave in my general direction, and it drowns me in her orbit.

Peach.

My life just went from messy as hell to fucking imploding in the span of a smile.

2

BLOWING UP THE WORLD AS WE KNOW IT

ROWAN

I step onto the gravel lot as Junebug sighs a cloud of thick black smoke. The engine chokes out a spluttering garbled noise, as though it's her last breath, and a pang in my chest has me rubbing my knuckles over my sternum.

My blood pressure spikes as I take it all in.

I kick the tires, but not out of frustration. No, what's happening is fear—forced change tends to bring it out in me, and I'm not in the habit of lying to myself about what my gut has to tell me, but I'm not ready to lose Junebug yet either.

"You've got one more fix in you, Junebug, you have to. Knock on wood." I knock against her tire twice because it's the closest thing to me. Wood, rubber, it's all the same.

A deep, rumbling chuckle floats through the fresh air, and I mutter a curse only loud enough for me to hear. Just my luck, I had an audience for that little outburst. Petting Junebug's tire one more time, I give her a silent apology, then lift a shining bright smile toward the laughter.

Four men stand at the bottom of the steps, staring in my direction. I recognize Lottie's brother, Elijah, but it's the man standing next to him that sends goosebumps scattering across my body.

Even with the distance separating us, the intensity of his stare licks at my skin, but it's the way he scratches behind his ear, so familiar, that has my lungs drop-kicking my ribs. It's as though he's reaching through space and time to hold me hostage with the determined expression that forms a little crease in the center of his forehead.

Is that...? No, Jesus, Rowan. One phone call with Pappy and the secret fantasies that got me through my scariest days keep filtering into my reality.

Good grief. Pappy would have a field day if he knew the only memory I have of the day my world collapsed that isn't covered in thorns is of his own freaking grandson.

The wind shoves my hair in my face, obscuring my vision for a moment. When I tuck it behind my ear and peer back at the men, the one causing all the uncomfortable skin sizzling has turned away and is walking into the woods.

Well, now we know that shot of—whatever that was— was one-sided. Walk away, big guy, walk away. Instinct tells me he's a complication I definitely don't need in my life. Now, or ever.

Elijah says something to the other two men, so I take my time approaching them, happy it's gravel beneath my feet so I don't have to constantly keep an eye out for cracks —the childish superstition about breaking mother's back always singsongs like a scary clown in the back of my mind.

The rich scent of the trees and the delicious heat of the sun remind me of the good times I had in my childhood. The weeks at summer camp before everything changed.

A shiver works down my spine, so I tilt my gaze to the treetops and decide it's the pollen making it hard to breathe, not the memories, and march my uneasy not-at-all emotional ass right up to them.

"Right on time, Rowan," Elijah says as I approach the office. Before I realize his intent, he pulls me into a hug. This man is way too touchy-feely for my liking—he's a carbon copy of his freaking sister and it's annoying. Who hugs every person they meet?

I pat his arms lightly and pull away.

"Hey, Eli. Where's Lottie?" I ask.

He peers down at me with a frown. "Didn't she tell you?"

Goddammit, Lottie. She may be my only friend, but she'll do whatever it takes to get what she wants. "Tell me what?"

Elijah curses out of the side of his mouth. "Well, you know about the Camp Nanny event in a few weeks."

"Yes, and?" I ask, squaring my shoulders to his. I'm aware that she's throwing Camp Nanny to launch the nanny side of her business. It's been a ton of work, and I'm proud of her. It's why I'm here so early—to help wherever she needs me leading up to it.

"And...you agreed to come early to help her—okay, me, you're helping me." He backs away quickly with his hands raised.

"Helping you with what?" My jaw ticks as I clench it.

The other two men are slowly backing up too, as if they're trying to make a sneaky escape.

"Well, this is my business partner, Beck Hayes." The tall man in shorts stops with one foot on the porch steps and lifts a hand. "And this is Leo, he owns the camp."

Beck radiates a *leave me alone* aura, but Leo seems more at ease with his yogi-surfer vibe.

"Elijah," I grind out. "What is the favor?"

"We have this huge deal in the works and our new partner's family literally crashed and burned. He needs help with his kids until Lottie can set him up with a permanent nanny at the date-a-nanny event."

"It's a meet and greet for nannies and families, not a date-a-nanny event," I growl.

His jackass smirk slowly morphs into a grin.

"Right. Well, we have a billion-dollar deal on the table, and if we don't get this guy some help his business will go under, which means our business will go under, so I may have strong-armed Lottie into helping us."

"You mean you got Lottie to trick me into helping you."

"Semantics, babe. If Lottie knew what the hell to do with kids, I'd have gotten her to do it, but...well, you know Lottie."

Yeah, I do. She had a million-dollar idea, but she's also possibly the most child-phobic person I've ever met. She's the brains behind The Single Dad Hotline, while people like me make it work.

"I promise, we're planning to make this worth your while, and since that death trap you refuse to give up on shit the bed, we'll start there."

"Junebug is not a death trap, and now you're just trying to change the subject. What is it you all tricked me here for?"

Leo and Beck grimace in unison.

"There are three kids..."

I narrow my eyes, and my right hand reflexively begins to twist the black tourmaline and rose quartz bracelets around my left wrist.

"It's only for three weeks, four tops. Okay, maybe five. Definitely two weeks with just them, one week helping them navigate camp, then one week, maybe more, until hopefully their new nanny will start." He holds up his hands with crossed fingers.

My foot starts tapping an annoyed rhythm into the dirt beneath me. Come on, black tourmaline. If your healing crystal power's going to work, now's the time to take the negative energy.

I peek down at my wrist. Nothing. I'm not even calmer. That's what I get for believing in crystals.

"Please, Rowan. You'd really be helping us all out, especially our new partner's family. They've had a rough go of it recently."

I do love helping families, swooping in to support them through big changes in their lives, and then slipping out as soon as they're back on their feet. I do anything and everything I can for them—except stay. But everything about this situation is screaming at me to run. These people are too connected, too close to my everyday life, and I go out of my way to keep clear boundaries in place at all times.

It's why The Single Dad Hotline has been so perfect for me—very rarely do people expect me to stay, and now Lottie, my friend and boss, has even made that a rule of my employment—I'm temporary. The fill-in. The substitute. The one who moves on at the end of the week.

"Lottie has a proposition for expansion that will be very beneficial for you, and my beach house will be open to you for an entire year." Elijah trips over himself to get the words out.

Someone's gone to a lot of trouble planning this little scheme.

My toe stops bouncing. Lottie said that she had something huge to discuss with me, but it's his personal concessions that make the itchy sensations in my palms evaporate as quickly as they came.

"You'll let me have access to a beachfront property for an entire year if I nanny for your partner for three weeks? That seems excessive. What's wrong with him? Are his kids the spawn of the devil? There's no way you're going to all this trouble to get me to babysit for a couple of weeks."

"It's important." Elijah shrugs as though it's no big deal, but now, up close, his stress shows in the wrinkles around his squinting eyes. I'm going to freaking cave because I understand this kind of duress. I really do get a sense of fulfillment from helping people. "Lottie said based on both of your personality tests that you're the best fit and honestly, you're the only one I trust."

Damn him and his stupid trust. I may not trust others freely, but I work hard to make sure those close to me can always count on me.

"I'll do it under one condition."

Leo and Beck exhale a windstorm between the two of them.

"What's that?" Elijah asks with a grin sliding back into place.

"I get the house whenever I want it this year, and you agree to host two events for The Single Dad Hotline, using your fancy-schmancy contacts at your fancy-schmancy spas for Lottie when she expands to single moms next year. The nanny program will be in full swing by then too."

Lottie has mentioned numerous times that Elijah's company owns the fanciest spas in the world—not that I've ever been—and that means the people who go to them have the kind of money that can afford Lottie's services.

"You have me over a barrel and can ask for anything you want, but you ask for something for my sister instead? You do remember that she grew up with the same silver spoon in her mouth that I did, yes?"

"I do. But she's the one who keeps my lights on. So do we have a deal?"

He shakes his head. "Deal. Leo, the camp owner, will fill you in and give you directions to the house. Beck and I have to get cleaned up for a meeting."

He hugs me tightly even as I press against his chest. I have a love-hate relationship with his brotherly affection, but finally, he releases me and walks away, and I shake off the heebie-jeebies.

"The Sinclairs are great," Leo says, walking up the steps and holding the door open for me when it's just the two of us. "But neither of them is cut out for the woods, so please tell me you've at least spent some time camping. Otherwise this nanny event is going to be a giant pain in my ass."

Now it's my turn to laugh. Lottie is a lot of things, but outdoorsy she's not.

"What did she do, fall into poison ivy or something when she was here last week?"

As I enter the building, I find a very large sleeping black freaking cat, and a groan escapes from deep in my chest.

Leo chuckles. "No, luckily the previous owner had the poison ivy removed last summer. But, last I heard, Lottie's struggling with the idea of sharing a communal bathroom, and it may have impacted her arrival time. That's Lucky," he says, pointing to the superstition of all superstitions. "You'll see a lot of him. He splits his time between here and the house." He shrugs as though that's normal.

"Good grief," I grumble. I'll ignore this damn menace of a cat for as long as humanly possible. "Any idea when Lottie's planning to show up?"

He walks around the counter to a numbered pegboard display of keys. "Your guess is as good as mine, but you'll be lucky to even get her into a cabin when she does show up, so be prepared to do the heavy lifting."

His grin tells me he's going to love torturing her. "My fiancée told me I can't give her too much shit, but with Lottie, I won't have to try very hard. She hates it here. I'm not sure why she thought this was a good place for a kickoff."

My face scrunches up, and I close my eyes. "That was my idea." Camp was my safe space growing up, at least until they took it away from me like everything else.

His laughter is rich and fills the room. "You and I are going to get along just fine. I haven't known the family all that long, but I know they'll be happy to have you. They bought the property on the other side of camp. You're welcome to bring the kids here anytime."

Leo's fingers trace over numbers on the board, and my gaze narrows in on the little pegs as he passes them.

He wouldn't.

"Here it is. Twenty-two Coastal Drive. The kids seem nice too. The oldest, a girl, is...struggling, I think. She didn't talk much when she was in here earlier."

Teenage assholery. This should be fun.

"If you need anything, I'll be around, getting the camp in shape. It needs a lot of work, but when I'm done, it's going to be amazing. Anyway, the fastest route to the house is the Tabby Trail. It runs behind the activities center and drops you right at the property." He points to the side of the building. "Go outside and take a left, you can't miss it."

The key scorches my palm. Freaking twenty-two. If I adopt one more superstition, I might need to seek out a support group, but the number twenty-two always, always, ends with heartache. It's happened too often to be coincidence, and now my fight-or-flight is kicking into high gear.

Nothing good will come from this.

"Thanks," I mutter, squeezing the key into my palm, then pushing open the screen door while trying to block out all the other times the number twenty-two has filleted me wide open.

"Nice to meet you, Rowan."

I pause, holding the door open with my finger, and he grins.

"I'll see you tonight. My fiancée will be here, and so will Beck's wife, and all the camp staff. We're having a little welcome party at the dining hall followed by a bonfire."

Wonderful.

I nod, then let the screen door slam with a deafening crack that makes me feel marginally better. Examining my surroundings, I follow his directions to the left of the building.

I'll give it to Leo—the trails are carefully marked, and I find the Tabby Trail easily. Birds chirp overhead and the tree leaves rustle in the breeze.

Removing my phone from my back pocket, I open the camera app and point it to the sky. The trees create a canopy that the sun shines through, so I lower myself to one knee for a better angle that captures the sky and the sign marking the trail. This will be a perfect shot for Insta.

Not that anyone follows what I post. No one cares enough, but it's not for them. These memories are for me. Adding a few filters, I press Done and stand back up.

It takes less than a second to realize I'm not alone.

Meow.

The freaking cat. I refuse to look down because if I do and I find I have a cat tailing me, a black cat at that, I'll have to soak myself in holy water.

Meow, Lucky says again, because I know it's Lucky, and

he's so insistent this time that I stomp my foot. He doesn't even scamper away. No, this asshole sits between my feet as though he has every right to smear his bad luck all over me.

"I don't need any more bad luck, Lucky. Can't you follow someone else home?" I growl.

Meow. The furry beast figure eights around my ankles.

Dropping down into a squat, I pet the little fucker, then try to shoo him on his way, but his beady eyes follow me as I walk along the path. He and I have unfinished business—I sense it.

Something crackles in the bushes, and Lucky, the scaredy-cat, runs off, leaving me with my whispering trees.

Closing my eyes, I tilt my face to the sky and inhale deeply. It's been years since I've spent any time in the woods —not since Pappy's camp—and those were the happiest times of my life.

I used to be able to hear music in my head out here that no one else could hear. It was magical. Now when I listen, all I hear is noise—voices, accusations, and threats have replaced the melodies in my mind. It's cruel, really, but that's life.

Still no music. I sigh and open my eyes, then head down the trail.

The past hijacks my mind as I walk, flooding me with memories. It feels so real that when the activities center comes into view and a sad chorus I recognize hits my ears, I nearly trip over my own feet. The melody creates a riot in my mind that seizes control of all my limbs.

This song is a piece of me that died years ago. The melody is ingrained in the fiber of my very being because I'm the one who wrote it. It's the song that ended my life as I knew it.

Trembling, I move forward with no intention of doing so, but this song, it calls to me through the pain.

Who's playing it? I haven't touched this song since I was a teenager. The key is off, and she's only repeating the chorus, then adding her own words, but that chorus? Those words were once the touchstone of my life.

I slip through the open door, shocked to find a tiny girl sitting at the piano with hunched shoulders. The sadness pours off her just as it used to me. If it weren't for her dark hair, this little girl could be me.

I'm staring at a ghost.

My body glides through the space as though each strike of a chord is pulling me closer, and when I'm able to reach the keys, I slide into place beside her without saying a word.

The little girl stops playing but doesn't look at me. Her anger and sadness assault me like tiny electric shocks that shoot from her arm hair and into mine.

She's hurting. It's there in her hunched shoulders and arms tucked tightly against her ribs.

Without permission, I place my fingers on the keys—it's a homecoming. "You almost had it. The tempo for the chorus is a little faster. Let every keystroke invoke anger for what's been lost."

Closing my eyes, I play the song as it was meant to be played, and suddenly, I'm a little girl again, playing to a forest full of campers who have yet to experience the pain that's suffocating me.

Hope is the line between happiness and me.
The instilled fears,
They still cause tears.
'Cause I must confess,
You broke me like all the rest.

Stained glass shines,
But not for me.
Now 'they' speak and their whispers scream,
The pointed fingers of sinner's sins.
Because you broke me just like stained glass,
Then left before I could shine.
Hope is the line between happiness and me.

My fingers rest on the last keys, my eyes remain closed, and my heart beats angrily, each thud stabbing at an old wound.

"How—how..." the little girl to my left stutters. "I only know three lines of the chorus."

"It's called 'Lullaby to Loneliness,'" I tell her.

"But how do you know it? My dad could never remember the whole thing, only a few words, but he hums the chorus when he's lost in thought. He said a little girl...he said."

Dread settles into my bones. Only three people paid me any attention that day, and they're all related. It's *him*.

"Sebastian's world fell apart." Pappy's words from our last conversation ring loudly in my ears.

There's no way they're here. I don't believe in coincidence. There's good luck and there's bad, and it's a toss-up which side you'll end up on. Someone, maybe this little girl's dad, just happened to be a random camper—the same as me. That's the only reasonable explanation.

"I wrote this song when I was a teenager," I finally say, dragging my gaze to hers. Our eyes meet and my stomach drops out. My soul understands the stories hiding behind her beautiful green orbs.

So, not a random stranger—I've never forgotten his eyes, and this little girl is the spitting image of her father.

Sweat pools in very uncomfortable places. Maybe there's good luck, bad luck, and then Pappy.

Right. Time to get the hell out of dodge. Forget what I told Elijah, this can't happen. I'll never willingly put myself in the position of caring too much again, and this family, the one who once showed me kindness in the violence of my life, is the one thing left in this world that could break me.

"It's so much better the way you sing it," she says quietly. Too quietly, ghostly, as if the words are pulled from her soul without her permission. "I've been trying to figure it out on my own. My dad used to sing it to me when I was little, but he made up his own words and it changed all the time. His attempt was mid at best, so it never felt right—except the chorus."

Well, shit. And also, what a strange choice to sing to a baby.

"What you were playing, you did that? On your own?" I scoot back a bit, trying to gauge her age. She's probably only a few years younger than I was when I wrote it.

She nods and picks at a fingernail on her left hand.

"You did it from what? Lyrics? Can you sing them for me?" What are you doing, Rowan? It doesn't matter. None of this matters. You need to get out of here before history wraps its grimy little paws around you and ties you to itself.

The little girl opens her mouth and sings my words with her own special twist.

"Because you broke me just like stained glass, then left before I could shine. Hope is that line between happiness and me." She bites the corner of her lip. "Well, that's how he always sang it, but it wasn't right, was it?"

I'm shaking my head and completely unable to force air into my lungs, but she's good. Really good.

"Ah, you were close." The words are pinched. My throat aches. Maybe I'm coming down with strep throat.

"Huh," she says with a roll of her shoulders. "He said he only heard it once, so I guess his memory isn't complete shit."

"You're very talented," I say, directing the conversation away from her father, then lifting myself off the bench.

Unease has me biting down on my bottom lip, and it's reflected in the way this little girl curls in on herself. Again, I'm struck by how much she reminds me of myself at this age. It has to be the camp atmosphere. That's the only similarity. I'm so on edge, I'm seeing things where they don't belong.

She lowers her chin to avert her gaze. "So," she says with discomfort clouding her tone. "You're Rowan?"

The air whooshes from my lungs, and I nearly topple over. "Uh-huh."

"Well, you don't look like you want to see my dad any more than I do, so don't worry. He's in a meeting."

How the heck do I process the relief that washes through me with that admission? I love Pappy, and Pappy loves his grandson, but it's the kind of love that grows roots, and I know better than anyone that all roots die eventually.

"But Pappy sure does talk about you a lot. He'll be happy to see you."

"What?" The walls tunnel in around me.

I'd bet my last cent that Pappy is behind this. This shit doesn't just happen, and it certainly doesn't happen to women like me.

"Yup, he's at the house with my brothers." She keeps talking while sweat collects into a stream down my spine. "The house is fine, but I have to participate in some bullshit camp activities with nine other girls for an entire week."

The adult in me screams that I should say something about her swearing, but twelve-year-old me understands. I allow my lips to tilt into a slight grin.

"I'm Seren, by the way. Thanks for sharing your song, it's a flex for sure. But don't worry, I'm not going to bug you. The last freaking thing I want right now is a nanny, so you're clear."

Nanny. Oh my God. I'm her nanny.

She slams the lid down on the piano and waltzes out of the cabin as though she didn't just shoot my carefully formed boundaries right to hell.

Danger has never looked so innocent.

3

FUCKING PERVERT
SEBASTIAN

I walk the trails without searching for a destination. That woman is a complication I shouldn't want or need, but I can't rid my mind of the full-body shiver I experienced when we made eye contact.

For one brief moment in time, I was the old me, the one who believed in true love and happily ever afters. For fuck's sake, when I was Miles's age, my life goal was to fall in love, have a family, the white picket fence—everything my father never gave me.

One glance at a stranger today had that sensation of pureness and love flowing through my veins.

I blame my ex, Mya, for fucking everything up.

Is it all her fault though?

If I could stab my own conscience, I would. Of course it's her fault. She fucked my best friend and VP, not me. I've always been faithful.

My phone vibrates in my hand, and I almost drop it.

Alexei: You doing okay?

Before answering, I scroll through my messages. It's something I've been doing obsessively since Mya left. Not for me, but with an overwhelming sense of sadness I have for my children. How can she go no-contact with our kids? At least the boys have stopped asking for her every night. That was like getting kicked in the nuts over and over again.

Seren made her position perfectly clear when she blocked her mother, but the boys aren't carrying that same rage, at least not yet, and their innocent questions electrocute my heart when I'm least expecting it.

Me: Fine. You on your way?

I'd told him he didn't need to come, but he wanted to meet with Elijah in person.

Alexei: Yes. Meeting's set for 10 tomorrow.

Alexei: How's Seren?

This. This is why I keep the womanizing prick around. He always has my back, and he loves my kids with a fierceness most children will never experience. He once said it's because he never intends to have his own children and showering mine with all his love ensures it doesn't fester in his body and make him soft.

He's an idiot.

Me: I'm giving her space to explore the camp.

Alexei: In the woods? Is that safe?

Me: You know that I've successfully parented for twelve whole years now, right?

Me: She knows not to leave the camp boundaries.

Me: I promise we'll be fine.

Alexei: …

A note of music flutters on the wind, tickling a memory I can't catch. Pocketing my phone, I walk farther down the trail and hear another note, followed by another that siphons the breath from my lungs.

Did Seren find the piano? Fuck, please let that be her playing.

I pick up my pace, and a large building comes into view around the next corner. The front door is propped open, but I walk around to the windows on the side so I don't disturb her. Even if she only ever plays for herself, I want her to play —I need her to play again.

It's been months since she's touched the piano at home. Before the divorce, there wasn't a day since she started taking lessons that she hadn't played…something.

The piano stops and salty emotions clog my throat when I hear Seren sing. But as I peer through the window, my body tenses and my mind whirls with questions. She's singing in front of that woman—no, she's singing to her.

Seren won't even hum in front of me, but she's opened her soul to this stranger.

Blood wooshes in my ears when she finishes, and I miss what the woman said.

"So, you're Rowan?" Seren's words kick me in the chest, and suddenly I'm freefalling without a net to catch me.

Rowan. Peach. Fuck.

Spinning away from the window, I press my back into the wall of the cabin. Visions of a broken Rowan have haunted my dreams for years. It's always made me feel like a fucking pervert, even if there was nothing sexual about those dreams. What grown-ass man dreams about a childhood friend from a moment in time twenty-five years ago?

"Don't run." I hold out my hands so I don't scare the girl sitting beside the dock. I think she scares easily, like my neighbor's puppy. "How old are you?"

Her little chin tilts to the sky. "Eight," she says, folding her arms in front of her belly. She's wearing a James and the Giant Peach *T-shirt but looks like that* Jane of the Jungle *cartoon I watched with her wild blond hair that's falling out of its braid.*

"I'm ten," I tell her proudly, and suddenly I'm pretty sure I'm the giant and it's my job to protect her. "This is my grandparents' camp. Is it your first time here?"

She nods, then gasps, and my chest gets itchy.

"What's wrong?" I ask, moving closer to her.

When she lifts her face to mine, my itchy chest crawls into my throat.

"Nothing." She smiles. She has a really nice smile. "A ladybug landed on me. That's good luck."

She's staring at her shoulder where the red and black bug crawls, but I just want to make her smile again.

The camp bell rings loudly. It's time for the next activity, but now her smile stretches all the way to her eyes, and I don't move.

"An angel just got its wings," she says, standing. "When you hear a bell, that's how you know. Sometimes there's a lot of angels." Her hands protect the ladybug on her shoulder as she walks away from me.

"Hey," I call after her. "What's your name?"

She doesn't hear me because she's talking to the ladybug, but she waves at me distractedly.

"Bye, Peach," I call after her.

"Her name is Rowan," Pappy says, scaring me so much I almost fall into the lake.

"Peach," I repeat, and he chuckles. "I'm going to marry that girl someday."

But she's not that little girl anymore. She's fucking hot and seems to have an instant connection with my daughter who is quickly slipping through my fingers.

Jesus Christ.

She's my nanny.

I'm going to kill my grandfather.

There's a snap at the front of the building, followed by a screen door screeching open, then slamming shut. I catch a glimpse of Seren's raven hair as she rounds the corner. I should go after her. I should check in. I should do something other than peer through the open window again.

Rowan stands perfectly still, her fingers resting on the closed fallboard, but she stares straight ahead as if caught in a memory. Leaning on the window frame, I wait, hoping she'll play again. When she doesn't, I announce myself.

"You still play beautifully."

She flinches, removes her hands, and slowly turns my way. When we make eye contact, she's wearing a receptionist's smile—it's not real.

"I don't, actually. I haven't played in years."

Suddenly I'm haunted by the memory of the last time I saw her.

She'd been having a panic attack on stage, so I joined her. I sat on the bench next to her and told her I'd flip her music for her. I had no idea she played everything from memory. As soon as she started her performance, I was transfixed, as was every other person at camp.

Until her narcissistic stepsister began to screech over Rowan's performance. Halfway through her song, Rowan was dragged offstage by a man I later found out was her stepfather—a man so consumed by appearances he worried Rowan's pain and her stepsister's outbursts would reflect poorly on him.

The stepsister's face as Rowan was carried off the stage like a ragdoll is something I'll never forget—it was pure evil, and I'd never felt so hopeless.

Rowan didn't return to camp after that.

But I know Pappy kept in touch with her. Over the years, he's given me bits and pieces of her life. Tiny ties that kept up my interest in her, but he never pushed. He's been a silent pillar for so many of his campers over the years, but Rowan has always been different.

He has an intuition about people that's uncanny. It's why I never understood how he ever allowed my mother to get tangled up with my father. Surely Pappy knew he was bad news from the beginning. When I've asked him about it though, he only shrugs and says you can lead a horse to water, but you can't make them drink.

I would have made Seren take the freaking drink.

"Are you okay?" Rowan asks. Shit. I've been staring at her open-mouthed and unblinking this entire time.

"What do you mean you don't play anymore?" Music is a part of her.

"The piano I had at home was destroyed." She shrugs. "I started playing again in college but then, well, I grew up."

There's so much to unpack in that statement, unease spreads through my veins—music is in her soul. I knew that the second I found her hiding at the pavilion with a keyboard when she was eleven.

Random memories, snippets in time flood my mind faster than an avalanche. All the innocent moments I'd been drawn to her over a handful of summers—a need to ease the pain that surrounded her—it hits me again now.

"What about now?" I ask in an attempt to tame my wild thoughts and keep us on track.

"Some things in life are best left as a memory." It's a nonanswer, and when she raises a brow at me, it's clear that's all she'll give me. "Are you going to keep standing at the window, or would you like to come in so we can have a proper conversation? Apparently, I'm your interim nanny."

My shoulders shake with silent laughter. She's blunt—she always was. It's refreshing to see that some things never change. "What are the chances that Pappy is behind this?"

Rowan frowns. "It's an almost certainty."

Shaking my head, I gnaw on my bottom lip. "It does feel like a scheme he'd dream up."

Her face softens. "So you don't believe in coincidences either?"

"No," I say, more harshly than I intended. "Believing in fairy tales is what landed me in this position in the first place."

"Okay." She glides toward the door without another word.

Is that it? She's just walking away—

I'm scratching the side of my head when Rowan walks around the building and plops down in the dirt, exactly as she did when we were kids, resting her back against the building. The instant she peers up at me with those big brown eyes that always tugged at my heart, I know I'm in a lot of fucking trouble.

"It's good to see you, Peach."

———

WE SPENT an hour going over logistics, but it passed in a flash. Her scent is still imprinted in my mind, and now I want fucking roses everywhere I go. What would it take to line the paths with rosebushes?

God, I'm an idiot.

The trail we're following opens up to the ocean, and she stops so suddenly I nearly crash into her.

"You okay?" I ask, surreptitiously scanning the sand in front of her for something ready to strike. I'm not even sure what I'm looking for if I'm being honest. A crab?

"Yeah." We stand side by side, close enough to feel her shoulders unfurl like a yoga mat as she exhales deeply. "The beach is my happy place. I'm never as calm as I am here. I wish I were able to visit it more often."

I'm still studying her face when a chorus of "Daddy!" wakes me from the surreal bubble I'm in.

Kade kicks up sand as he sprints toward us. Miles runs beside him with his hands outstretched as though he's ready to catch his little brother when he inevitably falls.

"Miles is protective," Rowan observes.

"He's a peacemaker, but yeah, he loves his little brother."

She eyes me curiously but says nothing as my boys wrap their arms around my legs.

"We saw sharks, and dinosaurs, and snails, and kites. I swam in a big wave and I'm going to be a surfer when I grow up." Kade's excitement for life is infectious. "Right, Miles? Right?"

"Right, buddy," Miles says with an indulgent quirk of his lips. He's much too old for his eight years.

"Are you having fun?" I ask Miles.

His pasted-on smile, a permanent fixture lately, lifts at the corners. I wish I could get my happy little man back—the one who didn't fake his emotions to make everyone around him comfortable. "Pappy promised me three scoops of ice cream if I kept Kade from diving into the waves without him."

"That sounds about right. At least he knows that at seventy-plus years old, he's in no position to dive into the waves to rescue a curious six-year-old." I grin at my little boy.

"Pappy did good watching us," Miles says, then dusts off his hands in the same no-nonsense way my grandfather does.

"Pappy's a stubborn old mule who believes he's still in his prime," Rowan mutters, then drops to her knees in the sand while Miles and I gape at her.

"Rowan, this is Miles and Kade," I say, pointing to the boys.

"Hello, Walker boys. My name's Rowan, and I'll be hanging out with you for a bit if that's okay with you?"

Kade pinches his face as though he's in deep thought. "Do you like bugs?"

"I eat them for breakfast," she replies without a moment of hesitation.

A bark of laughter escapes me.

"No, you do not," Kade says with his mouth gaping in between words. "What about snakes and mud?"

"Snakes and mud together or on their own?" Rowan tilts her head as she nudges the ball back to his court.

Kade's feeding off the silliness, and he scratches the back of his neck as if this is the most important question of his life even as his feet dance in the sand.

When was the last time anyone simply accepted my youngest's energy and vivid imagination? Even his own mother was exasperated by him most of the time.

"On their own," he says with a serious nod of his head.

"Well." Rowan sits back on her heels, pure sunshine radiating from her mischievous expression. "I prefer my snakes behind glass, but mud can make for excellent spa days."

Miles inches closer to me. It would seem he's as curious about my childhood friend as I am, but he's still partially hidden by my side, so I wrap an arm around his shoulder. We breathe deeply and in sync, the salt air settling into my bones.

"You play in the mud?" Because Kade can't do anything with subtlety, his skepticism shows in his comically raised brows and impossibly wide eyes.

"Sure thing, kid. I don't mind getting dirty." Rowan places her hands in the sand, then leans around my legs to address Miles. "What do you like to do?"

He shrugs. "Whatever Kade and Seren want to do."

She sits back on her heels and dusts the sand off her hands before placing them on her thighs and rolling her shoulders forward as though she's creating a bubble around herself. Is she pulling back for herself or for my boys? "What if they were busy? What's the one thing you want to do this summer?" Rowan watches him closely but allows Miles to make the first move.

As his shoulders hover around his ears, parental guilt rolls over and lodges itself in my throat. What does he want to do, and why the fuck haven't I asked him that myself?

"I heard you can find treasure on the beach sometimes," he says shyly. His feet move an inch in her direction.

"Treasure hunting it is! I'm sure we can find some metal

detectors, too." Rowan's voice is almost cheery, but she still keeps that bubble of space around herself.

Kade is a tiny wrecking ball who has no use for personal space, and I can't wait to see how he'll break down that wall she's putting up.

Miles takes half a step forward and scans Rowan's face. A silent conversation drags out between them, but no one moves.

Her body language relaxes, and her face is kind when she finally holds out her hand to my little man. He tentatively places his palm in hers. "It's nice to meet you, Miles." She lowers her face and whispers conspiratorially, "I keep my promises, and I never promise something I can't follow through on."

My fist clenches against my sternum when a shooting pain lances my chest just as Pappy shuffles toward us from the water's edge.

"How do you feel about spending some time with me for a few weeks?" she asks him. In fact, everything she's done so far seems to give him the power. What would she do if he said no?

"Sure," Miles says pleasantly, but his tone isn't sure at all.

"It's about damn time, Row." There's a fondness in my grandfather's tone that's generally reserved for my kids, and it tells me everything I've always suspected about Rowan Ellis—he loves her as if she's his own flesh and blood.

"Pappy," she sighs. Her expression opens, and for one moment in time, she's the frightened little girl she once was, but as quickly as it came, she shutters it behind a smile that will fool everyone.

Everyone but me.

$$4$$

LOVE LINES ARE JUST MIXED SIGNALS

ROWAN

"You look good, kid. It's been too long." The emotion in Pappy's voice tugs at those heartstrings I've spent years trying to cauterize, so I stare straight ahead and focus on the waves as they lap at the shore. Sebastian and the boys headed back to the house, so it's just Pappy and me out here now.

We talk a few times a year, mostly on our birthdays, plus he calls me on March twenty-second—the date is a reminder that my family will never hurt me again. When my stepfather pulled me out of camp that last summer, I secretly sent Pappy letters to stay in touch. We switched to phones once I turned eighteen and finally had access to a phone. But lately, he's been calling more often, and it's unnerving to me.

Pappy is as close to family as I've ever had, but even he's kept at arm's length, just in case.

The last time I saw him in person, not on FaceTime, was at my college graduation—May twenty-second. I hadn't invited him, but like every other major event, he presided over it as my stoic guardian. He took me out to dinner that night, and it was the last time I ever let him see me cry.

I'd told him that Jake and I weren't together anymore, but not why we'd split up. So when I refused his offer to drive me home, he reluctantly took me to the parking lot where Junebug was waiting—and he learned another of my secrets.

The next day, he signed a lease for my first solo apartment. It's the only time he's ever been harsh with me. He hadn't known I was living in my Jeep again until he dropped me off, but my scholarship only covered so much, and I learned early in life not to ask anyone for anything.

And it's not as though I was unsafe. I rented a parking spot in a lot near the police station and spent all my time in the library anyway.

I was good.

I always am.

But Pappy was heartbroken and said his wife was rolling over in her grave. The memory of Rosa he evoked was what had me relenting to the apartment. It wasn't until he'd left to go home that I found out he'd prepaid the year's rent.

It allowed me to save for my future. He gave me a leg up in life—again, after a lifetime of sinking in quicksand. My attempts to repay him sit in uncashed checks somewhere in his house.

"Free spirit, remember?" I say, bumping his shoulder with mine, but his frame is frailer than I remember, and it makes my lungs burn with the need for more air. Avoiding those feelings, I take a picture of the ocean, knowing it'll look perfect on my Instagram feed in black and white.

He grunts, leaning back on the bench we're sitting on, then reaches over and picks a piece of grass from the dunes.

"Pappy?" I wait until he turns his attention toward me.

"Did you do this?" I say, waving my hand in the air. What I really want to ask is why? *Why* did you do this? But I'm too afraid of his answer.

His eyes crinkle, but his features don't change all that much.

"Do what, exactly?" he asks with an easy drawl.

A familiar pang swirls in my gut. It's the same feeling I had when I learned about the apartment.

"All of this. Arrange this so we'd all, I don't know, be on the same path? I don't understand."

"Your skepticism has gotten you through life, Row, but you can let down your guard around me. I've always tried to keep an eye on you, but you're too stubborn for your own damn good sometimes."

He scratches at his head exactly as Sebastian had done earlier.

"Grams used to say that true love is the crossword puzzle of life." His eyes sparkle and shine. They always do whenever he mentions Rosa. "Your stories cross paths and intersect until that one moment in time, when all the stars align and you become the pieces completing both of your puzzles."

"Pappy," I whisper. How can those words make my throat close up? "You cannot seriously be talking about your grandson and me."

He sits there, staring expectantly. "You were friends once —good friends."

Were we? That's not exactly how I remember it. I always felt like more of an obligation for him because my dad worked for his grandmother.

"He's older than me." By two whole years. It's a weak excuse, so I swallow hard and try again. "He's some nasty caviar to my generic saltines."

"You think Seb's nasty?" Pappy chuckles because he knows that's not at all how I'd describe Sebastian Walker—not when I was ten, and not now. I've probably had giant hearts in my eyes since I was eight.

Sebastian always protected me.

"No, that's not...please tell me if you had a plan here."

He rests his hands on his little potbelly and leans back. "I told you, he's going through a tough time."

During our last conversation, he told me that Sebastian's wife had cheated on him, and I shiver remembering the specifics of how they all found out.

His sigh is bone-deep. "Yes, I did know you were working for the hotline. And I met Elijah about six months ago when he came to the house to meet with Seb. That's when Elijah told him about the hotline—that's fate's doing, not mine. And as far as putting you in his path? Nah, that's destiny, kiddo. Elijah told me, even when I asked about you, that his sister took her matches seriously, and would only place you with Seb if your questionnaires aligned."

He chuckles and chews on the piece of grass, so I'm sure there's more to it than that.

"I could have saved her a lot of time. You can't mess with the stars, Rowan. Your path was always going to collide with ours." He pulls me into his side and places a kiss on top of my head. "You can't run forever, sweetheart."

Watch me. Watch me. Watch me.

"Every instinct you possess is begging you to run," he says against my hair, "but for me, please stay. I won't ask you to stay forever, but stay for now, for me."

This man has never once asked me for anything and has given me more than I probably even know. How can I say no to him?

Instead of answering, I curl into his embrace and count

to five. Anything longer than five seconds will make those love lines I actively avoid sprout roots—a girl can only bob and weave for so long before she goes down.

———

"Thane," I groan. He's the most annoying hotline dad I have at the moment, but I lower myself with a thud to sit on the top step of the beach estate Sebastian is calling home. Not a second later, Lucky pops out of nowhere and slinks into my lap.

Freaking hell. I attempt to shove him off me, but he digs his claws into my thighs, and I give up. I'm supposed to be at the bonfire, but Thane's fourth emergency of the day saved me from having to be social.

"She's a teenager." I sigh. It takes a lot of effort to keep the exasperation out of my tone. "I'm not at all surprised she doesn't want to give up her devices and spend a week in the woods, but I promise she'll make the best of it when she gets here."

I need to find this guy a permanent helper. He's recently taken custody of his little sister and things are...strained, and I don't foresee that changing anytime soon.

"I'm going to throw every device she owns into the ocean." The words are angry, but his tone is almost sterile.

"That is not advisable—it's not that much longer. Do your best until camp starts, then she can go through withdrawals with all the other kids."

"Fine. Will Lottie be there?"

It's not the first time he's asked about my friend, and I'm beginning to wonder if there's a hint of a crush blossoming, but I wasn't aware that they even knew each other.

"She will. Is there anything else I can help you with tonight?"

He mutters something about deciphering my tone under his breath, but I've never been able to get a read on his emotions either.

"No. If you're sure I can't remove her bedroom door the next time she slams it, I've got nothing." His words are stilted, but somewhere in there is a man trying to do right by his teenage sister, so I keep my voice light.

"She'll come around. She's hurting and feels betrayed by your father. Be consistent with her and you'll be just fine."

"You're the expert here, Rowan, so you'd better be right. Talk to you later." A low hum vibrates through the phone, so I wait. "Thank you," he adds as an afterthought. I'm not sure what it is, but general manners seem to be a lot of work for him.

"You've got this," I say, distracted as awareness rakes over my body. The sensation of being watched usually kicks my fight-or-flight into high gear, but this—here—is different. A footstep lands on the porch behind me, but I don't turn around.

"You keep saying that," Thane mutters, and while I'd guess that he's hurting as much as his sister, there's no pitch change to indicate how he's feeling. "But I'll believe it when we get through this...whatever this is."

He hangs up without a goodbye, so I pocket my phone. Thane Wilder is trying so hard to be what his sister needs, but there are times when I wonder if he truly has no idea how emotions work.

"You've found a friend."

Sebastian's voice swirls and zings through my body, electrifying every inch of skin his words touch. The awareness from moments ago wraps around my body with the comfort of a weighted blanket. It must be his tone, right? It's soothing, in a strange sort of way. It's not familiar because when we knew each other, he was still a boy.

Tilting my head up, I find him looming over me. When he sits next to me on the step, a tad too close, I press myself into the railing. He takes up all the extra space because he's all man now—well over six feet tall and broad enough to pass for a football player.

"The cat isn't giving me a choice. I think he's following me too."

Sebastian laughs, and it warms all the dark corners of my soul.

"It's not funny," I grumble. "Black cats are bad luck. I can't be inviting more of it into my life." Even as I say it, I scratch the little jerk behind the ears, and he purrs. I swear he's gloating.

"Why the hotline?"

"Variety's the spice of life." Little white lies like this were the first survival skill I learned. It's also why I keep my promises when I make them—if I can't keep it, I won't make it.

He nods and holds out a bottle of beer in my direction. My hand is halfway to his before I pull back, hesitant to drink. Am I technically on the job right now?

"You're not on the clock twenty-four-seven," he confirms. "I figured we could both use one. I did speak to my grandfather, you know."

I nod. "Me too."

"He swears it's all some cosmic twist of fate or something."

A very unladylike snorts escapes, and I'm glad I hadn't taken a drink yet. "I had no idea that nannies were fated."

His lips twitch, and he doesn't break eye contact, but it's

not as unnerving as it should be. There's familiarity in the way he stares at me that stirs up long-forgotten dreams. When he raises a brow in silent question, I blink multiple times, forcing those old dreams back under the rug where they belong.

"That old man's been telling me about you for over twenty years, but in my head, you were still the saddest little girl I'd ever met. It's..." He takes a long pull from his beer, never releases me from his searing gaze. "It's disorienting."

I use fake laughter and stare out over the dunes to break the visual connection that tells me he sees too much—he always did.

"I haven't been that little girl in a very long time."

"No." The low, gravelly nature of his tone has me peering up through my lashes. His gaze bores into my soul as if he can not only see all my broken pieces, but feels them as viscerally as I do. "You're not."

His hand cuts through the night, coming at me in slow motion. "You've got..." His palm cups my face, and I hope to God that mewling sound came from Lucky and not me. His thumb brushes across my cheekbone three times, back and forth, before pulling away.

Holding up his thumb for me to inspect, he says, "Sorry, you had an eyelash."

I grab his wrist before he can pull away, and his pupils dilate. "Ah, I have to make a wish. It's good luck."

He swallows roughly, then nods as I lean forward until my lips are almost to his thumb. Allowing my lashes to flutter closed, I blow.

A wish never even entered my mind.

Heat gathers and swirls in my belly when I open my eyes. "Good luck," I repeat. His stare is hazy and unfocused as he licks his lips.

Good lord, what were we talking about? "Um, I'm pretty sure I've heard as much about you as you have of me." We need to steer back to a safe topic, and Pappy is as safe as they come. I take a quick sip of beer, hoping the effects of alcohol will settle whatever inappropriateness this man is pulling from me.

Sebastian's only being friendly, I remind myself. It's because I'm doing him a favor. The thought helps fuse those frayed edges back in place.

He leans back as though my words surprise him.

"What? You didn't think Pappy's storytelling was one-sided, did you?" A genuine smile pulls at my lips—my confidence returning with some space between us.

"No, we were friends once, so it makes sense."

Friends. There's that word again.

"I was just...remembering something Pappy said." He stares too intently at me, and my cheeks flush hot. "You only talk to him a few times a year because you hate talking on the phone, but you're a hotline helper by trade. You literally make a living on the phone."

I don't miss how his gaze follows my skin when I stretch my legs out in front of me. My denim cutoff shorts that I love now expose too much. "Do you always say what's on your mind?"

Seb nods. "And I always say what I mean."

"Huh. You're a novelty then." Lucky flops off my lap and takes his sweet-ass time crossing the porch to jump into a chair.

"And you're a masterful avoider, but it's okay. Pappy isn't the only one in the family who can get people to spill their secrets." He winks and heat instantly creeps up my neck.

"There's really nothing to say. The hotline is impersonal, easy, there are rules."

His chuckle ripples through my body like a wave hitting the shore. "How'd those rules work out for Beck and Stella?"

I know through Elijah, who's friends with both Beck and Stella, that they had a little helping hand in falling in love via the hotline—the helper being Elijah.

"There's always the exception to the rule. More than one now, I guess. Lottie's very good with her permanent matches, but I *am* the rule—I'm temporary."

Silence descends, and try as I might, I can't keep my gaze from sliding to his. A shiver rolls through my body when I find him already staring at me.

"That sounds...lonely."

I lift one shoulder. "People can be lonely in a room full of people or sleeping next to someone they love. Being intentionally alone means nothing else can hurt you."

Fuck. What am I doing? *Stop talking, Rowan.* Keep that shit in your head. Biting my tongue, I focus my attention on the quiet waves as they roll in and out.

The moon casts a long streak of white across the dark expanse of water, and I love that too—one streak of light in an otherwise dark world.

"Nothing else, or no one else?" His voice is thick, as though my words have struck a nerve.

"Same thing, isn't it?" The salty air licks my skin as a breeze kicks up, and I wrap my arms around my knees to ward off a chill.

"I'm not so sure," he replies, then finishes his beer with one gulp. "I do know my divorce was finalized months ago, but I still hate my ex-wife, my ex-best friend, and myself. But none of that means I want to be alone forever."

He's so open, too open, and I'm not as unaffected as I'm pretending to be.

"She cheated?" I ask, already knowing the answer.

Something about Sebastian Walker makes me want to be someone he confides in.

He leans forward, resting his forearms on his knees, and nods. "We all caught her at Seren's school recital with my best friend—who's now trying to blackmail me or threatening to sell his shares of the company my grandmother built from nothing to my biggest rival in the industry."

This poor family. The boiling heat of hatred swirls in my gut on his behalf. "That's on them, though. You're not responsible for other people's actions, Sebastian."

"No, I'm not. But I also didn't do anything when I felt lonely sleeping next to someone I vowed to love, so I do have some culpability."

How did this conversation spiral into something that's too personal, too intimate, too...everything?

"You, ah, you really are an open book, huh?" I welcome the cold that slips down my throat when I chug my beer.

Seb runs both hands through his hair, the action harsh and at odds with the man I imagine he's become. His arm brushes against mine with the movement, scorching my skin with his flame. But it's not that pain that jolts me to life—it's electricity, and lightning, and bombs in the night.

I stand quickly, and he peers up at me with a crooked grin that reminds me of the sweet twelve-year-old boy who'd check on me every time I'd try to hide.

"No one has ever called me an open book before." His whisper is a seduction I can't fall victim to. "Quite the opposite, actually. Maybe it's you who has some of Pappy's magic."

I swallow, and it might as well be cement going down.

"Listen, I didn't mean to dump all that on you." He sighs, and it's as though all his confidence expels from his body with each heavy exhale. "But it's good that you know. It all came to a head at Seren's recital, and she's so full of rage because of it. I can't even get her to touch the piano since, so that's actually why I'm here. I wanted to thank you for playing with her earlier. I—I haven't been able to reach her. She's completely closed herself off."

He stands a step below me, and it puts us so close that his scent envelops me—clean laundry, peppermint, and something so manly it causes me to lick my dry lips. Even though my inner self is screaming into the silence, begging me to step back, my legs refuse to put space between us.

"She's very talented, but she probably needs some time. Music is in her soul. She'll come around."

He tilts his head, and I can read the questions in his eyes. He wants to know why I don't play anymore, but that answer is a bit more complicated.

My hand lands on his biceps, and I'm so shocked, I stare at the connection for a beat too long before snatching it away. "Sorry. Um, I'm happy to help. We'll find you a permanent solution when all the nannies get here."

He opens his mouth to say something, but we're interrupted by a loud popping sound, and before I can blink, we're both covered in a thick, white, milky solution that smells like shaving cream.

Spluttering, we look up to find remnants of water balloons tacked to the roof of the porch. My gaze follows the rope I've only now noticed that's hanging on a Command hook. She must have used it to somehow pop the balloons. It leads to a giant bush that's already shaking, followed by the sounds of footsteps racing away from the scene of the crime.

"Are there other kids at camp already?" he asks, swiping a hand over his face.

I shake my head while wiping the goop from my eyes.

"Miles wouldn't do this, and Kade is too young. What the hell was Seren thinking?" His voice booms into the night even as he lifts the hem of his T-shirt to clear his eyes.

Dang. This man has never heard the term Dad-bod—I'd bet Junebug on it.

Before I can reply, a belly laugh overtakes me. "It's a harmless prank. I did much worse when my life was turned upside down."

I'd gone the self-destructive path. At least she's acting out in a way that's not harmful.

He paces the small porch while wiping angrily at his face. The muscles in his bare forearms bunch and jump with the movement, making my belly clench and nerve endings throb.

"This is so fucking disrespectful. It's unlike her and completely unacceptable. I'll speak to her."

Regardless of what he says, my body responds when he speaks, and I shiver.

Again, I reach out to stop him, then stuff my hands into my pockets. I really need to get a grip on my limbs. I haven't spent a lifetime avoiding people to have it all crash to hell now. "It's okay, really. Trust me when I say I can handle this. I can almost guarantee this was for me. She had no way of knowing you'd be out here tonight since you're supposed to be at the bonfire, but when I dropped my stuff off earlier, I mentioned that I'd love to sit on the porch and listen to the ocean."

"That makes it even worse," he thunders.

I point my thumbs at my chest. "I'm a professional, remember? I've got this."

His gaze follows my thumbs. What the heck am I doing? I basically drew him a giant arrow pointing at how my nipples are pressed against the wet fabric of my T-shirt.

"It won't happen again," he rumbles. The tension in his jaw flicks as he blinks hard.

I appreciate that he's attempting not to stare at my boobs even as a secret part of me wishes he would.

I simply shake my head, cross my arms over my chest, and focus on the real issue here—project Seren just took a whole different turn. "It's fine, really. I can handle Seren. But I'm going to, ah, get my stuff and clean up."

"Of course, yeah." He moves left when I move right. Seb steps right and I shift left and then it happens.

Our feet hit a slippery patch of goo, and before I can do anything, our limbs are flailing as though we're in some stupid romantic comedy.

His hands grasp my hips tightly and he spins us right before we hit the porch with a hard thud that knocks the air from my lungs. Well, Seb hits the porch. I land on top of him.

He lifts his head, his expression worried, and time stands still. Our faces are an inch apart. He exhales, and I breathe him in greedily. Sharing air has never felt so intimate before.

"Sorry," I whisper.

He brushes a wet strand of hair from my face. "Me too." His voice is soft as his thumb slides over my chin and across my bottom lip.

My heartbeat grows claws. Each rapid thud against my chest cavity slices through years of walls.

"Je-sus. What the hell happened here?"

The voice comes out of nowhere, and I scramble to my feet—or attempt to. Our limbs seem to fuse closer together the harder we fight to break apart. Leo and another man stand at the bottom of the steps, surveying this mess.

"Stop." Sebastian growls low in my ear, and once again, my body obeys his command.

His hands fall to my hips, then he lifts me over his body as though I weigh nothing and places me on my ass beside him. He stands before I've even blinked, then his big hands wrap around mine and he lifts me up.

"So, it's like that, is it?" Leo says with a chuckle. "Someone's going to have their hands full this week." He steps closer—not enough to be inappropriate, just near enough to study my face in the moonlight. "Are you okay? Your face is really red. Did you hit your head?" He glances over my shoulder at Seb, then back to me.

"Did you get hurt?" Seb growls.

"No, I'm fine. Really. I'm, ah, going to take a shower. Alone. I mean, of course alone. It's fine, really. I'm good. I can handle anything Seren throws at me. I'm good with kids. Really good. She's only lashing out because everything in her life feels unstable. I've got this. I said that already."

Shut up, Rowan. Close your mouth and stop talking!

The other man doubles over with laughter.

"Shut up, Alexei," Seb mutters.

Snapping my jaw shut, I give an awkward wave and rush into the house to grab my shower caddy and some clothes.

Twenty days. That's all I have left before everything goes back to normal. Twenty days. Easy peasy, right?

For the first time in years, I allow myself to believe in a lie.

5

NO ONE IS CHOKING ON YOUR MICROPENIS

SEBASTIAN

The room is too small.

That's my first thought when I sit down at the conference table next to my attorney, Raj. The wall of windows behind me overlooking Boston's Financial District does nothing to brighten the room. There's a cloying darkness that hangs in the air like death.

Which I suppose is fitting.

A death of a marriage.

A death of a friendship.

But if Nick thinks it'll be the death of my company, he has no idea how depraved his betrayal has made me. Just because I don't normally fight dirty doesn't mean I can't do it. Did he really fucking forget who raised me? Marcus Walker didn't know any other way to play—dirty was in my father's blood, and it's in mine too.

"How are the kids?" Raj asks, genuine affection tugging at the corner of his lips.

There's no denying that the last week with Rowan in my home has been insanely good. Well, good if you can ignore the fact that I have a constant erection knowing she's down

53

the hall—filling every room with the scent of roses and sunshine.

She's good with my kids, and she's good for Pappy. The only reason I was able to leave my kids in North Carolina for this meeting in Boston was that my children seem happy with them.

"They're good," I say quietly, while secretly praying for that to stay true.

"That's great," Raj says. "Now to the business at hand. No matter what Nick says, keep yourself in check, Seb. We've been playing the long game, don't throw it all away now. He'll have enough rope to hang himself, so let him do it."

Nick enters the room with his trademark swagger turned up a notch and my knuckles drain of blood as I clutch the arms of my chair, but my face remains impassive while Raj clamps his lips closed. Nick is followed in by an attorney, an older man I've seen with Mya's father. Anger bubbles in my gut—he worked on our prenup.

Nick's smirk flares into a snarl as he studies me and his attorney, but I offer no pleasantries to either of them.

Raj leans over the table and quickly hits the record button. My gaze hasn't left Nick's, and because I've spent a lifetime reading him, I know when his nostrils flair that he wasn't prepared to have this meeting recorded.

He'll have to work much harder to keep his lies straight now.

"Is that really necessary?" He scoffs. "Your choices are very simple."

He's a fucking idiot. Did either of them even read his contract?

The Pappy Clause is going to hang him. Once again, that old man is saving my ass, and he has no idea. But Pappy's the reason I added the morality clause to every contract when I took over Walker Meridian.

Meridian Industries has been in my family for generations, but when my grandmother's MS overwhelmed her life, the only one who could take the helm was my father. I was still in college at the time, and my mother had passed years prior.

In the few years he controlled my legacy, he managed to nearly destroy it. It's why I had to rebrand as Walker Meridian, and it's why I looked to my grandfather for guidance. He'd never wanted to be part of the corporate world, but he knew people, and it's his instincts that are saving me now.

"There are certainly some choices," Raj replies, shuffling papers in front of him.

"Why'd you do it?" I ask, unwilling to wade through this bullshit.

Raj's hands freeze—he doesn't move a muscle. This isn't how we'd planned to get this information, but I can't sit here and stare at Nick's smug face any longer.

Nick's nonchalant shrug is a farce. He picks nonexistent lint off his lapel, and it's the first sign that I'm right—he's nervous, and he should be.

"You've always gotten everything you want, even when it doesn't belong to you," he says blandly. The only emotion he emits is hatred in the twitch of his eye—it blinds him, and it will aid in his downfall.

"What you're saying is your jealousy goes way back?" I'm goading him, and I don't regret it. I handle my shit, while he's always been on the verge of exploding.

Raj places his palm flat on the table in front of me—a warning, but I lean back in my chair as if facing this fucker isn't tearing me apart inside.

"Everything was always so easy for you. You take everything for fucking granted," Nick snarls. His attorney gives him a less subtle warning with a hand on his forearm.

"I gave you everything," I spit out, and immediately roll my shoulders. I won't allow him to hurt me ever again. With a deep inhale, I continue more calmly. "You lived with us in the summers during college. My grandparents paid your tuition, got you the most coveted internships, I gave you a stake in my company, and this is how you repay me? Sleeping with my wife? Embarrassing and traumatizing my children? Spreading lies about my character?"

At the mention of my kids, the corner of his eye quivers. At least he knows he's a scumbag.

"You may be at the top of your game in every other arena, but you couldn't keep your wife happy." His voice pokes at my temples like tiny needles injecting me with his poison. "It's not my fault she came looking for someone better. If it hadn't been for your last name, she would've chosen me in college anyway. Now we're correcting a long overdue lapse in judgment, and my shares of your company will secure my future with her father's organization."

"How long?" I grind out. "How long were you fucking my wife behind my back?"

An ugly thought sets off cannons in my chest. My kids— what if? No, fuck that. I'm their father. I always have been and always will be, regardless of their DNA.

"You see, the thing about not taking care of your relationships is you have no idea when they started crumbling. Was it before Seren was born? Where did Miles get the blond hair from? All questions that are probably eating away at you right now, huh?"

He leans forward on the table. The face of the man I would have taken a bullet for is now unrecognizable. "Don't worry. They're yours. The last thing I want is a kid ruining my life."

"How. Long?" It's the only answer I need.

His attorney must sense something's off because he leans over and whispers into Nick's ear, but Nick's grin never falters. His ego is toxic.

"Nah," Nick says, shrugging off his attorney. His cockiness was always his greatest weakness. "This is rock solid." He speaks to his lawyer but never looks away from me. Seconds of silence raise the tension, but I've asked my question.

Raj clears his throat, and I cut him off with a slight shake of my head.

"You've got me over a barrel here, Nick." His name burns my tongue. "You want me to buy you out at a crippling rate or you'll sell them to Skyview, my biggest competitor. I know you're dying to rub salt in my wounds. You're itching to tell me every despicable thing you've ever done with my wife."

"Ex-wife," he snarls.

"Yeah, ex-wife." I chuckle sardonically. I should probably focus on the fact that losing her didn't hurt as much as it should have, but the truth is, I just don't give a shit anymore. The hit to my pride stung, but the only pain I felt was for my children.

I should have listened to Pappy all those years ago. An arranged marriage was never what I wanted.

Rowan's face flashes in my mind, and I cross my legs, resting my right ankle against my left knee, then clasp my hands behind my head while staring straight into the soul of my enemy. It forces the thoughts of my childhood friend out of my head—I can't focus on her right now.

"I'm assuming it started after Kade was born," I say casually. "Suddenly, I was traveling more, thanks to you and the deals you were finding. It makes perfect sense. Get me out of the way so you can slide in like the cancer you are."

Nick lurches forward, as I knew he would, slamming his open palms on the table. "Mya came to me," he seethes. "She was ignored and lonely. I was only too happy to let her feel wanted by choking on my cock."

A demonic-sounding chuckle gurgles in my chest. "You forget we've been to the gym together, Nicky. No one is choking on your micropenis."

He snaps, leaping over the table and wrapping his hands around my neck. I allow it and lift one side of my mouth, which makes the vein in his temple throb. It must be my lack of action that finally breaks through his rage.

"I fucked your wife," he snarls. "I own her now, she's mine, and the next thing I'll take is your company. By the time I'm done with you, you'll have nothing left. Not even your fucking brats."

I shove him off me with the strength of a pissed-off father protecting his kids. He crashes into the table, but it's his possessed snarl and his wild, vacant gaze that has me flipping through old memories. Was he always this fucking crazy, or did something make him lose his goddamn mind?

To my left, Raj picks up the phone, and moments later, security stands in the doorway. Nick rounds the table to his side, attempting to straighten his now crooked tie, but he doesn't sit.

"So that was your plan? Take my wife? Ruin my name?" I goad.

"Ruining your name was the easiest fucking thing I've ever done. Everyone was all too ready to believe that you are your father's son."

Violence as I've never known tightens the muscles in my arms until they burn. My father manipulated people, used them, blackmailed them, and ruined them with all his schemes—I'll never be like him.

"What's your choice, Sebastian? Buy me out? Oh, and by the way, my price has now gone up. Or do I sell to Skyview?"

Finally. This is what I've been waiting for.

A sneer spreads slowly across my face. For the first time since Nick crashed onto that stage with his hands all over my wife, I smile. It's broad, and freeing.

"But there's always a third option," I say with a menacing grin. "We learned that in business school, remember? Oh, that's right. You got through school copying my homework, so I'll give you the *CliffsNotes*. It's the basis for every story since the dawn of time—there are always three sides—his, hers, and the truth. Did you truly believe I've gotten to where I am by luck or on the lies my father raised me on? No, Nicky. You of all people should know me better than that."

His jaw clenches, the muscles in his face bunching, but he doesn't say a word.

"I always have a safety net, Nicky. Always. Even from my best friend." I grin at Raj, who removes a stack of papers and hands them to Nick's attorney.

Nick snatches them from the lawyer's hands and angrily flips through them. He's not a stupid man. He'll understand what's happening in three, two, bingo!

"What the fuck is this?"

"I call it the Pappy Clause. You might be more familiar with the term morality clause. Those"—I point to one stack of papers—"are your exit papers. You've been terminated, effective immediately."

His shoulders relax. "This, this is what you have up your sleeve, you fucking idiot? Working for you was never going to happen again. It's the shares that are the ticking bomb here."

"Oh." I laugh humorlessly. "About those. Thank you for reminding me."

Raj leans forward again and hands the pale-faced attorney a check.

Nick glares over the older man's shoulders and his face turns crimson. "Don't fucking insult me. I know what my shares are worth."

"You're right, and that's why you're getting fifty grand."

"That's not—"

"But it is," I hiss. "Tucked away in the contract you never bothered to review right out of college is a morality clause. Since you just admitted to fucking and carrying on an affair with my then-wife, plus your planned character assassination and deals with a competitor, you fail. It all falls into the morality clause, as does blackmail and corporate sabotage. I'll hand it to you, four for four. I couldn't have predicted you'd manage all of them, but when you do something, you go all out. So congrats. You're fifty grand richer because the clause clearly states that by engaging in those acts, you forfeit any rights to company shares, and you'll be compensated fifty thousand dollars, or five percent of their worth—whichever is lower. And fifty grand is much, much lower."

Buttoning up my coat, I signal the end of the meeting. Raj reaches over and takes the flash drive that contains the recording of this meeting and slips it into his pocket with a silent nod.

"We're done here."

"You asshole. I trusted you." Nick's anger isn't allowing him to think clearly.

I raise a brow in mock surprise. "Funny how that works, isn't it? But so we're clear, I trusted you too. I never would have turned on you. Now you've made the worst enemy you'll ever have in your life. I never forget a betrayal."

Ushering Raj in front of me, I nod to the additional security personnel who enter the room and create a wall between us and Nick.

"This isn't over," Nick shouts. "Money isn't the only way we can get to you."

Ice floods my veins. Is he seriously threatening my children right now?

"I don't care how long it takes or what I have to do. You *will* get what's coming to you," he warns.

"I wonder how many vibrators Mya's using to compensate for what she no longer has." It's a dick thing to say, but the dig feeds a sickness in me. The sickness for revenge.

He's always been insecure, and now he should be.

———

THE AIR CONDITIONING in my car blasts at full power against my heated face, but it's still not enough. I held up in Raj's office, and now, alone, the effects of the betrayals threaten to drown me.

But underneath all the pain is relief.

Relief that my marriage is over.

Relief that I had the foresight to protect myself, even from someone I had trusted my children with.

Relief that feels like freedom.

It's unsettling. When did I start feeling trapped in my own life?

Yes, marrying Mya was easy. It looked good on paper, it made our fathers exceedingly happy, and for the most part, she was easy to get along with. We had a good life, or at least I thought we did.

But not once did I have that jolt of longing I get staring at a very grown up Rowan Ellis, and that's where the guilt comes in.

I don't agree with how Mya handled things, but if I'm truly honest with myself, I have to wonder if either of us were ever actually in love. Even searching my memories of us, I can't begin to fathom how we went from the white picket fence to this.

She loves our children, in her own slightly detached way. I know she does, or maybe she did?

It's all too much. My head spins when I try to make sense of something I'll never understand. I may not regret our time together—she gave me three precious gifts—but I do regret my part in our downfall, even if we were doomed from the beginning.

Closing my eyes, I lean against the headrest. My phone vibrates in my lap, and I almost ignore it because it's sure to be Alexei.

But when I lift the phone to my face, it says The Single Dad Hotline.

Quickly I swipe up and open the message.

SDH: Mud pies.

The text is followed by a series of pictures of the boys. In one, Kade is caked in mud and only his bright white teeth are visible on his face, but his easy happiness makes my chest ache. At least he's happy—for now. It's always the *for now* that gets me. How long until they fall apart like their sister?

Kids don't forget their mom, even if that's what she's hoping will happen.

I hit the green button and listen as the phone rings. She finally picks up right before it goes to voicemail.

"Single Dad Hotline, I'm your helper. How can I help you?"

"Rowan?"

"That's me. How can I help you?"

Doesn't she recognize my voice? And why am I strangled by jealousy that she doesn't?

"Ah, it's me. Sebastian."

There's a pause of dead air that wraps around my lungs and squeezes. "Um, do you always answer your phone that way?"

"This is my hotline phone. All calls are routed through Lottie's agency, so I only see Single Dad on the caller ID."

"Oh." The memory of her talking to another dad the day we sat on the porch hits me much harder than it should, and my brain scrambles in an attempt to come up with something else to say.

She clears her throat. "Since I have all of your children, I have to assume you're not calling for parenting advice right now."

"Do you have another phone? A private one?" The question is out before I can censor myself.

"Ah, no, actually. Why?"

"Do all calls show up as The Single Dad Hotline?"

"I guess so. Well, except Pappy and Lottie. They're the only ones who call me besides my hotline dads."

Pain rolls through my chest hotter than heartburn. "Your friends don't call you?"

"I move around a lot. Is there something I can help you with, Sebastian?"

Jesus Christ. My name from her lips makes my mouth go so dry you'd think I was sucking on cotton balls all day.

"Shit. Um, yeah, I was calling to check up on things. The pictures of the boys are great, thank you. How's Seren?"

I didn't want to leave them in Sailport Bay so soon after our move, but I had to return to Boston to handle this shit. And now I'm in damage control mode, which means I'll probably have to travel much more than I'd like.

I thought Pappy was out of his mind when he encouraged me to go to this nanny mixer, even more so when he encouraged me to pack up my life and move for the summer, but the man has literally never steered me wrong, and the boys were so excited about the idea. Seren was just happy to get the fuck out of dodge.

My baby girl feels broken, and for the first time in her life, I don't know how to put her back together again. Care Bears Band-Aids can't fix this hole in her life.

How does a little girl come back from her mother's infidelity literally falling onto center stage in front of all her peers? I'll never understand what Mya was thinking, but I'm sure the gossip from high society over her actions on school property is the reason her father insisted she leave the country—appearances are what matter to them.

"Well," Rowan singsongs, dragging me into the present and wondering about the future. "She short-sheeted my bed last night, but we had a good laugh about it. Today she's quiet. She's probably planning her next attack, but I'm ready for her," she says good-naturedly.

"I haven't been able to help her," I say quietly. The pain that statement brings hangs heavily in my chest. "She's in therapy, but it's obviously not doing any good. She's never acted out against someone like this before." Internally I cringe. "Well, except the nannies we tried in Boston."

We lived through a shitty version of *The Parent Trap* for a few months. Any and every prank Seren could pull on those poor women, she did, but for some reason, I wasn't prepared for those actions to follow us to North Carolina.

"It's hard to know what to do with all those big feelings when you're twelve, Sebastian. She'll come around. I had Leo pick up a blank music book from town. I'm going to show her how to write her own music, and I gave her a journal. She can write whatever she wants in it without fear of repercussions. Sometimes it's easier to talk without talking, you know? And her new nanny might have suggestions I haven't even thought of. You'll get through this."

This woman has been back in my life for one week and the thought of her leaving heats my blood more than the end of my marriage.

Maybe I'm the one who needs counseling.

"That's really great. Thank you, Rowan."

"No problem. We're good. You do what you've gotta do. Pappy and I have things covered here, but if you want to FaceTime them at any time, just call. Right now, we're taking Kade boogie boarding. I figured it's safer than surfing."

An image of her in a bikini has my body reacting in a way it most definitely should not.

"Thank you again. Tell the kids I love them and I'll be back as soon as I can."

"You've got it. Have a good night, Sebastian." She hangs up before I can say goodbye. She's completely unaffected by speaking with me, and that's enough to tell me that this life-long infatuation is one-sided and I need to get my shit together.

I can't always have what I want, or who I want, no matter how much damage they do to my blood pressure.

6

WHEN DID FIGHTING TURN INTO FOREPLAY?

ROWAN

I t's been a long-ass day. I haven't spent this much time with a six-year-old in ages, especially a six-year-old like Kade. That kid has so much energy I'm surprised he doesn't combust, and yet I hope he never loses that spark that makes him special.

There's nothing sadder than a child beaten down before they have the chance to fly.

Like Seren. I've put the boys to bed, and Pappy is on the porch reading through Leo's plans for his new summer camp. It won't surprise me one bit if he's also making notes for improvements out there too.

With a low groan, I reach for the door to my room. I can't hold off talking to Seren any longer, but I need a few minutes to strengthen my armor. Warily, I enter, wondering what kind of shit she has planned for me tonight.

The door swings open and I kick my foot through it first, trying to trip any traps she may have set. When nothing happens, I lean my head in and scan the ceiling, floor, and all the open space.

Nothing looks out of place. The room was decorated

with clean lines and a beachy theme before I arrived. The light-gray walls offset the bright white and aqua bedding. I hate to admit that it's exactly what I would have done if I'd decorated it myself.

I'm about to enter my room when I hear the softest whimper and sniffle coming from Seren's room down the hall, and my stomach twists into a knot.

Reminding myself that this is temporary does nothing to squash the heartache that burns at the sound of her pain. Moving quickly into the room, I set my shower caddy on the desk, and the sight of the journal I'd given Seren catches my attention on the corner of my bed.

A beautiful guitar graces the cover. I open it and am not the least bit shocked by what she's written.

I hate you. I don't need a nanny. I don't need anyone. Just leave me alone.

The pain she's suffering is parallel to my own life. Different situations, but it hurts the same.

Taking my pen from the nightstand, I go back to the hallway and sit outside her room, then flip the notebook over to a fresh page.

I was ten when my dad died, eight when he got sick.

Shit. Am I really going to do this? I've never talked about this with anyone. Seren sniffles, and my hand glides across the paper. I'll do whatever it takes to help her through this. It's why I went to school for music therapy—if only I'd been able to stay in one place, I could have put it to better use.

At least the hotline still allows me to help.

The need to help a child in pain is a living, breathing part of my makeup with no off button, and it's why my pen glides across the paper almost as fast as I can think.

Pappy's camp was important to my dad. He loved music too, that's why I'd gone. And why he left money in his will for me to keep going as long as I wanted.

My stepfather had other plans though.

When I was twelve, my mom remarried. Suddenly I had a new dad, and a stepsister. If you look up the name Haley Ford in the dictionary, you'll really see what the devil looks like.

She wanted everything, and she got everything.

My room. My piano. My life.

But she didn't have my camp. It's what I waited for all year. It made all their terrible treatment and punishments worth it.

They came to the camp recital when I was thirteen. The one where I played that song your dad sang pieces of to you. I had my first-ever panic attack before I even started playing, and your dad came to my rescue. He sat with me while I faced my stage fright, my family's glares, and began to play.

I got lost in the song.

I didn't hear Haley screaming at her dad to make me stop.

I didn't hear him approach, or when he scolded me for embarrassing him in front of strangers.

But I felt it when he ripped me away from the piano with such force that my feet left the ground. They removed me from camp that day, they took away my music, and my life changed forever.

My mother never stepped in. Not once.

I know how much it hurts to be let down by someone who is supposed to love you.

For me, things went from bad to worse, and I did what I had to survive. My only regret is that I allowed them to silence the music in my heart—even temporarily.

Don't let that happen to you. You have a family who loves you and will support you always, so lose yourself in your art, not your anger. Express all those big feelings through music because you deserve to be heard. You're allowed to tell the world how you feel.

You're too special to allow someone else's mistakes to rob you of your gift, and what you have is a gift. Don't waste it because someone was too blind to see it for what it is.

XO,

Rowan

Closing the book, I knock quietly and enter after a few beats of silence.

The room is pale pink with light gray accents. It's exactly what I would picture for a princess. Music notes decorate the walls, and a guitar sits in the corner with broken strings.

I place the notebook next to Seren on her bed and sit at the foot of it. Her little body shakes with silent tears, but her hand slips out and draws the notebook to her. I hear pages being flipped and hitches in her breath, so I move a few inches closer and place a hand on her back, hoping she's read my note.

"My mother loved me once—in her own way," I say softly. "After my father died, she lost herself. She became indifferent. It's the indifference that hurt the most."

Seren stops shaking, so I push on, even though she hasn't poked her head out from her blankets yet.

"After that, nothing could hurt me. I took her indifference and made it my entire personality."

"What did you do?" she whispers.

"Well, my situation is different than yours, but I think some of the feelings we've experienced may be similar."

"How?" She still doesn't pull her blankets down, but the tremor in her voice is lessening.

"You have a dad who loves you and will do anything for you. I had a cruel monster parading around as a doting step-father. I haven't experienced love since I was ten years old. But you can. You have your dad, and Pappy, your brothers. It's easy to want to punish everyone around you, to make them experience the pain you're feeling, and I don't even fault you for it. You're going through a tough time, but you can learn to handle all those big scary things while still allowing people to love you."

I tap the notebook that has slipped out from beneath her blanket and she finally peeks out at me. "Write it down. Get it out. Sing about how unfair it all is until your voice is raw. I think you'll be surprised by how much it helps. Musical therapy is a thing for a reason."

"How did you handle it if you didn't play anymore?"

When she scoots back to sit up, I flash her a wobbly smile. "The difference there is that I couldn't play anymore. That choice was taken from me with a sledgehammer to my piano."

She gasps and her eyes well. If she blinks, I'll be forced to witness her tears as they fall.

"Things can be taken from us, Seren. But it doesn't define who we are."

"What did you do after your piano was ruined?"

I ran. I ran as far from home as I could get because I had no doubt the rage building in that house would be what ended me if I didn't.

She doesn't need to know that though. Instead, I say, "I

left as soon as I could. I didn't have anyone to lean on, but it was my only option. You have a lot of people who love you and a lot of people who want to help. All you have to do is ask."

"I hate my mom," she blurts, and immediately tucks herself under her blankets, but it's too late. I saw the truth, the pain, and the confusion that confession causes her.

"I understand that emotion more than you could know," I say. "She hurt you, and forgiveness is something that takes time."

"She doesn't care about my forgiveness."

What do I say to that? I haven't asked much about her mom, and suddenly that's feeling like a massive error in judgment on my part.

"I hate my dad too," she whispers so quietly I could almost convince myself I made it up. But when her body trembles, I know I didn't.

Her statement makes my skin prickle. "Why do you hate your dad?"

"Because he didn't make her stay. He didn't try to fix us. Daddy always fixes us."

Oh, sweet baby Jesus.

"Sometimes things can't be fixed, sweetheart. But you will be happy again. I promise you."

"Are you happy?"

Her question catches me off guard. Happiness isn't something I've ever reached for. Survival is my way of life.

"There's happiness to be found every day," I say instead. I'm already in too deep with her. These are conversations for people who stay, for lifelong nannies who never plan to leave. They're not for me—someone who only knows how to move on.

"You're not so bad, I guess," she mutters.

"Neither are you, kid." I give her a crooked smile.

"Maybe—maybe we can help each other be happy again."

The lump in my throat explodes like shrapnel.

"I'm happy to help," I choke out. "And I'll personally help you choose your permanent nanny too. Things will get better, Seren."

She doesn't reply, so I stand and place the notebook on her nightstand. I'm at the doorway and turning off her light when she speaks.

"I'm sorry," she whispers into the darkness.

"I know." Seren doesn't elaborate, she doesn't need to. I think I understand her more thoroughly than anyone else in my life.

Quietly, I pull her door shut and then nearly run to my room with my heart in my throat. I can't get into my own bed fast enough. I'm running even though I haven't left the house because the love lines of this family are slowly tying me to them one thread at a time, and I don't know how to get free—or even if I want to.

I'm almost asleep when a tear falls down my face, startling me awake, and Seren's words ring loud in the silence.

Maybe we can help each other be happy again.

The fucking noose I've been running from pulls tighter against my throat, and this little girl might be the one holding the rope.

———

"Single Dad Hotline, I'm your helper, how can I help you?" I ask, then gasp as my foot hits a slippery patch of grass and I'm forced to slow my run to a steady walk.

Without my music blasting in my ears, the sounds of the forest accentuate the dark shadows caused by the early morning light hitting branches far above my head.

"Hi, did I wake you?" Seb's tone is husky. Did he just wake up?

"Ah, no. I had a daddy emergency at four forty-five, so I decided to get up and work out. But I happen to know that all of your children are still sleeping peacefully and nothing has changed since we spoke last night, so what can I do for you?"

"I'm not sure. I just, I needed to call."

Danger. Danger.

Keep us on task, Rowan. Do not go off the rails.

"Are you okay?" There go my fucking rails.

"Yes," he says too sharply. "Yes, thank you." He's not fooling anyone with his forced softer tone.

"Is there anything I can do?"

"No. Not really. My ex-VP made a thinly veiled threat against the kids. I haven't been able to sleep since."

I ran into Leo on the trail this morning. He told me a little more about Sebastian's situation. That conversation also taught me that I shouldn't tell Leo anything important. The man is a bigger gossip than TMZ.

Sweat dots my skin. This damn family makes me so freaking uncomfortable, but Sebastian especially.

"I can promise you that they're safe, and they will be safe here. They're in their own little bubble for now—it's good for them."

"Logically, I understand that. But not being there with them, it's hard. I'm all they've had since their mother left—maybe even before that. I tried to do it all, I really did. I wanted the perfect family for them."

The hair on my arms stands on end. "You know that

perfection isn't something tangible in a family, right? Families, the way families should be anyway, are full of imperfections that are applauded and revered. It's the unconditional love in the face of those imperfections that make a family perfect."

Or so I've been told. Thank you, Family Psych 101.

I swear I hear him swallow over the line. "I've spent most of my life trying to create the family I never had but always wanted. I wanted so badly to give my children a childhood without the trauma that shaped me, and I failed. Miserably failed."

A crack of thunder sounds overhead, drawing my attention to the dark clouds that rolled in while I was solely focused on the timbre of Sebastian's voice.

"Being aware of what you want to give them, in spite of whatever you've gone through, is already doing better than your past."

"What about you?" he asks. A drop of rain hits my forehead, so I turn around on the trail that will lead me to the house.

"What about me?"

"Well, you didn't have an idyllic childhood. Did that shape you and the kind of family you want and surround yourself with?"

My laughter is a little unhinged. "No, actually. I stay away from entanglements altogether. I'm temporary, remember? I use my history as a reminder to help children find people who can give them the love and affection they need."

"You make it sound as though you don't give those things."

My feet squelch in the mud, and I slide down a small hill. When I've gotten my footing, I focus on what he said.

"I don't. Not really. Don't get me wrong, I give the children in my care what they need, but I'm more of a wordsmith than a hugger. But I do realize children need affection, so I make sure I'm always—"

"Temporary." His tone is low and whisper-soft, almost as though he's repeating something so unfathomable, he doesn't dare say it too loud. "That's a lonely fucking existence, Peach."

That knife only he can wield slips between my ribs. He's always called me Peach with so much affection my body would go numb, but when he says it now, it's a wildfire, blazing hot as it races across every pore.

And yet, I don't, can't, acknowledge the stupid nickname that means so much I tattooed the damn thing to my body —a small peach on the inside of my wrist that's always covered by my crystals.

"It's survival, Sebastian." I don't know what makes me hiss his name, but I do know he has no right to judge how I live my life. "Not all of us get the happily ever after. Not all of us have the same capacity to give or receive love, and that's a fact."

"Do you think this is weird?"

His subject change has me spinning in a circle, glaring at the clouds as if someone up there's to blame for all the turmoil uncoiling in my mind.

"What? Do I think what's weird?"

"That we're bickering like we've known each other our entire lives?"

My stomach lurches up to my throat, but the rest of my body behaves in a very different way.

When did fighting turn into foreplay?

"We're not—"

"We are. I remember finding you behind the snack

shack at camp. You were crying, but you wouldn't tell me why."

"I was eleven. What's your point?"

"I was thirteen, and I came to your rescue then. You hated it and did everything you could to make me leave you alone. You did the same thing when I found you at the pavilion, hiding from swim lessons."

"I was a chubby kid who hated bathing suits."

"You were perfect. You were my friend."

I snort, thankful he can't see the blush heating my cheeks.

"And after that asshole dumped paint water on you, I chased you into the woods, sat with you against that giant tree, and talked at you until you eventually gave in and talked back to me."

"Okay, so you're relentless. What's your point?"

"My point is, in the end, I always made you laugh and would sit with you until you were ready to face the other campers, but it was the story you hid behind your eyes that has always stayed with me."

My throat itches. I must have formed a new allergy in the last ten minutes. Can I sue him if I go into anaphylactic shock because of him?

No. I do not get worked up and emotional. I just don't, so I reach for anger instead.

"Yeah, well, I remember you taking pity on me when I was twelve, and no one, I mean no one would choose me to be on their team—for anything. In whiffle ball, they pretended they didn't see me. Arts and crafts, oops, sorry, there wasn't enough room at their table. I know you always felt bad for me, but honestly, you didn't need to do it then and you certainly don't need to do it now. I. Am. Fine." My nostrils flare with my last three words.

"That wasn't pity, Peach. That was friendship, and we can—will be friends again. I know we could fight about this all day, but I have a meeting with an office in London that's about to start, so I'll leave you with one thing to remember. It's never been pity I felt when I looked at you. Not when you were ten, not when you were thirteen, and definitely not now."

"Then wh—"

Ping.

Did he? That asshole hung up on me.

"Rowan?" A little voice breaks through the torrent of words and memories swirling in my mind. I spin to find Miles standing in front of me holding an umbrella. He's on his tiptoes trying to share his shelter.

"Miles? What are you doing out here?" My surroundings come rushing back as if time had forgotten to move and now it's speeding up to fit in all that it's missed. How long have I been standing outside of the house in the rain? Nothing's penetrated my armor since I first put it on. Nothing but Sebastian, and that's a huge problem.

"I saw you standing in the rain. I don't want you to get sick. Come inside before you get sick, please." The worry in his voice makes my body tremble.

"Oh, right. Let's go." I usher him toward the porch. "Sorry, buddy. I was on the phone and then got lost in a daydream."

He smiles shyly. "I like to daydream."

"Oh yeah?" I ask while shaking out his umbrella under the cover of the front porch.

"Yeah, in daydreams things can be however you want them to be. You don't have to feel any sort of way but happy."

Suddenly I hear a ticking in my soul—a time bomb

waiting to go off. I haven't learned what the triggers are yet so I have no idea when it will explode—but I know with certainty that it will.

7

LIQUID LAXATIVES ARE NOT ALLOWED

SEBASTIAN

"You're pretty anxious to get back to Sailport Bay," Alexei says with a teasing lilt that grates as we head from the airport back to the beach house.

"I'm excited to see my kids." I ignore his prodding by keeping my face pointed toward the passenger side window. "I haven't been away from them since their world imploded."

"Of course. And it has absolutely nothing to do with the nanny I heard you verbally sparring with last night."

My glare cuts to him, and the temperature in the SUV rises to scorching levels. At least he has the good sense to keep his eyes on the road, though that doesn't stop his lips from twitching and curling into a smirk I want to wipe away with the back of my hand.

"That's not how it is. Rowan and I, we have a weird history. I knew her when I was a twelve-year-old kid, for fuck's sake."

"And as a fifteen-year-old lovesick puppy," he reminds me.

I'd forgotten he was working at camp with me that summer. He witnessed the same things I did.

"I remember how distraught you were when she was taken away from camp," he presses.

"She was thirteen, Alexei. I'd known her for five summers, and there was something about her as a little girl that made me protective of her, but it was never anything more than that. She was my friend."

I won't tell him how I panicked when she didn't return the next summer, or the one after that. I don't tell him that I worked that camp every summer until my father put a stop to it because I'd hoped she'd return. And I definitely don't tell him that the only thing that kept me from finding out where she lived to make sure she was safe was that Pappy told me she was writing to him, so I let it go. At that point, I was eighteen years old. I had no business worrying about some kid I knew for a few summers, no matter how intense our connection had always seemed.

"Jesus, Seb. I didn't say you were inappropriate with her, but you can't deny that she's always had an effect on you."

I fiddle with the AC because the air in here is stifling. "I never saw her again, Alex. I think it's safe to say I wasn't the only one concerned for her safety after witnessing how that asshole manhandled her, shouting about repenting for her sins."

It was the first time I'd seen an adult actively destroying innocence just because he could.

Alexei tilts his head in silent agreement. "And what's it like seeing her again now?"

My pulse accelerates as I roll his question around in my mind. The truth is, I haven't had time to process my reactions to her—my old friend. That pull, the string that kept me checking on her day after day is still there, but now it's edged with heartache, trauma, and enough sexual tension to light up the entire sky—it has claws and barbed wire and strikes to kill.

"Different," is the word I settle on to answer his question. It is different. I'd always worried about the little girl from summer camp. In my mind, she never aged, she stayed that sad little girl. But now, she's a sad, beautiful woman who chooses to live her life in temporary situations.

I'm still trying to reconcile the two versions of the same person when Alexei pulls onto the gravel road that leads to my new home.

We round a corner, and the large house comes into view. It's much more space than we needed, but as soon as I stepped inside, I could feel us making it a home. The large light-gray house sits on a hill overlooking the ocean. Windows cover most of the walls, giving ocean views from almost any vantage point.

My palms itch as though I'm nervous, so I wipe them on my shorts. Alexei notices, but simply raises a brow in recognition.

"If, at any time, your plans change, say the word and I'll be happy to jump in as your wingman."

I swing my head in his direction so quickly I'm surprised my eyeballs don't roll around in my skull. "What's that supposed to mean? I'm here to solidify this merger, to remove my kids from the fuckery at home, and to find a nanny—a permanent nanny—that's it."

He opens his door and climbs out, but not before mumbling, "And plans have a funny way of changing."

God, he infuriates me sometimes. Not even Nick could get under my skin as Alexei does, and Nick always had a bit of a mean streak in him.

Thinking of the man who is still actively trying to turn

investors against me reminds me of the betrayal that led me here in the first place. It's the reminder I need. The reminder to put my children first—nothing else matters as long as they're happy, healthy, and safe.

Not even the sexy Rowan Ellis.

———

"Okay, well, I'm out of here." Alexei's sly grin is annoying. He's spent all morning trying to witness the chemistry between me and Rowan in person and it makes me want to kick him out and lock the door.

Instead, I focus on wiping down the kitchen island and wait for him to show himself out.

"You're not staying with us, Uncle Alex? I have a bunk room. You can sleep with me and Kade. It's, ah…" Miles scratches the side of his head. "We've been having fun. Right, Ser?" He looks to his sister, almost as if he's asking permission to be happy, and acid crawls up my throat.

"Right," Seren says. At least she attempted to hold back her sarcasm for him, but I'm starting to miss the Gen-Z slang that used to send me to Google with every conversation. This version of my daughter is muted and much too old for her years.

"I love you, kid, but my bunk bed days are over. I'll be at a hotel in Corolla, it's not too far away. I'll come by in the morning to pick up your dad for our meetings, then we'll be back to explore the camp with you in the afternoon."

"Uncle Alex is scared of bugs," I whisper to Kade as he sits in my lap at the island with a coloring book and crayons. He's been attached to me since I walked in. My little boy gasps, and mischief sparkles in his shining eyes.

"That's silly." Kade giggles.

"Uncle Alex is silly," I stage-whisper.

A knock on the kitchen doorframe has us all turning toward the sound. Rowan stands in the open doorway with the sun filtering in behind her. Her dirty blond hair is piled high on her head with random strands spilling out as though she just rolled out of bed and didn't bother brushing it, yet it's so sexy I can't drag my gaze away. She's so fucking beautiful.

She's wearing a form-fitting black tank top with a pair of very short running shorts, and the strings of a pink bikini sneak out through her top to wrap around her neck.

"Good morning," she says cheerily. Glancing around the room, she pauses only briefly on Alexei. A perverse sense of satisfaction hits me when she doesn't show an ounce of recognition.

"Good morning," I reply. Kade wiggles from my lap and barrels through the room toward her.

Rowan crouches down, but he doesn't ease up on his speed and almost knocks her over. She catches herself with her free hand and keeps them both upright. He wraps his arms around her tightly and she pats him awkwardly on the back.

That's...strange. I've seen her pick him up before. Is she really that awkward about a hug? Is it because everyone's staring at her, or did I reinforce her walls by insisting we'd be friends again?

She stands, but Kade immediately slips his hand into hers, and I watch as each muscle in her body relaxes once she has a little space.

"Are we going? Are we going on a hike now?" Kade asks, bouncing on his toes.

Rowan's face erupts like the first rays of sunshine on a cloudy day as she slowly reveals her perfectly straight teeth and dimples my fingers ache to caress. I purposefully fill my lungs with air, so I don't do something stupid, like pass out in front of her, but that's the effect she has—the ability to make me forget basic human functions like freaking breathing.

"We can head out as soon as we cover you with sunscreen."

"All done," he grins. "Daddy sprayed us."

"Oh." She seems surprised, but I've always been a hands-on dad. "Well, if you get your hats on, we can go." She turns to Seren, and her lips dance around a smile—somehow it conveys understanding.

"Did you decide to come with us?" Rowan asks. Everyone tenses, waiting for my little girl's response.

Seren shrugs her shoulder. "I heard the wild horses are pretty epic, so I guess I'll go." I can tell it took a lot of effort on her part to keep her excitement at bay, and that gives me hope.

"I'm so glad," Rowan says. There's a hint of relief in her tone that sinks all the way down to my bones.

"Okay if I tag along?" I finally ask. "It's a rare free afternoon for me."

"Oh." Rowan's eyelashes nearly hit her hairline, and she manages to frown at the same time. "Ah, of course. We're going to hike through the Ruby Rolls Trail. It's a little longer than I'd normally do with them, but it spits us out at the beach near the wild horses."

"Sounds good. Pappy went into town with Leo to get some fishing supplies, but Leo's fiancée dropped off a picnic lunch. I guess he told her your plans."

She stares at me as if I've grown three heads while I spoke. Alexei, who has been silently observing our interactions with a smug expression of appreciation on his face, finally steps forward.

"Hi, Rowan. You might not remember me, I'm Alexei. I attended Pappy's camp for a few summers with Seb."

Her face remains neutral, but the muscles around her eyes tighten. "It's nice to meet you," she says. "There were a lot of people at camp."

He nods, glancing between the two of us as if an answer to an unasked question will magically appear. When it doesn't, he simply chuckles. "Well, I'm heading to the hotel to get some work done. I'll be back to grab you tomorrow at seven, Seb."

"Thanks. If anything—"

"I'll have everything ready for Hayes and Sinclair. I've got this, you do..." He waves his arms around the kitchen. "Everything else."

Alexei Stepanov might be a pain in my ass, but he cares about my family, my business, and me. I should have listened when he told me Nick was bad news.

I nod in appreciation and stand back as he hugs all my kids, then exits the kitchen with a wave.

Rowan moves around the space as if she's always been here and starts collecting the kids' water bottles. Kade still has ahold of her hand, so she gives him one of the bottles to hold, and they fill them at the filter on the refrigerator door.

She's slipped into our lives seamlessly.

"Miles, can you grab the bug spray from the porch and stick it in one of these bags?" she says, pointing to a couple of backpacks on the floor with her foot. The movement drags my attention to her long slender legs.

"Yup," he runs past me and out the door.

"Seren?"

My daughter doesn't quite glare at Rowan, but she isn't exactly pleased either.

"Leo said to tell you they got your Amazon order, but all packages to camp have to be inspected, and they don't allow liquid laxatives. But you can go to the infirmary if you have a stomachache." Rowan smiles sweetly at Seren.

I spin on my daughter. "Are you sick?" Was she ill while I was gone?

Seren's face flames red, setting off her bright green eyes. "Geez, Dad. I'm fine."

Worry festers in my chest. "Then why did you need a laxative?"

Rowan walks between us and chuckles. "It's all good, Sebastian. Seren and I are still coming to a truce, isn't that right, Seren?"

My daughter rolls her eyes, and her fingers twitch before they clench into fists. "Leo's flyer said we can have packages delivered to camp. So much for two-day shipping," she grumbles. "I ordered it before..."

"Before what?" I demand, unease rolling down my spine. She wouldn't seriously try to make Rowan sick, would she?

"Before we came to an understanding," Rowan fills in. "It's all good. You ready?"

I can't decide if I want to look at Rowan or my daughter, and it results in a rushed glare between them both. "Yeah, I'm ready. But this conversation isn't over, Ser. As much as I want to be, I can't be with you guys every second. I have to work, and we need the help, so you have to accept that."

My daughter stomps out of the room, and Kade chases her out the door.

"I'm sorry if she's...being difficult," I say.

Rowan bends over to pick up the backpacks, and I'm a

prick because my gaze is glued to where her running shorts stretch over her perfect ass.

She stands quickly, and I immediately stare at the ceiling. What the hell is wrong with me?

"No problem. It's probably better if she gets it out on me rather than the permanent nanny." She smirks and walks out the door.

Why does it feel as though I'm being electrocuted every time she reminds me that she's temporary?

She's never hidden the fact that she has an end date, and my kids need stability. Even though my head understands that, my heart isn't getting the message because every time she's near, it beats for her—to her song.

Yes, my kids need stability, but they also need someone they can relate to, right? Someone they can tell their secrets and their fears to. And when I think about who that someone could be for them, the only person I see is Rowan.

The wild horses have nothing on the wild contradictions floating around my mind.

8

OBNOXIOUS PROTECTOR

ROWAN

"**P**ranks would have been a lot easier if I had two-day shipping when I was a kid," I whisper, catching up to Seren. The trail curves to the right, blocking us from her father's view for a few steps.

She cringes, and I laugh.

"It wasn't for you," she mutters.

Shock must register on my face because she shrugs. "It wasn't."

"Who was it for then?" Who the hell is she trying to give the shits?

She glares over her shoulder to where Sebastian is walking with Kade on his shoulders and Miles at his side as they round the bend.

"Promise you won't tell my dad?"

Ah, crap. Don't do this to me, kid.

"I promise not to tell your dad as long as you promise not to do anything without running it by me first."

Seren rolls her eyes and her lashes flutter along her brow line with the movement. I'd forgotten how many times teenagers do that. "Whatever. I'm going to get in trouble either way. I was going to stick it in the coffee of whatever full-time nanny he plans to stick me with."

I was the kid trying desperately to hide and blend in, but some of the kids I met on the street were always looking for trouble, anything to get their parents' attention. Is that what she's doing?

I peek back at Sebastian. He doesn't seem to be a man who would ignore his children, but he's had a lot going on.

"Are you trying to get in trouble?"

She stares at the ground and kicks at a rock. "Not like it would matter."

"Why do you say that?"

"It doesn't matter. My mom was gone long before she took off, and my dad tries, but his work comes first."

"Your dad loves you, Seren." Anyone can see that. "And he's worried about you."

She doesn't answer, but she does pick up her pace.

How do I keep her from sabotaging all the prospective nannies?

"What if we pull some pranks on your dad and Pappy instead?" She stops walking and stares at me with wide eyes full of cautious excitement.

"Are you serious?"

"Very. Your dad could stand to loosen up a bit, and camp prank wars are part of the experience."

"I'm so in." She grins without a moment's hesitation.

"Done. But one rule." Her grin slips from her face. "No pranks that can cause lasting damage or make anyone sick."

She rolls her eyes again. "Deal," she mumbles. "What happens if we get into trouble? What if he fires you?"

Now I roll my eyes. The action must be contagious. "If he fires me, I'll tell on him to Pappy. I'm pretty sure Pappy likes me more."

She laughs, and Sebastian's sharp intake of air tells me they've caught up enough to hear it.

"My turn, my turn, my turn," Kade squeals. His little feet stomp on the trail in circles around me. "I need a stick."

"A stick, huh?" I ask, smiling down at him.

"Yup. I gotta fight the bears."

"A stick it is then. But we can't hurt the trees, so we need to find one on the ground already." We move closer to the edge of the trail at a slower pace, and everyone else goes ahead of us.

"Oh, there's Lucky," he says, waving with both of his hands.

I stand still, scowling at the black furball. Would anyone notice if I took him to an animal shelter? That cat is a bad omen, and no one's going to tell me otherwise.

I *accidentally* stub my toe in the ground, and Lucky scurries back toward camp.

"Let's find your stick," I say, thankful that Kade is so easy to distract.

We walk in silence for a while, well, as silent as Kade is capable of being. In between the ground crunching beneath our feet and the tree branches sighing with each gust of wind, he happily hums to himself, lost to the land of make-believe in his head.

He doesn't have a single fear. It's pretty incredible to witness.

Leo told me that the property is only about four acres, and that includes the land Sebastian's house is on, but for little kids, I can see how this would feel like an entirely new world.

"Holy crap." Seren gasps, and I lift my head to find her stopped in the middle of the trail.

Sebastian and I hurry the boys along to see what's caught her attention, and I immediately blame Lucky.

"Oh, wow." We all stare down at the washed-out trail. "It's a pretty steep hill. All the rain a couple of days ago must have done this."

"But the horses," Seren whispers.

I glance up at Sebastian, and I swear we share thoughts without saying a word. She wants to see the horses more than she was letting on. Raising my brow, I nod toward the trail with a shrug.

"Worst case, we can get Leo or Alexei to come pick us up," he whispers.

"You think we can get them down the embankment safely?"

Sebastian takes a few steps down, testing the ground. "It's pretty dry. The rain probably unearthed all these tree roots." He flashes a pointed stare at each of his kids. "If we go down, you all have to be very careful and go slowly."

They all agree, and Sebastian goes first with Miles. Seren goes next, and then I help Kade down. It's easier than it looked. Sebastian, Miles, and Seren make it down without breaking a sweat. It's taking Kade and me a bit longer because he insists on checking every root for bugs.

"Go ahead and have a water break," I call down to them. "We'll be down in a minute."

Sebastian waves and tugs the backpack off his broad shoulders.

"It's so cool," Kade says, tugging free of my hand.

Then I see it.

The snake.

Everything moves in slow motion until a scream breaks the silence—my scream.

"No," I shout, lunging for Kade. I grab ahold of him

when he's less than three feet away from the copperhead that's clearly agitated. I pull Kade back toward me and away from the snake as quickly as I can, but my foot slips on an old root and we hit the ground.

Hard.

We slide for what my fear says is an eternity, but in reality is probably less than five seconds. Sebastian must have sprinted as soon as he heard me scream because he reaches us just as we stop moving.

I have Kade tucked into my chest. I think I protected him from the worst of the fall, but I can't be sure.

"Ch—check him," I gasp. The air hasn't returned to my lungs yet.

Sebastian lifts Kade easily from my chest, and I heave for oxygen. "Buddy. Are you okay? What happened? Does anything hurt?"

"That was the coolest snake I've ever seen," Kade says excitedly.

"V—venomous. Copperhead," I wheeze.

"Kade, are you hurt?" Sebastian asks again, and finally I sit up, trying to take inventory of my body, but everything aches. It takes a few more seconds to register the stabbing pain from my ankle, but when I do, I force myself not to whimper.

That's going to be a bitch.

"Nope." Kade pops his P with a full-body wiggle.

"Snakes here are dangerous, Kade. That snake was venomous, it has poison that could have killed you. You can't just charge after things like that." Sebastian's voice is tight with fear, and it unlocks a piece of my heart that my own father used to hold.

The little boy's eyes widen as he registers what his dad is saying, and then his tears fall.

"It's okay. You didn't know," I say. My voice is a little breathless still, but hopefully I'm doing a bang-up job at hiding my pain.

"Are you okay?" Sebastian asks, scanning my body now.

I'm covered in dirt and scratches, but it's my ankle that throbs. "Yeah. Go ahead, take him down. I'll be fine."

Sebastian frowns but does as I ask.

With his back to me, I slowly lift my body from the ground and gingerly take a step on my injured foot. Fuck, that hurts. But it doesn't feel broken, so I slowly make my way down. It's only a quarter mile to the beach. Seren isn't missing those damn horses because of one stupid sprained ankle.

When I reach the bottom of the hill, Sebastian is tossing all the kids' water bottles into his backpack. If I get my hands on Lucky, I'm going to ring his furry little neck.

"Are you okay?" Seren asks.

"I'm sure I look much worse than I feel," I say, forcing a laugh.

Sebastian examines me again, but this time his gaze licks flames across my skin.

"I'm fine. A few aches aren't going to keep me from these horses, and we're almost to the beach. Let's go. I'll pull up the rear."

"Rowan," Sebastian groans. He's not convinced, so I place my hands on my hips and instantly wish I hadn't when needles press into my skin, but I'll be damned if I give him the satisfaction of inspecting my injuries when he's studying me as though I'm his own personal pop quiz.

"When I say I'm fine, I mean it. I'll need to go a little slower, that's all."

He grumbles something about a stubborn ass, then takes Kade's hand and starts on the trail again.

Seren hangs back with me, which makes it much harder because now I have to hide my limp. Something pokes my side, and I find a few sharp prickers sticking out of my skin. Shit. How the hell do I get those out?

"Are you sure you're okay?" Seren asks, staring at my injured ankle.

"I'm fine." I smile tightly, though it probably comes across as more of a grimace. "So, these pranks you're planning on playing. You can't do that stuff to the nannies coming in a few days."

She scowls at me.

"Listen, if it were a normal camp, I might turn a blind eye, as long as they were harmless pranks. And by the way, laxatives do not fall into the harmless category. But the thing is, this event is really important to my friend, so I can't let you sabotage it."

We walk a few steps in silence. Sebastian glances back, and I give him a thumbs up when really, the urge to flip him off is strong, and I have no idea why other than he draws such volatile reactions from me.

"I don't really have any friends. Not anymore." The sadness in her voice claws at all my old wounds.

"It's hard," I admit. "I've only ever had one or two real friends, not a big circle of them, so I've never felt as though I'm missing anything, you know? It must be so much harder to suddenly not have them anymore."

She nods, but I can tell she's flustered by my honesty. "Everyone started making fun of me after my mom. Their parents wouldn't let them come to my house anymore, and then they started excluding me from everything."

"Well, those parents sound like idiots." I huff. "And twelve is a tough age, especially for girls. Someone is always the bad guy, the one they push away. But it also changes faster than the wind. I'll bet when you return to school in the fall, something else will happen to make them forget all about this and your friends will be back."

"I don't want them back," she snaps, but her welling eyes tells a different story. "They're punishing me for something I didn't do. Why would I want friends like that? And what kind of friend are they if they throw me away so easily?"

Her reasoning is solid and shockingly sound for a twelve-year-old.

"Well, you're more mature than I was at your age, that's for sure. But you're right. Maybe they're not your crew. Sometimes it takes these harsh realities to show you who you can really count on."

My mind drifts to my hotline dad, Thane. He's raising a sister who's around Seren's age and is dealing with something similar. I make a mental note to ensure his sister is in Seren's group during Lottie's event.

"I think you'll find a lot of the kids are dealing with similar feelings when the other campers get here."

"Oh yeah? Are there a lot of moms cheating on dads, then vanishing as though their kids never mattered?"

Oof. Okay, Seren is pissed off. She's working through those stages of grief pretty quickly—I might need a refresher course to keep up with her.

"Not exactly, but trust me, you'll be surprised by how much you have in common."

The trail turns to sand, making it even more strenuous for my ankle, and with each step, I have to work harder to school my expression.

Eventually, Sebastian and the boys come into view. They're up ahead, standing at a fence with a Jeep behind them.

Sebastian's expression darkens when he locks in on the

limp I can no longer hide. Walking in the sand is a fucking bitch.

He jogs toward us with a scowl. "What the hell, Rowan? You said you were fine."

Before I can process his actions, he swoops down and lifts me in a wedding hold to his chest. I'm too shocked to push him away.

"She's been limping for a while, Dad."

"Hey, I thought we were on the same team," I grumble, and she shrugs.

"Why the hell do you have to be so damn stubborn about everything?" He curses under his breath so only I can hear.

"About everything? You don't even know me. Do you have a knight in shining armor complex? I'm perfectly capable of walking."

He stomps toward the Jeep, pulling me more firmly to his chest, which presses those damn prickers deeper into my skin, but I refuse to flinch. When he reaches the Jeep, he sets me down in the front seat, then his hand is on my shin—his touch branding me with something scarily like desire, and I refuse to acknowledge it. Lifting my leg, he sets my foot on the dashboard, and I flinch.

"Okay, maybe fine was too mild a word," I grumble.

"For fuck's sake, Rowan. Are you trying to do permanent damage?"

I shoo him away. "It's just swollen. It hardly even hurts," I lie, then search the space for something made of wood. When I don't find anything, I knock on the dashboard—I can never be too careful when it comes to attracting good luck. "Nothing is broken, and I *am* fine. Where did you get this Jeep?"

"You're infuriating."

Kade climbs up into the Jeep and holds out his hand to me. We spent all day yesterday working on our secret handshake. Once it's complete, I return my glare to his father.

"And you're obnoxiously overprotective," I hiss.

Seren laughs, and we turn our heads toward her. That's when I realize how close Sebastian is—our cheeks are nearly touching, and the scent of him scrambles my brain. He's clean and minty and something musky I can't define.

"How ya doin'?" Kade asks, causing me to lurch away from Sebastian.

"I'm good, buddy. You ready to see some horses?" I clear my throat when it croaks like a frog.

"Yup. Daddy said I don't even need my car seat."

I frown at *Daddy*, and he shrugs.

"It's a tour Jeep, they don't provide them. Leo dropped it off for us because the horses are further north today."

Leo is on top of everything, and I'm not going to complain about it.

9

WHAT'S WRONG WITH THAT WOMAN?

SEBASTIAN

"How the hell has she survived thirty-plus years without killing herself?" I fumble through my house toward the kitchen in the dark because I couldn't find the damn light switch.

"She's independent," Pappy responds, scaring the shit out of me. He flicks on the kitchen light, and I move toward it.

"Why are you sitting in the dark?"

He holds up a pint of ice cream, and I chuckle. I've never met anyone with a bigger sweet tooth than this old man.

"Alexei read to the boys, so I came for a little snack," he says, digging into the container again. "Want some?"

I shake my head. "No, I'm grabbing some damn ice for my pain-in-the-ass nanny."

I'd called Alexei on the way home to get some ice for her ankle, and the freaking guy showed up with brand new ice packs, from the store, that need to be frozen.

"Go easy with her, Seb."

I huff out a breath through my nose, roll my shoulders back, then turn to face him.

98

"She's not had anyone take care of her since her dad passed. She doesn't know how to accept it, even from me. I can see that you're feeling a certain way, but you can't take over her world like you do with everything else."

"I'm not feeling any certain way," I grumble, sounding worse than a sulking teenager.

"No? Haven't you always though? You're the one who got her to play the piano again after her father died. And then you spent that whole summer showing her how to play guitar with the stuff you learned on the internet."

"I wasn't teaching her. I only learned the basics, so I gave her enough direction to get her started."

"And when she was nine and her canoe tipped over, you were the one to fish her out."

"She was my friend, Pappy. My friend! Would you rather I let her drown?" White stars form in my vision as the first signs of a tension headache appear.

I don't appreciate that he's watched us so closely. I've never understood why I did the things I did for Rowan. I certainly never paid close enough attention to any of my other camper friends to know when they were sad, but with her, I knew before I even saw her face. It was a feeling I'd get deep in my chest back then, and one I haven't been able to get rid of since she crashed back into my life.

"It's not in you to let anyone suffer, Seb, especially not your *friends*." I don't like the inflection he uses on the word friend—at all. "My point is, that thread that connects you two has always been there. Don't run so fast that it snaps before it has a chance to braid those love lines together, is all I'm sayin'."

Rubbing my temples, I attempt to ward off the pounding headache rolling in. "Pappy, for the last time, that's not what's happening here. I don't think she even likes me as a boss, let alone a friend. She's helping out, and she's made it abundantly clear that she's temporary."

Pfft, he tuts. "She's just never had a reason to stay."

Arguing with him will get me nowhere.

"Why have you spent all these years filling us in on each other's lives?" I ask while rummaging through the freezer. For some reason, his answer makes me uneasy, so focusing on why this house has everything except a damn ice maker feels safer.

"Why wouldn't I? You're two of the most important people in my life."

Skeptically, I glance over my shoulder, and it makes him belly laugh.

He pulls the spoon from his mouth and taps his chin with it. "You can steamroll, and she can run, but neither of you will ever outrun your destiny. Those love lines were created long before you knew what love was."

"Pappy." Exasperation laces every letter. "Just because there's a connection does not mean we're destined to be together. I want forever, and she wants what's next. That will never work out."

He shrugs as if I'm the town idiot. "Unless what's next is forever. We'll see, Seb. We'll see. Don't go scaring her off. You can be rather pushy when you're...worried."

My nose scrunches up with the need to defend myself, but he's right. I'm generally relaxed, but there are five people in this world who change me from relaxed to a raving nervous jackalope in the blink of an eye, and nothing has ever worried me more than Rowan Ellis.

"I'm going to sit on the porch," Pappy calls over his shoulder.

"Sure," I grumble, then go about twisting the old ice cube trays and tossing the ice into a zip-top bag. "What's next for me is giving my kids stability. And there's nothing stable about Rowan's lifestyle. Great. Now I'm talking to myself."

Refilling the trays, I carefully set them back in the freezer, then turn off the lights and head upstairs to Rowan's room.

When I knock, it's Seren who calls out, "Come in."

Opening the door, I find my little girl on Rowan's bed scribbling in a notebook that she quickly snaps closed.

"Are you all right?" I ask.

"Yup."

"Did you have fun with the horses today?" I'm standing in the center of the room now, so close yet so far away from my sweet little girl.

"They were pretty, and seeing them with the sunset on the ocean was so cool," she says, lowering her chin to her chest. "But I feel really bad. Rowan was hurting but made you keep driving so I wouldn't miss the horses."

"She wanted you to have a good day. So did I. I haven't seen you smile in a long time, sweet pea. It made me very happy."

She nods with watery eyes. "It was a good day." She twists her hands together in front of her but keeps her chin pressed into her chest. "Rowan's not so bad."

"No, she's not," I say through the thick glob of emotion sticking to my throat. "Speaking of, where the heck is she now? She was supposed to stay put while I got her ice."

Spinning in place, I search the empty room for clues.

"I told her that, Dad. Really, I did. But she said you were not the boss of her, and she needed a shower." Seren tries and fails to hold in her laughter.

I stare blankly at my daughter, mesmerized by the beautiful smile I've missed so damn much.

"I don't hear the water running," I say as a grin of my own creeps across my face.

"Ah, the bathroom upstairs is really cool. It has a rain shower, and you can see the ocean, so we claimed that one as the girls' bathroom."

"She walked up another flight of stairs to shower?"

Seren nods while biting her lip.

"With an ankle the size of a soccer ball?"

My little girl starts chewing the side of her nail. "I tried to help her, but she told me to try and hear the music because she was *fine*." She accentuates the word with an eye roll.

"What's wrong with that woman?" I say more to myself than anything.

Seren opens her mouth and closes it multiple times while I wait her out. She appears to be collecting her thoughts, and I don't want to rush her. This is the longest conversation I've had with her in months.

"She doesn't have anyone to count on, Daddy." My gaze snaps to my little girl. Daddy is becoming a less frequent moniker, and I miss the hell out of it. "She doesn't even have any friends other than her boss and Pappy. Like, none. It makes me…" She peers down at her notebook again. "It makes me sad for her. She must be so lonely, and it hurts to be lonely." She won't lift her gaze to mine, but it doesn't take a genius to figure out that she's talking about herself now. "But I think she's been lonely her whole life, and that hurts. I didn't want to like her. But now I kind of do, and I'm sad for her."

I didn't think my heart could shatter any more than it already had, but my little girl just proved me wrong.

I stride to the bed, drop the ice bag on the blanket, and place my palms on either side of her. "I like her too, and I'm so glad that we're on the same page, Seren. But..." I swallow and roughly tear my gaze away. "Rowan is only our temporary nanny. She moves around a lot and enjoys experiencing new things. She's going to leave at the end of the month. You understand that, right?"

"I know that's what she said." Pouty, moody Seren is back. "But..."

"We can't get our hopes up for something that has very clearly been explained as a termination date."

Goddamn it. Will Seren view the loss of Rowan as another sledgehammer to her already fragile heart?

"She said she'll write to me when she writes to Pappy." My little girl loses the life that filled her words only moments ago faster than water escapes a broken dam.

"I'm sure she will, baby. I think Rowan is someone who keeps her promises." Even if that promise is to run.

Seren leans back against the wall, staring straight through me.

I hold up the bag of ice, and she nods. "I'm going to go find little Miss Stubborn and make sure she puts this on her ankle."

She graces me with a curious smile. "It's okay if you like her too, Dad. Maybe she needs a friend like you."

Oh, sweetheart. My biggest fear is that I'll end up wanting to be much more than friends.

"Maybe," I say instead.

She stands and wraps me in a hug. It hits harder than a baseball bat to the head. "I love you," she whispers. "I'm going to bed." I can't speak, so I kiss the top of her head and allow my gaze to follow her as she walks down the hall to her room. As soon as her door closes, I stomp up the stairs, flittering between anger and annoyance with each step.

I reach the third-floor bathroom and pause at the door. I hadn't really thought this through.

But I'm suddenly so pissed that thinking clearly isn't a priority any longer. How dare she get my daughter to like her. Yes, I'm aware that I'm being unreasonable, but what the fuck am I going to do when Rowan runs? It's not as though I can force her to stay with us.

Can I?

No.

Freaking hell, she's making me lose my damn mind and it's only been a week.

Glancing over my shoulder, I'm relieved that the door to the bunk room is closed. I stand in the hallway and bang on the bathroom door.

"Rowan," I bark. Generally speaking, I'm not a yeller, but damn, does it relax me right now.

No one has ever riled me up this way before, and the sad part is, I'm fairly certain she's not even trying to do it. Lucky me.

The water turns off, and she says, "Sebastian? What is it? I'm in the shower."

"Are you decent?"

"What?"

"Are you covered?"

"Ah, yeah?" she says like a question.

"Can I come in?"

"What?"

"Can. I. Come. In?"

"It's your house." I swear she growls at me.

And I've lost all my brain cells because I storm into the bathroom.

Rowan stands behind a curtain that isn't see-through, but it does show the silhouette of her body.

"What the hell, Sebastian? If you storm in on all your nannies in the shower, you're going to have a freaking lawsuit on your hands."

"You told me I could come in, and don't change the subject. You said that you'd wait for me, and you didn't. You're injured, Rowan. How can you take care of my kids if you can't even fucking walk?"

"Yeah, well, I also have prickers stuck in my skin that hurt like a bitch, so I needed to try and open my pores."

"You...what?"

"My back and hips are on fire with tiny pinpricks. I must have slid down, at least partially, on a pricker bush. The damn things hurt like hell."

My gaze darts all around the room in time with my frustration. "But Kade doesn't have a scratch on him."

She steps up onto her tiptoes to glare at me. "No, he doesn't. Because I take my job very seriously. Do you really think I'd let him get hurt if I could do something about it? Hand me my towel."

Reaching over, I pull her towel down from the hook and hand it to her. "Let me get this straight. You twisted your ankle, possibly broke it—"

"It's not broken," she huffs and lowers her toes so I can no longer see her eyes, but her hand slips out from the curtain, and she knocks on the cabinet two times.

"Did you knock on the cabinet for good luck about your ankle?"

"You can never be too careful. I don't want to jinx anything."

I pinch the bridge of my nose and count to five. "Fine. You hurt your ankle, badly," I modify. "Then you sat in the Jeep for hours—hours, Rowan! —with slivers in your skin and you never once thought to speak up?"

Her towel flops over the top of the shower rod, and I clench my jaw tightly to keep a groan from escaping.

"Hand me that towel robe thing," she demands, pointing to the sink.

I pick it up and hand it over the curtain. If she were anyone else, I'd feel so uncomfortable I probably wouldn't be able to form words, but with her, I have no control over myself, and the need to get everything out is stronger than my willpower. It's a strange thing unique to this woman— the guard I protect myself with crumbles in her presence.

She rips the curtain open, and I might swallow my tongue.

She's wearing a tiny purple towel with elastic that holds it up over her breasts like a tube dress.

"Would you have rather I let Kade take the brunt of that fall?"

"Don't be daft."

"Daft?" She turns her fiery gaze my way. "Since you're the one standing in a bathroom, with your hired help, I would say you're the one who's daft. Are you trying to get sued for sexual harassment, Seb?"

She's never called me Seb before. It's...intimate.

"Because Pappy told me that you're working your ass off on fixing a false image some asshole is painting of you. A lawsuit from whatever nanny you hire will not help your case."

It's interesting that she's talking about a future nanny but says nothing about herself in this situation. But she's right, I can't believe I barged in on her in the shower. What in the actual fuck was I thinking?

She turns her back on me, and that's when all the rational thoughts attempting to make an appearance evaporate into thin air. Not only are her shoulders and legs scratched all to hell, but there are tiny burrs sticking out of her skin.

I reach out and touch her shoulder because regardless of what else is going on, I will always be drawn to this woman. The second my skin touches hers—she halts. Her only movement is a sharp intake of air as though I've just jump-started her lungs.

Her skin is silky under my touch, and Pappy's words about destiny and love lines become a living, breathing entity, pulsing where our skin connects.

"You're touching me," she whispers.

"I know asking for help is right up there with scratching out your own eyeballs, but Peach, you need help before these get infected. Is your entire back covered in burrs?"

She drops her head to her chest.

"I don't want Seren to do it." She sighs. "She already feels guilty enough about the horses, and I wasn't going to take that experience away from her."

The anger and annoyance that filled my limbs only moments ago are replaced with admiration and so much affection my knees grow weak.

"Pappy's eyesight isn't what it used to be, and there's not a fucking chance in hell I'm letting Alexei touch you." My voice carries an edge to it that sounds an awful lot like jealousy.

Her spine stiffens.

"That leaves you with a couple of choices," I say, lowering my voice while simultaneously stepping closer. I really should remove my hand from her shoulder, but I don't because I don't want to, and she hasn't asked me to, so my thumb continues to run soft circles on her skin. "We need supplies from the infirmary to get these out, so we can call Leo and see if his fiancée can meet us there."

She shakes her head, and droplets of water cascade from her hair down her back and over my hand. "She has a new baby. I won't bother her with something so dumb." Her voice is barely above a whisper.

"Then your only option is to allow me to carry you to the infirmary where you can ice your ankle while you lie on your stomach, and I use tweezers and alcohol to remove all this shit. I'd do it here, but we don't have a first aid kit, and I think some of these spots will need to be cleaned out."

"You have three kids, Seb. You really need a first aid kit, and I can walk." Feisty as an uncontrollable fucking fire.

"You can walk, but you won't, and I'll buy a first aid kit first thing in the morning. So what's your choice, Rowan? And I'll warn you, I'm already pissed off that you A, walked up here on that ankle and B, suffered for hours while your body was a live version of a fucking voodoo doll, so choose wisely."

She spins and my fingers drag across her skin from her shoulder to her collarbone before I pull my hand back.

The flush that covers her body is an aphrodisiac that causes my cock to stand up and take notice.

"Let's get one thing very clear here, Sebastian." My name is hellfire coming from her lips. "You are not the boss of me. I mean, you are, but I have agency over my personal life, got it? I'm not a scared little girl who needs rescuing anymore. That part of our relationship is over."

I step forward, crowding her against the sink because I love how the words *our relationship* fall from her pouty lips.

"This...relationship...has always been about more than that and you know it. Everyone needs someone to cover their back, and luckily, I'm the man for all things Rowan Ellis. Now grab your shit."

Her jaw drops. "Don't you dare."

"Fine, we'll come back for it." Leaning down, I place my arms on either side of her so she knows I'm not fooling around here. She swats her hands in my direction, which makes me want to pin her to the vanity with my body.

"Rowan," I bark. "You're only wearing a robe. If you keep moving, it will not hold up." I lean down so my mouth hits that sensitive spot below her ear. "Not that I'd mind that show. In fact, I'd fucking love it, but if that's not what you want, climb on my back and let me take care of you."

"You can't carry me through the woods naked, Sebastian."

My eyes flare and her hand immediately flies to her robe while she glares at me, and I take two steps back.

"Grab your towel." She does it without any more questions and wraps it around her waist. "Good girl." Those two words rumble through my body, but I don't miss the reddening of her cheeks as I kneel down and wait for her to climb on either. She's affected too, and when she squeezes her arms around my neck, I realize I might give up everything but my kids to keep this woman in our sphere.

10

TRAITOROUS VAGINA

ROWAN

"**G**ood girl," he murmurs in my ear. What the hell? Did I suddenly come down with a praise kink? Or maybe I'm losing my damn mind because my core spasms as though it's a hairsbreadth away from orgasming.

From freaking words.

"Good girl," I shoot back when I'm mostly convinced that I have control of my traitorous vagina. "I told you, Sebastian Walker, that you are not the boss of me. I'm not a child in need of saving. I don't need rescuing or any other bullshit princess constructs that are constantly shoved down our throats."

"And I told you, Rowan Ellis, that sometimes you have to let down your guard and count on someone else."

"You never said that."

"Maybe not, but I'm telling you now. Sometimes you have to trust me." He opens the door and fires off his glare to the left, then the right, and I hear Pappy laugh. "I'm taking her to the infirmary. We'll be back."

Slowly, he turns his head. Our cheeks are too close for this conversation and I'm far too naked. My lips are pressed into a thin line, and my jaw is clenched so tightly it clicks in my ears.

He shakes his head, but I don't miss the sadness in his features.

"I don't need your pity either," I say haughtily.

"Trust me, pity is the last thing I'm feeling." The way the words rumble in his chest knocks loose something in mine, and I chew on my lips to keep every catastrophic idea from escaping my mouth.

He stomps through the night, holding me up by the backs of my thighs as carefully as he can. He can't help himself, he's a natural-born caretaker. His kids are very lucky to have him.

"Who do you trust?" he asks quietly, so quietly he's almost drowned out by the crickets and frogs.

That's too broad a question for me to ever answer. "Trust with what?"

"I don't know, Rowan. Who's your emergency contact?"

"I'm not ten. I don't have school forms my mom is supposed to fill out anymore. What the hell would I need an emergency contact for?"

He stops walking, cranes his neck, and forces me to look at him in the moonlight.

"If you were in an accident, who would the hospital call?"

"Who knows. If I'm dead, it doesn't matter, right? And if I'm not, I'll take care of myself again as soon as I get out."

The man growls. Actually growls as though he's calling his wolfpack to meet us out here in the dark.

"And you don't think it would absolutely crush Pappy if he suddenly never heard from you again?"

Shit. He had to play the Pappy card.

"Well, there are only two numbers in my phone. They'd either call him or Lottie."

"And if your phone was submerged in a lake or thrown from the car?"

I don't answer, and eventually, he starts walking again.

"You need a damn emergency contact. Who do you call if your car breaks down?"

"AAA."

"What if you're sick?" he shoots back.

"Then I would have some freaking chicken noodle soup delivered. Listen, I get that you've spent the last twelve years in dad-mode, but I had one of those and I'm not looking for another. When I say I can handle my shit, I mean it."

"You're impossible."

"And you're infuriating."

He grins back at me with a wolfish gleam that has me loosening my arms around his neck to create space.

"You like me," he says, and I swear to God he adds a sexy swagger to his gait as he jogs up the steps to the camp infirmary while wearing a smirk that shows off dimples I've just now noticed. Dimples I want to lick.

Lick? What the what?

"Did I hit my head in the fall? How do you get that from me telling you that you're infuriating?" I ask, but I've lost the bite that made it easy to keep him at bay.

"Because you keep going. If you didn't like me, you'd simply walk away, you wouldn't engage." He tilts forward, resting me on his back so he can use one hand to enter a code to unlock the door. The adjustment places the bag of ice dangling from his hands on my upper thigh, and I hiss in a breath right before Lucky meows on the steps below us.

Of course that little fucker is here. Now I'm certain he's the reason I slid into a pricker bush in the first place.

"In case you've missed it, Sebastian, you're carrying me. Carrying me! I don't have the option of walking away."

He gently sets me down on a doctor's table, then picks up Lucky and places him outside.

"I like our banter," he chuckles, striding back to me with purpose. "Lie down on your belly so I can put this ice under your ankle."

I do what he says and then grumble into my hands when I'm face down. After he positions the ice, I hear him searching through cabinets and drawers.

"How did you even get in here? Do you have any idea what you're doing?" I ask.

"I'm a silent owner of the camp, and what I'm doing is keeping you from getting an infection," he says as if this is just another day.

He exhales, and it shifts the air at my back. He moved so stealthily I hadn't heard him approach. "Okay, we're going to have to lower the towel some."

I choose to ignore the throaty tone of his voice.

Holding the towel to my chest, I lift up and undo the Velcro holding it together so it can slide down my back, then drop my face back to my folded hands.

"Could this be any more humiliating?" I groan.

His laughter catches fire in my veins. "Well, yeah. You could have them in your ass too."

Mother forking jackoffs. I groan in answer, and his hands hover above my skin. The heat of them ghosts over my shoulder blade.

"You have them in your ass too, don't you?" He sounds tortured, and I shudder to admit it, but he also sounds turned on, and that ignites every naughty thought I've ever had about this man.

"God, why me? I couldn't get through this with a shred of dignity?" My voice doesn't sound any less needy than his.

"I can always call Leo's fiancée, Tabby, if you want."

God. Did his voice drop and become even more silvery?

"No, forget it," I mutter. "Let's get this over with and then never, ever talk about it again." As mortifying as this is, he's right. My ass is on fire from sitting on it for so long in the car.

He rips open a package, and then his hands are on me, gently caressing my back with the softest touch. Then he stops, and my skin pinches as he plucks a burr out, and I hiss in a mouthful of air.

"Sorry," he whispers, leaning so close to my ear that I shiver. "I'll be as gentle as I can."

And lord help me, but I believe him.

We're silent as he meticulously makes his way down my spine. When he leans down to get one close to the side of my breast, I hear him swallow. It shouldn't turn me on, but like everything else in my life right now, nothing behaves as it should.

His fingers skim the sensitive skin of my side, so close to my breast that it grows heavy with want.

Holy shit. I want this man to touch me.

I'm over thirty. I've had sex, but it's usually better when I take care of things myself. A single touch has certainly never stolen my breath before.

"Sorry, I'm not trying to feel you up, I promise."

A whoosh of air releases in a semi-choked laugh.

"Not your type, huh?" I have no idea how those words left my mouth. Maybe I should have seen a doctor. I must be concussed.

His fingertips rest on my back. All ten connections press

at different times into my skin, and after a few moments, I lift my head to peer up at him.

His gaze is searing into my soul, and I wish I'd never looked up.

"Why would you say that?" His voice is rough and low. He has me pinned to this bed, not by where his hands touch me, but by the way his gaze devours me.

My mouth opens and closes a few times—I'm finally speechless. He walks to the head of the table, and I arch my back to maintain eye contact. Slowly, he lowers into a squat, so we're face-to-face.

"I think you're the very definition of my type, Peach. Maybe you always have been, but I have children to consider, a career that is one wrong turn away from collapsing. My wants and needs can't factor into my life until my children feel stable, but make no mistake, whatever you thought my type was, you're wrong." He never breaks eye contact while he speaks—he doesn't even blink.

If ever there were honesty in words, I'd bet Junebug that he's offering pure truth.

He stands suddenly, and my eyes expand when I come face-to-crotch with a very defined cock that's pressing the limits of what his khakis will allow.

Sebastian sees my reaction and chuckles before returning to my backside.

Ugh, what am I doing?

Thankfully, he's quiet after that little spiel, but the silence makes scenarios run amok in my mind. It doesn't help that his hands have been on me for an eternity now.

I've never let a man touch me for this long. Sex is just that, sex. I don't even mind the phrase wham, bam, thank you ma'am because that's exactly what I've wanted. But this? With him? It's too much.

Goosebumps explode over my skin, and there are times when he touches me that I can't contain a shiver. Like now, when he's at the base of my spine. He can probably see the dimples above my ass, and he has his face so close to me that his hot breath flutters against my skin. It's erotic in a way I don't know how to handle.

His breathing has also changed. It's more erratic and panting?

Is he panting on me? I don't dare to look, but suddenly his heat is gone.

"Fuck, Rowan. Maybe we should call someone else to do the rest." He sounds as tortured as I feel.

Rolling my face to the side so I can stare at him, I blink away moisture that shouldn't be there and hope he doesn't notice. "Why?" I finally ask.

"I can't tell you that."

"Why?" I repeat.

His heated stare bores into my skin. His jaw ticks, and the muscles in his neck jump three times as though he's chewing on his words. "Because if I tell you why we need someone else to finish, I'll have to tell you why I can't do it, and that will sure as fuck scare you away. I won't do that to you or my kids. They like you, and they need you."

"I'm temporary," I remind him, but unfortunately for me, it feels like the start of a lie. "But I also don't scare easily, Seb. When you've fought the demons and won, nothing else can hurt you. And I've won. Over and over again."

"You don't know what you're asking."

I raise a brow in his direction. "Don't I?"

His palm rests at the curve of my back, and he lowers his face so we're cheek to cheek. Every nerve ending in my body comes to life. This is what it means to be alive.

I almost moan at the intensity of it all.

"I think we should find someone else to work on your ass, as much as it pains me to say that, because simply touching your back for the past hour has my cock fighting against my zipper and weeping for a taste of you. Because if I touch your ass, I'm going to want more. Because if I hear you moan one more time at the touch of my hands, I'm going to flip you over and worship every goddam inch of your body, and then I'm going to make you come until your body seizes up and begs for a break before I do it all over again."

His fingertips dance at the curve of my ass.

"That's why I can't do this, Peach. I can't take the risk of losing you while my children are just beginning to make progress, so unless you're willing to give me more than three weeks, we need someone else to work on your ass."

He places the most chaste of kisses to my cheek.

"Do you—"

"Well now, this is interesting." Lottie's voice bursts our overly erotic bubble like an explosion in a silent night.

I gasp and scramble to right myself while Sebastian takes his time unfurling himself to his full, upright position.

"What are you doing here?" I ask.

"I got in this afternoon and was in the office with Leo. He got a notification that Sebastian had unlocked the infirmary, but it never said he left, so when we finished there I decided to come see how things were working out with you," she says, but her eyes miss nothing as she scans the situation she's found us in. "It appears I had nothing to worry about."

"She's injured," Sebastian says. How the hell is his voice so calm? "I've been working on her back for an hour plucking these little fuckers out." He holds up a pair of tweezers as if that explains it all. "But, as I was explaining, for the sake of professionalism, we should call in someone to help her with a more delicate area."

He walks toward Lottie and hands her the tweezers.

"Rowan," he says my name when he's at the door but waits until I lift my gaze to his. "I'm really." His throat works to swallow. "Really glad I could be the one to help you. I understand why you don't trust easily, but you can always come to me." His jaw ticks, and his gaze darkens as it sweeps over me one final time. "For anything. I'll wait outside to carry you home."

Then he exits, and the door snapping shut makes me jump. My mind is a battlefield, and I don't know which side of the war I'm on anymore. It takes several minutes for me to realize Lottie's talking.

"Are you okay?" Her question finally registers in my brain.

"Mm-hmm. I slid in some burrs. I have some poky things in my ass. Can you get them out?"

"It's a good thing I love you, Rowan Ellis. But don't for one minute think you're going to get out of discussing whatever the hell that was with Sebastian—your client, I might add."

Guilt turns my stomach. She's worked so hard to build this company, but at the same time, far too many of her nanny matches have ended up with the title of wife. I know it's just not for me, and something about that makes my insides tremble violently.

"It's nothing," I mumble.

"Don't give me that when it smells of sex and happy endings in here."

I scoff.

"Not that kind of happy ending. The kind that ends in a white dress and a picket fence."

"No," I nearly scream. "That's not what this is. At all. I just—he's Pappy's grandson."

She freezes with the tweezers held in the air. "Your Pappy? The one who showed up to graduation? The only other person on this planet that you talk to regularly. That Pappy?"

"Mm-hmm." Words are getting twisted between my mind and heart, so I simply hum. One drunken night with Lottie, I spilled a lot of my secrets. I've never regretted it before now though.

"Whoa. So, how long have you known Sebastian?"

"I don't. Not really. I knew him, past tense, from the age of eight to thirteen. But we weren't really friends. It's more that he felt the need to babysit me. I haven't seen him since that last summer at Pappy's."

I hear a thud and lift my head to find that she's dropped heavily into the chair beside the table. I recognize that starry-eyed gaze, but I want nothing to do with it.

"This is not a fairy tale or those spicy love stories you read, Lottie. It's not some second-chance—or even a first-chance romance. I'm leaving in a few weeks. It's what I know. It's how I protect myself, and I'd rather be safe than live my life waiting every day for someone else to leave me. I can't go through that again. I can't." My voice breaks, and so does her happy expression.

"Oh, hon. You're beyond fucked up, huh?" She sniffles and giggles at the same time. It causes a very similar, but snotty reaction from me.

"I am," I admit.

She nods, but I can almost hear the gears of her imagination spinning this tale into something fit for a princess. What she doesn't understand is that sometimes it's the princess who has to hurt the prince to survive—and that's something I'd never want to do to Sebastian.

"Let's get this over with then. You do have an amazing ass, but this is the very last thing I was expecting to do tonight."

I lie down, and she swings the towel to expose one cheek. She gasps. "Holy crap, Rowan. What the hell did you do to yourself?"

"It's a long story. Just do what you can, and I'm sure I'll be fine."

With a throaty chuckle, she gets to work on my butt. That's an image that will need to be bleached from my mind in the morning.

Well, if I still have a job in the morning. Where will Sebastian and I go from here? Where will I go from here?

11

BAND OF MERRY FUCKING MEDDLERS

SEBASTIAN

The sound of a chair scraping along the floor has me lifting my blurry gaze from the conference table we've set up in Beck's home, and I find three sets of eyes staring at me.

Well, two staring and one glaring. I've learned that Beck Hayes has two modes, laid-back family man and takes-no-prisoners businessman.

I can't say I blame him. It's probably what people say about me. But lately, my mind has been stuck in the infirmary with Rowan last week, and this is not the time for my focus to splinter.

"You've taken care of the Nick problem in Boston, at least for now," Elijah says to the group, wearing a toothy grin that's a little too happy for my liking.

"And we're working on the public image issue he's attempting to create," Beck grumbles.

"I also have most of the investors recommitted to moving forward once those image issues are resolved," Alexei says. The shit-eating grin on his face makes me believe he can tell exactly where my mind has gone. "The recording of that douchebag was a nice touch."

"I haven't seen any issues with the merger." Elijah's face nearly splits in two when his clownish smile takes over his entire face. "But I have seen this sullen, pissed-off expression before. Recently actually. Does it look familiar to you, Beck?"

Beck tosses his pen onto the table. "I don't play games, so here's the deal. I've been where you are before, so if you're in love with your nanny, tell us what you did wrong, and we'll help you fix it before things spiral out of control."

Affronted, I nearly leap from my chair, and then begin pacing like a caged tiger. "I'm not in love with my nanny, she hasn't been here that long, and I didn't do anything. It's... complicated."

"It usually is." Beck sighs, pinching the bridge of his nose in what I assume is annoyance. "Tell us what's going on so we can get back to work."

I open my mouth to argue, but he points a finger at me and shakes his head.

"I know firsthand how fucked up messy love can make a man. We're in this together now, Sebastian, because if you go down, we go down. That means if there's a crisis in your home life, there's a crisis in ours."

"I'm not in crisis. Rowan is a temporary nanny—"

"Who you've had feelings for since you were twelve years old." Alexei chuckles.

"You"—I point my own finger at him—"stay out of this."

He holds up his hands in mock surrender, but it's obvious that he has absolutely no intention of staying out of it.

"Come on, Seb. Tell us your story," Elijah urges, then reclines in his seat and runs his thumbs under the bright yellow suspenders he's wearing today. Even at the beach, this guy is wearing suspenders. I'm not sure if I should laugh or get him an appointment with a personal stylist.

Since we're not going to move on from this until I tell them something, a shortened version of how we met as kids is probably the way to go. But once I open my mouth, it all spills out, every memory I have of her right up until the sexually charged night in the infirmary.

When I've finished, everyone's faces have glazed over. They're not even blinking. Did I bore them to sleep?

Beck is the first to come to. When he clears his throat, the other two blink as though they have sand in their eyes.

"Okay, well that's..." He shakes his head. "That's quite the history. And you haven't seen or heard from her since you were a teenager?"

"No. Well, Pappy always gives me updates, but I'm not a fucking pervert or a stalker. We were kids—friends, and I didn't feel this way about her then, at least I don't think I did. She was always fucking sad. It made my stomach hurt to see her that way, even when I was just a kid myself."

"And how do you feel about her now?" Alexei asks with a serious tone he doesn't use often.

Tugging on the ends of my hair, I shake my head and fall back into my chair. "I don't know."

"You're not going to get anywhere until you figure out what you fucking want," Beck says harshly.

"Do you want her?" Elijah asks.

I press the heels of my palms into my eye sockets, trying to arrange my wild thoughts. "I want my children to be happy. I want them to feel safe. I want to be a great dad and protect them from any more pain."

"That's what you want for your kids, and I commend that," Beck says patiently. "But what do *you* want?"

"That's the thing. My children will always come first, and what they need may not align with what I want."

"Why?" Beck asks. He's calmer than I expected he'd be at a commandeered business meeting.

"Because my children need security and stability, and what I want, who I want, lives her life in temporary situations. Rowan is always searching for an end date."

"So, give her one." Alexei rubs his jaw with his thumb, and I can almost envision the dumb fucking idea taking root in his mind.

He looks at Elijah, who shrugs and turns to Beck.

Beck shrugs. "It might work."

"What might work?" They're making me dizzy.

"Give her an end date that keeps extending." Elijah is obviously proud of this plan, but I'm even more confused.

"What makes you think that she, the woman who moves across the country yearly, and never takes permanent positions anywhere, is going to accept an extension?"

"We don't," they say in unison.

"But if she accepts the first one, she might be more likely to accept the next one. And, if we get the town involved, she'll be rooted here before she even realizes what's happened." Beck actually smiles. "It happened with my wife. Trust me, this town has a way of wrapping their limbs around even the most stubborn people."

"This all sounds a little...I don't know, high-handed and disaster-ish?"

"Do you have a better plan?" Alexei asks.

When I don't answer, he changes tactics. "Is seeing where things can go with Rowan worth it?"

The word "yes" flies from my mouth with absolutely no thought, filter, or planning.

"Then it's worth a try, right?" Elijah asks.

I lean back in my chair and scan each of their faces.

"This is, without a doubt, the most ridiculous business meeting I've ever had. I came to discuss floorplans and building strategy, and instead, I got Prince Charming's band of merry fucking meddlers."

Elijah and Alexei high-five each other while Beck drops his head against his chair to stare at the ceiling.

"There are worse things we could be called." Elijah laughs. "Now that we've got a plan, let's bust out these floorplans so Prince Charming can head back to his castle on the beach."

My groan vibrates through my veins. I might not survive this shit show.

———

I WOULDN'T SAY Rowan's been avoiding me for the last few days, but it does feel as though she's actively running from me. Which I admit is highly impressive, considering we live in the same house. That's put to a stop when we're both called to Leo's office to meet his new camp director, Maria DeLuca.

"Pappy's doing arts and crafts with the kids at the pavilion," she says without looking at me. She's standing against the wall of the office giving off *don't fuck with me* vibes.

"Good afternoon, Rowan. How are you, Rowan? It's good to see you, Rowan." Jesus. I've reverted to a teenaged asshole, except I wasn't even this prickly when I was fifteen.

"Good afternoon, Sebastian," she hisses. "I'm fine, how are you? It's good to see you as well." I think she'll end it there, but I should know to expect the unexpected with her. That fire that sizzles inside of her won't allow her to back down. "Although I also saw you this morning, and twice yesterday, so it's not as if it's been years since we've spoken."

I'm smiling so broadly my lips are dry. My tongue runs along the corner of my mouth, and her gaze follows the motion. I swear her reaction causes my stomach to tighten and desire to swirl through my veins. Leaning in so only she can hear me, I whisper, "This time, Peach. It hasn't been years, this time."

She scrunches up her nose and purses her lips into an angry scowl, then uses two fingers to push me back a step.

"You've been spending a lot of time with Pappy, and I can tell you that I've never seen him so at peace. He loves being with you every day, Peach."

Some of the ice leaves her features. "He's probably the only person I've ever missed."

That one sentence gives me hope in the harebrained scheme the merry fucking meddlers came up with.

"Well, hello." Lottie drags out the word *hello* like a Broadway performer. "You two are awfully cozy. Again."

Rowan shoots eyeball daggers at her friend.

"Anyway," Leo says, clearing his throat. "This is Tabby, my fiancée, and our son, Ryker." A small woman with a baby strapped to her chest and flour dusting her cheek steps forward with a wave. Her dress is a patchwork of uncoordinated colors, and she's wearing a rainbow apron beneath the sleeping baby.

We share greetings, then refocus on Leo. "And this is Maria. She's our new camp director, and she'll be taking over all our needs for the next few weeks while she prepares for a full July session. I'll be in and out, working on refurbishing various parts of the camp and running yoga sessions on the beach. You have my number should anything come up, but Maria will be your point of contact for the nanny mixer."

Tabby dances on her toes. "And we're having a sand dance tonight, so you have to come." She clasps her hands under her chin, and her happiness bounces off her as she continues brightly. "Bella Moonbeam, she's my friend. Well, she's everyone's friend. She's the town party planner and the sweetest human on the planet. Anyway, she pulled this one off at the request of Beck and Elijah which is just, gah, it's so nice of them. They don't usually get involved in these. So basically, that means you all have to come. Okay? Great. I'll see you all there."

She bounces out of the office. Did she even breathe through that entire spiel?

"She's, ah, excitable," Leo says affectionately.

"She's lovely," Rowan says with her eyes pinned straight ahead.

Just to test her, I step forward so I'm in her peripheral vision and grin. She can't ignore me, no matter how hard she tries.

"It's nice to meet you, Maria." Rowan steps forward and shakes the woman's hand.

Rowan steps back, and I repeat the greeting, returning to stand a little closer to Rowan.

Lottie and Maria discuss some things about her date-a-nanny event—I mean, her *hire*-a-nanny event—and I take the opportunity to speak quietly with Rowan.

I don't necessarily intend to crowd her space, but when she takes a step back, I follow until she's pressed against the wood paneling.

"Sebastian," she says through gritted teeth. "What are you doing?"

"I'm saying hello to my friend."

She narrows her eyes and screws up her lips. "I know what you're doing, but I'm your nanny. Your temporary nanny, not your friend."

I dramatically clutch my chest. "Rowan Ellis, I've known you since you were eight years old. Are you saying you won't be my friend?"

Her nose twitches, reminding me of a baby bunny, and she twists the pink and black bracelets she's always wearing around her wrist. Something partially hidden by her bracelet catches my attention, and I pull her hand up high.

A vision of pinning her naked to the wall floods my mind, and I bite back a groan.

When I push down the beads, the air in my lungs turns to cement. A sea of memories washes over me while I gently rub my thumb over the tiny tattoo on her wrist.

"It's a peach," I say, dumbfounded. The words are a guttural sound I have no control over.

She shrugs. "It's just a tattoo."

"Just a tattoo?" My throat rumbles with the words. "Does anyone else call you Peach?"

"No. It's a tattoo, nothing more."

"When did you get it?"

"When I turned eighteen."

She won't look at me, but a smile erupts across my face, and the emotions I've been holding at bay break free.

She didn't forget me.

"You see, Peach. I think that this tattoo proves that we are, in fact, friends and always have been."

"You're reading too much into this," she says, attempting to pull her hand away, but her gaze darts around the room as though she's guilty and needs an escape.

"Are you trying to tell me that this tattoo has nothing to do with me?"

"That's exactly what I'm saying," she hisses, but she can't hide the truth in her brown eyes.

"You're a terrible liar, Peach. But I'll wait for you to tell me about it on your own." I release her wrist, and she quickly covers the tattoo with her bracelet.

"What do you want?" she whispers.

The thing is, I have no idea what I want, and the revelation of her tattoo has my mind spinning, so I say the first thing that pops into my mind. "Dance with me at the sand dance."

Her jaw comes unhinged, and she begins tapping the black bracelet.

"I like those," I say, reaching out and pressing my thumb to her wrist again, right above the tattoo. "You wear them a lot."

Confusion has never looked more beautiful than it does on her pretty face.

"The pink one is a reminder to love yourself and the black one absorbs negative energy," she mutters.

"You believe in crystals but not Pappy's ideas on destiny?"

Her hands fall to her hips. My little warrior is coming out to play. "Who do you think gave me these?" she asks, holding her wrist in front of my face.

"Sounds like something he'd do." I tilt closer to her. "So, will you dance with me?"

"Are you seriously asking me to a dance like we're in high school?"

Suddenly, it feels imperative that that is exactly what we do. "I am."

"I'm not going," she fires back.

"Oh, you're going," Lottie calls over her shoulder. How the hell did she even hear us?

Rowan flips her friend off, but Lottie laughs while Rowan grabs me by the sleeve and drags me outside and around the corner of the building.

She faces me with her arms crossed over her chest, fire in her eyes, and her toe tapping aggressively against the dirt.

I tap my middle finger against my thigh in sync with her toe just to have another thread connecting us.

"I. Am. Not. Going. To. The. Sand. Dance."

"Why not, Rowan? When's the last time you were properly asked to dance?"

"Never." Poison laces every syllable. "I never went to a dance. I wasn't allowed, and when you run away and become homeless, by choice, at sixteen, there's not too many people asking you to dance."

Shock and fear show in her eyes while she rolls her lips in to keep herself from saying any more.

"You were homeless? At sixteen?" That knowledge slices my throat wide open, making speech painful.

"Just drop it, okay? And don't you dare talk to Pappy about it. Not a word."

Involuntarily, my hand rises. I watch it as if I have no control over its movements until it cups her cheek. My body releases tension that's been there since the last time I touched her.

She is perfection, and when she melts into my touch, even for the briefest second, nothing else seems to matter but her and this connection.

"I'm so sorry." I take a step closer, and she tries to lower her face, to break the thread tying us together, but I shake my head. "I'm sorry that so much of your childhood died with your father."

"Sebastian, don't." Her voice is whisper-soft. The words barely touch the air. "Please don't."

The pain that etches each word solidifies a decision that's out of my control. It's the only option—I want to erase all the heartache that makes this woman run from every good thing life has to offer. I want to show her that even when things break, it doesn't mean they're broken forever. And I need to show her that not all families hurt—that not all families turn their backs when you're suffering—to show her what it means to be loved, truly loved.

"There's a very good chance I'm going to get hurt here, Peach. But I'm okay with it if it means a little bit of happiness."

She shakes her head free, but her chin trembles.

"I'm sorry that life has shown you the worst sides of humanity. I'm sorry that you've never had someone to trust. And I'm really fucking sorry I didn't kick your stepfather's ass when I had the chance."

At least that makes her choke on a giggle.

"What do you want, Seb? Don't you see it's not your place to apologize? Nothing in my life has anything to do with you." It's a plea that calls to the injured pieces of my soul.

She's wringing her hand around those beads at her wrist, and I reach out, pulling it to me, holding it hostage while my thumb runs light circles over her tiny tattoo. Her pulse thrums rapidly beneath my finger.

This simple touch rocks the foundation of my world.

"My life has always had something to do with yours," I say gently. "I knew it the first time I met you, but I felt it that day you sang that fucking lullaby that's haunted me for years. That's when I recognized what the ache in my chest was. I was just too young and stupid to do anything about it. I didn't know what it meant before, but I do now. So I want you to keep an open mind and come to the dance with me tonight."

"I can't."

Leaning away from her, I hook her chin with my pointer finger and lift her face to mine. "You can't or you won't?"

"Does it matter?" she whispers.

"More than I can explain. Tell me why."

Her eyes close and she steps back, tugging her wrist free in the process, and I swear the earth moves with her.

"Because." She dips her chin and kicks at a rock on the ground. "I don't know how to be part of a group, okay? Getting through camp with fourteen fathers, twenty-four kids, and thirty-six other nannies is going to be hard enough, but I'll be working. My role will be clearly defined, and I understand what I'm supposed to do and what I'm supposed to say. The sand dance is a free-for-all, and I just can't. It's too much, okay?"

I nod, unsure how to respond to that. She's isolated herself more than I realized.

"Then promise me two things," I plead.

Her weight shifts from foot to foot. "I can't promise anything."

I chuckle, and it's a sad sound—the lone trombone that's out of key in an orchestra of perfect harmony. "Then try to do two things. One, answer your door when I knock tonight, and two, remember it's only one father you have to worry about next week. The rest of it's on Lottie, and I have no doubt she can handle it. Your job, for the next few weeks, is me."

"You mean your kids," she clarifies.

"Sure." I smirk. "My kids." Stuffing my hands in my pockets so I don't reach for her again, it still takes all my willpower to turn my back and walk away. "Oh, and Peach?"

I ask over my shoulder, turning enough to catch her expression. "How's your ass?"

Frustration bursts free, and she stomps her foot while shaking out her hands. "It's just fine, no thanks to you."

Well, fuck me. She turned those tables quickly.

"I'll have to see what I can do about that next time." I walk away with a newfound purpose, one that leaves me feeling lighter and happier than ever before.

12

LATE-NIGHT WISHES AND ALMOST KISSES

ROWAN

"How's your ass?" I mutter, adding the final filter to my Instagram post of a flower I found on the trail before burr-gate happened. Jackass. Of course he would bring it up.

Seren pokes her head inside my partially open door. "Ah, are you talking to someone?"

"What? No, sorry. I was talking to myself. Come in." I soften my grumpy tone for her.

Seren stands in the doorway with her right hand holding her left elbow tightly to her body, a serious expression on her face, and the little black furball Lucky sneaks past her and jumps on my bed. Like I need any more bad luck in the bedroom.

"Everything okay?" I ask.

She nods, but I'm not convinced.

"You can always talk to me if something's up, about anything, okay?"

Her shoulders roll forward, and she takes a seat on the floor, so I mimic her crisscross position and sit in the silence. She'll talk when she's ready.

Seren picks at her fingernails and chews on her lip.

"I'm trying to write a song," she whispers.

My heart pitter-patters. I have no doubt this is what her soul needs.

"That's amazing, Seren. How's it going?"

She lifts one tiny eyebrow and peers up at me. "Not well," she grumbles. "The chorus is crap and there's something wrong with the melody that I can't figure out."

"Would you...do you want me to take a look at it? Maybe we can brainstorm something that will knock loose whatever creative block you have right now."

Skepticism feels too familiar on her face, but eventually, she straightens her shoulders and stops picking at her fingers.

"You'd help me with it?"

"Yes."

She nods, and her cheeks flush pink. Did she think I'd tell her no?

"I don't think it's very good," she admits quietly.

"That's why there are drafts for all things in life. Very few things are right the first time."

Silence settles around us. I wish I knew what she was thinking.

"Maybe tomorrow?" she asks.

"Absolutely. I've been meaning to spend some time in the music room anyway. It might be time I put some of my old ghosts to bed too."

Seren's eyes blow wide enough for me to see white all around her irises.

"Memories can haunt like ghosts sometimes," I explain. "The only way to exorcise them is to face them head-on."

"There was a dance at school," she says softly.

The sudden topic change should give me whiplash, but something tells me she's about to face one of her ghosts too.

"Oh yeah? Want to talk about it?"

She shakes her head. "I didn't get to go. I had a dress. It was really pretty, and my mom said we could get my hair and nails done. She even let me get shoes Daddy would hate."

I have a feeling I know where this is going, and my heart drops into my belly.

"What happened?" I ask gently.

"My mom ruined my life," she says. The lack of emotion in her tone covers the room in an arctic frost.

"I see."

Seren finally lifts her gaze to mine. "My friends didn't want—or weren't allowed—to go with me, and everyone was making fun of me. I had to hide in the bathroom at school sometimes."

God, do I know how that feels.

"I've spent my fair share of time hiding in bathrooms, Seren. I can imagine how hard this has been on you."

Her face morphs into a frown, and I'll take that over sadness any day. "Why did you hide in the bathroom? You're beautiful, and you talk back to my dad."

My laughter is sad. "First, you're beautiful too. It's just hard to see that when you're twelve sometimes. I didn't always stick up for myself. I was homeless when I was sixteen and had to learn to be tough."

"What?" She gasps. "Sixteen. What did you do?"

"My home wasn't safe anymore. My stepdad was violent, and my stepsister was malicious and abusive in her own way. Being homeless felt safer than being home. But the reality is, I didn't have much. So the kids made fun of me for showering in the locker rooms, and for wearing the same few outfits until they were in tatters. Kids can be cruel."

"You really lived on the streets? The teachers didn't help you?"

Her innocence makes me want to protect her at all costs.

I nod. "A few tried, but the system is sort of broken. And I didn't really sleep on the streets. My dad had this Jeep, and I knew it had been left to me. His friend stored it in his barn until I turned sixteen, and on my sixteenth birthday, I showed up to get it."

Her eyes are the size of saucers, so I continue with a story I've never told anyone. "His son was home from college, and he took me out into a field and showed me how to drive the thing. Then I went to see Pappy and Rosa. I couldn't tell them what was happening, but he always knew when something wasn't right. When I refused to tell them why they couldn't write to me anymore, they helped me register the Jeep and get insurance on it, then I lived in that until I graduated. I had a really great counselor who helped me apply to college, and I got a lot of scholarships."

"Pappy loves you so much. Why would he let you be homeless?"

"Oh, Ser. He does love me. That's why I couldn't tell him. I was a dumb kid who was afraid of what my family would do if they found out he was helping me." Admitting that makes my palms sweat. "My point is, I know how hard life can be sometimes."

"Geez. You had it a lot worse than I do."

"Just because someone's story sounds bad doesn't make yours any less valid. Your feelings matter. You're going through something really tough, and that matters. Don't ever diminish your story or your feelings so someone else can shine, sweetheart. Use your story to empathize and make yourself stronger. That's how you win in all of this."

She jumps to her feet and throws herself at me. Her arms wrap around me in a vicelike hug that makes my lungs shrivel, then stop working altogether. I'm not a hugger. Pats and high fives are my comfort level, but the longer she holds on to me, the more the frayed edges of my past braid together to make something stronger than I've ever known.

"I want to go to the sand dance, but I don't know how to do my hair or anything," she admits, then pulls out of the embrace.

My arms stay awkwardly frozen in the air, almost as though I wasn't ready for her to end the hug. But that can't be right, so I quickly drop them to my lap.

"Well, I'm not really a girly girl, but I can do some fancy braids. And because it's at the beach, I'm pretty sure that means it'll be super casual."

"You'd braid my hair for me?"

Oh, sweetheart. "Of course."

"What do I wear? Daddy said there would be a lot of kids." She lowers her lashes and stares at the floor. "Kids who don't know what my mom did."

It hits me then. She's lonely, and the idea of making new friends, friends who haven't heard about her history, feels like a new beginning, a breath of fresh air after nearly drowning. It's how I felt every summer when I'd go to camp. No one there knew how shy I was, or how bad my panic attacks were. I could be whoever I wanted or needed to be, and it was such a freeing experience.

"I think it's an excellent time to start a new chapter," I say, peeling myself off the floor.

"You do?"

"I do. Let's get you ready for all those kids who are about

to meet their amazing new best friend." Covertly I knock on wood for good luck because you seriously never know with kids. Sometimes they truly are little assholes.

"Okay. Will you..." She picks at her fingernails again. "Will you come with me?"

Shit. My entire body is screaming *hell to the no*, but one look at her little face, and I dive headfirst into the deep end, not caring that I don't know how to swim. "Sure. I'll go."

She runs forward again and envelops me again. "Thank you."

I pat her back uncomfortably, but my blood pressure settles and my mind clears in a way that feels suspiciously similar to peace. "You got it. Let's get you ready."

For the next thirty minutes, I help Seren with her hair, and we role-play introductions and ways to approach the topic of her family without oversharing. I explain them as tools she can use to meet whatever kids may be in attendance, and her confidence grows with each passing minute.

And then there's a knock at my door that has my blood pressure spiking again.

"Are you okay, Rowan?" Seren asks.

I nod quickly.

"You're turning a little pasty. Are you sure?"

"Yup. I'm good. Why don't you get the door while I grab a sweater." There, easy. Let her open it for her dad.

I hear the door swing open, and his voice covers the room with warmth.

"Look at you, sweetheart. You're beautiful," Sebastian coos.

"Rowan did it. She looks beautiful too, doesn't she, Daddy?"

He lifts his head at the exact moment I spin around, and our gazes collide like a meteor shower. I've never felt chemistry so forcefully before. Whenever he's near, it's as though he's thrown a lasso around my body, and no matter how hard I run, he just keeps reeling me in one inch at a time.

"She sure does, Seren," he says, staring straight at me. "You're both absolutely stunning."

"Looking good, Row," Pappy says from the doorway. Crap, I hadn't even noticed him there.

Miles pushes through the doorway to hand his sister a small bouquet of flowers, then runs to me and hands me the other. They're wildflowers, and they're my favorite.

"Those are from me and Kade, but Kade kept shaking them and they'd lose all their petals, so I had to give them to you alone."

Lowering myself to one knee, I give him a high-five. "How did you know wildflowers were my favorite?"

His smile eats up his entire face as he looks over his shoulder at his dad. "Daddy said he had a hunch."

"A hunch, huh?" Why can't I stop staring at this man? The right side of Sebastian's mouth tips up into a devastating smile as I stand.

"Yup," Miles says, walking back to his dad. "Didn't know what a hunch was, but now I have a new word."

"New words are good," I say absentmindedly. Vaguely, I hear Kade skipping back and forth in the hallway.

Sebastian takes a step forward. "Wildflowers seemed... fitting."

"Because I'm so wild?" I ask.

His eyes twinkle at my sarcasm. Sebastian slowly shakes his head. "No one is trying to tame them or make them something they're not, but they do add beauty to the world around them when they're allowed to thrive."

The moment is too intense. We're not talking about wildflowers anymore, and if he's talking about me, I'm too flustered to process what that means. Is he saying he isn't trying to tame me?

The butterflies in my belly morph into a pissed-off hornet's nest.

"Come on, Seren. Help me get the boys down to the sand dance. Dad and Rowan are goin' to meet us there," Pappy drawls with a pleased expression on his face.

Oh, Pappy. Please don't read too much into this. I'm temporary. The thought has always grounded me. Knowing that I'm not locked into anything, that my situation will change again soon, has always brought me peace. But right now, peace is the last thing I'm feeling. No, right now, I'm terrified that the thought of leaving is causing an emotion I haven't allowed myself to experience in a very long time.

Regret.

"We—we'll come with you," I say too loudly for the enclosed space, but Pappy shoos me away and Sebastian stops my forward motion with his fingertips splayed across my chest and collarbone.

A full-body shiver courses through me from the point of contact. It's a claiming, a branding that keeps me stock-still.

I'm not someone who can be claimed or tamed or, or—

"Thank you," Sebastian says in a smooth tone that makes it hard to swallow. His fingers press a rhythm into my skin. One, two, three, four, five. Then he does it again as his palm falls flush against me.

My heart thrashes wildly beneath his touch.

"For what?" I croak.

"For what you told Seren earlier. I didn't mean to eavesdrop. I was coming up here to make sure she had what she needed, and your door was open. I know you don't talk about your past, maybe ever, but I appreciate that you shared something that made her feel less alone. That's not something I could have given her."

I shrug, but it's hard to think with his hand still pressing into my skin.

"She's a good kid," I finally say when the silence begins to chafe.

"She is," he agrees. "But you're pretty special too."

I'm shaking my head, but if I'm disagreeing or just trying to get my brain cells to start working again is anyone's guess.

He's so close that his body heat warms me from neck to shins and every time my chest heaves a breath, it pushes me harder into his palm. I nearly moan from this contact alone.

"You have no idea how badly I want to kiss you, Peach. You've invaded every waking hour and disrupted my dreams. You're everywhere, and I fucking like it. A lot."

I gulp, and he leans in painfully slowly, as though he's giving me the chance to pull away. Oh God, I'm going to hell because I want him to kiss me. I want him to touch me in a way I've never allowed before, and I'm a horrible person because I'm only capable of hurting him in the end.

When his lips hover above mine, the deafening sound of my phone breaks us apart like two virgins caught by their parents.

"That's, uh." My fingers press to my lips. The ghost of his minty breath still lingers there, and I press harder, holding the essence of his kiss to my mouth. Lowering my fingers, his gaze darkens. "That's the hotline. I, uh, I have to get it."

I practically sprint across the room and retrieve my phone from the nightstand.

"Single Dad Hotline, I'm your helper, how can I help you?" I answer shakily.

"Rowan, my sister's trying to give me a heart attack. We're supposed to leave for camp tomorrow, but she's locked herself in her room and refuses to pack. She says she's too old for a nanny and won't come out. I told you I should've removed her damn door."

Freaking Thane. He might be the biggest pain in the ass, but he also just saved my ass from doing something monumentally stupid.

"Thane, calm down." I almost burst out laughing. Thane isn't the one who sounds like they need to calm down. He's as monotone as ever while I'm a hyperventilating fool.

Sebastian waves his hand to get my attention and motions toward the door. I nod, grateful that he's leaving, but also almost sad that he is.

I'm leaving, I remind myself. I always leave. It's how it is and will always be. I'm the runaway.

The reminders aren't doing anything to ease the unfamiliar sensations filling my body and mind though. If anything, they're causing more thunderous storms to rage below the surface, searching for a place to touch down.

"Calm down," Thane mocks while Sebastian silently closes my door. The sound of it clicking sets off a ricochet of pain I try to ignore because it's a terrible freaking sign.

Absolutely no more late-night wishes or almost kisses. Girls like me have no place wishing for anything but survival.

13

ROWAN, ROWAN, ROWAN
YOUR BOAT

SEBASTIAN

I'd better not meet that jackass Thane this week because I'm liable to strangle him for interrupting what would have been, undoubtedly, the best first kiss in the history of kisses.

So good, poets would've written about it. It would've been the kind of kiss that changes the trajectory of my life, and he fucking ruined it with his whining.

The kind of energy I experienced was a full-body ache feeding a growing hunger for Rowan Ellis. It both spurs me on and fucks with my head because if I'm wrong, I could end up hurting my family all over again.

Seren is growing attached already. The boys don't stop talking about her. And Pappy? Well, he's as happy as a psychic watching their fortunes come true because this is what he's wanted since we were kids.

But how do you get a runner to stay?

Closing my eyes, I let my head fall to the porch swing with a dull thud and use my feet to sway in time with the waves breaking on the shore. The calming effect of the ocean hits the second I allow myself to acknowledge it—the gentle waves, the salty air that always feels a bit thicker at night, all of it peaceful without the seagulls of daytime stealing its beauty.

My phone chimes with an incoming text, and I reluctantly open my eyes. A harsh bark of laughter surprises me so much the porch swing crashes into my calves.

The notification reads: *Elijah named your group chat Band of merry fucking meddlers.*

Opening the text thread, I reply immediately.

Me: Is this a joke?

Elijah: It's a good name.

Beck: We have a plan.

Elijah: It'll kill two birds with one stone.

Leo: I'm here for the show, but I set up the cove just in case.

I groan and rub my temples.

Beck: Tell her you need seven more days.

Alexei: Seven days in seven cities.

I'm going to regret this.

Me: What are you talking about?

Beck: At the end of her contract, tell her you need her help winning back seven investors in seven cities.

Elijah: It's sort of true. And you'll spend quality time alone with her, while also securing these fuckers Nick was hand-feeding bullshit to.

Me: I'm not sure that's a good idea. And it's not even a little bit true. The seven investors we need are all in two cities, and I'm pretty sure she'd never go for it anyway.

Me: Also, it's a little creepy that you're all conspiring against her.

Beck: Not against her, for her. We care about her, and we care about you for some reason. There's a difference.

Me: I'll think about it.

Beck: Either way, you need to go. The events I'm sending you to will be better suited for a date, but asking Rowan is your decision.

Leo: We'll all help with the kids while you're gone.

Fucking perfect. This isn't exactly what I had envisioned when they said to extend her stay. What happens if she won't come with me? Would she stay with the kids?

Pocketing my phone, I flop against the porch swing again and attempt to reclaim the calmness the waves had given me moments before.

Rowan's voice carries out through her open window. I gave her privacy by coming out to sit on the porch, but there wasn't a chance in hell I was leaving here without her.

I can have compassion for the guy and still hate him for his shit timing. It sounds as though Thane has his hands full with a teenage sister who is seriously fucking with him. I'll have to get her name and keep her far away from Seren. That's the last thing I need.

My mind drifts to Seren and Rowan's conversation from earlier. My daughter confided in her so easily, but she'd never have done that with me. Not because she doesn't trust me, she does, but because while I can sympathize, I can't relate to what she's going through.

It's as though Rowan was sent here just for us. Perhaps Pappy is on to something with his theories on destiny.

The door opens, and Rowan exits, staring down at her phone with pinched brows and turned-down lips.

"You're good at your job."

She screams and jumps into some messed-up version of a karate chop that has her bobbling her phone. I catch it right before it hits the porch.

"What the hell, Sebastian? We're in the middle of nowhere. You can't sneak up on people like that! I thought you were a chainsaw murderer here to chop off my fingers and toes one by one while feeding them to the pigs or something."

"That's...oddly specific." I chuckle.

"Some kid told me a crappy story at camp when I was nine. I never went pee in the middle of the night again."

Taking her hand, I weave it through my arm and head down the stairs, taking it as a win when she doesn't pull away. "I promise to save you from all the chainsaw murderers."

She stiffens next to me, and I hold my breath. Is this where she'll pull away?

"That's the problem," she mutters. "I'm not the kind of

girl you need to save. I've been saving myself for a very long time. It's all I know."

I stop walking and take her hands in mine so she can't escape. I almost chuckle when her clammy palms settle in against mine.

"Are you saying you're too old to learn new tricks?"

"Are you calling me a dog?"

"No, but I wouldn't mind collaring you," I deadpan.

Her expression is priceless—wide-eyed and blushing. I bend at the waist and bring my lips to her ear. "I'm joking, Rowan. Unless you're into that kind of thing...and then I could be persuaded." I stand upright, so close her body heat penetrates my armor. "I'm all for trying new things with you."

My soul is already lighter. This banter, these exchanges with her are so real, so raw. There's none of the practiced etiquette my father shoved down my throat from the time I could sit at a table or pretenses meant to trick me into love.

Rowan Ellis is the light shining through on my darkest days.

Her cheeks flame a delicious shade of pink before she slaps me in the chest with the back of her hand. I recapture it and begin walking again.

"What's wrong with you?" She attempts to sound offended, but the tremor in her words gives her away.

"You're excited by that idea, Rowan, don't try to deny it. The pulse point in your neck is beating so fast you'd think it was following Dave Grohl's drum solo, and you blush so prettily I want to trace it with my tongue."

I feel more than hear her sharp intake of air, and this time, she's the one to stop so she can poke me in the chest. "I've spent the last seventeen years of my life making sure I'm not tied to anyone's rules, oppressive standards, straight-up lies, or vicious outbursts. I'm not about to start any of those now because of a stupid flutter in my belly."

Her righteous indignation would hit harder if she didn't shiver as I run my palms down her biceps. But she's also given me more than she intended to, and hope blooms in my chest as wild and uncontrollable as the flutter in her belly.

"You get butterflies around me?" My voice is six shades past husky—I want this woman with a passion I can't control.

"What?" she demands, and her lashes flutter as though her wheels are spinning trying to figure out what she said. Her mouth pops open into a perfect O-shape the moment realization hits. "No, that's not what I mean. Did you hear anything else that I said?"

Entwining her clammy hand with mine, I lead us down the beach. What will make her tug it away this time? I might be a sick fuck because I love this push and pull with her.

"Oh, I heard you." I don't even attempt to mask the lust in my tone, though I do lower my voice. "I heard every word. But if there's any part of you that thinks I would ever try to contain you, or hurt you, you don't know me very well."

She leans in closer.

When my lips reach her ear, I say, "And I know that you know me. So the only thing that matters is that you get butterflies around me. It's a very good sign."

"It's not a sign," she squeaks.

I hold up our joined hands and tap my thumb against her tattoo. "Sure seems like a sign."

She tries to tug her hand away, but I lift our joined ones and kiss the back of hers, one knuckle at a time.

She stops struggling to get free. Her gaze is locked on my lips kissing one finger and then the next. I nearly groan when her breaths turn shallow, and her chest rises and falls in short pants. She's as affected by me as I am her. The difference is, I can admit it—Rowan isn't there yet.

"I don't believe in signs," she huffs. "There's good luck and there's bad luck. That's it."

"I didn't believe in signs either, but then you came along."

"I'm not your sign."

"That's not how it works, Peach. You don't get a say in what my signs are."

"You're impossible."

"And you're gorgeous. It's a good thing we're about to be surrounded by people because my thoughts about you are not rated PG right now."

Her blush deepens, and she drops her gaze away from mine. "You can't say that stuff."

"Sure I can."

Rowan digs her heels in, and I wait expectantly for her fire to burst free in the dark night.

"You can't, Sebastian. You know this is temporary." She twists those black and pink bracelets around her wrist, pausing with every circle to tap her thumb to her tattoo. She doesn't even appear to notice that it's become her touchstone—but now it's clear. She's always been mine.

"What makes something temporary to you?" I ask, feigning a careless shrug. The merry fucking meddlers' plan is sounding more and more like a reality.

"Ah, an end date?" Her sarcasm is biting as it passes her lips. "There's always an end date."

"Okay. And we have one, so what's your problem?"

Her gaze shifts to anywhere that's not me. I'm not sure if she's searching for an escape or a comeback.

"My problem? It's not my problem. We set my end date. We put it in writing, and I can't stay after that."

I make a tsking sound with my tongue. "Again with the can't. It's not that you can't, Peach. It's that you won't." My brow lifts, daring her to contradict me. "And I'm aware that you have an end date. What I'm asking you to do is give me your now."

"My now? What the hell does that even mean?"

"It means you give me your todays and your tomorrows. We'll worry about the rest when we get there."

"This sounds like a trick."

That's because it is, my beautiful Rowan. I smile so sweetly that I know I've just invited a handful of cavities into my life, but her frown makes it all worth it. I'd love nothing more than to kiss away the worry line between her brows.

"Today and tomorrow, Peach. And your now starts with a dance. Our first dance."

"Seb." She sighs, and I love what that sound does to my battered heart. "We can't. There are people around, and more importantly, your kids. They've been through a traumatic event—you don't want to confuse them any more than they already are."

With a sharp tug on her hand, she falls into me. Her body was meant to fit against mine.

"I love that you're so considerate of my children. They will always be my priority, which is why I've already spoken to them."

"You did what?" she whisper-hisses, and it's kind of adorable.

"I told them that you're my friend. And that sometimes friends hug and dance."

She aggressively pulls away from me to yank her hair into a ponytail and fastens it with a hair thingy she always has around her right wrist. Then she faces me with her hands on her hips, and I can so easily envision her charging me like an angry bull.

"Seren is struggling, you jackass." The fire that makes her Rowan blazes to life behind shuttered eyes. "She's hurt that her mother ruined things for her and that she so easily abandoned her. You can't just fill that space with the next asshole that walks by."

Irritation prickles my neck, and I stare up at the stars to rein in my wild thoughts before I say something I'll regret. When I'm sure I can control my tone, I lower my chin to my chest and wait until she meets my eyes.

"You are not a random asshole. And our situation is nothing like your mother and stepfather."

She stumbles back a step as though my words have physically pushed her. "You know nothing about my life," she blurts.

I step forward, fueled by her utter lack of self-awareness. "But I do, Rowan." Our bodies are nearly touching. "I know that whatever your mother did was enough to make you run from everything that could potentially hurt you ever since. I know that your life irrevocably changed the second your stepfather entered your life. I know that you're, unfortunately, not my children's mother, and if their mother ever gets her head out of her ass, she'll be welcome to try and rebuild those relationships. I'll never stop that from happening unless it's causing them pain. And I also know that you will never intentionally hurt my children, and if you did, you'd make it right. That's why our situation is different. You're not your mother or my ex. You're so much better than they could ever be."

"That's the thing, don't you understand?" Her voice breaks, and it eats away the volatile feelings of a moment ago. "I'm the result of my mother's indifference. I wouldn't mean to hurt them, but it would happen anyway when I inevitably had to leave. It's why I have an end date, Seb. To protect them, and to protect myself."

Oh, my beautifully broken, stubborn-ass peach.

"There are no promises or requests for the future here, Peach. Only today and tomorrow, remember?"

"It's going to hurt."

"I know." I take her hand and guide her closer to the beach.

"You know? Then why are you pushing this?"

Because I'm starting to believe in Pappy's love lines and theories on destiny. Because my heart is telling me that if I can only show her what she means to us, she'll come back. Because I have no doubt she'll leave when her end date arrives—it's all she knows. I can only hope we'll have made enough of an impression that she'll return to us.

Lifting her hand to my lips, I kiss her knuckles again. It's as intimate as she'll allow right now, but it's never felt more right.

"I'm pushing because I can't live with not knowing what it's like to have you in my life, for however long you'll allow. If this past year has taught me anything, it's to live for today, and that's what I'm doing."

We reach the clearing between my house and Beck's, and we both stop, awestruck.

When this town has a sand dance, they don't mess around. Tent structures have been constructed with wispy flowing panels that sway in the ocean air and fairy lights are strung across anything and everything they could reach. Round tables and chairs are set up at various spots on either side of a dance floor, decorated in shades of navy and aqua and topped with flickering candles.

"Wow," Rowan whispers. "This is—"

"Magical."

"Yeah." She pulls her hand free from mine. "I mean, if you believe in magic and everything."

"Row-Row, Row-Row," Kade sings, spotting us first and running through the middle of the party.

"Is he calling you Row-Row?" I ask.

Her laughter washes away on the sea breeze—it's a reminder of how fragile this beginning really is. "Yeah, he thinks my name sounds like *Row, Row, Row Your Boat*. You know, Rowan, Rowan your boat?" When I stare are her, she shrugs. "It sounds funny, and it makes me laugh when he sings it."

"It must be because you're rowin' right into his heart."

Her jaw drops. "Oh my God," she says, covering her mouth with both hands. "You did not just dad-joke me."

I frown at her. "I mean, I am a dad."

"Row-Row. Come dance. Come dance with me." Kade drags her forward.

Was I seriously just cock-blocked by my six-year-old?

Rowan appears to read my thoughts. "Guess you need to up your game, old man. Little Kade here could teach you some things."

I drop my head back and allow the laughter to overtake my entire body. "Challenge accepted, Peach," I call out loud enough for her to hear me.

She stutter-steps but keeps her balance.

Game on, Rowan Ellis. Game fucking on.

———

MILES FELL asleep in my arms an hour ago. I should carry him to bed as I did with Kade when he fell asleep in Pappy's lap, but I can't bring myself to move from this spot. This is the perfect vantage point.

To my right, Seren is sitting on a large piece of driftwood with three other girls who don't appear to be troublemakers. If I turn my head slightly, I can see Rowan at a table on the other side of the dance floor surrounded by women. They've commandeered her for hours, and if her body language didn't suggest that she was actually enjoying herself, I would have stolen her away a long time ago.

Rowan throws her head back, and her laughter barely touches my ears, but it covers me from head to toe as if she's my missing piece. She's mesmerizing. The way her throat works when she swallows. How her hair blows wild and free as if it's a symbol of the personality she's adopted. Her eyes crinkle when she smiles, and I swear I can see them sparkle from here as if she's a real-life toothpaste commercial.

"Daddy?" I roll my head to the side to find Seren peering down at me. I guess my time observing my girls hasn't been split evenly after all. She stands there with the girls she's befriended but appears nervous.

"Hey, sweet pea. What's up?"

I scan each of the girls, and they offer a polite wave. Then each of them steps forward and introduces themselves, referring to me as "sir."

Welcome to the South, I guess. That never would have happened with her old friends in Boston.

"Um, the girls invited me to the beach tomorrow. Marlo's mom will be with us," Seren adds quickly. She really wants me to say yes. The silent plea shines in her eyes and shows when she picks at her fingernail.

I'd give anything to say yes, but I haven't even met Marlo's mom yet.

"Marlo's mom, Jenny, grew up here," Beck calls across

the table. "They're a good family. They all come from good families."

He's vouching for them, for Seren.

I nod in thanks and focus on Seren again. The excitement in her pretty green eyes gives me hope that this was the right move for us all.

"Both Rowan and I will need Jenny's phone number."

"Yes, sir," the three new friends say in unison. A little of the weight that's been sitting on my chest for months dissipates.

"Okay, then. You can go."

Seren wraps her hands around my neck and hugs me tight. I blink away the wetness that belies my relief. My little girl is still in there buried under all the hurt.

"I love you," I whisper.

"Love you too," she whispers back. "Can I show the girls my new room?"

Emotion dances behind my eyes each time a piece of her old self resurfaces.

"Of course. Kade's sleeping, and maybe Pappy too, so you'll need to keep it down."

She grins, and I stare after them as they run toward the house.

"They really do come from great families. I wouldn't bullshit over safety," Beck says, pointing his beer at me.

"I appreciate it."

The firelight is blocked by what I can only assume is a body. Rolling my head along the back of the Adirondack chair, I find Alexei staring down at Miles with a lazy grin. For a man dead set on not having kids of his own, he certainly loves mine.

How long will he continue to lie to himself?

"Why don't I carry him to bed," Alexei suggests. "I'm

heading that way already. I'm going to walk Maria back to camp."

It takes a moment for the name to register. Right, Maria DeLuca, the new camp director.

Oh shit! Maria DeLuca, the new camp director. That's a terrible idea.

"Alexei," I warn.

He rolls his shoulders, then folds at his hips to take Miles from my lap. "I'm walking her home, Seb. Relax. I'll put him in bed, and you can finally ask a certain nanny to dance."

My gaze immediately jumps to Rowan's last known location, and there she is. Staring at me with an easy smile that's either from the cocktail the women handed her as soon as she sat down. Or maybe it's something else, something more rewarding—something like peace.

Alexei lifts Miles's dead weight off me and hefts him up on his shoulder. "He's getting a little big for this."

"It happens fast."

Alexei pats my shoulder and walks toward the house with Maria at his side.

"That could get messy," Elijah chuckles.

He, Beck, and Leo have been sitting with me for the last couple of hours.

"Only for Leo," Beck says, holding his hands up in mock surrender.

The party is winding to a close, and it's now or never if I want to get my dance with Rowan. Finishing the last of my beer, I set it on top of the table. "Gentlemen," I say with a nod as I stand, and then I stride toward Rowan.

It's time for our first dance.

14

COLLARS AND TOMBSTONES

ROWAN

"Dance with me." Sebastian's quiet words silence the table of talkers. Again, he doesn't ask. He demands, and freaking hell, does my body respond. Even the ocean breeze has settled as if he's commanded it too.

"I'm busy with the girls," I say without looking at him. Doing so is like being frozen by Medusa herself—it's dangerous.

Tabby and Beck's wife, Stella, don't hide their laughter. The fruity concoction they made with more parts tequila than juice might have something to do with it.

"Oh, that's hot," Bella whispers to my right. I still haven't figured out how she fits into this trio, but there's no denying she's one of them.

Their eyes widen comically as they all sink lower into their chairs at once. Then, of their own volition, my lashes flutter closed when Sebastian presses his lips into my hair.

"Dance with me, Rowan," he says for my ears only, "or I'm going to tell all your new friends exactly what I want to do to your tight little body, and trust me, I'll be very thorough in my descriptions." Those gravelly words scrape across my skin more sensually than a Wartenberg wheel.

He's barely finished speaking before I stand so quickly that I almost topple my chair over.

"What do you think he said?" Tabby asks out of the side of her mouth. The alcohol has apparently made them incapable of whispering.

"Oh, it was something dirty all right." Lottie grins. "You don't get that red from a grocery list."

"And she's breathing hard," Bella says behind her hand.

"Are her hands shaking?" Tabby chuckles.

"Okay, that's enough of...whatever this is," I say, spinning to face Sebastian up close for the first time in hours.

Damn. That was a mistake. His charcoal gray T-shirt is stretched at the neck where Miles must have weighed it down and a tiny tuft of chest hair pokes through it.

"You." I point at his chest because I can't bring myself to lift my gaze from how his shirt clings to his pecs. "Let's go."

I march toward the dance floor, but he takes my hand and walks me right over and past it.

"I thought you wanted to dance?"

The moonlight bathes his face in dim light and shadows.

"I do, but not here. Leo and Beck told me about a place on the other side of the house. It's up the beach a bit." He pauses and glances down at my feet. "Is your ankle okay to walk?"

Eye rolls around here seem to be contagious. "Yes, I told you I was fine when it happened. It's not the first time I've dealt with a sprain. A couple of days of ice and elevation at night and it was good to go."

He frowns at my answer but takes me at my word and leads me away from the party that's starting to wind down.

Were they all waiting for him to fetch me?

"It looked like you were having fun with the girls," he says, breaking our silence as we walk along the shore.

"Well, they're very pushy and sneakily kind. They're the kind of people you never intend to befriend and before you know it, you're a bridesmaid."

His eyes crinkle with a secret, but he says nothing.

"Did you put them up to this? Oh my God. Did you coerce them into hanging out with me and tricking me into helping plan something for the camp kids next week? That's so embarrassing, Sebastian. You can't force people to befriend me."

The hand still holding mine spins me, and I dizzily crash into his chest.

"There was no coercion, sweetheart." Oh lord. Please don't call me that. "They like you, and it appears that you like them. Is it so hard to believe that you might have made a few friends?"

"That's not, I didn't—"

"You're easy to like." He presses a gentle kiss on my forehead, and everything I've ever said about not being a girly girl or wanting romance shrivels up and dies because at this moment, I want him to give me all of those kisses that turn my insides into molten lava.

"You're also incredibly intelligent and have a way with kids, so I'm sure they understand that you're a great benefit to whatever it is they're planning. I'm also sure they realize you're an asset as much as a friend. You have a lot to offer people, Rowan. You just have to allow them to see it."

Keeping our hands clasped together, he tugs me along beside him as we pass the house on our left. It's a tactic to keep me from responding, and it's for the best because my mind is a muddled mess of woulda, coulda, shouldas.

Would I be able to maintain a friendship?

Could I even form real friendships?

Should I try for...more?

"Breathe, Rowan. None of this is a trick. I swear the sound of your mind racing could scare off an entire ocean of creatures."

"It doesn't seem to be scaring you off," I mutter.

His thick, velvety laughter skims down my body, heating my skin to uncomfortable temperatures.

"Not much scares me anymore, sweetheart."

I have to put a stop to this. He can't use those endearments with me. I'm leaving in a couple of weeks.

Before I can open my mouth to tell him so, the beach curves inward, creating a little cove. On the beach ahead of us is a blanket, a picnic basket, and gas torches lighting our way.

The words *I'm leaving* curl up in my throat and kick at my neck until it's so swollen air can barely pass through.

"Don't freak out," he says, physically pulling me forward now. "It's only so we can have some time to talk, in private."

We reach the blanket, and he kicks off his flip-flops, then sits down and leans back on his hands as he scans my body in a slow perusal that tickles my skin and causes the flutters in my belly to ricochet off each other.

And I am totally fucking freaking out.

"I agreed to a dance." The words are stilted and thick.

"We'll dance," he promises, holding up a small Bose speaker, then he pats the blanket beside him.

"Seb..."

"I love when you call me that."

With one sentence of praise, my shoulders drop, and I give in. I've never felt so weak yet so emboldened as I do when I'm next to this man. Lowering myself to the sand, I kick my legs out beside his.

I don't want to be a broken record, but he knows I'm not planning to stay, so why is he putting in all this effort?

"Two weeks," he says, acknowledging our expiration date, and possibly every thought sprinting through my mind.

"Two weeks," I repeat, but the words cut like glass leaving my tongue.

"I think I've gone through a lifetime of emotions in a very short amount of time with you, Peach." He lowers himself to his elbows, then lies flat on the blanket.

It's uncanny how easily he reads my mind.

"The kids are adjusting well," I say.

He smirks up at my weak attempt at keeping us on safer topics.

"They are," he agrees. "Thanks to you."

I wave him off. "Any nanny could have done it, Seb."

His hand snatches mine out of midair. He places the softest of kisses on the inside of my wrist, right over the tattoo that's kept me tethered to him even when I thought I'd never see him again. When did that become so damn sexy?

"No." He swipes gentle kisses across my wrist. Back and forth. Back and forth as if he understands the tattoo is a reminder of the only time I've ever truly been happy. "Not everyone could have gotten through to Seren as you have."

His movements on my wrist steal my attention, jumbling my thoughts and making it impossible to form a coherent sentence.

"We have two weeks left, Rowan. Do you really want to wonder? Years from now, will you regret not jumping in and taking a chance on something that in our souls we know is right?"

"Maybe, if things had been different," I say, then shake

my head. "But they weren't. And now I'm this version of me. You may not like that, or who I've become, but this is me, Seb. Every broken promise, every bruised rib, every hardship I've ever faced is tied together with fraying ribbons that sometimes slide this way and that, but never allow me to stay because if I do, they'll eventually untether, and I'll never find myself again."

He simply continues to kiss my wrist, and then up the sensitive skin on the inside of my arm.

"What if I want to undo all those fraying ribbons and tie you back together with something stronger, more stable?"

A tear slides down my cheek. Years' worth of sadness constricts my lungs, and every time he speaks of a future, or of not wanting to change me, the sadness squeezes harder.

"I am stronger." I am. I'm not the little girl who gets crushed anymore. I did that. I made myself strong.

"You are. But are you stable? Is your foundation stable?"

At some point, he's risen to his knees and climbed between my legs. How did I miss that?

His languid kisses now reach my shoulder, and the ties that hold my dress together feel flimsy at best.

I'd be a fool if I didn't know exactly where this was headed the second I saw the setup. And perhaps a small piece of me, the piece that has been denied for so long, is fighting against everything I've made to be true.

I want to know what it's like to be held and not equate the sensation to fire ants feasting on my skin.

I want to know what it's like to be cared for and adored.

Taken care of.

"For today." The words, my final attempt at keeping my armor in place, hit the air with a hiss when his tongue darts out to touch my collarbone.

I wouldn't mind collaring you.

His sexily inappropriate comment from earlier flitters across my conscience, and for a split second in time, I can easily envision what being tied to another person would entail.

And for the first time in my life, I don't run.

"For today and tomorrow," he agrees, giving me this, my safety net, because I need it despite my best efforts, and he understands me in a way I never imagined another living soul could.

His tongue sweeps up the side of my neck, hot sensation pouring down my throat and into my belly, and a low, wanton moan escapes me.

"This isn't why I brought you here," he whispers against my skin. His lips fall away, but his forehead stays pressed to my skin.

I arch my back enough that we're nose-to-nose and flash him my best *yeah right* expression with one raised brow.

"I swear I didn't." This time, he puts some space between us and pulls the basket closer to him.

I attempt to even my breaths as he pulls out a...a cribbage board?

So many things hit me all at once. I'm being swept away at sea with nothing to grab ahold of.

I'm adrift.

Officially untethered.

"How? How did you remember this?" I'm so emotional my mouth goes dry because all the moisture in my body is pooling in the corners of my eyes. The tremor in my hands makes a tap, tap, tap sound against my thigh, and it's all I can do to keep myself from breaking down and sobbing right here on the beach.

No one has ever paid this much attention to me. Not

even my father, the one person who always gave me uncon-ditional love.

"Sweetheart." He groans as if what he's about to say hurts him. "I remember every single thing you've ever said. Every memory was locked away for safekeeping in my mind as though it always knew I'd find you again."

"My—my dad." I cover my mouth to force a choked sob back into my throat. I can't break down. Giving him this piece of myself, it's...too much.

"You learned to play when he was ill," he says quietly, and I exhale with a shudder. "And it was the first thing your mother ever took from you."

She blamed me. Not for my father's illness, but for occu-pying all his time in his last months.

"I didn't want to make you cry, Peach. I only wanted to give you back something you should have never lost. I wanted to show you that I care, and I really want your todays and your tomorrows."

That's it. He's finally taken my strings and weaved them with his magic because I no longer recognize what's holding me together.

I'm in a freefall where I can't predict the consequences or the next steps. It's only the here. The today.

And today, I kiss him.

I kiss him like I'll never let go. And I kiss him so I'll have the memory for a lifetime because no experience on earth will ever hold more meaning than this one, right here.

On my tombstone, I want it to say *I kissed him today.*

15

COCK-SIZED IMPRINTS

SEBASTIAN

Her legs wrap around my waist, the cribbage board caught between our ribs, but I'm so consumed by the press of her lips against mine that I ignore the stab of pain the rough edge causes. Instead, I'm consumed by the way her tongue tentatively touches my bottom lip and how, when I open for her, she pours her soul into mine.

Without breaking the kiss, I ease the board out from between us and reposition my legs so I'm no longer sitting on my knees. I want to be as close as humanly possible to her body. We meld together as one, as if we're finally where we were always meant to be. The new position pulls her tighter against my cock, and stars of every color explode in my vision.

As soon as we connect, a mewling sound I plan to remember forever slips past her lips, and I greedily swallow it down.

Rowan slides her hands beneath my T-shirt, and I hiss. Her skin against mine causes a searing sense of rightness, and each press of her fingers sends a jolt of emotion through my body I've never before experienced.

And I swear on my life, I will never mock Pappy's thoughts on destiny and fate again because with Rowan wrapped around my body, I resolutely felt the world shift. It tilted on a new axis that's meant just for us, and I'll gladly spin in her orbit for the rest of my life.

"Rowan," I groan. She kisses along my jaw until her warm lips are at my ear. "We need to stop before this goes too far."

She freezes, but I press her body tightly against mine so she can't run while I scramble to explain. "If we don't stop now, I don't know if either of us will be able to. So if any part of you is unsure about moving forward." I'm not sure if she grinds down on me, or if I press up into her, but the heat of her core melts us both through her thin cotton dress, and my entire body vibrates.

Need should always be felt this profoundly.

"I don't want to stop," she whispers into my chest. "For today, and tomorrow, I don't want to stop."

Those words steal my breath. For today and tomorrow. She still needs an out, maybe she always will, but I'm not strong enough to walk away from this moment either.

"Are you sure?" My voice shakes with desire for her.

She nods against my shirt. "I'm sure."

"Fucking Christ, Rowan."

My hands fall to her ass, and I lift her up so I can lay her out on the blanket. Hovering over her, I take a moment to memorize every perfect inch of her face.

"Your eyes twinkle in the moonlight, did you know that?"

She shakes her head and bites her plump bottom lip.

"You're so beautiful."

"So are you," she says, and I chuckle. I've never wanted

to be called beautiful before, but it's a compliment I'll carry like a badge of honor coming from her lips.

Rowan's hands slide up my chest, lifting my T-shirt as she goes until I shift to toss it to the side. I stay braced above her as she maps my body with her fingertips, until my muscles begin to shake.

Her hands sear my skin, and my cock swells in my shorts. I don't ever remember being so hard that my cock twitches and aches to be set free. It should serve as a warning that everything with this woman will be explosive, but instead of pulling away, I allow my hips to press into hers.

She moans on contact, arching her back and rolling her hips more firmly into mine. I bite back a groan and pin her still so I can fight back my impending mind-blowing orgasm —at least for the time being.

Knowing how she handles physical contact, I allow her to set our pace. I refuse to do anything that will scare her away. Not when everything in me is screaming that I've been waiting for her my entire life.

She sinks her nails into my skin, not hard, but enough that it causes goosebumps to race across my body and a hiss of pleasure to escape my clenched teeth.

"Seb." She peers up at me through long lashes, her confidence draining from her with each passing second.

"What do you need?" I lower my mouth to hers, not quite touching.

Her tongue darts out to lick her lips, and mine are so close I steal a taste of her too.

"I'm not a...touchy-feely kind of girl."

I kiss the right corner of her mouth.

"I know."

Another kiss to the left corner of her mouth.

"But I—I..."

I interrupt her with a kiss, slowly exploring the softness of her lips. She tastes like sugar, sweet, with a hint of tequila that gives her some bite.

Leaning on my elbows, I cup her cheeks with both hands and stare directly into her eyes. "Whatever you need, whatever you want, all you have to do is ask, and I'll do everything in my power to give it to you."

I kiss her cheek.

"Today," she whispers.

Our connection never breaks as I rub my nose along hers.

"And tomorrow." I correct.

Her chest heaves, and her body vibrates beneath me.

"Just ask, sweetheart. Whatever it is, ask me."

"I want you to touch me, to hold me, but I've never been comfortable with the—the intimacy of it before. I'm not sure how I'll react." The words spill out of her as if they're in a race with each other, and I give her a slow smile.

"We won't know until we try. Can I try, Rowan? Can I touch you?"

"Yes," she mewls.

Thank fuck. Paying close attention to her reactions, I rise up to my knees and place my hands on her thighs. She squirms, attempting to press them together, but she can't with me between them.

My girl wants to take control, but she needs to let it go.

"The second you say stop, for any reason, I'll stop." It might kill me, but I will. "If you don't like something, if it makes you uncomfortable, or you're unsure about anything, say stop. Do you understand?"

"Yes," she sighs when I skim my palms to her upper thighs, and her lashes flutter closed.

"One more thing."

She blinks open.

"Keep your eyes on me, and let me hear you. I'm going to move based on the sounds you make, so don't hold anything back."

She twists her head around, taking in our surroundings as though she's just remembered we're outside.

"It's private property. No one will see us."

"Are you sure?"

"Positive. I'll give you anything you need, sweetheart, except one thing." My body fights against memories, and the muscles in my neck strain against my skin. "I don't share. Ever."

Events from my past bubble up in my throat, causing my words to sound haggard and a little ruthless. I count to five before I'm sure I can remain calm. "Whatever happens between us, out here or behind closed doors, is not for anyone but us. And there's not a fucking chance I'd allow anyone any piece of us that we don't explicitly give. Understood?"

"Okay. Yes."

She's quick to answer with words but also her eyes—for once, she allows me a glimpse past her shield, and it's more than I could have ever asked for. When I lift her dress higher, exposing pale pink lace panties, her lashes flutter against the creamy skin of her cheeks.

Heaven. That's the only word that comes to mind. She is fucking heaven.

I lift her dress higher, exposing the expanse of her silky skin, and she writhes beneath my touch. Her body leans into mine as much as it tries to pull away, so I take my time in my exploration of her, allowing her time to adjust to the feel of me.

There's not a mark or blemish anywhere on her, and as I snake my hands up her ribs, my body shudders.

"You're perfect," I groan, tugging her dress over her head.

A crimson flush expands from her neck to her cheeks, and down lower to her chest.

"Seb..." It's a low, throaty plea that my cock responds to.

"What, baby? What do you want?"

"You," she cries out when my mouth captures her nipple with my teeth through her lacy bra.

Her tits are the perfect size to squeeze, pinch, mark. I sink my teeth into her flesh, and her back arches off the blanket.

"Fuck, Sebastian. Fuck, fuck, fuck."

I undo the clasp in the center of her chest and peel the bra from her skin, groaning when I find my mark below her nipple.

I trace a finger around the teeth marks three times. *Mine.* It roars throughout my body and rings in my ears.

She shudders beneath me, and I drop my lips to her other breast while my hand caresses down her body to her panties. Cupping her, I savor the wetness already soaking the material. Then, I lap, lick, and suck her nipples while I tug her panties to the side and delve into her silky heat.

Her pussy sucks me in greedily, and if I had any less self-control, I might come on the spot.

"Seb," she whines.

I press on her clit with the palm of my hand while my fingers explore, fuck, and curl to the most sensitive space inside her.

"Oh, God, please," she moans, and I can't wait another second.

Releasing her nipple from my teeth, I kiss down her body, each one rushed in my efforts to find home.

She wiggles and pushes her panties down, and I thank my lucky stars she's not pushing me away.

Lowering my body to the ground, I place my hands under her ass and lift. Waiting for her to look down at me, I inhale deeply.

So fucking sweet.

When our gaze connects, I don't give her a warning. I deep dive into her, searching for her clit with my tongue and teeth as she rocks beneath my touch.

"Oh. Oh, God." Her thigh muscles lock around my ears, and I chuckle against her.

I'm a man possessed, and I don't slow down. Not when her moans and pleas urge me on, showing me what she needs as if she's writing a road map of her pleasure for me.

I slide two fingers inside of her, and her hands fall to my head, pressing me harder against her, and my grin feels just this side of maniacal.

"You need more?" I growl into her sensitive flesh. "Harder? Faster?"

"Yes, yes, please."

I don't know what will happen after this, but I'm an enthusiastic prisoner to her demands and will give her everything I am.

I sink my teeth around her clit and flick at it relentlessly with my stiffened tongue while adding a third finger and crooking it, reaching and stretching until I find that magical secret button.

As soon as the pad of my finger connects, I press my free palm into the skin above her mound, hard, while sucking her clit like a goddamn vacuum.

Rowan screams unintelligible words that spur me to

move faster and harder until she falls completely silent. I almost pull away, sure something's wrong, but then her body stiffens and shakes violently through her orgasm. Her inner walls squeeze and throb against my fingers, so I don't stop my ministrations.

No, I press again on her pelvis, suck even harder, and fuck her ruthlessly until her orgasm rolls into another and she covers my face with her juices.

Lapping, licking, sucking all that I can until her body relaxes into a boneless heap.

Rowan's eyes are open wide, and if I hadn't been the one to bring her to this precipice, I might worry that she's in shock.

Or maybe I am.

I've never witnessed anyone come like she did. Silently beautiful as she twisted and came undone in the moonlight.

She opens her mouth, but no words come out.

"Are you okay?" I crawl up her body dropping random kisses whenever I can't control the compulsion to taste her.

She nods enthusiastically, but exhaustion is also creeping in.

I did that to her, and my chest expands with the pride of a fucking caveman.

"Do you want to stop?" I whisper, hovering above her lips. Her scent and taste cover my lips, and I know she can smell her desire on me. Her eyes dilate as she stares at my mouth. "Peach? Do you want to stop?"

Tears dot her lashes, but her lips spread into a slow smile as she shakes her head no.

"Are you sure?"

She nods.

"Can you speak?"

She shakes her head again, then laughs. It's a delicate

sound, one I don't recognize. It's then that I realize, in all the time I knew her when we were kids, I never once heard her laugh.

Whatever I thought was going on between us shifts as my goals become clear. Rowan Ellis was always meant to be mine, and now it's time to claim her in every possible way so I can hear that sound for the rest of my life.

I sit up and remove my shorts and boxers, reaching blindly into my pockets for my wallet.

Fuck, no. Please, baby Jesus, don't do this to me. Where the hell is my wallet?

My movements turn manic. Our night cannot end this way. I stand up, my aching cock bobbing angrily against my stomach as I search the sand. Maybe it fell out somewhere.

"What's wrong?" Rowan asks lazily. I pause mid-freakout to soak her in. Her smile is unlike any I've ever seen from her. She's relaxed, and she's at peace.

It's how she should always be, and I swear on my life, I'll make sure it happens.

"I can't find my wallet," I admit, hearing the panic in my voice.

Silence hangs heavily when I finally admit to myself that my wallet is probably on the entry table at home.

I turn to face her, pinching the bridge of my nose as I do because when her naked body comes into view it's going to be a fucking kick to the balls.

"Have you been tested?" she whispers.

My hand immediately falls away from my face, and I scan her eyes.

I won't do this to her. I won't. Even as I think it, my resolve huffs out a laugh straight from the devil himself.

"I have." Fuck. I'm a weak asshole. "After my ex, I got

tested. There hasn't been anyone since her." I barely breathe as she processes my words.

Finally, she looks at me, but I can't read the expression.

"I am too. And I can't get pregnant."

I must frown, because she continues. "It's a long story, but endometriosis happened and honestly, I never wanted to saddle innocent kids with my DNA anyway."

Something about that makes my chest ache more painfully than I could have ever imagined.

"Why?" I ask, falling to my knees before her.

She sits up and tucks her knees to her chest. It takes all my concentration not to stare at her swollen pussy.

"My dad loved me, but I'm the spitting image of my mom. So I obviously have her genes, and I refuse to pass that coldhearted bitterness on to innocent children. I'm not even sure if I'm capable of love, so when I had to have surgery for the endometriosis, I made sure there would never be an accident by having my tubes tied. I've known I didn't want to have kids of my own since I was a child. I can't take that risk."

My mind is a firestorm of questions. But only one of them screams in panic. "You don't want kids, yet you've always planned to work with them. And then you were a nanny. And now you help single dads. So, you do like kids, right?"

Logic says the answer should obviously be yes. But what if it's not? What if that's why she doesn't want to nanny anymore? My children are the one thing I won't give up.

I'm not a praying man, but in that moment, I find myself searching my life for anything I have to bargain away to God. I'll give Him anything else if He doesn't take her away from me before we've began. My career? It would be a bitch, but I'd do it in a heartbeat. My wealth? Done.

I'd give it all up for her.

She shrugs but shifts her focus over my shoulder to the ocean. "I do, I love kids. If things had been different, if my dad hadn't died, maybe—" She stops abruptly. "I gave up wishing on stars a long time ago, Seb. This is me. Broken, messed-up me."

I inch forward. "I won't lie, Rowan. The idea of never seeing a mini-you is fucking heartbreaking, but it's not a dealbreaker. And more importantly, you're not broken."

You're mine. It's a roar made in silence, but I'm not sure either of us are ready for those declarations yet, so I bite my tongue until I taste copper to keep it inside.

It might be one of the hardest things I've ever done, and that's what tells me I'm in for one hell of a bumpy ride to happiness with this woman.

She turns her face toward me with questions swirling in her soulful brown eyes.

"You're not broken, you're just you. Perfection," I murmur. Silence passes as she stares at me, lust and anxiety vying for dominance in her gaze. I hate the worry she attempts to hide, but it's always there, lurking beneath her surface.

"Do you want me?" I ask, closing the space between us, ready to pull away at a moment's notice. "Do you want me bare and buried so deep inside you that you'll be thankful your tubes are tied because when I paint you with my seed, it'll reach the deepest recesses of your womb?" Her eyes dilate, and she licks her lips. "Do you, Rowan Ellis, want me to make you come on my cock so hard that when you spasm around me, I'll leave a cock-sized imprint on your walls?"

"Jesus," she pants.

"Mm," I hum. "You like it when I talk dirty to you, Peach. Your body doesn't lie."

I grab the back of her neck and hold her forehead to mine. My grip is unyielding, but not enough to bruise, and she relaxes into my touch. We share air and secrets without speaking a word.

My lips tick up into a half smile. "Do you want that? Do you want me inside you, Peach?"

"More than my next breath."

That's all it takes. The leash holding me back snaps, and I press her body into the sand.

16

TODAYS AND TOMORROWS AND BROKEN HUGGERS

ROWAN

Sebastian's body weight sinks onto me, pressing me deeper into the blanket on the sand, and the noise that always fills my mind becomes silent.

Gone are the voices telling me to run.

Gone are the memories reminding me why I can't stay.

Gone are the fears of what will happen if I care too much.

It's just...quiet.

Closing my eyes, I focus on the sounds of life that are normally drowned out by my fears. The ocean licks the shore, and far off, the tree branches whisper in the breeze. These are the sounds of freedom.

"I think I've been waiting for you my entire life," Sebastian vows, and I open my eyes to stare at him.

His cock rubs torturously slowly along my seam, pausing to pump against my clit. It's not nearly enough friction to get me off, only enough to keep me on edge.

He's in control here. I wait for the panic to come, but it never does. My body submits to him as though it was always meant to be his.

178

What the heck did he do to me? Even on my own, I've never experienced an orgasm like the one he just gave me.

I actually blacked out.

"Please," I sigh when the blunt head of his dick presses against my entrance. He lifts his weight off me, and we both look down at where we connect.

He's big. Thick and long and veiny. I'm not sure what I was expecting, but it wasn't this porn-sized cock.

I'm not naïve—I know he'll fit inside me because even if I don't repeat his words, my body understands that I've waited my entire life for this moment and God wouldn't be so cruel.

His head slips inside, a physical representation of the connection our souls innately understand, and I memorize how Sebastian's body tenses. The muscles in his neck cord with the strain of holding back until he hooks one of my knees over his arm and he sinks in deeper.

My moan vibrates throughout my body.

I've never been so wet, so lubrication isn't the issue. If I wasn't so embarrassed, I'd have confirmed that he made me squirt, but instead, I'm ignoring that for the moment. I didn't even know I could do that, but when it happened, the deep growl in the back of his throat confirmed my suspicion—he loved every moment of it. Right now though, the sheer size of him is new. Nothing this big has ever come close to me.

"You're so goddamn fucking perfect," he says through clenched teeth as he attempts to wedge himself deeper.

His body rocks in tiny motions. In and out. In and out until his dick glistens from root to tip.

We're both mesmerized by the point of contact. It's the most erotic thing I've ever witnessed.

Then his gaze jumps to mine. He's wild, untamed, and free. I've never seen him this way.

"Are you ready?" he snaps. The vein in his neck throbs with each word. He's straining to hold back, but that's the last thing I want him to do.

"Yes. I need…"

My words are stolen when he slams into me, then grinds his pelvis into my clit.

He fills me to the point of pain before my pussy pulsates around him and the pain gives way to unimaginable pleasure.

"Perfect," he hisses. "You're fucking perfect, and just for me."

He pulls back before I can respond, and when he slams home this time, he doesn't stop.

My tits bounce with each thrust. The air is forced from my lungs when he lifts my other leg and holds them both against his chest.

He ruts into me as though he's claiming me, marking me, and it's that thought that makes my body seize around him.

I want to be claimed by him. My heart shatters because I can never allow it to happen.

"Fuck," he roars as my walls contract around him. Shaking away my intrusive thoughts, I wrap my arms and legs around his body like a sex-drugged koala bear.

Shooting stars light up the sky, or maybe that's my vision, but when he thrusts up while buried to the hilt, everything flashes white-hot and life-altering.

I'm in a full-body tremor that lifts my back from the sand as if I'm experiencing an exorcism. And maybe I am. Maybe Sebastian is exorcising my demons one orgasm at a time.

"I'm going to come," he groans. "If you don't want me to come inside of you, say it fucking now."

My vocal cords don't work. Instead, I hold his body tightly to mine, clawing at his back and tightening my clasped ankles.

He comes with a chorus of curse words and promises he shouldn't be making, but I allow them into my heart, and I cling to them, pretending I deserve them—if only for a moment.

When his body stops spasming, he drops with his forearms on either side of my face.

"I don't know what the fuck just passed between us, but for the love of God, please tell me we'll do it again."

He lowers his face and places a gentle kiss on my forehead. I shouldn't melt when he does that, but I'm too shaken not to. Then he slowly slips out of me. His cum slides down my legs, and he pulls back to watch it with carnal pride on his face.

I'm too scared to ask what it means. After a while, his gaze returns to mine.

"I don't like to cuddle," I blurt as I sit up and move quickly to drop my dress back over my head.

He doesn't get angry. He laughs, then falls down beside me, causing a surprised squeak to escape when he tugs me into his side.

"I literally just said I don't like to cuddle," I tell him as he wraps himself around my body.

"But I do, so we'll compromise like the adults we are. I'll give you an end time. How long can you handle?"

"How long has it been?" I snip.

His laughter melds with the ocean sounds into a harmonious symphony in my mind. "Let's start with five minutes. Think you can handle five minutes of my body holding yours?"

The truth is, I don't know.

"Try, for me," he whispers.

His quiet words weave through my mind, pulling the anxiety from me as I sink into his touch. I'm painfully aware of every connection our bodies make. How his chin rests on the top of my head. His arm, hanging heavy but strong as concrete across my belly—his hand a vice on my sternum. How his legs curl into the bend of mine and our ankles tangle together.

My mind screams at me to pull away. I've spent years lying to myself, telling myself I don't desire affection, that I don't need it, so it doesn't hurt as much when I hold myself at night. But with his arms around me, the pins and needles poking at my skin slowly fade to a full-body hum.

Five minutes. I can do it. I can handle anything for five minutes.

"Relax," he says quietly into my ear. "I've got you. I've always got you."

———

I FROWN and force my eyes open as I settle into something soft.

"Seb?"

"Shh, go back to sleep. You're in your bed. As much as I wanted to carry you to mine, I'm afraid we won't wake up before the kids. But don't, for one minute, allow that mind of yours to think that I don't want you lying beside me."

He kisses my forehead, and that quiet peacefulness slowly relaxes my muscles. A genuine smile tugs at my lips while my lashes flutter closed and darkness takes me under.

———

INCESSANT BUZZING near my head has me swatting away the fly before I even open my eyes.

Oh. Not a fly. It's my phone.

What the hell? Am I hungover? How did I get here?

My pelvis aches with the delicious memory of what made me sore, but before that vision can turn into a nightmare in my mind, my phone buzzes again, and I answer it blindly.

"Single Dad Hotline, I'm your helper. How can I help you?" I rasp.

"You are alive." Seb's voice is silky and smooth, and it makes the hair on my arms stand at attention.

It also makes my clit pulse with memories, but I won't allow those thoughts into my mind right now.

"What?" I glance down at my phone. Nine in the morning! What the hell? I'm always up by seven in case the kids need me. "Shit, I'm sorry. I'll be right down."

"Stop." His command does unthinkable things to my body.

"We're fine. The kids are all still sleeping."

"Then...why are you calling me? This number is for the hotline."

"And you're still assigned as my helper." His smile sounds through the phone.

"Is that right? Then what's up? What do you need help with?" I ask, pressing myself back into my pillow.

"Right now, I'm in bed with a raging hard-on, remembering how you came around my cock last night. Every." He groans, and I imagine him stroking himself. "Single. Thing."

My hand slips closer to my pussy.

I can't do this.

I shouldn't do this.

Maybe just once?

"Sebastian," I scold. "This is a hotline for daddy help. You're so lucky these calls aren't recorded."

"If it eases your mind to call me daddy that's fine by me, and I'd listen to this recording over and over again, Peach. Imagine how fucking sexy that would be."

My body goes up in freaking flames, and my fingers tap an uneven rhythm at the top of my mound.

"That's not...can I help you with something?" I ask, attempting to keep this professional, which is already idiotic considering what we did last night.

"Your hand would feel a hell of a lot better than mine. Your mouth might ruin me."

My hand moves on its own and circles my clit. I can't contain the gasp that escapes on contact.

"Fuck, sweetheart. Are you touching yourself?"

"Hotline," I say in a near sob.

I attack my clit the same way he did last night. I had no idea I wanted it so hard, so rough, so...everything. How the hell did he read my body better than I have in a matter of minutes when I've been with it for over thirty years? It seems completely unfair, if you ask me.

"I can still taste you on my lips." He growls. His words are choppy, and relief makes my shoulders sag into the mattress. I'm not the only one losing their mind here.

"Seb." Apparently, I'm now reduced to one-syllable words.

"Do you wish it were my tongue on you right now? Do you want it to be my hands that make you come undone?"

The sounds of him jacking off spur me on, and before I can process what I'm doing, the world around me flashes white and my mind falls silent. I vaguely hear his muffled curses. Even after I remove my hand, everything is so over-sensitive that the thin material of my dress is threatening to make me come again.

"Shit." Sebastian's words are loud, and then he chuckles. That's when I hear it. The knocking.

"Daddy. Your door's locked. Let me in. I'm hungry."

"Oh my God," I gasp.

"Sweetheart." There's rustling in the background, and I picture him jumping around his room so he can open his door. "I really fucking love your job."

"*No*," I shout. "We cannot do that again."

"Oh, Peach. We can, and we will. Today and tomorrow, remember?"

"I remember but...no, that's not right. Tomorrow is today. Now you only have today."

He laughs, and then I hear Kade squealing with carefree happiness. He must have opened his door. "No, sweetheart. You promised me today and tomorrow, that's what I'll have. Your todays and your tomorrows. Take a shower and come down for breakfast."

He hangs up. Sebastian Walker hung up on me. And I think he tricked me into giving him all my days.

———

MORTIFICATION.

Idiocy.

Embarrassment.

Orgasms.

What? No. Focus on being mortified, Rowan Melody Ellis. That way when you enter that kitchen, every blissfully sinful thing you've done in the last twelve hours won't be reflected on your face.

Gah. Why am I so bad at giving myself pep talks?

"Are you going to stand there and hover all day, or are you going to join us?" Seb's teasing voice filters down the hall.

How the heck did he know I'm standing out here? I'm plastered to the wall and haven't made a sound.

Little feet thwap against the hardwood, and Kade slides to a stop in front of me with a toothy grin. "Row-Row. Seren just went to sing her songs. You missed her," he squeals with arms held high. Everything this kid does is done with the careless energy of a circus clown, and the overwhelming compassion he inherited from his father.

Even though my breathing hitches and sweat dots my upper lip, I pick him up and hold him on my hip but arch away from him a bit. This kid might be part spider monkey.

I've been this way around kids since my last long-term nanny position with a little girl named Lucy—she nearly killed me when I had to leave. I'd known I was becoming attached, but leaving her affected me as though I'd cut off my own arm. I vowed to never feel that way again. Before her, I'd only have a visceral reaction to affection around adult men, or the occasional overly huggy female.

"Your huggers are broken," Kade says, staring at the gap between his body and mine.

Sebastian drops his spatula, and it bounces off the pan in front of him with a clatter. "Kade," he scolds. "That's not a kind thing to say."

"But look," he says, pointing to the space I've created between our bodies.

"Kade," Miles whispers, trying to tug on his leg to pull him down. "Not everyone's huggers are the same. It's not nice to say that."

The mortification I felt not three minutes ago is quickly overridden by a six-year-old's blunt observation.

Sebastian is quick to my side, attempting to pull Kade away, but there's a big thorny pit in my throat, and the pain of it makes me cling to Kade. I shake off Sebastian and stiffly carry Kade to the table and place him on the wraparound bench of the kitchen nook that overlooks the ocean.

"Maybe my huggers are broken," I say sadly, sliding in beside Kade.

"Rowan," Pappy says from across the table. I attempt a small smile for him, but it's forced as hell, so I angle my body toward Kade.

"Want me to teach ya?" Kade says, flapping his hands together in front of him like a seal waving its flippers.

"What made you think my huggers are broken?" I ask him. And unfortunately, I really want the answer. I thought I'd been doing so well hiding those pieces of myself.

Kade grins wide, then stands up on the bench. "Because, silly. When you hug, you're supposed to do this." He wraps his arms around himself and jerks around with the grace of a wacky waving inflatable tube man at a car dealership. "But when you hug, you do this." The kid holds his hands out in a half O-shape and is as still as a freaking statue.

Intuitive little shit, isn't he?

He pats my head, then sits beside me. Squished up against me, not leaving a centimeter of space between us. "Don't worry, Row. Daddy's the best hugger ever. We'll teach ya."

The way his eyes crinkle when he's happy is the spitting image of his father.

Kade holds up his hand. "But we can still high-five if ya want, too."

Sebastian drops a plate of pancakes a little too forcefully onto the table, then slides them over to his youngest son.

He uses the gentle scraping sound, and the appearance of leaning over the table to whisper, "He's six."

I nod, but it's evident that everyone in this room has had the same thoughts as Kade.

"Gram wasn't a hugger," Pappy says after a sip of coffee.

I frown but drop my gaze to Kade's plate and busy myself cutting his pancakes.

"She really wasn't," Sebastian chuckles. "She was a cheek pincher." He reaches over me again and playfully pinches Kade's cheeks. It's made easier because Kade still has a little of the baby chub in his cheeks that he's sure to outgrow soon.

A wave of sadness hits me when I realize I may not see him outgrow his baby face, and I focus on the pancakes again.

"I don't remember that," I grumble. Miles stands at my side, silently asking me to scoot down the bench, so I slide Kade over, then myself, and Miles slips in next to me.

Sebastian and Pappy continue discussing Gram's "spunky" side. They make her sound grumpy, but that's not how I remember her. She was always so...perfect.

Miles ducks his head away from the table and into my space to whisper, "Your huggers are not broken, Rowan. Daddy said being different isn't the same thing as being bad, and I don't think being different means you're broken either." He smiles, and it's not the practiced one he wears all damn day.

This is the smile of a little boy who isn't hiding or making sure everyone else is okay.

His little fist raises, and he gives me a fist bump that might just be the catalyst for my undoing.

Sebastian eyes me curiously, sandwiched between his

two sons who both managed to obliterate my walls in under five minutes. "You okay?" he mouths over Pappy's head.

My fake grin is as shaky as my thoughts, but I nod, then remain a silent observer as this family goes about their morning as though they've done it a million times before while my heart and mind go to war. Again.

Todays and tomorrows and broken huggers. What the hell is happening to me?

17

DON'T PANIC!

SEBASTIAN

Thane. What the hell kind of name is that anyway? When I pulled it up on Google, it said it means warrior, and I immediately shut that shit down.

Fucking warrior. Give me a break.

"Any reason you're sitting here sulking like someone stole your girlfriend?"

The glare I shoot Alexei makes my eyes sting, but the prick sits next to me at the picnic table and follows my line of sight since I can't tear my gaze away for longer than thirty seconds.

"Damn, man. Do you know who that is?"

I cut him a side-eye, but my ire is quickly masked when Miles looks up between us. We're sitting here making a cat's eye with sticks and yarn while nannies join us every thirty minutes.

Thirty freaking minutes is a long-ass time to hold a conversation with a stranger, especially when the one woman you want is flittering around the camp with Thane fucking Wilder.

Why isn't he going through this shit? Clearly, he needs a nanny too. At least Kade keeps the current nanny sitting at our table occupied with his stream of never-ending questions about bugs.

Then Thane steps closer to Rowan, and jealousy so blinding I can't see anything except Rowan clouds my vision. He better not be trying to move in on her. I don't care who he is, I'll ruin the bastard before I let him take her from me.

"Yes. I know who he is," I grumble.

Anyone who uses technology knows who Thane is. He's just always held himself apart from everyone in our social circle, until recently. And if I wasn't being a jealous asshole, I'd cut him some slack, remembering how uncomfortably awkward he was at a fundraiser last year. The guy spoke the emotions he saw on everyone's faces as though he were trying to understand them.

He might be a genius, but I've always wondered if he's lonely. That doesn't mean he can take my girl though.

"Thane's working on some real cutting edge shi..."

I glare at Alexei and give an exaggerated nod toward the kids.

"Stuff. Whatever app he's working on right now has the tech industry in a tizzy they haven't seen since Steve Jobs and Apple."

That information takes my sour mood and spoils it completely. I knew Rowan had a client named Thane, but I hadn't cared enough to look into it more. Now that I see her client is freaking Thane Wilder, I want to rip his goddamn head off, and not because of his tech—I have no doubt whatever he's working on will be revolutionary. My issue is that he's monopolized her time all damn morning.

The bell chimes, indicating it's time for the nannies to move to the next station. I nod politely at the third prospect of the day.

"Are you supposed to be interviewing them or something?" Alexei whispers.

I shake my head, but keep my gaze glued to Rowan. "Today's a meet and greet—a time to see how they interact with our kids. From here we choose our top ten, and Lottie will arrange for us to spend time with each of them throughout the week."

"How many have you seen today?" he asks.

"Three," I groan.

"What's the matter? No contenders?"

As if she senses my attention, Rowan scans the crowd until she finds me already staring at her. The smile she wears doesn't falter because it's not real.

At least that fucker isn't getting the real her.

"One," I grumble.

"Ugh." Seren makes a gagging sound. "If you care about her, ask her out already, Dad. Geez. It's kind of creepy how you stare at her."

I spin toward her so fast I pinch a nerve in my neck. "What?" I bluster while Alexei hides a laugh behind his hands. Without so much as looking in his direction, I swat him across the back of the head.

"I'm not a baby, Dad. And I heard the merry effing meddlers talking at the sand dance."

"Hey," I warn.

She flashes her lashes with fake innocence. "I didn't say it." And there's the eye roll of preteens everywhere. "We don't mind if you like her," she says contritely.

Miles tucks his head into my side. "Yeah," he mumbles quietly, but his face is obscured by my chest.

"Hey, guys. That's not...it's not..." Fuck. "I don't know how long Rowan will stay," I finally admit.

It's the ticking time bomb in my chest because while I got her to agree to give me her todays and tomorrows, there's nothing actually keeping her tied to me.

Perhaps I should be taking these nanny meetings a tad more seriously.

"It wouldn't be the first time someone left, Dad. We'll be fine." Seren stands abruptly. "Can I go back to the house? I want to get my stuff together for tomorrow afternoon, and they have crap scheduled for the rest of the day."

I should demand she stay. Whatever nanny we end up with will need to get along with Seren too, but she's so damn excited to go to Beck's house tomorrow. More accurately, she's excited that the friends she's made are going to meet her at Beck's and show her around Sailport Bay.

If Beck Hayes is wrong about these girls Seren's hanging out with, I'll string him up by his ears.

Seren stands expectantly, and when Alexei elbows me in the ribs, I realize I've been staring too long without giving an answer.

"Sure, Ser. I love you."

She swallows while lowering her lashes. I get a flash of the little girl she's trying so hard to outgrow. "I know," she whispers, then hightails it out of the pavilion and toward the house.

She's at the mouth of the trail when she's intercepted by Rowan. The two exchange words, and it's the first time I've witnessed Rowan use almost parental or authoritative body language with her. I'm rising from the bench because every dad instinct is telling me something's up but freeze when Rowan holds out a hand and they perform an elaborate secret handshake, then hip check each other with matching bursts of giggles.

I think my heart just smiled.

I'd seen her execute a simpler version, minus the hip check, with Miles yesterday.

She may not believe she's offering them much affection, but there's no doubt in my mind that my children know she cares about them—even if she hasn't gotten that memo herself yet.

Lottie announces lunchtime over the loudspeaker, thank God. These nannies are all fine, probably, but they're not who I want.

Thane's grin reminds me of the Cheshire cat, but instead of following Rowan in my direction, he stalks off toward the office.

"Everything okay?" I ask when Rowan sits opposite me. "With Seren I mean, not Thane."

Okay, Alexei's right. I am a petulant teenager.

Her brows shoot to her hairline as she fights off a smirk. "Is there a problem with Thane?" she asks.

"Lover boy over here is mad he's taking up so much of your time," Alexei deadpans.

A lovely flush creeps over Rowan's cheeks. Is she wondering if I told him about the beach or our late-night hotline calls that are most definitely not child-related?

When her worried gaze cuts to mine, I shake my head, and her shoulders relax.

"Okay, kids. Have a good lunch. I'm heading over to Beck's now to review some contracts," Alexei says.

"Wait," I say as he quickly attempts to make an escape, his long legs tangling in the child-sized picnic table. "Why did you come here this morning? I thought you were meeting with Elijah."

For the first time in all our years of friendship, something flashes on his face that I never thought I'd see—unease. Alexei has been unflappable our entire lives—a rock, unmovable, so much so that I've teased him about being a robot. His gaze cuts to the stage of the pavilion. When he realizes what he's done, he returns his focus, almost begrudgingly, back to me.

But the damage is done.

Alexei Stepanov is in deep for the camp director. And judging by the glare she shoots his way—he's fucked up big-time.

"What did you do?" I ask warily. Rowan's gaze is bouncing around the camp comically, trying to figure out what we're talking about.

"I may have..." he squeezes the back of his neck. "I may have screwed up."

Maria DeLuca walks by like a storm cloud, and he doesn't hesitate to follow her.

"Ah, what was that about?" Rowan asks.

"Maybe I'm not the only one falling in love at kiddie camp." As soon as I say it, I wish I could suck the words back into my mouth. Not because I don't mean them, but because I know without a doubt that the panic running through her expressive eyes tells me she wasn't ready to hear them.

Thank God, Miles and Kade are too busy playing tag on the other side of the table to hear what I said.

"Okay, well. Um, I'm going to make sure Seren isn't setting traps for the nannies tomorrow."

Nerves set off fireworks in my head. "Is she still planning that? I thought she was over it."

Rowan shrugs. "I just have a hunch. Better I intercept them than have her run off all your prospects." Her face falls. She shakes her head, and it turns into a shiver that has her shoulders shimmying before it's replaced with practiced brightness.

"Today and tomorrow," I say, almost absentmindedly. How long until my tomorrows run out?

She nods and forces a tight smile. Then gracefully unfolds herself from the ridiculously small table and nearly runs for the trail.

Alexei may also not be the only one screwing up at camp.

————

"You look like shit," Beck comments when I join him at the conference table. I'm glad he's the only one here so far this afternoon. I'm not ready to face the firing squad of merry meddlers. The last two days of nanny meet and greets have been brutal—and this morning's session nearly made my head explode.

"It's hard interviewing nannies when the only one you want is the one who may not stay."

He tosses his pen onto the table and leans back in his chair, then releases a heavy sigh. "Listen, I spent most of my adult life closed off and never allowing anyone in because of the betrayals in my life. The fact that you're even in the position to want someone to stay tells me you're ahead of the game. I certainly wasn't that intelligent. But it also means that I understand what it means to not fully be able to trust anyone in your life. If that's how Rowan feels, then the only thing that will change her mind is time. Or..."

"Or what?"

"Or an igniting event," he says, sitting up straighter and staring at the wall as though he's masterminding world peace.

"I'm not going to trick her into staying."

He shakes his head. "Then, it's pretty simple. You either pick one of these nannies to take over in two weeks, or you let us help so you can figure out a way to keep her."

My phone buzzes as Alexei enters the room, and I welcome the intrusion.

Rowan: Don't panic.

I finally changed her number in my phone. I don't care if it's technically the hotline number or not. It's my only direct connection to her.

Me: Rowan! Don't panic is the very thing that makes people panic.

The three dots next to her name start and stop four times before a picture comes through.

"Oh, shit."

"What's up?" Alexei asks. Whatever I'm doing with my face has him frowning even harder than he was.

"Ah, I think I have to..."

Rowan: I said DON'T panic.

Rowan: It'll wash out. For most people. But you may get a salon bill for the blond.

Alexei's impatient ass hovers over my shoulder to stare at my phone.

"What the fuck?" he asks, taking the phone from me.

We grapple with it for a few seconds, but the asshole has

the leverage of standing over me, and he zooms in on the photo.

Our squabble has Beck rising from his chair too. "What's going on?"

Alexei tosses my phone to Beck, and he doesn't even attempt to hide his grin.

"Who did this? And what did they do?" Beck asks.

I grab the phone out of his hands as another text comes through.

Rowan: Don't take away her trip into town tonight with her friends.

Rowan: I mean, I can't dictate how you punish her, but what I have in mind will be the punishment of all punishments without isolating her from her new friends.

Rowan: I've got this, just wanted to give you a heads-up because Lottie is pissed.

Rowan: Ah, and Leo isn't thrilled about the state of the showers.

Rowan: And Maria might be looking for you.

Rowan: But I've got Seren handled.

Rowan: Bye.

"What is she, an Olympic texter?" Beck mutters. "How the hell did she get all those messages out before you typed a single one?"

Before I can type a reply, Leo walks in. His face is equal parts amused and pissed off.

"She's creative, I'll give her that," Leo says, dropping into one of the conference room chairs.

"What the hell did she do?" I'm staring at the photo of three very pissed-off nannies. All three are dyed red—their hair and skin.

"The good news is it's temporary dye. The bad news is my bathhouse now resembles a bloodbath."

I stare at my phone in a state of shock.

"She unscrewed the shower heads and filled them with dye tablets so when the water turned on, it sprayed through the quick-dissolving casing to the dye tablet. They had been at the beach, so the nannies were in their bathhouse when it happened. She only targeted that one, thankfully."

"Thankfully? My daughter dyed human beings, and you're sitting here grinning as though there's a bright side?"

He shrugs. "I figure you'll get enough shit from Lottie because two of the nannies you chose for tomorrow have already bailed." Leo's gaze shifts from me to Alexei. "And for some reason, Maria had to shower there too instead of going back to her cabin on the other side of camp."

Alexei mumbles a half-assed apology and storms out of the room. I'm also closing in on the door.

"Sure," Beck calls after me. "It's not as though we have a billion-dollar deal on the table or anything. Go do what you've gotta do, and then get your ass back here so we can finish this shit."

I run into Beck's wife Stella at the front door. "Don't worry about him. He's a big teddy bear who values family above all else, so take care of whatever you need to. We'll see you tonight." She pats my arm.

"Thanks, Stella. I think Seren's trying to kill me."

She laughs and despite myself, I chuckle too. Parenting is not for the faint of heart.

"Nah, she's just a kid going through a tough time. Tough times still call for tough love sometimes though." She leans in conspiratorially. "I heard about the dye. I don't envy your walk into camp, but it's kind of impressive."

"That's not the adjective I had in mind," I say grumpily. "But yeah. We'll be back later tonight."

18

ORPHANAGE FOR LOST SOULS

ROWAN

"Some people pay good money for hair that color," Seren grumbles as she carries the cleaning supplies to the next stall.

"They do when they ask for it," I reply. "You're lucky Leo is accepting this as reimbursement."

"Aren't there child labor laws or something?" she asks when she enters a stall and gags. "Why are boys so gross?"

"That, my dear, is an age-old question. When you're done with this bathroom, you're done for the day. But you'll do this daily until the end of July."

"Did you tell my dad what you're making me do?"

"This is much more lenient than I would have doled out." Sebastian's voice echoes against the metal dividers of the stalls. He can't see Seren from where he's standing, but I can.

Her little body freezes, and her face crumples, making me think this might be the first time she's ever really been in trouble.

"What were you thinking?" Sebastian yells. "I understand that this is hard for you, Ser. It's hard for us all. But lashing out isn't the answer. You're lucky those women aren't suing us."

The little girl slams the stall door closed and locks it.

Sebastian's face shows his shock. His jaw is still reaching for his chest when he stalks toward the stall, and even though it's not my place, I hold up my palm, and he stops immediately.

"Talk to her later," I whisper.

He stares at me for long moments with his jaw twitching and the vein in his throat throbbing while I prepare myself for when he inevitably tells me to go to hell. But it doesn't come, and after an intense stare-off, he spins on his heel.

"Find me in my office the second you're done, Seren. Don't make me come to you."

The toilet flushes, and Seren exits the stall, washing her hands and studiously avoiding eye contact. But I catch her reflection in the mirror—it's a mixture of sadness, regret, and rage.

Crap. She's not done—I recognize the anger swirling in her pretty green gaze.

"What else do you have planned?" I ask gently.

This catches her attention, and she defiantly lifts her chin. "Nothing."

"Seren, I thought we had an agreement. You said you'd tell me, and we were going to prank your dad instead. What changed?"

"What does it matter?" she yells, catching me off guard.

"I know you're angry, but you don't get to be disrespect-ful. I'm on your side here."

She scoffs and pushes the mop bucket toward the exit. "That's the biggest lie of them all. If you were on my side, you wouldn't already be planning your next job. I heard you talking to your boss this morning—you can't wait to get away from us."

"What?" I ask, genuinely surprised. I did speak to Lottie this morning. She said she wanted to schedule a meeting to discuss something big for my next assignment, but nothing's set in stone yet. Is that what Seren heard?

"Forget it. I didn't expect you to stay. You're all just like her."

Seren's words knock me back a step, and it doesn't take a genius to guess why, but the worst part is, she's right, and it hurts so damn bad. How can it hurt this much after only a few weeks?

She slams the door on her way out, but I stand mute.

I'm not her mother. I'm not even her real nanny. I'm a stranger helping out for a couple of weeks. She couldn't have grown attached in such a short amount of time—could she?

The ache in my chest won't go away. Instead, it festers like a rotten apple. But I'm so confused. The plan was always for me to leave. She knew that. Sebastian knows that. So why are my hands shaking and my stomach rolling as though I'm about to be sick?

Todays and tomorrows.

That ache ignites until my entire chest is on fire.

"Hello?" Leo's voice rings loudly in the empty room. "Anyone in here?"

"C—come in. She's all done," I reply.

Leo walks in and inspects a few stalls. "Looks good to me. She doesn't have to do this all summer, a few weeks is sufficient for me."

I puff my cheeks on a slow exhale. "Let's get through the next few days and then see if you still agree."

His brows rise in question, but I shrug.

"I don't know anything about anything anymore. But I should go check on her."

Leo tilts his head to the left with a frown. "Are you okay, Rowan?"

My chin trembles, and I hate it. There's an overwhelming burst of energy coursing through my veins that I can't contain.

When I attempt to swallow the ball of emotion that's gagging me, it cuts and tears at my sensitive skin.

Gulping for air, I drop my chin to my chest so he can't read what I know is flashing brighter than a neon sign in my eyes—sadness. "Yup. I'm fine. I, ah, have to go check on her though."

He steps out of the way, and I make a hasty escape. I walk back to the house feeling more unsettled than I have in years.

———

"You know," Lottie says, taking a seat next to me. "I came here with something I thought would make you over-the-moon happy, but now, after seeing this." She waves her hand toward the kitchen. "I'm not so sure I even want to say it out loud."

Tension creeps in and heats my skin. "What do you mean?"

"You know I'm expanding."

"Yes." Why is she stalling? What doesn't she want to tell me?

"I came here to offer you a partnership, in Paris. You'd basically be doing what I do here."

Sweat breaks out over my body. It's literally my dream job. It's everything I want. I'll still help children and families, but I won't have the emotional attachment that comes along with it.

"Row?"

"It's...that's...everything I've ever wanted."

"Are you sure about that?" she asks gently.

I swallow hard as emotion prickles in my throat.

It is everything I want.

Or wanted, a traitorous voice says in my mind.

It's freaking Paris, with minimal human contact and zero chance of me growing attached. So why does it suddenly feel like a death row pardon coming in too little too late?

"I just want you to be happy, Row. That's what matters. Take your time and think about it, okay? Just make sure the decision you make isn't one made out of fear."

"Lottie," her brother, Elijah, calls from the kitchen. "Come tell everyone that Beck's lying."

She pats my thigh. "Really think about it, okay?" she asks before walking inside. I don't know how long I watch them, but my eyes are dry from barely blinking.

I've been in my own world since we arrived at Beck's house, but the bomb Lottie just dropped had me zoning out even more, so it takes a few seconds to register that someone's talking to me.

"Are you okay?"

Beck's wife, Stella, sits beside me on the oversized sectional on their deck. Their vibe, this house, it's all so surprisingly casual. They obviously have money, but their home has been designed and furnished with children in mind.

Even the ocean air is lighter here. Maybe the storms only brew over my head.

"Yeah, I'm fine," I say with a smile that hurts my soul.

"I heard you had a rough day," she says gently. This

woman is a fixer. I sense it the same way I know when someone is bad for me. What did she go through that made her the way she is?

That's the thing about remaining a loner. Those kinds of questions have never occurred to me before. But now I'm finding questions everywhere I turn.

Closing my eyes, I remember Seren's face when she exited Sebastian's office. But the devastation she expressed was nothing compared to Sebastian's when he followed her out.

"They're all hurting," I say evasively.

"I can only imagine how hard that is. I don't mean to pry, but it doesn't seem as though you're completely unaffected by it either."

I mindlessly run my hand over Miles's head. He crawled up next to me after dinner and now he's passed out with his head in my lap. It's taken the full hour, but I no longer feel the need to claw at the itching sensation where his cheek presses against my thigh.

Once I was able to settle, I was startled to find that my mind was quick to quiet again. Is it really the healing power of the ocean, or is it something else, something so terrifying I don't even want to think the word into existence—home?

"I'm okay." Even I can hear how hollow I sound.

Loud laughter in the kitchen draws our attention to the open glass doors.

I'd come out here because inside was...too much. People are everywhere, and I've never felt like such an outsider—given my history, that's saying something.

But I haven't been able to stop staring at them either. Beck and Stella's family, Leo and his fiancée, and even a couple I've only met in passing have all opened their arms to Sebastian, Pappy, and Alexei as if they've always been a part of their blended family. The kids run wild and happy while the adults move around each other in a perfectly choreographed dance that I never learned.

Beck's loading the dishwasher while Sebastian washes pans in the sink. Leo walks behind them, saying something that makes everyone laugh.

Alexei, who must be drying dishes on the other side of Sebastian, holds up a pot, and Beck points to a cabinet in the island.

Pappy and Elijah sit on the other side of the deck with their heads together as though they've known each other their entire lives.

Leo's girlfriend, Tabby, joins us on the sofa holding a sleeping baby boy. "It's so much quieter out here," she laughs.

"Yeah," I choke out.

I catch her in my peripheral vision, tilting her head back to find what has my attention.

"It's a lot, huh?" Tabby asks.

My throat is too dry to respond, and I'm saved when Kade runs full speed into my side. I hold my hands out to stop him from jumping on his brother's head.

"Row-row." Excitement shines in his eyes. "I love Ruby."

Tabby and Stella laugh out loud, but my palms feel clammy.

"I'm glad, buddy. You're having fun?" I ask, praying that I can keep the internal trembling I feel from the words.

"Yup. I'm goin' to marry Ruby."

"Oh boy." Stella giggles. "You'd better see what Uncle Beck has to say about that."

My face snaps to hers. Uncle Beck? Does that sort of thing happen that fast? Can you just say someone's your family and have it be true? I can almost feel the color drain from my face.

Kade must have taken her words as a challenge because he runs back into the house, yelling for Uncle Beck.

"I'm sorry," Stella says, her unease softening her tone. "Did I say something wrong?"

I shake my head even as sweat trickles down my spine. What the heck is happening to my body right now?

"Do you have a big family?" Tabby asks. Her demeanor has changed as well, and she's approaching me as you would a wounded animal.

"I don't have family," I admit. I don't even know why. I've always evaded the question before. "Not since I was sixteen. They're alive, but not to me."

What in the ever-living hell is wrong with me? I don't share. I don't open up. And yet, here I am spilling my freaking guts like we're at a sleepover having alcohol for the first time. I eye the wine glass on the table beside me, but I didn't even drink the first glass Sebastian handed me.

"I'm so sorry for what you've gone through," Stella says. The sincerity in her voice is unnerving. "My whole life, it was just me and my mom. We moved so much I never even truly learned how to make friends, so when I entered this" —she sweeps her hands out in front of her to encompass the chaos happening in her kitchen—"it was completely overwhelming."

"But now you're all related?"

"Hey, guys." Bella sits beside Tabby, holding another baby.

"Hey, Bell," the other women say in unison.

"Rowan's overwhelmed by the family dynamic," Tabby explains. I've learned quickly that Tabby doesn't have a filter of any kind.

"Oh, no. I was—I was just thinking out loud," I say.

"Good grief. It's so overwhelming." Bella giggles. Her voice is wispy and gentle. It matches her personality. "I still have to hide sometimes."

"Tabby and Beck are cousins. Leo grew up with them," Stella says. "The rest of us are all loners who found our hearts and souls here in Sailport Bay. We've made our own little family. Well." Stella laughs. "Obviously not little. And even though Beck has a loud bark when it comes to business, I knew the second he told me he was partnering with Seb that our family was about to expand again. Especially after learning what they've been through."

"Yeah." Tabby's expression is soft—warmth radiating from her with gentle ease. "We're an orphanage for lost souls—a place to belong. All of us have felt lost at one point and had resigned to never finding love or happiness, and in some cases, ourselves. But Sailport Bay is magical— destiny's landing spot."

My gaze snaps to Pappy. Did he put them up to this?

"Oh, we've heard all about Pappy's thoughts on destiny, and I'm not sure he's wrong," Bella says. "But what Tabby said is true."

My attention returns to the kitchen. Sebastian's smile is easy and carefree. He belongs here, with these people who are taking him and his kids in as part of their own.

Inexplicably, moisture collects on my lashes. I'm happy he and the kids will have this. They deserve all the love a big, mostly sane family can give them.

"We've seen how Seb looks at you," Stella says, bumping my shoulder with hers. "Applications to the messy mansion are always open. So, if you're thinking about staying, we're all here for you too."

Todays and tomorrows.

"Oh," I splutter. "That's very...kind of you." I shrug with a sadness that makes the movement sluggish. "I'm not really the sticking around kind, you know? I'm always ready for a new adventure."

Roaring laughter comes from the kitchen, stabbing me in the chest with each shake of their bellies.

"I'm...temporary," I mutter so softly I'm not sure anyone heard me.

"I thought I had an expiration date once too," Stella says ruefully. "But sometimes you really can't fight destiny."

I replay her words in my head as they change subjects and talk around me. By the time the gathering comes to a close, my mind is still challenging her sentiment because what happens if your expiration date is stronger than your destiny?

LIKE CLOCKWORK, my phone rings at eleven. I've been in bed for close to an hour, but I haven't been able to sleep.

"Single Dad Hotline, I'm your helper, how can I help you?"

"Technically we were together all night, so how come I still miss you?"

My throat catches. I knew it was Sebastian calling, but the way he unabashedly lays out his feelings still catches me off guard.

"You were pretty busy all night. It was nice to see you so happy. You belong with them, Seb. They care about you and the kids."

"Yeah. The boys are happier too. They have a freedom here they never have in Boston."

"Are you thinking about staying in Sailport Bay? P—permanently?"

His sigh flows through the connection and kisses my cheek. "It would make work easier, at least for now, but I'll have to talk to Seren and probably her therapist because I have no idea what the right call is for her anymore."

"You're a great dad, Seb," I whisper. "Those kids are very lucky to have you. The boys have made this transition almost seamlessly. I'm sure they miss their mom, but you've done an amazing job of being there for them. That's a testament to the kind of dad you are."

He grunts on the other end of the line. "Honestly, not much has changed from when I was with their mother. I was the parent who did carpools and doctor appointments. I took them to extra curriculars and playdates. The more I recall of our past, well, I'm realizing Mya acted more as a warm body to be present when I had to work. Physically she was there, but she was never really emotionally available to any of us. I chose not to see it because I wanted that nuclear family so badly."

"Have you...have you heard from her?"

Sebastian growls as if the pain is being ripped from his throat. "I tried to call her a few weeks ago. I wanted to lay into her for not even attempting to contact the kids, but she must have changed her number. I called her father, but it didn't seem as if he knew it either."

"Isn't that a little...suspicious? I'd think that even the worst narcissist would make contact if only to keep their claws in them."

"Probably," he admits. "But I don't have the energy to put toward her, not when I'm doing everything to be both parents for all of them."

I nod, even though he can't see me.

"My mom never wanted me," I blurt, then squeeze my eyes shut and drop my forehead into my open palm.

Silence fills the line until I pull the phone away from my ear to check the connection. When I do, my door opens, and Sebastian's silhouette is backlit by the hallway light.

I push to a sitting position and lean against my headboard, waiting for him to make a move.

He enters quietly, shuts the door, then crosses my room and climbs in beside me. I'm still holding my phone in my hand, so he takes it and places it on the nightstand.

"Tell me," he whispers.

19

SHE STAYED

SEBASTIAN

I didn't ask permission to enter her room or to climb into her bed, and I have no right to demand her story, but I want all of her. Once again I find myself praying that she'll give me more, so I wait patiently, clasping my hands over my lap so I don't fidget.

The second I heard the words *my mom never wanted me,* my body moved on instinct. That invisible thread that has always tied us together pulled hard at my core—she needed me.

But that's not the only reason I want her secrets. The more I learn, the more I understand how similar her life is to Seren's, and I now know with resolute certainty that I'll do anything in my power to protect them both.

"Why?" she asks, her voice low as she stares at her hands. She's highlighted by a sliver of moonlight that slips through her sheer curtains.

We sit shoulder to shoulder, but my face is angled so I don't miss a single expression.

"I thought that would be obvious," I say gently.

Finally, she looks at me—really looks at me—and I allow her to see into the very depths of my soul.

"I want to know everything about you, Rowan, whatever you're willing to share."

Her forehead creases as she lowers her chin to her chest.

When she speaks, my entire body tilts forward to hear her.

"She never wanted kids, but she loved my dad almost obsessively, and he wanted a big family. My birth was...difficult, I guess." She shrugs, pressing against my shoulder with the movement. "I don't remember how she was when I was a baby, but from my very first memory of her, I don't think she ever tried to bond with me. Then, when Dad got sick, she blamed me."

"You were a child."

Rowan shrugs as though that one very important fact doesn't matter.

"When we knew that the chemo wasn't working, he wanted to spend all his time with us. She resented that I was there and that he always included me. She hated that I was always his priority."

"That's what parents are supposed to do," I mutter. She shrugs again as if it doesn't matter then reaches for her wrist, probably searching for the bracelets she always wears. But her wrist is bare, and her thumb just taps against the tattoo.

Whether she admits it or not, she seeks comfort from me, or at least the memory of me.

"After he died, she became...indifferent. When she remarried, I quickly learned that it made her happy to see me punished for everything and nothing. My stepsister was the golden child, and since she never stole my father's time, my mother decided Haley was worthy of her time and attention." She curls in on herself.

"My stepfather was a cruel, cruel man. He hated my existence—said I was a constant reminder that someone else had been with his wife, even though he happily lived in a house that my father paid for."

Rowan peers over at me but doesn't hold eye contact.

"They were happy when I left home—all of them were. I ran into my mom once, and I panicked. I thought for sure she'd attempt to drag me home. Instead, she simply told me good luck. That she wouldn't be looking for me, and that as far as she was concerned, I'd died right along with my father."

"Jesus Christ." My stomach revolts. Sixteen is too young for those words not to cut. Not that they'd hurt any less at sixty, but teenagers still need their parents. "Maybe I should be grateful Mya left without a word."

"Maybe," she says absently. "Seeing you tonight, with all those people at Beck and Stella's house, it made me happy for you and the kids. I'm glad you'll have that kind of family —the kind that chooses you. It'll be good for the kids to have that stability and love too."

She's pulling away again. I saw it in her eyes at Beck's. It's always one step forward and two steps back with her. How do I get her to believe I'm willing to perform that dance with her for eternity though?

Her phone vibrates on the table, and anger crawls up my spine. If that's fucking Thane interrupting us again, I'm going to lose it.

Picking it up, I sigh with relief when Lottie's name lights up the screen.

I hand it to Rowan, and she answers as my mind whirls

with ways to prove to her that there's a place for her and it's by my side.

"Oh no," she groans, putting me instantly on alert. "Have you checked in on Seren tonight?"

I go lightheaded. My blood pressure has probably spiked dangerously high. "She went to bed around nine, right when we got home."

"We need to have a talk with her. Leo just found a walkie-talkie strapped to a beam in the nanny cabin. Apparently, *someone* was talking in it, scaring the crap out of the nannies and making them think someone was watching them."

What the hell am I going to do with my daughter?

"And…Lottie wants to meet with us first thing in the morning."

"What in the actual fuck?" I grumble.

We're both climbing out of her bed when Miles screams. Rowan's terrified expression matches mine before we both burst from her room, down the hallway, and up the stairs to the bunk room.

Miles is in the middle of the floor, writhing in pain and clutching his side. He's panting and covered in sweat, while Kade is curled up in the bottom bunk with tears streaming down his face.

The world turns upside down and everything is wrong.

I'm momentarily frozen to the spot. I've never seen any of my children this way, and my body constricts as though his pain attacks my own flesh. Fear pushes the air from my lungs and twists my insides. For the first time as a parent, I don't know what to do.

Rowan rushes past me and drops to my little boy's side. "Miles, buddy. Where does it hurt?"

He can't talk through the violent sobs that wrack his

little body. Instead, he clutches his right side, then chokes as vomit spills from his mouth. It spurs me into motion, and I drop to his other side.

Rowan's hands roam his body. "He's burning up," she says with a shaky voice.

Pappy and Seren enter the large room and both rush to Kade's side.

"It might be his appendix," Rowan says in a rush. "He's holding his right side. I don't know what else it could be. We need to get him to the hospital."

I nod and try to lift him, but his scream chills me to my core. "C—call an ambulance. Please. Someone call."

Rowan jumps to her feet and rushes out of the room. Pappy ushers Kade and Seren out after her.

I've never felt so helpless in my entire life.

It's an eternity before Rowan returns, but when she does, she lowers her face to Miles and whispers comforting words in his ear while rubbing his back.

The next few minutes pass with agonizing slowness, until finally, paramedics enter the room with a stretcher. Rowan is the one who speaks to them. She tells them about the scream and everything that's happened since. She mentions that he fell asleep in the middle of a party, something I hadn't even thought twice about.

I hold his hand as they load him up but have to release it so they can get him down the stairs. Rowan and I rush outside, each holding his hand on either side until we reach the ambulance.

"Are you his parents?" the paramedic asks as they load Miles into the back.

"I—I am," I choke out.

The man looks between us and nods. "Immediate family only. You can come with us," he says, pointing to me.

My gaze darts from him to Rowan. But he's right, she's not family. No matter how much I need her with me for this, she can't be because she's not ours yet.

The fear that fills Rowan's face matches my own.

I climb into the ambulance, wishing things were different. Wishing she were Miles's mother so she could help us through this, but my focus has to remain on Miles, so I do the only thing I can.

"Rowan." She lifts watery eyes to mine. "Take my keys and meet us at the hospital."

She nods but returns her focus to Miles.

"Now, Rowan. Go," I say, more loudly this time, as they shut the back doors.

As we race toward the hospital, the image of Rowan standing in the dark with her hands over her mouth quickly fades away.

———

It feels like hours since they took Miles back for an emergency appendectomy. I've paced miles in these hallways all by myself while my little boy has been spread open on an operating table as they remove his appendix and clean out his abdominal cavity.

Rowan never showed up. I really thought she would. Even with her hang-ups, I thought she cared enough to at least come. The pain she's caused by not being here for me is only rivaled by the fear of seeing Miles on his bedroom floor.

I called Mya's dad, Michael, and told him what was happening, and once again, he said he can't get in touch with her. He's an asshole who leveled his rage at me when I divorced his daughter, but I have to believe he loves his grandchildren in his own way.

I refuse to call Nick myself but told Michael that if he thought Nick could reach Mya, he was welcome to try. I didn't get an answer either way, and I don't give a fuck.

The nurse was nice enough to let me borrow a phone charger when my phone was about to die, so I called Pappy and told him what was happening. Rowan didn't come to the phone, and I didn't ask for her.

The sharp reality of her connection to us—or lack of connection—will have to be a problem for another day.

I really thought she'd come. I've never felt loneliness this acutely before.

Finally, a doctor enters the hallway I've been pacing, followed by the nurse who asked me for Miles's health history earlier.

"Mr. Walker?" The doctor asks.

"Yes, that's me. Is he okay?"

The doctor fills me in on the specifics of what happened, but all I hear is that he's out of surgery, and he'll make a full recovery.

I shake his hand, and he retreats through another door.

"Mr. Walker," the nurse says, drawing my attention to her. "I can take you to him now, though he'll be sleeping for a while. Also, I apologize, we've had several emergencies, so I was unable to get to you, but your friends are in the waiting room. They've been there since shortly after you arrived. I wanted you to know so you could give them an update when you're feeling up to it."

"Friends?"

Her puzzled expression searches my face. "Yes, sir. Are you okay?"

"Do you know their names?" I refuse to let hope in.

"No, I'm sorry. There are three women and one, excuse me for saying this, but one very rude man."

Despite my situation, I chuckle. That has to be Beck.

"Are you sure Miles will be asleep for a little longer?"

Her kind eyes crinkle as though they're used to smiling. "Yes, he'll probably sleep through the night."

"Oh. Okay, maybe I'll give them a quick update before I settle in with Miles."

"That's fine, a nurse is still with him monitoring his vitals. Come to the nurse's station when you're ready, and I'll take you through to your son."

"Thank you."

My heart hammers in my ears as loudly as the incessant beeping that happens in every hospital. I'm warring with so many emotions, but I keep reminding myself that Miles is safe. He's safe because Rowan sprang into action as soon as she saw him.

Why didn't she come?

I enter the main waiting room and peer around a couple of privacy screens before I find them—Rowan sits against the back wall. The moment she sees me, she hiccups on a heavy breath as though she's trying to swallow her emotions. Tabby and Stella flank her, and Beck paces the room, cursing about all the donations he's made to this hospital and how that should entitle him to at least an update.

She's here.

The fear of the last hour morphs into relief and gratitude for these people. Rowan looks as though she's been in a trainwreck though, so I go straight to her.

The second I move in her direction, she leaps from her chair, and everything in her lap tumbles to the floor.

"Th—they w—wouldn't let me in," she sobs, and the

first tear seems to open the floodgates of her emotions as though I'm her safe space. "I'm n—not family."

I was right. She's been trying to hold in her tears.

"They wouldn't even give us a goddamn update," Beck grouses.

"Shh," I say, pulling Rowan tighter against my chest. She fights me because that's what she does, but after a few choked sobs, she begins to calm down. "He's okay," I whisper. "He's okay."

Beck is hovering close by, so he hears and relays the message to Tabby and Stella, who both break into tears.

I've never seen Rowan cry this way, and it guts me, but it's the way she's clawing at me as if she can't decide if she wants to pull me closer or climb over me to get to Miles that fills me with love.

"She needs this," Beck whispers. "She's been holding everything in, not allowing comfort from any of us even though we knew she was terrified."

I don't know if Rowan hears him, but I nod in thanks, then tell them what the doctor told me, and the wave of instant relief I felt hearing the same words registers on their faces.

"I'll call your grandfather and Leo to give them an update," Beck says, though his voice is suspiciously rough.

"Thank you," I say. Rowan still clings to me, though her body has lost most of its tension.

"They wouldn't let me in," she mumbles into my chest.

"I know." I run my hand down her back with the same soothing motions she'd used on Miles hours earlier.

"I tried. I tried to get in."

"I know," I repeat.

"Rowan?" Stella asks gently. "Why don't we give you a ride home, okay?"

It's not noticeable to the eye, but her body tenses in my arms before she nods, wipes her nose with the sleeve of her sweatshirt, and finally lifts her gaze to mine. "Will you call if anything happens?"

I want to glue her to my side and tell the hospital rules to fuck off, but I can't risk upsetting anyone and getting kicked out. Not when Miles is so vulnerable.

"You know I will."

She dips her chin, but I catch it with a finger, lift her face to mine, and place a gentle kiss on her forehead. Her body sags against me only momentarily before she spins in place and allows Stella to lead her to the chair where all her stuff is. I nod in thanks, then go in search of the nurse's station.

When I enter the recovery area, I find Miles hooked up to machines but sleeping peacefully.

"I'm here, buddy," I say, placing my hand over his. "You gave us all quite the scare." Leaning in, I place my lips on his forehead and breathe him in for long minutes. The tiny puff of air that escapes his mouth hits my chin, and I allow it to comfort me.

He's breathing. He's going to be fine.

Eventually, I pull a chair closer so I can sit next to him, and I sit, watching him sleep.

A couple of hours later, we're moved to a private room, and a new nurse comes in to check his vitals, then assures me he's doing great.

"Your friend is still in the waiting room. Apparently, she refused to leave. Someone named Beck called and asked that we relay that message to you."

The ache in my chest roars.

She stayed.

20

CARING IS A GIFT

ROWAN

I wake with a start when strong hands touch me. My eyes fly open, and I tense, ready to protect myself, when Sebastian's easy smile comes into view.

"Shh," he whispers, lifting me into his arms. "Your neck is going to hurt like hell if you sleep curled up that way any longer."

I hadn't meant to fall asleep, but I forgot how exhausting it is to give yourself over to a full-body cry.

"Miles," I say, stiffening and wiggling in his arms until he finally sets me on my feet, but he keeps me close.

"I'm taking you to him," he says.

"But..." Oh, crap. Please don't cry again. "I'm not family." Those words have been causing so much anguish for hours, and I don't know how to process that.

"You stayed," he says, his voice rough as commercial-grade sandpaper. "I'd love to see them try to take you away now." Then he takes my hand in his and leads me through a maze of hallways.

"I needed to know that he was okay. I... It's my fault for not noticing he wasn't feeling well earlier."

He stops abruptly, and I stumble into him. Curling up in the fetal position on a hospital chair was probably not my smartest move. All of my limbs are stiff, making me more wobbly than normal.

"It's not your fault," he says vehemently. Then he bends at his knees, so we're nose to nose. "The doctor said it would have been almost impossible to detect any sooner than we did. Even if he had pain earlier, we would have assumed he had a stomach bug first."

I don't reply because it was my job to take care of him and while he slept on my lap, I was too busy freaking out over stupid family dynamics.

Thankfully, Sebastian doesn't press and takes my hand in his, or tries to. I'm still clutching a piece of paper between my fingers.

Holding it up, I hand it to him. "I—I made you my emergency contact."

Sebastian's entire face shines with emotion. "I see that," he says quietly as he scans the form I handed him. He gently folds up the piece of paper the nurse gave me and puts it in his back pocket. "Thank you for this, Rowan. I don't think you have any idea how much it means to me."

Does he know how monumental it is for me too? Holding my hand tightly in his, he pulls me down the hallway and into Miles's room.

As soon as I enter, my knees knock together. He looks so small, so fragile lying there completely helpless and pale.

"They moved us to a private room about twenty minutes ago."

I drift closer to his bed without thought and scan Miles to confirm he's breathing, resting, healing.

Sebastian comes to my side, and together we just...stare at his little boy.

I was sad when I left little Lucy and her family, the first child I became dangerously attached to. I've clung to the pain of that leaving as a reminder to not get too close, but it's nothing compared to the fear of thinking Miles might not survive.

Sebastian rests his hand over mine and rubs my knuckles, encouraging them to relax their shaking hold on the railing of the hospital bed.

"He's going to be fine, Rowan." His assurance doesn't placate the fear still surrounding me with a sickening aura. I don't think anything will ease the death grip it has on me until I see this little boy open his eyes.

"Did you call his mom?"

His fingers tighten their grip on mine.

"I tried," he sighs. "I got ahold of her dad again, but the results are the same. She's gone off the grid, and I have no idea how to reach her."

"At least you tried," I say. "You're a good man, Sebastian Walker."

He wraps an arm around me, and for once, I welcome the embrace.

But there's also a sickening sense of dread swirling in my gut because I'm already in too deep with this family. The ticking clock that lives inside my head as my own life's metronome is out of sync. The rhythm is now wild and unpredictable.

I don't know how to survive its new beat, and I fear that when the clock finally stops, I'll be the one blown to bits.

———

"How you doing, kiddo?" Pappy pushes a cup of tea my way, then slides onto the bench next to me.

We're sitting in the kitchen, awake hours before Seren or Kade will stir because we're both anxious for Miles to come home today.

"I'm fine. How are you holding up? It's been a tough couple of days."

He pats my forearm. "It's been tough on all of us, Row. It's hard to see someone you love in so much pain."

I open my mouth to tell him I'm sorry for his pain but can't. He was talking about both of us and even though my mind is saying it's not love I'm feeling, my heart is rapidly beating those thoughts into submission.

"Everyone loves in their own way," he says, his voice coarse with age. "Just because your love looks different doesn't mean it's any less powerful. Seren and Kade needed you these last couple of days, and you gave pieces of yourself I've never known you to share. That's love, Rowan."

That's love.

Is it? I'm not sure I ever thought about what love looks like other than what's fed to us through movies, filled with laughs and hugs, or how my family presented it filled with intentional pain.

It never occurred to me that neither of those scenarios fully encompasses what love is.

Because you've never allowed yourself to think about love in terms of anything but how it ends.

"I'm glad I could be here for them," I say. Lifting the mug of tea to my lips, I blow on it and chance a peek at Pappy.

He sits, smiling at me as if he can hear all my thoughts before I can.

"Have you told him about Lottie yet?"

Shame heats my cheeks. Lottie dropped not one, but two bombs on me in the last couple of days. One, she has to kick the Walkers out of the Nanny camp event because Seren has apparently become a legend among the other campers who are now attempting to continue her reign as prank-a-nanny queen.

But it's the other reason that makes the tea scald my throat on its way down—my dream job.

Or what I've always thought my dream was...but today, that job feels closer to a betrayal. I just haven't sorted out what to do about it yet.

"Not yet," I finally admit without making eye contact. "Sebastian's had a lot on his mind. It wouldn't be fair of me to drop either of those on him while he's still in the hospital with a sick kid."

"Mm-hmm," Pappy hums. "Don't run from love because it's scary, kiddo. You're stronger than that. Running only allows your family to keep winning because it keeps all the power in their hands. Maybe instead of running away from what you fear, it might be time to run toward it and face it head-on—" He stops abruptly and stares over my shoulder.

"Hey," Seren says. Her tone is solemn, and she doesn't appear to have slept at all.

Guilt is written all over her face. She's had two pranks go off recently. One was nanny cabin with the walkie-talkie incident, but it was last night's prank that was Lottie's final straw. Somehow, she managed to climb up to each ceiling fan in one of the cabins and line each blade with baby powder.

When the nannies settled in for the night, someone turned on the switch for the fans, and the entire room was covered in white powder.

No one can prove that one was Seren, but her history was enough for every nanny to refuse any job offers from Sebastian.

The worst part is how my chest flooded with warmth at

the knowledge that no one would replace me while my head was screaming the same sentiment with a much different feeling attached to it.

My emotions and my mind have never been at such odds before.

"Hey," I say. "Are you hungry?" There's no sense in ripping into her again. I've already explained how she'll be cleaning the cabin today and will probably be grounded for a long time to come. But I'm pretty sure it's the lecture her dad will deliver that's weighing the heaviest on her.

"No," she mutters as she slides in next to Pappy.

I smile. He's who I would turn to if I were in her shoes too.

"He's going to kill me," she whispers.

"Life always has consequences, kid. It's better you learn to face them now than grow up to be an adult who can't handle hard truths." Pappy doesn't sugarcoat it and tell her it'll be fine. But he does tuck her into his side and hug her tightly.

"I just don't get why you kept at it. Surely you understand that while you're older, your brothers need more care when your dad's at work." Okay, so maybe I'm not going to push it under the rug this morning.

Seren picks at her fingernail with her head down, but I still see the slight tremor of her chin.

"I'm here for you. I thought we had an understanding and we were going to do this stuff to your dad. What changed?"

Pappy chuckles. "He could use some loosening up, but Row's right, this isn't you, kiddo. What's goin' on?"

"Those nannies are all highly qualified, and trust me, Lottie has thoroughly vetted them," I say. "I know nothing is easy right now, but having someone you can count on will be a good thing."

She lifts her gaze to me, and her glare sends a shiver racing over my exposed skin—she's never looked so cold. The ice in her green eyes could cover the room in frost. "Like I can count on you?"

Her words hit hard. "I—I was never supposed to be permanent, Ser."

"And you're going to leave. It doesn't matter who takes your place as long as someone does, right?"

"No, that's not—"

"Forget it," she says, standing abruptly. "Everyone says we need a nanny. We need to bring someone else into our lives, but no one has ever asked me who I wanted. No one cares about me or how I feel. No one cares that the one person I want to stay is already planning to leave. No one cares."

"That's not true." My voice wobbles, and she probably doesn't even hear me as she runs from the room. "I might care too much," I whisper.

"Oh, Rowan. I thought you were smarter than that," Pappy chides. "There's no such thing as caring too much when you're caring about the right people."

He's slow to slide off the bench, but as soon as he's close enough, he places his hands on my biceps. Holding me at arm's length, Pappy stares directly into my eyes.

"Carin' about someone else is the greatest gift on earth. I'd sure hate to see you miss out because you're too scared of your past to embrace your future." His thumbs caress the skin on my arms, and I drag my watery gaze to his. "I'm gonna go track down Seren."

With a final squeeze, he releases me and leaves me

alone, his words and my thoughts screaming into the silence.

———

WHEN WE ENTER yellow cabin number twenty-two, because of course it's that wretched number, my mouth drops open.

"Oh, Ser. You're in big, big trouble," Kade says with eyes the size of saucers.

And he's not wrong. I've never seen anything as jaw-dropping as this. White powder covers every square inch of the place. The only clean spots are where the nannies must have removed their stuff. Covertly, I take a picture of the scene before me for Instagram later.

Leo had all their items professionally cleaned and will send the bill to Sebastian.

Seren doesn't say anything as she rolls in the vacuum behind her.

"How did you even get up there?" I ask, pointing to the rafters. For a camp cabin, the ceiling is remarkably high.

"I didn't," she grumbles, then crouches down, running her hands all over the vacuum cleaner.

Has she ever even used one of those things?

"What do you mean you didn't? Who did?" Unease begins to crawl up my spine with spider-like tingles.

"Does it matter?"

Kade drops to the floor and starts drawing with his finger in the powder.

"Yeah, it does matter."

Her gaze cuts to mine, and I read all the doubt, fear, and loneliness swimming in her irises.

"You didn't do this, did you?" I ask.

Now that I've seen the mess myself, I'm sure she

wouldn't have had time to pull off this prank. She wasn't alone long enough at any point in the day to have done it.

"No one's going to believe me anyway, so can you please show me how to turn this thing on so I can get this over with?" The sadness in her voice makes my stomach twist painfully.

I cross the room and bend at the knees so we're at eye level.

"I'll believe you. Even though you've gone back on your word not to prank the nannies, if you tell me that you didn't do this, *I* will believe you."

"Why?" She grunts. Her gaze darts around the room frantically, attempting to avoid my eyes.

Why is a great question. But there's only one answer, so I go with the truth.

"Because apparently trust is earned, but it goes both ways, and I need you to trust me even when I make mistakes too. And because I care about you. I'm not good at this part of things. I don't know what to do when I care too much because I never let it happen, but here we are."

"Are you going to leave?" she whispers. Her gut-wrenching gaze fills with unshed tears that she aggressively tries to wipe away.

"I—" The truth is, I don't know. My answer has always been that I leave—it's what I do. I don't know how to stay past an end date. "I can't make any promises, Ser." Her entire body heaves, and Kade runs over to wrap his arms around his sister's neck. "What I can promise is that I'll stay until your dad finds someone that you all love. In September, I'll have to...well, I'll have to reevaluate my assignments."

What if he never finds someone?

I push the thought from my head. I can only deal with

today—my insides seize. I can only deal with the todays and tomorrows.

What if todays and tomorrows turn into months and years?

"That plan stinks," Kade grumbles. "Just stay with us. Why won't you stay?"

"I'm not sure I know how." It's a truth that has them both staring at me as if I told them I was an alien.

Kade's face crumples in confusion, but Seren? She stares at me as if she understands something I don't, and it's unnerving that a twelve-year-old can have that type of insight.

"I didn't do this," she says quietly.

"Do you know who did?"

She shrugs and won't look me in the eye. She doesn't want to be a snitch.

I brought her here with no intention of helping her clean up her mess, but when I find nothing but honesty in her glassy eyes, I pick up the vacuum handle and turn it on.

I toss Kade a rag and show him how to wipe down the walls. He makes more of a mess than he is helpful, but it keeps him busy while Seren and I tackle the impossible feat of eradicating baby powder from every nook and cranny.

21

I'LL NEVER TELL YOU A LIE

SEBASTIAN

"Single Dad Hotline, I'm your helper, how can I help you?" Rowan asks.

"Will you please add my fucking number into your phone?"

Her soft laughter rings through the phone and under her bedroom door.

"Can I come in?" I ask, pressing my forehead to the cool wood surface separating her from me.

"What? Where are you?"

I knock softly on the wood frame, and her gasp soothes my racing mind. I've been home from the hospital with Miles for three days, but the second I walked through the door, life sped into fast-forward mode. I've been putting out fires ever since.

Her door opens, and she stares up at me through her lashes, wearing something resembling pajamas, but I'd be forced to blind a man if anyone else saw her in them.

"Are you okay?" she asks, holding on to the doorknob as if it's the only thing keeping her upright.

I nod, basking in the sight of her. "Can I come in?" I ask again.

She sucks in her bottom lip and bites down on it before nodding and moving to the side.

The entire room smells of her light floral scent—roses. It engulfs me, and reminds me that this is home, here, with her and my children.

Rowan quietly closes her door and climbs back into bed, pulling the covers up to her chest. I follow her but sit on the edge.

"I got a pretty hefty cleaning bill today," I say with raised brows.

She rolls her eyes. "I've already sorted that out with both Leo and Lottie. Seren didn't do it, but because she didn't want to rat out who did, we cleaned the place together. I'm not sure what to say about the bill. Do you want me to pay it?"

"Why would you pay it?"

She shrugs. "Because I didn't force her to tell me who did do it?"

I shake my head with a huffed snort. "No, it's okay. I'll pay it. I'm glad she trusts you to tell you the truth. She cares about you, Rowan. A lot."

Her swallow is loud in the otherwise silent house. "I know. I like her too."

"I was kicked out of the nanny camp program." Saying it out loud sounds ridiculous.

Rowan lifts her knees to her chest and cradles them while resting her chin on top.

"I heard," she says. "I'm sorry about that. Lottie didn't see any other way to stop the prank wars from snowballing."

My shoulders have been a permanent accessory to my ears since finding out because what the hell do I do now?

"How's Miles tonight? By the time I got Kade into bed, the light was already off in your room." Her voice is my own personal lullaby—soft and melodic, but with a hint of sadness that never goes away.

I have Miles sleeping with me right now so I can keep an eye on him. Letting him out of my sight for too long brings back the fear of seeing him crumpled on the floor.

"He's good. Kids are a lot tougher than we are sometimes."

"It's easy to be resilient when the world hasn't crushed the belief of goodness from your spirit yet," she says absently.

That's the truth she's lived with, and perhaps she doesn't understand that it's not normal to be so beaten down by life that you give up before adulthood.

"He asked for you when he woke up from anesthesia. It wasn't me, or Pappy, or even his mother he wanted, it was you."

"That's…" Her brows pinch down. "I don't know what to say." The words are barely audible.

"In a very short time, you've left a mark on my kids—and on me. That's not something that happens all the time."

"Pappy did say I was fated, right?" Her joke falls flat, probably because we're both starting to believe that maybe he's been right all along.

"Seren said you promised to stay until we found a nanny she approves of."

Rowan tugs on her bottom lip, pinching and rolling it between her thumb and forefinger.

"I did, and I've been thinking about it a lot." She lifts her head, and a multitude of emotions flash in her eyes. There's a healthy dose of fear, but also something akin to excitement.

Bending my knee to rest on her bed, I angle my body toward her. It brings me within inches of touching her.

"You realize she may never approve of anyone." That's my biggest fear. That Rowan's made a promise she won't be able to keep and Seren will hate her for it.

She nods for a long time, her gaze going distant as she mulls over my statement.

Then she shrugs. "She likes me though."

My face breaks into the first smile I've had in days. "She does like you."

The way she lifts her gaze to mine, staring at me through thick lashes as though she's shy and worried about my response, does unthinkable things to my blood pressure.

"I don't know how to stay."

And my smile falls into crushing despair.

"But maybe, if I keep giving you my todays and my tomorrows, you'll...teach me."

I'm struggling to understand what she just said because I could have sworn it sounded as though she had no plans to leave at the end of the week.

"I'm going to need you to explain what that means." She has my full attention, but I've lost the ability to control my reactions, and my fingers twitch while I wait.

"I can't promise forever, it feels too... I don't know. When I think about that, my palms get sweaty and my vision blurs. Then the walls start closing in on me as if I'm slowly drowning and I can't break the surface."

Whiplash would be easier to handle than this conversation.

"Okay," I say, dragging out the word. Forever with me feels like a slow death, got it.

"And, well, Lottie offered me a dream job, but it would

start in September, and now because of you, it's not really feeling like a dream job."

I'm trying to follow along, but I can't tell if she's coming or going and it's fucking killing me.

Dropping her face into her hands, she groans. "I'm not explaining myself very well. I don't know how to do this, Seb. I've never cared enough to even try before."

That little asshole called hope springs anew in my chest.

"You're saying you care—about us," I clarify. It's hard to keep my grin in check, but if we have to walk through this taking baby steps, I'll hold her hand through every single stage.

"I think I do," she sobs, as if it's the worst tragedy since *Romeo and Juliet*.

It's not nice, but I laugh, and it makes her cry even harder, so I climb onto the bed and pull her into my side.

"Is caring really so bad, Peach?"

"Yes," she chokes out. "It is. That's why I never, ever do it, but you assholes sucked me in with your voodoo powers, and now" —she hiccups—"I think I care. A lot. And I spent years not crying in front of people, Seb, years. Then you come back into my life and now I can't s—stop."

"Oh, Rowan." I'm trying to be compassionate, but I also want to shake her a little.

"It's good that you care because I, *we* care about you too. So much that the thought of you leaving has made me sick to my stomach for the last three days."

"W—w—why do you people do this then?"

Her hair sticks to the tears on her face, so I brush it behind her ears. "Because, sweetheart, a life without love and caring isn't a life at all. It's going through the motions but never experiencing the beauty of it. Human beings are capable of the greatest love and the most brutal heartache, and sometimes you wouldn't have one without the other, but that doesn't mean you don't try. If anything, it means you keep reaching for it until you find the place where you belong."

"I don't know that I belong anywhere."

"Jesus, Rowan. Of course you do. You always have. You've just been too stubborn to see it. You belong with us, with me and Pappy, with the kids. You belong here in Sailport Bay, where everyone who has met you is ready to adopt you into their lives without hesitation because of who you are and the heart that you have. Even if you can't see that, it's all here, waiting for you."

"Stella said they're an orphanage for lost souls." She chuckles and blows a snot bubble at the same time. It's something I've only seen babies do, and it makes me laugh harder. "Ugh. I'm disgusting."

"You're amazing." *And you're mine.* Someday, when she's ready for that level of commitment, I'll tell her that, but for now, I keep it to myself.

I hand her a box of tissues from the nightstand and wait patiently while she pulls herself together.

With a handful of dirty tissues, she squares her shoulders and offers the smallest smile.

"Tell me what you want, Rowan. How can we make this work?"

She blanches, the little color she had draining from her face.

"What's the matter?" I ask, already knowing I'd move heaven and earth to fix everything I could.

"Nothing."

I don't even have to fully form an expression of disbelief before she's correcting herself.

"It's just that, Lottie, well...honestly, never mind. I'll deal with Lottie."

"Will there be an issue with you giving me your todays and tomorrows?" The excitement fizzing through me now is the same as when I was a kid on Christmas morning, waiting for my parents to get up so I could run down to see if Santa had come.

She swallows heavily.

"No," she nearly shouts, and I pull back to search her face. "It's just, todays and tomorrows until September. Then..."

"Then we'll renegotiate?"

"Um...renegotiate what?" I've never heard a person's voice actually quiver as Rowan's does now. She lives with very specific fears I've never experienced, but that doesn't mean I can't learn to help her overcome them.

"From now until September, you'll give me your todays and tomorrows as our nanny while we work out exactly what's happening between us on a personal level. In September, we'll decide if we need to adjust your title."

"That's not really what I meant."

"No?" I question, then drop my lips to her cheek, absorbing her tears with my lips. With my mouth next to her ear, I whisper, "Then be very clear about what you did mean, Rowan, because there's no part of me willing to walk away from anything we've already started."

"September," she mumbles as I kiss and nip down her neck.

I press my smile into her skin. "I'm glad we're in agreement then."

"I feel like you tricked me." She moans as I trail a finger along the hem of her V-neck T-shirt.

"It's only a trick if it's not the truth, and I'll never tell you a lie, Peach. Never."

22

YOU'VE HANDLED WORSE THINGS THAN PLAYDATES

ROWAN

"Honey, we're home."

I stand quickly from where I'm bent over searching the fridge and whack my head on the refrigerator door. I'm still rubbing my scalp when Bella and Tabby walk around the corner. They both have a baby attached to them with a baby carrier.

What the heck do they put in the water here? A baby boom has exploded all over town.

"Ah, hi?" Was I supposed to be expecting them?

"We come bearing gifts," Tabby says cheerily. I've yet to see her offer anything but golden retriever energy. It's as though her only setting is sunshine and rainbows.

She places a tray of cupcakes on the counter with one hand, holding the hand of a little girl in the other, all while bouncing the sleeping baby she's wearing.

Talk about multitasking.

"They're beet cupcakes," Bella clarifies. "Tabby uses us as guinea pigs for her bakery downtown."

"Oh, that's...nice."

Tabby waves me off. "Kids will eat anything with frosting and it's their opinion I trust."

"The guys have taken over Beck's house, and Stella's oldest wasn't feeling well, so we grabbed Ruby here and are invading your space for a playdate," Bella explains. "I hope that's okay."

"Oh, does your husband work with them too?" I saw him in the kitchen at Beck's house, but I thought he was a teenager at first.

Bella holds up her hand. "Fiancé, but yes. Teddy's Crystal Waters' legal counsel."

Ruby wiggles free from Tabby's hand and bounces excitedly. "Where's Kade?"

Her enthusiasm draws a chuckle out of me. These two are going to be trouble together.

"He's all the way upstairs on the third..."

She's tearing off through the house in search of the staircase before I finish.

"How's Miles doing?" Bella asks, keeping her gaze downcast. She's a wispy little thing that floats around as though she has wings helping her along. She's also painfully shy but attempting to be social, that much is clear. I thought I was shy, but now I know I'm just closed off because I've got nothing on this woman.

She stands two steps behind Tabby as though she needs a shield, and for her part, Tabby seems to understand her triggers and moves as though she's trying not to startle her.

It's similar to how the guys were in the kitchen the other night at Beck's house. They all move in perfect harmony with each other, as if they've been doing it their entire lives.

"Um, Miles is doing well," I say, finally remembering she asked a question. "He's still recovering, so he basically has unlimited screen time."

Tabby ushers Bella to a stool while she openly helps herself to a tour. "Where is he? I wanted to give him a cupcake."

"Oh, he's in Sebastian's room for now. Kade has too much energy for them to both be in the bunk room right now."

"And Seren? Where's she?"

My nose wrinkles and my palms begin to itch because I'm not sure how to handle this inquisition.

"She went to use the music room at camp. Leo said it was fine now that Lottie's crew is gone. I'm not sure what will happen when he has actual campers, but for now, it's a good place for her to be."

"Good, good," Tabby says. She scans the place as though she's planning to rob it.

"Is...everything okay?"

"So with the littles in the bunk room, Miles in Sebastian's room, Seren at camp, and the babes unable to speak, we're basically alone?"

"Uh, yeah. I guess so."

I didn't think it was possible, but Tabby's smile grows three sizes, then she places a hand to hold her baby to her and scurries across the room. Once she's seated next to Bella, they both prop their chins in their hands and stare at me expectantly.

"Can I get you a drink?" I'm so out of my element here. I don't play hostess. I don't do girls' nights, and I live alone for a reason. I have no idea how this is supposed to go.

Tabby makes a show of checking her watch. "Nope. Not five yet. But if we're still here at five we'll share a bottle of wine with you."

My gaze immediately whips to the clock above the oven.

It's just after one. Are they seriously planning to be here for four hours?

"Take a breath, Row." Bella should be the yoga instructor instead of Leo. Her voice could calm most people with simple words, but I'm a tornado touching down.

I can't entertain these women for four hours.

"Um, will you excuse me for one minute?" The panic must be showing on my face because they nod sympathetically.

I scramble up the stairs to my room, where Sebastian wrote down his number, and I dial it. Well, I try to. My fingers are shaking harder than a freaking leaf on a gusty day and instead of the number six, I press the number nine, three times in a row.

Finally, I get the number correct, and it rings four times before he picks up.

"Sebastian Walker."

That's how he answers the phone? Rude.

"It's me," I squeak.

"Rowan? What's wrong?"

"Nothing really. The kids are fine. They're good. Actually, they're great. Pappy's taking a nap on the porch, and Seren walked over to the music room at camp, so everyone's accounted for."

"That's good. So tell me why you sound as though you're about to hyperventilate." Damn him for using that commanding tone my body wants so badly to heed.

Sticking my head out of my room, I look up and down the hallway, then quickly shut the door.

"Tabby and Bella are here."

There's a long pause as if he didn't hear me.

"Yes," he says slowly. "They said something about a play-date when they picked up Ruby."

He knew they were coming and didn't warn me? Double rude.

"But it's not just a playdate for the kids. Miles is in your bed, Seren is at camp, Kade and Ruby are in the bunk room, probably tearing it apart, and the babies don't play. So it's me, Tabby, and Bella. And they want to...hang out," I hiss. "They said if they're still here at five o'clock they'll share a bottle of wine with me. Five o'clock. That's four freaking hours. How the hell am I supposed to entertain them on my own for four whole hours?" I'm aware that my words are pitching higher and gaining speed with each passing second, but fuck me if I can control it.

"I'll be right back," Sebastian whispers, but he isn't speaking to me, so I press my lips into a tight, thin line. Then I hear a door close and the chatter that was coming from his end ceases. "Row, when's the last time you had a girlfriend?"

"I don't have girlfriends."

Another long pause.

"Ever?"

Good grief, guy. Don't pity me now. Not having friends is the least sad thing about my life.

"I mean, I have Lottie, but we don't really hang out. Not even in college." Though not because she didn't try. "She lives in Tennessee and I...don't. But I watch TV. Mostly reruns of *Gilmore Girls* and *Friends* and sometimes *The New Girl*, and when they host, they put shit out. Like snacks, and I don't know, games or something. I'm a Cheese Whiz kind of girl, Seb. Cheese Whiz. Out of a can. I can't go around giving them hits of Cheese Whiz."

When he doesn't immediately say anything, my stomach gurgles as if I'm about to be sick.

"Can I give you some advice?" His voice is soft and kind. It relaxes me more than anything else.

"I guess," I mutter.

"Be honest with them. They're there because they want to get to know you, not because they're trying to take something from you or harm you in any way, I promise. If you tell them what you told me, you'll find it a lot easier to relax and maybe even enjoy yourself."

"You want me to tell them that at thirty-three years old I don't know how to make a friend? What if they ask why?"

"I'm sure they will."

I gasp audibly, but he speaks over it.

"I also think they'll respect your boundaries if you set them. They're good people, Rowan. You should give them a chance. You enjoyed hanging out with them at Beck's house, right?"

Did I? I thought I was more of an observer, an outsider looking in on a family I'd never be part of, not really an active participant.

"But I didn't have to do anything there. I don't know how to host." And that's the crux of it. I'm embarrassed I can't do something as simple as host a playdate. I never arranged them as a nanny. I always brought the kids to the library or the kiddie gym. And something about hosting in Sebastian's home makes it feel more...domestic. I don't do domestic.

"You do, Rowan. That's your home too. Share it with them and see how it goes. If it all blows up and you get the impulse to run, tell them you need to check on Miles and hang out with him for a bit, but I'm confident the time with them will go by in a flash."

"You could have warned me," I say petulantly.

"I did, sweetheart. Try checking your text messages

sometime. I've got to get back into my meeting. Are you okay?"

"No."

"I believe in you. You can do this." His smile broadcasts through the phone.

"That's supposed to be my line," I grumble.

"I'll call you later."

"Fine. And Seb?"

"Yeah?" The noise around him picks back up.

"Thank you."

He's silent for three long beats.

"I'm always here for you, Peach. I'm really glad that you called me. Try to have fun."

I nod and hang up before he hears how his words affect me.

In a panic, I called him. I don't think I've gone to anyone for help or comfort since I was eleven years old.

I'm in so much trouble.

Tabby's distinct laughter fills the silence, reminding me that I can't stay up here forever.

Okay, Rowan Ellis. You can do this. It's only two women. It'll be a piece of cake. No problem. You've handled much worse.

With that embarrassingly inadequate pep talk complete and two knocks on the doorframe for good luck, I march back to the kitchen as though I'm entering the death chamber. I just hope this isn't my last meal.

"Okay," I say far too loudly. *Wow, get it together, Row.* "Um, so here's the deal. I don't know how to do this." I wave my hand frantically between me and them. "Or this." My hand extends around the kitchen. "I've never done any of it before. It's making my hands very sweaty, and my heart might stop any second. Either that or my breakfast is about to evacuate in a very disgusting way. It's a toss-up, really."

There. I did it. That wasn't so hard.

They both stare at me with wide eyes, and I'm forced to wipe my palms on my shorts.

"You don't know how to do what, babe?" Tabby's voice doesn't carry anything but kindness.

"This." I point from me to her. Doesn't that explain it all?

"Are you nervous?" Bella asks, and I swear understanding flashes in her pretty blue eyes.

"I passed nervous when you two sat down." If I speak any faster the words will be a jumbled mess.

"Are you saying you don't know how to hang out?" Tabby's brow furrows, but I'm also pretty sure she's seconds away from climbing over the island to wrap me in a hug.

I take a step back.

"Hang out. Host. Make friends. Whatever you want to call it."

Huh. That wasn't as hard as I thought it would be.

"You didn't have any friends at home?" Bella asks.

And the nerves are back twofold.

"I never stay in one place very long, so it wasn't worth it."

"And when you were a kid?" Tabby asks.

"Not sure. Maybe in elementary school, but after my dad died, everything changed."

Bella sucks in a gasp, drawing my attention to her pale face. "We might have more in common than you think." She smiles, but it showcases a sadness I thought I'd buried years ago.

"Let me get this straight." Tabby paces the length of the island while mindlessly patting her son's back. "You're telling me you never had any of the traditional girlfriend-type experiences?"

I shrug. "Like what? I don't feel as though I missed out on anything, if that's what you mean."

"No." She stops abruptly with her index finger pointed at me. "So, you never had sleepovers, got ready for prom with friends, or got so drunk at a party the cops brought you home?"

"I'm pretty sure having the cops bring you home isn't a traditional anything," Bella interrupts.

"Sneaking out in the middle of the night to watch the stars?" I shake my head and keep shaking as she keeps going. "Camping? Shopping? Wine nights? Clubbing? Pajama parties where you do spa treatments? Nothing?"

"Tabs, you're making her feel worse," Bella mutters out of the side of her mouth.

The truth is, I don't have any feelings about missing any of that. I've never thought about it because it wasn't an option.

"Did you at least go to a school dance?" Tabby's wobbly chin says she's about to burst into tears. How the heck did this get so heavy so quickly?

"No," I say as unemotionally as I can, even if my body is gearing up for an epic fight-or-flight response.

Tabby exhales harshly, then pulls out her phone and rage-types a three-minute message while I stand shifting from foot to foot and Bella tries to ease my worries with her gentle smile.

"Okay." Tabby finally disengages from her phone. "We've got a lot of time to make up for. We'll start by hanging out today, and maybe have a wine night tonight, but don't you worry, we're going to give you all the experiences."

"No, that's not...I mean, I don't—"

Tabby stalks me with catlike intent and I almost laugh at how fitting her name is. Then she launches herself at me while managing to turn her body to the side, so when she wraps me in a crushing hug, she doesn't squish her baby.

"It's okay to be scared, Row. I've been there. I spent years not being able to trust anyone because of what Leo put me through when we were younger. They were very lonely years, but slowly, I learned to let people in. And we'll be here for you while you find and expand your limits on trust. We've got you, babe."

Good God, how long is she going to keep me locked in this embrace?

"Now I understand why you were hiding on the deck at Beck's house at dinner the other night, but no more. We're going to give you the ultimate girlfriend experience." She finally releases me, then takes me by the sweaty hand and leads me to the sofa and tells me to sit.

Reaching over, I angle the baby monitors so I can hear Miles if he needs something and turn up the volume on the video one in the bunk room. Kade and Ruby appear to be making a fort using every blanket they can find. I'm still busy silently begging for one of the boys to call for me when Tabby and Bella walk back into the family room with a charcuterie board I've never seen before and three bottles of sparkling water.

Then they sit around the coffee table and start talking about their day, their plans, and past experiences. I excuse myself a couple of times to check on Miles and take deep, shaky breaths.

Kade and Ruby came down for a snack, bounced around the house, and are now cuddled together in yet another fort watching a movie. Even Miles felt well enough to come down and join them. He's now sprawled out on the sofa with his head in my lap, and I don't even really hate it. Seren texted a few minutes ago to say she was on her way home, and Pappy made his way in about an hour ago. When our eyes locked, I swear he shed a tear.

Tabby turns to me with a giant smile and a mischievous glint in her gaze. "It's five o'clock, Row. You ready for that wine?"

I nearly topple over the side of the sofa when I twist my body to look at the clock. Five-twenty-five.

Holy shit, I did it.

23

DANCING TO HER BEAT

SEBASTIAN

"I think this is the best course of action," Beck says, tossing his pen onto the table and removing his glasses. "The rest of us should take turns joining you, but it's imperative you're at them all."

"I agree," I say, even though the idea of leaving again makes my chest itch as though I've been rolling around in poison ivy for days.

"Due to Miles and his surgery, six out of the seven investors have agreed to push everything back by one month." I can tell by the tick of Alexei's jaw he's pissed.

"Let me guess, the seventh who's refusing is Coleman Industries?" Elijah's eye roll could rival Seren's.

Old man Coleman is a hypocrite of the highest order. He's looking at the scandal with my wife and using it as the reason for pulling out of our deal, but he's married to a twenty-year-old and has never been faithful.

"You guessed it." Beck stands and rolls his neck side to side. "The only way we can get to him is by pulling some strings and getting you into the Hearts of Hope annual gala in New York City. It wasn't easy either, as the guest list is curated by the Broken Hearts Network years in advance."

"But you pulled some strings." Elijah chuckles.

"Never underestimate how far money will take you," Beck says with a wide grin. "You'll have to donate a pretty penny once you're in there, but between your donation and mine, you'll be seated with old man Coleman, his wife—who is young enough to be his granddaughter—his son, Jacob, who is in the process of taking the reins, and his wife. It's a table for eight, but I haven't been able to suss out who the other couple will be."

"Okay," I say, taking notes on my laptop. "I know Jacob. His father did business with mine a few times, and I've heard of Hearts of Hope. That's the organization that provides free surgeries for children in need, right? It makes sense that he'll be there. If I remember correctly, Jacob volunteered with one of their other charities. It's why he worked at my grandfather's camp the summer before he went to college—it's how we met."

A thought occurs to me, and their voices fade away as I put the pieces together in my head. I may not need fucking old man Coleman.

"Yes. They're doing amazing things with all the money they raise," Beck says.

"And this year, the MC is the CEO of Bryer-Blaine Industries, correct? He's somehow related to the founders of the charity."

Beck stares at me for half a second before realization dons on him too. "That man doesn't ever accept meetings that aren't thoroughly vetted."

I know this about him, but all I'd need is five minutes of his time.

"It's doubtful you'll even get close to him," Elijah says.

He's also right, but if I do? If I do, this could be a coup for our newly formed partnership. If I can't get old man Coleman on my side, I'll have to get close to Blaine—whatever it takes.

"You have to bring a date with you. This can't come across as an ambush, or the old man will double down. If Rowan won't go with you, ask a friend, hire someone, I don't give a fuck, but you can't show up alone," Beck says.

What are the chances she'll agree to this?

Our phones chime at the same time, and we all reach for them.

Band of merry fucking meddlers:

Leo: The girls' playdate is rolling into a wine night.

Leo: So, looks like dinner's at your place tonight, Seb. You have burgers and hotdogs at your house, or should I grab them on my way over there?

Me: Everyone is on board with that?

"You worried about Rowan?" Alexei asks, uncharacteristically somber. He's the only one in the room who has a little knowledge of her background. But the thing about this group is they don't need the details to give her exactly what she needs, and they've never once hesitated to bring her into their circle.

"She had a minor freak-out when they first showed up, but I haven't heard from her since."

Leo: Yessir!

Me: Okay, we had a grocery delivery yesterday, but probably not enough for everyone.

Leo: On it.

Beck: I'll see if Stella can put together a pasta salad.

"You could have just said that. We're all right here." Elijah chuckles.

"Leo's not. What if he doubled up on tuna macaroni and no one likes tuna macaroni?" Beck's deep frown says he is one hundred percent serious.

Elijah's laugh shakes his entire body. "Oh, how times have changed."

Alexei: I'll grab some cookies at the store when I run to the hotel to change.

Elijah: Samira's out of town, but I'll grab some beer.

We all lift our gaze to Elijah.

"What? I wasn't going to be the only asshole not chiming in," Elijah says.

The room explodes into laughter and finally, some of the tension that's been suffocating us for weeks starts to dissipate.

"Well, we better get going. Tabby's amazing, but she's also a little troublemaker," Beck says, straightening his papers. "Guess we'll see you at your place in a bit."

I nod. There was never a question of if they'd be there. The girls are there, so that's where they'll be. This is exactly the kind of family my kids need—and maybe it'll be what helps to convince Rowan to stay for good.

The drive home is short. I could have walked to Beck's house along the beach, but the idea of sitting through meetings all day covered in sand and saltwater was less than appealing.

Opening the door to my house, the laughter and chatter of a happy home hit me.

It's disorienting, and my emotions sit heavy in my chest. My kids have never had this. I've never had this, unless you count my time spent at my grandparents. It's overwhelming, but so damn right. This is where we were meant to be—all of us.

Following the voices, I stop at the edge of the family room and observe. Tabby talks animatedly while Bella and Rowan listen attentively. Rowan smiles at the right times, but I can tell she's still holding herself back—keeping herself on the periphery—but at least she's really trying.

There's a Pack 'n Play set up next to the chair Pappy's reclining in. He wears a contented grin as he stares at whoever is inside it. Ruby and Kade are lying on their bellies with their chins in their hands, watching a movie. They both burst out laughing when the cartoon dog says something I missed.

But it's Miles, stretched out on the sofa with his head in Rowan's lap, that hits me right in the chest. He feels safe with her, and that's more than I could've ever hoped for.

"Seb, you're here," Tabby says, jumping up. "We've been waiting for one of you to show up so we can open the wine. You're on kid duty. The other guys will help out when they get here."

My entire body relaxes with the happiness in this room. "Sounds like a plan."

Rowan studies me with a hint of amusement ticking at the corners of her lips as I make my way closer to her.

Without thinking too much about it, I lean over the top of her and kiss her forehead. Then move to Miles, and when he grins up at me, I'm pretty sure I grow to ten feet tall.

"Hey, bud. How you feeling?"

He turns that brilliant smile of his to Rowan. "Good. Rowan's the best."

Surprise lights up her face. "You're the best Miles I've ever met." Her voice is soft and velvety, as if the words touched her soul as much as they did mine.

Tabby and Bella are already heading toward the kitchen, so I wait until they're out of earshot.

"How are you holding up?" I ask Rowan as she scootches over so I can slide in next to Miles.

She takes a minute, and her lips twitch as if she's pondering my question. Is she even aware that her fist is clutching her chest? "Okay, I think. I mean, I didn't contribute much to their conversation, but I guess it wasn't as bad as I thought it would be."

Unable to stop myself, I fist the back of her neck and pull her to me, pressing another kiss on her forehead. "I'm really happy to hear that."

"Daddy!" Kade abandons his movie long enough to run to me for a hug.

I hadn't realized he'd been watching me, but when he shifts to Rowan, and waves with both hands so she'll come closer, he presses a kiss to her forehead too.

"I like you too, Row-Row."

The muscles in her neck pull taut as she nods. She won't look at me, but when her lashes flutter and stick together with moisture, it's obvious how profoundly my little man has affected her.

Seemingly unaware of the power he wields, Kade skips back to his friend and continues watching the movie.

"It sounds as though the girls are waiting for you," I whisper, right before a cork pops in the other room.

"Hope you don't mind us raiding your wine fridge," Tabby shouts from the kitchen.

My shoulders shake with silent laughter. Tabby told Rowan they were an orphanage for lost souls, and I couldn't have come up with a better description if I tried.

"Have at it," I call back. Lowering my voice, I say, "You should get out there before they come to get you."

Rowan's face pales, and it becomes apparent how much of a toll this day has taken on her already. Dark circles are forming under her eyes, and her shoulders only relaxed for a moment when I kissed her forehead.

Squeezing her hand in one of mine, I tilt her chin to face me with my free hand. "I get this is a lot, but I need you to know how proud I am of you for trying. Have you had fun so far?"

Her gaze jumps around the room before she finally nods. "They didn't push me or anything, and Tabby is really funny. It was just...different."

"Different is good for ya, Row," Pappy chimes in, apparently not at all perplexed by how intimately we're sitting. "You've been more alive these last few weeks than I've ever seen you before. Don't cut yourself off when things get hard. Take breaks and try again. You were never meant to walk through life as an empty version of yourself. You've got so much more than that to offer the world. Explore it, thrive in it, and live."

"Row, get your skinny ass in here." Tabby has no boundaries whatsoever, and she might be exactly the kind of friend Rowan needs.

There's a knock at the door, followed by footsteps. This

crazy chosen family seems to knock as a warning that they're entering, not as a way of asking permission.

Twisting my neck to stare at the door, I grin when Leo walks in holding about twenty shopping bags.

"All set," he calls out. "Let me drop this in the kitchen, then I'll come help with the kids."

"Is it just a known thing that when their wives have a wine night, they're on dad duty? No one puts up a fight?" Confusion clouds Rowan's tone, but I simply shrug.

"Yeah, Peach. That's what a partnership is. Give and take, take and give in every aspect of the relationship. When one person is fighting to maintain at twenty-five percent, the partner steps up to handle the other seventy-five. The best you can hope for is to find someone who gives as much as they take so as a couple, you're always at one hundred percent for yourselves, your children, and each other."

"He's right," Pappy says, lifting a fussy baby into his arms. "If you give yourself a chance, Row, you'll find out that life can be so much more than you've ever experienced."

She sucks in a breath but doesn't say anything.

"Hey," Seren says from behind us. "I'm home."

I lean away from Rowan, and we both tilt our bodies to include Seren in our conversation even though the sofa is separating us. Her gaze dances from one person to the next, but I can't tell what's going on in that head of hers. She's so guarded these days.

"Hey, sweet pea. How was camp?"

She looks from me to Rowan and shrugs. "I played a little and wrote some music, but it's probably not any good."

"That's part of being an artist—you never think your work is good," Rowan says, then stands and walks around the sofa to face Seren. "How did it feel to do it?"

"Angry," Seren mumbles.

My gaze ping-pongs between my two girls, but I stay where I am because this conversation was meant for Rowan. She might be the only one who can truly sympathize with my little girl.

"It's very therapeutic. And lots of music can be angry, but still beautiful. Maybe tomorrow we can go together, and you can show me what you've done? I—I might have some feelings to get out too."

Her gaze snags on mine, and my heart beats to her tune.

"Really?" The hope in Seren's voice cuts me to the quick. How many times has her mother let her down in her short life?

"Really," Rowan laughs, and I swear the tension melts from her body. "It's been a...day around here."

At that moment, Tabby's loud, rich laughter fills the air, and Beck walks in, holding a large bowl in one hand and an infant car seat in the other.

"What's going on?" Seren asks, unease coating her words.

"Family dinner, kid," Beck says, entering the fray. "Mind helping me with this?"

Seren takes the large bowl from him.

"What am I supposed to do now?" Seren's gaze follows Beck as he rounds the sofa and removes the small child from the car seat.

"Well, apparently, it's family dinner and girls' night," Rowan says in a light tone. "I have no idea what a girls' night entails other than wine, but if your dad says it's okay, you can come hang out with us in the kitchen with a soda if you don't want to be on kid-duty out here."

"Really? You'd..." She drops her chin and stares at the floor. "You'd let me hang out with you guys?"

"Sure," Rowan says lightly. "Why not? You're too old to

play with the littles, unless you wanted to play with them, which is totally fine, but you're old enough to be in on whatever Tabby has up her sleeve. With a house full of people, it can't get too wild, and if it does, you'll be my escape plan." Her face glows with happiness.

"My mom never even let me be in the same room with her when she was with her friends."

Rowan's face falls to sadness in the blink of an eye. She may feel as though she's not good with her emotions, but she takes on everyone else's with the empathy of a survivor.

"I'm so sorry about that, Ser." I say the words, but they slice open my mouth on their way out. "Your mother..." What do I say to her? *Your mother's a selfish asshole* doesn't seem appropriate.

"All adults are different," Rowan cuts in. "But I think we can make up some new rules for a while, if that's okay with you, because I'm most definitely a little different."

The smile Rowan shares with Seren makes me want to drop to my knees and beg her to marry me right this second.

"Seb," Rowan cuts an inquisitive stare my way. "Are you alright with Seren joining us in the kitchen?"

"I'm all for different." My tone is rough, and I clear my throat before continuing. "I trust your judgment, Peach, always. And as much as I hate to admit it, you're not my little baby anymore, Ser. If you want to sit in on girls' night, that's fine with me."

My little girl's face nearly splits in two. "Why do you call her Peach?"

My gaze floats between the two of them, and I shrug. "Because the very first time I saw Rowan, she was wearing a *James and the Giant Peach* T-shirt."

"I love that book," Miles says, smiling up at me.

"And he declared that he was going to marry her right there at first sight," Pappy supplies, drawing all eyes my way.

"That's...sweet," Seren says, then grabs Rowan's hand and drags her toward the kitchen with Beck's bowl tucked under her arm. Rowan glances over her shoulder at me, and all her unasked questions and fears flash across her face.

I wink at her just before Seren tugs her out of sight.

"She's going to pull away," Pappy says, bursting the light-hearted moment of a second ago. "It's all she knows, Seb. One step forward, two steps back. All you can do is dance to her beat until all her old trauma is put to bed. You're good for her, son. You all are, and I've never been more proud of you than I am right now."

Jesus, Pappy. Way to make a grown man cry.

"Thanks, Paps. I'm only who I am today because of you."

"Bull," he barks. "You were always a good boy, Seb. But now you're a great man, and that all comes down to you."

24

OUTSIDE LOOKING IN

ROWAN

Stella stayed behind with their sick daughter, but everyone else in Sebastian's life is here. Again. I'm not even sure if they asked him or if they all decided that because Tabby and Bella were here, they'd have an impromptu get-together on a random Wednesday night.

One bottle of wine has turned into two, mostly thanks to Tabby, who manages to keep our glasses topped off without me even noticing.

Seren has stayed close to my side, not offering much to the conversation but observing and listening. We're very similar that way. And her smile hasn't faded once since we sat down at the island with Tabby and Bella.

What I would have given to belong anywhere when I was her age.

As soon as we sat down, Tabby poured Seren's lemonade into a long-stem wineglass the rest of us are drinking out of, and right before our eyes, the girl's confidence grew.

We've talked about everything from Tabby's peculiar baking habits—pickle cupcakes were a hard pass for me—

to how Bella had drifted into town a few years ago and instantly knew she'd found her place.

Seren and I had both shifted uncomfortably on our stools as Bella recounted her story, but neither woman pushed us to share more than we were comfortable with.

By my second glass of wine, I could even admit, at least to myself, that I was having fun.

"Are you getting along well with the kids in town?" Tabby asks, startling Seren, who chokes on her lemonade.

"Yeah," she says with a slight frown as I pat her on the back. "They've all been really nice."

"Does that surprise you?" Bella asks gently.

"It's just..." Seren turns her gaze to me. "Different. The kids in Boston weren't nice unless they were trying to get something from me. At least the kids at my school, anyway. It's all about who you know and how much you have."

Sebastian steps in from the deck, holding an empty platter. "Everything will be ready in about ten minutes."

We all hum our acknowledgment while he walks into the pantry.

"All kids have their moments, and small-town kids are no different, but I do think the beach and the South in general can feel a little more welcoming of a place sometimes. It's why I came here in the first place," Bella says. "I love the beach, but the people are why I stayed."

"Going home is going to suck," Seren mutters. Sebastian stops cold in the doorway of the pantry, but Seren is staring at her glass and doesn't see him. "I wish we could stay here."

"Is that what you want?" Sebastian asks, causing Seren to jump.

She shrugs but won't look directly at him.

"We'll set the table," Tabby says while she and Bella back away from the conversation.

In all honesty, Seb hasn't brought up his long-term plans much, and I never thought to ask because I've been too busy trying to get through the todays and tomorrows.

"Ser, talk to me," he begs, setting a box of tinfoil on the counter.

"I hate it at home now," she says, her voice hollow and broken. "The kids will never let me live down what Mom did. The mean girls will only get meaner, and even if I change schools, people in Boston will still talk. I get sick to my stomach anytime I think about going home."

Lord, she could be talking about my childhood. Sebastian's gaze locks on mine, and I get the uncanny sensation that he's comparing my situation to Seren's, but I can also see his wheels spinning as he runs through every option they have.

"I can understand how you feel," I say. "I used to have physical reactions like hives and throwing up every time I had to walk back into my house. But the difference is, you have so many people who love you."

Beck walks in off the deck. He takes one look at our faces, grabs the tinfoil, and heads back outside.

He cared enough to read the room and our faces, then give us a few more minutes of privacy. It's still strange to me, how these people care so easily.

"Okay," Sebastian says. "I can't promise you'll get what you want, but I do promise to see if it's an option for us. I've been thinking about it anyway."

Seren's head jerks up. "Really?" The hope in her voice tugs at the little girl in me who had hoped and prayed for a way out of her misery.

"Really," he says. She jumps down from her stool and runs to him. He wraps her in a giant hug the instant she reaches him. "Remember, I can't promise, Ser. There are so many moving pieces, but with the bulk of my company now tied to Beck's, I might be able to work something out."

I don't realize she's crying until she chokes out a "thank you, Daddy." The hairs on my arms stand on end as I stare at them, and then goosebumps creep over my skin.

"Oh, sweet girl. There isn't anything I wouldn't do for you." He's talking to Seren, but staring intently at me as though the words are meant for us both.

Beck walks back inside. "Sorry to interrupt, but the food's ready."

"It's okay," Sebastian says, waving him in.

Seren pulls away from her dad and stands next to me. Then she buries her face in my chest, and sobs with what feels like relief.

When her cries turn into hiccups, she meets my gaze but doesn't immediately release me. "Thank you, Row," she whispers.

"For what?" I'm truly dumbfounded. I haven't done anything.

"For including me."

My heart no longer belongs to me because she just reached inside my chest and wrapped both fists around it.

Sebastian hands her a box of tissues, which she takes, and wipes her eyes and nose while I stand frozen, unsure if there's even any air left in my lungs.

"You're good for us, Peach." He glances over to his daughter. "All of us." For the third time tonight, he kisses my forehead, then walks around me toward the dining room.

His laughter jump-starts my lungs, and I suck in a large gulp of air.

"I'm going to need a bigger table if this happens a lot around here." Sebastian chuckles.

"Get used to it," Leo says with a teasing lilt to his tone. "You're one of us now."

Sebastian lifts his head at that moment and snags my gaze.

"Yeah, I think we are," he says, before helping Miles into a chair.

My palms sweat, my vision tunnels, and I might be seconds away from passing out. This is the beginning of a panic attack, and I need to get out of here before I embarrass myself.

"Row," Seren calls to me. She sounds far away, and I barely make out her silhouette. "Come on, out here."

I follow the sound of her voice, then out onto the deck where the salt air washes over me with the force of a ten-foot wave. I'm instantly calmer, but it takes several more deep breaths before I'm sure I can speak.

"Thanks, Seren. How did you—"

She shrugs. "Sometimes I feel like I'm drowning too. Pappy said the ocean is a natural stress reliever—the air or something. I just wanted to try it out on you first before I believed him."

Miraculously, this kid not only pulled me from my panic, but she also got me to belly laugh.

Her lips tilt up on one side. "We have to take care of each other, right?"

"Yeah," I choke out.

"Seren, come make a plate," Sebastian calls, oblivious to the moment I shared with his very special little girl.

"Coming," she calls. "Want me to save you a seat?"

I exhale a heavy puff of air through my teeth. "Sure, Seren. Thanks."

Her cheeks blush, and then she scurries away as only

preteen girls can—with a bounce in her step, her arms swinging side to side.

Meow.

"Not today, Lucky."

Still a little shaky on my feet, I'm not ready to return to the party yet, so instead, I stand on the outside, peeking in on what it means to be part of a family.

"Look at them, Lucky. They make it appear so easy. It's a dance that everyone knows but me."

Meow.

"I swear you're out here just to curse me."

Sebastian laughs, and my gaze returns to the window. It's truly a dance that they do, passing plates and touching shoulders as they move around each other so as not to collide. They're in perfect harmony while I'm still out of key.

———

I ENTER my room after a very long, hot shower, and open my mouth, but the scream dies on my lips when I find it's Sebastian sitting on my bed with the lights off.

"What the heck are you doing sitting in the dark? You nearly gave me a heart attack."

"We haven't really had a chance to talk," he says.

No, we didn't because the house was overrun with people for hours.

"It was a pretty busy night."

"How are you doing?" He keeps his voice low, but the tendril of worry is a caress around his words.

Unwrapping the towel around my hair, I hang it up on the back of my door so I don't have to face him yet.

"I'm okay. Peopling is really exhausting though." The

words are barely out before the air shifts and his gaze blazes across my skin.

"Yeah, I guess it is. Especially when you're not used to it."

Mindlessly, I brush my hair, nodding in agreement. He sits patiently until I have nothing left to hide behind and sink into the mattress next to him.

His arm snakes around my shoulders as he pulls me into his side as if he never heard me say I'm not a cuddler. I actively choose to ignore that some small, tiny, insignificant piece of me is beginning to crave the connection.

"Do you have any idea how much you've given us these past few weeks?"

"Seb," I whisper.

With his free hand, he cups my cheek and tilts my face up to his. "I'm serious, Rowan. When we first arrived, Seren was so angry. It was all she could see, and it was eating her up for months. Three weeks with you, and she's smiling again. And hearing her laugh, God, it's been so long since I heard her laugh, and you did that—you connect with her in a way I couldn't. You pull Miles out of the old man mentality and allow him to simply be a kid, and you've always accepted Kade for the cannonball that he is."

"I really haven't done anything. They're good kids, Sebastian. Good kids going through a tough time, and they're more resilient than us. They would have been fine regardless of who their nanny was or will be."

"I disagree." Those two words are laced with frustration, but he doesn't push the subject more. "I have a question, and a favor to ask." He sounds almost nervous, and when I look up into his green eyes, I see the hesitation in the windows to his soul.

"Okay, this sounds ominous." Damn my sweaty hands.

Placing my palms on my mattress, I wipe them, then scoot myself back against the headboard to give me a little space.

Sebastian kicks off his shoes and crawls up the bed. With a hand on each knee, he separates them so he can settle himself between my thighs.

"Not ominous, my little rain cloud. Optimistic, yes. Pragmatic is fair. Hopeful for sure."

His hands run long, smooth patterns up and down my legs from my shins to my thighs where my sleep shorts end. His thumbs swirl in a circular motion that causes my brain to short-circuit. He's making it really hard to focus on his words.

"What's the question, and what's the favor?"

The smile that spreads across his face could belong to the devil himself.

"They're connected." His thumbs turn inward on my thighs and run along the hem of my shorts.

"And?"

"I want to take you out on a date."

I frown, and my face scrunches into something that must resemble smelling a dirty diaper, but I can't help it. "A date? With me?"

"Yes, Rowan. Only with you." His hands stop moving, but his fingers press a little harder into my skin. "You've been on dates before."

Sort of, though Jake and I never really cared to go out. Did we actually ever go on a date that wasn't in one of our apartments? I reach for my bracelets to find my wrist naked —I never put them back on after my shower—and now all my nervous energy zaps from my fingertips into my tattoo. Each time my thumb taps against it, my blood sings Sebastian's name.

"You've never been on a date before?" His entire body

has turned to stone, and the way he's glaring, you'd think I told him I wanted to be a virgin again or something.

Geez, Seb. Don't stare at me as though you want to fix my whole world. Lowering my chin, I chew on my lip before answering.

"I had one long-term relationship in college, but neither of us were very social. I mean, we went to the movies a couple of times."

"Fucking idiot," Seb growls.

"What's the favor?" I ask. Anything to change this subject.

He's quiet for a long moment while he studies my face, and a flush instantly creeps across my skin. What's going through his mind when he stares at me that way?

"I have to go to New York in a couple of weeks for a big charity gala. I want you to come with me, and we can have a date in New York, away from responsibilities for a couple of nights."

"You want me...to go with you...to a charity gala...in New York City?"

There's no way he's asking that. What the hell would I do at a gala?

"Yes."

"Yes?" My voice reaches a decibel that only dogs can hear. "Then what's the favor?"

His grin morphs into a sheepish expression, and he lowers his lashes. They flutter against his cheeks before opening again. "My question is will you go on a date with me. My favor is going to the gala."

Sweet baby Jesus.

"Sebastian," I say breathlessly. The way he's staring at me is frying my brain cells. I almost freaking said yes. "Trust me when I say this, I'm the last person you want to take to a gala. I can't walk in heels, I don't own a formal gown and I never have, I can barely apply makeup without looking like a clown. I wouldn't even begin to know what to do with more than one fork on the table. Stella! Take Stella. She'd be great at this."

Even as I say it, the green-eyed snake of jealousy slithers up my spine.

"Beck tolerates me most days, but he doesn't like anyone enough for them to cross state lines with his wife. And that's beside the point because you're the only person I want to go with. All that other stuff, the dress, the shoes, that's all stuff we have plenty of time to figure out. Plus, the girls would love to take you shopping."

Suddenly Tabby's statement about making up for lost time makes a lot more sense. Every ounce of self-preservation I have is screaming at me to say no because this is truly a terrible idea.

Then I study his face, and my mouth disconnects from my brain entirely.

"Fine, but don't say I didn't warn you about this. If I make a fool out of you, you only have yourself to blame." I pout, crossing my arms over my chest, because the second I give my consent, Sebastian's dark gaze changes from one of hope to all-consuming lust that burns hot enough to scorch my skin.

He slides down the bed, grabs both of my ankles, and gives me a sharp tug until I'm flat on my back. Then, he goes to work. He unties my pajama shorts, pausing to give me a chance to say no—yeah right. I'm not saying no now. With a smirk, he pulls the shorts down my legs. He's so close to my body that his short puffs of hot air hit my skin with the intensity of a blowtorch.

"There's my girl," he says, staring straight into my eyes as his thumbs hook the straps on my panties. Then they're gone too.

He slowly scans my body, only stopping when he reaches my pussy, and it's so intoxicating, the insides of my thighs grow damp with my arousal.

The first swipe of his tongue along my slit might as well be my last crumbling wall. He separates me with his thumbs. It would be embarrassing, how intensely he stares at my pussy, if not for the way his entire body vibrates with a satisfied growl.

"So sweet," he says as his tongue dips inside my channel.

My back arches off the bed. How can he play my body so effortlessly when I don't even know my own song yet?

He pinches my clit, rolling it between two strong fingers, then taps it relentlessly in time with his tongue that dips in and out, licking, and sucking, and lavishing me with the most sensitive of kisses.

"Oh, God," I moan. This man always makes me forget myself. He slips two fingers inside of me, curling and stroking. It's too much sensation all at once. I twist and writhe, but he holds me steady. Sebastian's long fingers strum me from the inside while his tongue mercilessly attacks my aching bundle of nerves.

"I don't want to scare you, sweet, sweet Rowan, but you are mine." He squeezes a third finger inside of me, and my body bows to his command. "Your pussy is mine. Your heart is mine."

Words that would normally send me running only add to the erotic tension coiling within my body. Ripping the pillow from beneath my head, I bite down on it to muffle my sounds.

He wants me. He wants to keep me. And he's the only one I'd consider staying for.

"Come for me, Rowan. Give me everything you have." His words tear the sound from my throat. A cry of pure ecstasy, a cry of surrender that can't be muffled by my pillow, even as I bear down on it.

My body tightens as everything goes silent in my head. Seb rips the pillow away from my face as wave after wave of pleasure drowns all my fears until the only thing that's left to do is freely hand myself over to this man.

Slowly, the buzzing of my thoughts rolls back through my mind. But they're quieter than normal, less antagonistic in their brutal truths.

I may as well be floating on a cloud high above the thorns of life.

Sebastian chuckles softly. Did he say something? His lips trail kisses up my stomach, to my neck, and finally my lips. Tasting myself on him is like a drug, something you never meant to try, but once you do, you want more.

I fumble with his belt, but a heavy exhaustion is rolling in, and my fingers tremble uselessly. He clasps my hands in his and shakes his head.

"Not tonight, sweetheart. Tonight, we sleep. We have a lifetime to explore."

He shifts over me, pulling my back into his front, molding my body to his, but my mind settles on two words —a lifetime.

"A lifetime is an awfully long time."

"Or maybe it's not nearly long enough," he whispers into my hair.

My heavy lids drift closed before I can remind him that I'm not a cuddler.

25

LIES MADE ME THIS WAY

SEBASTIAN

The front door slams shut with a deafening crack. What's with all the screen doors at the beach? Have they not heard of hydraulics?

"Pappy, what the hell are you doing? Get out from under there." The worry in Rowan's tone has me leaning over the kitchen sink and pressing my nose to the window. She stands in front of her beat-up old Jeep with her hands on her hips and the toes of her right foot tapping aggressively into the gravel.

My little spitfire is probably about to shoot flames from her eyeballs.

Pappy's body slowly crawls out from under the death trap she calls a car. This should be good.

Scanning the baby monitor, I find Kade on the indoor trampoline in the bunk room. Miles is busy at the counter, organizing his fishing lures.

"I'll be right back, bud. I'm going to check on Pappy."

"Rowan doesn't sound happy with him," he says as his face splits into a wide grin, showing off his big dimples I don't see often enough anymore.

I chuckle too. "No, she doesn't, does she?"

He shakes his head and continues sorting his fishing supplies while I slip around the corner to the front door.

I hit the front porch as she holds out both hands and lifts Pappy from the ground. She's not wrong—the guy is well into his seventies—but I might truly believe in magic if she can stop him from doing anything he sets his mind to.

"I don't think there's any quick fixes this time, Row."

Leo had Rowan's death trap towed here a few days ago.

"What do you mean? There's always a fix." I hate how her voice quivers.

"Not this time, kiddo. For what it'll cost ya to fix, you could buy a newer, safer one. I know how much Junebug has meant to ya, but it's time to let her go. You can't keep dumping money into short-term fixes, especially when it's already unsafe."

"It's not safe?" I ask. I knew she'd been hoping to have it fixed, but I had no idea it was unsafe to drive.

"You stay out of this," she says, pointing her finger at me.

I hold up both of my hands while leveling Pappy with a stern glare. We have a conversation in the silence, and finally, he nods to confirm we're on the same page. She cannot drive the death trap anymore.

"Okay, I'm taking Miles fishing. I'm sorry about Junebug, Peach."

Her angry foot tapping intensifies, displacing gravel with each heavy stomp, while the muscles in her jaw set into a hard line.

Instead of going back inside, I jog down the stairs and tug her into my arms. The pull of her is impossible to ignore, especially when she's trying so valiantly to shut everyone out and tuck her emotions away. "I am really sorry. I know you're...attached, but please don't put yourself at unnecessary risk to hold on to the past. We need you here, now."

She nods against my shoulder, and her arms come up my back to hold on to my shoulders as though she's afraid to let go. Her tears soak my shirt, and the shock of it has my stomach rolling with acid. My gaze lands on Pappy, silently imploring him for help.

Rowan doesn't react this way. I'll do anything to fix it, but unless she opens up, I have no idea what I'm fighting against.

"Junebug was home for Rowan for a lot of years. It'll be hard to let go of that security."

"Pappy," she groans.

Jesus Christ. "Years, Rowan?"

"It's not as bad as it sounds. Pappy shouldn't be blabbing all my secrets when I'm literally standing right here." If we needed a poster child for Grumpy, she'd be it.

She pulls away and attempts to shield her face from me while I openly gape at her.

"Not bad? Are you kidding me? How would you feel about Seren living out of her car in a few years? Would you consider that safe?"

"Obviously not, but I was a different person. I *am* a different person. My circumstances weren't normal, so I did what I had to, and it made me who I am today." Her words tremble, but the conviction is clear. She did what she had to do to survive.

Anger festers in my gut. At her mother, at the world, and at Pappy for knowing what was going on and not doing anything about it.

"How could you allow that?" My voice cracks as I glare at him, and he slowly shakes his head.

"I didn't know, Seb," he says sadly. "After I found out, she promised she'd never do it again. Then, her junior year, that bastard—"

"Pappy," she snaps. "It's not his fault, Sebastian. He didn't know because I didn't want anyone to. It wasn't anyone's business but my own, and I refuse to be indebted to anyone ever again. End of story." Turning her watery gaze to Pappy, she nods. "I'll let her go." Then she spins on her heel and takes the stairs two at a time. The front door slams shut behind her, the sound cracking another wall around my heart.

"So goddamn stubborn," I mutter.

"Stubborn is just another layer of protection for Row. So much of her life has been out of her control. Now she holds on to every bit she can get with an iron fist because she's scared to repeat history."

"What I wouldn't give to find her parents in a dark alley."

"Trust me, it wouldn't do any good. I tried," he says sadly.

Talk about a day of bombshells. "What do you mean?"

"I paid a visit to her house after I helped her get Junebug registered when she was sixteen. Something wasn't sitting right for me and Gram, so I wanted to check on her. That's when I learned that they had no idea where she was. That worthless piece of shit stepfather of hers may have gotten acquainted with my right hook."

"Pappy," I gasp. "You hit him?"

"No, son. I knocked that fucker out cold, and trust me, after hearing him talk for less than five minutes about our Row, I was too easy on him."

Pappy brushes his hands off on his work jeans, then makes his way up the stairs while I mentally calculate how old he would have been—early sixties, maybe. My grandfather knocked someone out cold in his sixties. I guess age doesn't matter when it comes to the safety of someone you love. I'd have done the same thing.

With a shake of my head, I follow them inside.

"Miles?" I call toward the kitchen. "You ready?"

He walks down the short hallway with a small tackle box in hand. He's still moving slowly from surgery, so we won't stay out long, but Rowan insisted he needed some one-on-one time, and the smile on his face now tells me she was right once again.

"Ready, Dad."

I pick up the two fishing poles Pappy fed with new line this morning, then follow him out the door and down the path to the water.

It's an hour before either line even moves, but his excitement as we reel it in together is worth everything.

"Holy cow, Dad. It's a big one."

"It really is," I say, slightly out of breath. The fish might be too big. As soon as the thought enters my head, the line snaps.

"Ah, bummer." Miles sighs.

"It would have been hard getting that thing all the way up to the deck anyway, bud. You hooked a giant."

The happiness shining on his face is everything to me. He's missing a canine tooth on both sides, but he hasn't smiled big enough for me to see that lately.

"It's okay, Dad. We can try again. I don't mind sitting here." I have him set up in a beach chair on the dock. It was easier for him than getting up and down in the sand, so I take a seat next to him with my legs hanging off the side.

"Me either. I love doing stuff with you, buddy. I'm sorry things have been so crazy I haven't been able to do this as much as I'd like, but I hope you understand that it's not because I don't want to. I love spending time with you. I always have, and I always will. You're a very special kid, you know that?"

He doesn't reply, so I tilt my head, blocking the sun from my eyes to stare at him, and my entire stomach drops out when his chin quivers.

"Hey, Miles. What's the matter? Did I say something?"

He shakes his head violently, and I immediately set our fishing poles to the side. Standing, I gingerly lift him from his chair, then spin around so I can sit in it with him cradled in my lap.

When he curls into me the way he hasn't since he was a toddler, that unease from a moment ago turns into a turbulent storm in my gut.

"What's up, buddy? What's wrong? You can always talk to me. I'm your dad, and even if I'm busy, I promise I will always make time for you. You, Seren, and Kade are the most important pieces of me. I'll always be there for you."

Miles buries his face into my chest, so I hold him tighter. Time passes, and I rub his back as horrible fears play through my mind. I hug him until his body stops trembling and the sun begins to set.

Eventually he shifts in my lap enough to peer up at me through wet lashes. He opens his mouth twice, as though he wants to say something but can't find the words. Tears fall down his cheeks, and he tucks himself into my side again to hide them. He clings to me as though he's trying to claw his way inside of my chest to hide, and parental fear as I've never experienced sits solidly in my throat.

What the hell have I missed?

"Is it…" His little voice shreds my heart, peeling back layers one at a time, and it's fucking brutal. "Is it my fault she left?"

So many emotions war inside of me. Hatred for his

mother for doing this to him. Fear that I won't be enough for him. Sadness that he's carried this question around with him for months.

"God, no, buddy. Why would you think that?" I mindlessly pat his back as images dance in my memory of doing the same thing to him when he was a baby and needed help burping.

"She didn't like me much."

My hand freezes in midair, and another layer of my heart is ripped from my chest.

"Of—of course she did, Miles. She's your mom."

He shakes his head, and I run through the memories of our lives together. What happened to make him believe this?

"She liked Kade when he was a baby, but then she didn't like him anymore either. She yelled at us a lot. And, before she left..."

My entire body fills with icy dread. Whatever he's about to tell me has been crushing him. The weight of his fear crashes into me with each violent shake of his body, knocking the air from my lungs as I wait for the final blow.

"Mommy was having a meeting with Uncle Nick, and we were always supposed to leave them alone during their meetings. But." He chokes on a sob, and all I can do is hold him to my chest and rock him while my world falls out below me for the second time because of my lying, cheating fucking ex.

"K—Kade fell down the stairs." In slow motion, my muscles lock together like the teeth of a zipper from my toes to my scalp. "We weren't supposed to go upstairs at all, but he wanted his trains and—and I thought we could be quick."

The lump on Kade's head the days before Seren's performance flashes in my mind—the scene a horrifyingly vivid nightmare.

"He hurt his head, and I went to tell Mommy, but she, they...he told me I ruined everything."

Breathe in, breathe out. In. Out. I focus on my physical reactions, because my mind is veering off to every way I can inflict the most amount of pain on two people who not only betrayed me but did this to my son. I have to stay calm for my little boy.

Focus on Miles. Focus on Miles. Focus on Miles. I chant it in my head. He is what matters. I'll fucking destroy them later.

"Are you mad at me?" His voice is so small I barely hear it over the sea breeze.

"What?" I pull him away from my chest so he can read the truth in my eyes. "No, Miles. I'm not mad at you at all. I would never be mad at you for trying to help your siblings —never. But why did you tell me he fell off the swings?"

I fear I already have the answer, but I need confirmation.

"Mommy said you'd be mad, and you wouldn't love me anymore if I told you what I did to Kade."

My jaw is clenched so tightly that when something cracks, it brings the smallest hint of relief. The rage, the need to rip apart my ex-wife's world, is a force I'm not sure I'm strong enough to control anymore.

He clenches my shirt in one hand, and it takes a Herculean effort to tame the rage festering in my soul, but I do it because he is my priority. The hatred that's consuming me will never touch his gentle soul—but I'll blast it toward those who hurt him if it's the last thing I ever do.

"Buddy," I say, blowing out a harsh breath as if I'm releasing the toxicity his mother has infected us with. "Trust me. No one is to blame for that except your mom. It was her job to keep you all safe. That was not your responsibility. Is that why you've been hovering around him, protecting him?"

He nods as fresh tears fill his eyes. "I didn't want to be bad again."

"Oh, God, Miles." The words barely make it past my lips before a sob is ripped from my chest. "You're the best kid in the whole wide world. There's not a bad bone in your body, I swear to you. I'm so sorry, Miles. So, so sorry." Tears stream down my face, but I make myself say the words he needs to hear. "It's my job to protect you all too, and I haven't been doing a very good job of it. The only thing you have to do is love your siblings. Everything else is my job, and I will do better, I promise."

His body is wracked with tremors of emotion he isn't old enough to deal with.

"Miles, if you ever have something bothering you, no matter what anyone says to you, you have to come to me, okay? I will never punish you for telling me the truth, do you understand?"

He nods against my shirt.

"It wasn't fair of your mom to say that to you. But I promise, I'll never lie to you, okay? And as far as Uncle Nick, he had no right to blame you for anything. He's the adult who made bad decisions, not you. And he'll be punished for hurting you."

"Do you think Mommy will come back?" No kid should ever sound this broken.

"I don't know, buddy. I just don't know. But I promise you that if she does, I won't allow her words or her actions to hurt you ever again."

Eventually, his body goes limp in my arms, so I stand with him cradled against my chest. The fishing poles and tackle box can be put away later. I need to get back to the house and finally make a long-term plan for all of us.

Mya Fitzgerald had better hope I never cross her path again, because if I do, she won't recognize the man she's turned me into.

———

"HEY." Rowan meets us on the stairs, but Miles doesn't stir. "I put Kade to bed. You missed dinner, is everything okay?"

Unable to form words, I shake my head.

Concern crawls across her features as she glances from me to Miles.

"Okay." She nods, gently patting Miles's legs as they flop over my arm. "I'm about to drop Seren off for her sleepover at Marlo's, and Pappy went to his room about an hour ago. I'll find you when I get back."

My entire body is hollow, but I manage a nod, then turn sideways to walk past her on the stairs without jostling Miles.

I forgot that I'd agreed to a sleepover. Such a stupid thing to forget. What else am I failing at?

I watch Miles for a long time after I tuck him into bed— his heart-shaped lips press into a thin line and fear still mars his angelic face, but he never even flinched as I tucked him in. I can't begin to imagine how exhausting all those lies were for his confused eight-year-old mind.

Eventually, I push away from the bed and quietly shut the door behind me. In the hallway, I turn left toward the stairs, but I only make it two steps before I spin in place and quietly enter Rowan's room.

Without turning on the light, I strip down to my boxers and climb into her bed. Her scent envelops me in goodness I don't deserve but greedily hold on to with both hands.

How many ways have I let my children down? I count them in my head like sheep, over and over again until the bed dips and I jolt awake. I hadn't meant to fall asleep.

"Hey, sorry. I didn't mean to startle you, but you are in my bed," Rowan says lightly. "What's going on?"

My nerves are shot, so I pull her into my side. She stiffly rests her head on my chest, and her fingers tap in time to my rapidly beating pulse that I'm trying desperately to calm.

"Seb, are you okay? You're scaring me."

"They told Miles it was his fault." The confession is ripped from my throat. It roars in the silence of my mind until my throat is raw, and Rowan stiffens against me. My voice fills the room, but it's jagged and broken as I relay what Miles told me at the beach.

"Oh, no," she murmurs when I pause to collect my thoughts.

"It gets worse."

Rowan shakes her head against my chest before wrapping her arm around my belly and hooking a leg over my hips. She willingly holds on to me as though she's trying to protect me, and it all breaks free.

"Mya told him that if he told me the truth, I'd be mad at him and not love him anymore."

Her stiff body goes full-on rigor mortis. "That cunty bitch," she seethes.

It's so unexpected I choke on a bitter laugh. "That's not a word you hear every day."

"I hate the C-word, but if anyone deserves it, it's Mya. I've never even met her, but I want to rip her tongue out."

"My girl chooses violence. In this instance, I wholeheartedly approve." This time, my shoulders shake with a morbid chuckle, and some of the tension in my shoulders eases as my hand finds its home on her spine.

"This isn't funny, Seb." Her fist slams against her mattress with all the outrage that's consuming my body. "That's a horrifying thing to say to a child. And he's been carrying that guilt all this time because of her. It's so unfair." Her voice cracks, and I've never been so thankful to have someone at my side.

"I know. I broke in a million different ways I didn't think I was capable of when he told me. H—how did I not see any of this? For fuck's sake, he told me she didn't like them when they weren't babies anymore, and when I replayed our life in my mind, he's probably right. He's eight years old, and he saw the truth when I couldn't."

Rowan's arm and leg squeeze me more tightly—she's offering support in a way that goes against everything she's held true, and she's doing it for me. Rowan Ellis has just taken ownership of my heart and swallowed the key.

"She loved them until they started having their own opinions. But then we'd have another baby, and I attributed her behavior to being postpartum or adjusting to life with multiple kids, so while she focused on the baby, I did what I could with the big kids. How did I fail them so completely?"

"You didn't, Seb. You thought you had a partner, and you trusted her."

"I have to find her."

Rowan attempts to peel herself away from my body. She couldn't possibly believe I'd want Mya back after this, could she?

Holding her tightly to my side, I say, "I have to make sure she can't waltz back into their lives whenever it suits her. She's done enough damage to last a lifetime."

"Okay," she says, but it doesn't sound okay, but I'm just too tired to dig any deeper tonight.

"I want to stay with you tonight. Is that okay?"

"What about the kids?"

"I'll get up early and go back to my room. Tonight, I need to hold you close. Please give me that."

She squeezes me tighter, then kisses my chest, right over my heart. "This doesn't mean I like to cuddle now—you know that, right? I'm only doing it because you need me tonight."

"I need you every night, but God forbid I bring you over to the dark side of something as nefarious as cuddling." My chuckle shakes my shoulders. "Yes, Peach. I know you're putting yourself through the misery of allowing me to hold you for my benefit only."

"Good. Good night, Seb."

"Good night, my sweet Peach."

With her by my side, I feel a little less powerless, and I'll hold on to her with both hands for as long as it takes to make her mine.

26

EVEN BETTER THAN A PRINCESS
ROWAN

The doorbell rings, and I roll over, but Sebastian's side of the bed is cold. Something changed the night he took Miles fishing, and he hasn't slept in his own room since. I try not to worry too much about how my pulse spikes every time he leaves.

What if the kids see him sneaking out of my room?

What if Pappy gets the wrong idea?

What if Sebastian thinks I can stay?

What if I do too?

Meow.

My gaze darts to the end of the bed where Lucky sits, staring at me like an evil wizard.

"How the hell did you get in here? Shoo. Go away. I don't need your bad luck today."

Lucky stands, spins in place, then plops down to glare at me as if he has every right to curse me.

Excitable voices echo up the stairs, and I groan, pulling Sebastian's pillow over my face. Why does his scent have to be what calms me? Groaning, I attempt to suffocate myself with his pillow.

"Rowan?" Seren calls through my door with a soft knock.

"Come in," I reply, tossing the pillow to the side and sitting up. The movement startles Lucky enough that he jumps down and scurries from my room when the door opens.

She walks through the door, worrying her bottom lip with her teeth and shifting her weight from foot to foot.

"What's wrong?" I ask. When did I start holding my breath every time I ask that question?

"Nothing, but..." Her gaze jumps around my room before falling back to me sitting in the middle of my bed. "Miss Stella and Miss Tabby are downstairs." She twists her hands together in front of her belly. "Um, they're here to take you dress shopping."

My chin falls to my chest in exaggerated exasperation. "I hate shopping," I whine.

"It can't be that bad, can it? They said they have a whole day planned."

Something in her tone has me searching her face a little more closely. She's nervous.

My lips twitch as a plan forms.

"Do you want to come with us?" I ask carefully. She said her mom got her a dress, but did she get to choose it?

Her gaze snaps to mine, and I recognize the lost emptiness in her emerald irises.

"You mean it?"

I nod, my chest expanding to welcome her in even more as her tentative smile grows.

"I do. But here's the thing. If we go, we're in this together." I wave my hand back and forth for emphasis. "Those two think this stupid gala is a chance to give me a stupid Cinderella fairy-tale moment, but that's not me. I have no desire to look like a helpless bumbling princess, so no matter what, you'll have to tell me the truth. Got it? Even if you think it'll hurt my stupid feelings, promise me you'll tell me if you hate something stupid they make me try on."

She flushes with happiness, and her smile shows off a dimple I've never seen before. Warmth spreads through my chest because something I did made her smile so real and genuine that it transformed her entire face.

"You said stupid a lot of times." She laughs. Perhaps I'm more nervous than I'm allowing myself to believe too. "But deal. No princesses. Got it." She darts across the room, jumps onto my bed, and wraps her arms around my neck.

I'm not prepared for it, so my arms hang listlessly at my sides until the sight of Sebastian leaning against my door reminds me to move.

Awkwardly, I pat her back, but the reality is, it's not as uncomfortable as it once was.

"What's going on in here?" he asks. His body is relaxed, and the softness of his features tells me everything—he loves the bond I'm forming with his daughter.

Seren pulls back and hops off my bed. "Row asked me to go shopping and wants my opinion so the girls don't turn her into a pumpkin." She runs past her dad, leaving him even more confused.

I shrug and scrunch up my nose. "I asked if she wanted to go shopping with us. It seemed as though she wanted to come, and she's the only one I trust not to turn me into Gala Barbie."

Without breaking eye contact, he quietly shuts my door, locks it, then stalks me with sexual intent in his bright green orbs.

He doesn't stop until he's on his knees, hovering over me. Then he clasps my face with both of his hands.

"I'm going to say something to you right now, and no matter what kind of reaction it stirs in you, I won't let you run. You need to absorb these words, feel them, think about them, then react. Got it?"

Oh, lord. What's happening? My sweaty hands lock over his as air whooshes from my lips. I'm glad he's holding me up because I'm suddenly hyperventilating, and he hasn't even said anything yet.

Lowering his mouth, his lips ghost over mine, feeding me air. "Breathe, Row."

Sebastian makes a show of inhaling deeply then releasing it slowly. Before my brain catches up, my body follows his lead, and he smiles.

"Do you have any idea how special you are?"

Like a mewling cat, I lean into his touch.

His kiss is a dusting across my lips. Why does that feel more intimate than anything else we've done?

"Are you ready?" he asks, a mysterious glint shining in his eyes.

"There's more?" I squeak.

He nods as unspoken emotion passes between us. "Remember. Absorb, feel, think, then react, okay?"

"Jesus, Seb. You're scaring me."

He laughs. "Then I'm really about to fucking terrify you."

My mind goes blank, but before I can conjure up all kinds of horrors, he winks.

"Rowan Melody Ellis, I love the fuck out of you. All of you. The pieces you consider broken, the parts you attempt to keep hidden, the bits you can't see that make everyone around you better. I love all of you, and I think a part of my soul has been yours since the very first time I saw you. I was just too young and dumb to understand what the flutter in my chest meant. But now that I've had you in my life, my heart won't beat without you next to it. You're it for me."

He hit me with something far worse than anything I could have dreamed up, and I wait for all the fear to come crashing down, but...it doesn't.

Instead, a peaceful silence washes through me. He's the only person in the world who has ever been able to give this to me—a break from the torment that haunts my mind.

The voices telling me I'll never amount to anything.

The ex's face that was burned into my soul when I caught him.

My stepsister's cruel laugh.

My mother's painful indifference.

It's all...gone, vanished into the abyss of my tortured mind.

"Row? Are you okay?"

I blink him into focus, but it's as though his words have choked out all my fears. I'm not sure who I am when I'm not fighting through the trauma.

It's just me, and him.

"Rowan, say something. I know I told you to absorb the words, but Jesus, I can't even tell if you're breathing."

I nod. "I—I'm absorbing."

His face lights up like a little boy at his first baseball game. "Good." He leans in and presses his lips to my forehead, but he isn't quick to pull away. His lips burn into my flesh as though he's tattooing his love there, and from that one touch, the first flickers of hope I've had since I was ten years old take root in my heart.

When he pulls away, I'm still in a state of shock, but as he stands, he slowly releases my face, willing my gaze to follow him.

"Thank you for everything you do. Especially with Seren. I'll never be able to express to you how much that means to me. It's..." He scans every inch of my face, as though searching for answers before staring at me with a content grin. "It's everything, Rowan. You are everything."

Before I can say anything, he's off the bed and opening the door.

"You'd better get ready." His smile is disarming. "Stella and Tabby are on a mission, and I can only hold them off for so long."

I nod, then shake my head, then nod again. I keep waiting for the noise that's filled my mind for more than a decade to return but it...doesn't.

My body moves of its own accord through the motions of getting dressed while I attempt to figure out what the warmth in my limbs means. I keep glancing over my shoulder as if those voices that have controlled me are lurking behind the next corner, but as I make my way down the stairs to the sound of nothing but my own heartbeat, I feel free.

I feel like myself.

And I don't hate it half as much as I thought I would.

———

"Just come out and show us," Tabby says, rapping her knuckles on the dressing room door.

For my part, I'm sitting on the small stool in the corner of my dressing room with my head between my knees, sweating like an ice cube in July in the Texas heat.

"Row?" Seren's hesitant voice comes next. "My dad wants to talk to you."

"Shit," I curse. "Who called him?" The accusation shoots from my mouth before I can adjust my tone.

Seren's hand waves under the door, holding her phone out to me. "No one called him, he called me."

Grabbing the phone, I retreat to my corner. "What?"

His soft chuckle fills the small room, and I hit the button to take him off speakerphone.

"Things not going as well as you'd hoped?" he asks.

"I've tried on over ten dresses, Seb. I'm soaked in sweat from the sticker shock on these ridiculous gowns, and they all make me look like some sort of cupcake."

"Rowan." His voice is deep, commanding. "Didn't the girls tell you?"

"Tell me what?" I sulk. When the heck did I turn into this girl—the one who seeks comfort from a man? Blowing my hair out of my face, I stare at the ceiling because even I can't deny that simply hearing this man's voice has calmed my racing anxiety.

Danger signs flash before my eyes. What will happen to my heart when this is over?

The memory of full-body sobs in the back of Junebug after I caught Jake fill me with a foreboding sense of dread that has my walls stacking up faster than the last few rows of Tetris.

"This entire day, from the dress, to shoes, to fucking flame-throwing and whatever the hell else it is that goes on for girls' days are all paid for."

What does that make me? A kept woman? A whore? Wait, flame-throwing?

Pressing the phone into my chest, I stick my head out the door. "Are we flame-throwing?" My voice is pitched so high it sounds as though I've been sucking on helium for half my life.

Tabby taps her chin as though she's considering it, but Stella laughs. "No flame-throwing, but there is ax throwing in Corolla. We could do that on the way home."

I frown at them, then slam the door shut again.

"Leo, Beck, and I all chipped in." Sebastian is still talking. "None of you should be pulling out a credit card for anything. Not even a fucking glass of wine."

Okay, so maybe not a whore then.

"I don't understand," I hiss.

"Sweetheart..." He sounds pained.

"Are all your dates as difficult as me?" The words meant for my head slip out through my insecurities. I'm so embarrassed I attempt to crush the phone with my bare hand.

This is what happens when I'm not fighting through the noise of life. My own shitty thoughts push through the barrier and escape into the world.

"There are no other dates, Rowan. But if you think I'm going to ask you on a date and then expect you to spend thousands of dollars to get ready for it, you've lost your damn mind. All three of you have events coming up, so try to enjoy this day."

"Are they coming with us to New York?" The thought settles the unease making my hands shake.

"No. You're going with me to New York. Stella is accompanying Beck to LA for a similar event, and Tabby is going to a military ball with Leo in the fall. You'll all get your dresses, your nails done, whatever the fuck it is you do at these things, and enjoy yourselves. If I find out that you've spent even a quarter on the meter to park the car, there will be hell to pay. You hear me?"

"That goes for us too," someone hollers in the background. Beck, maybe?

"You're impossible," I grunt.

"And you're a stubborn mule sometimes, but I still love you."

Sucking in a breath, I open my mouth, but my lungs burn because I've forgotten how to exhale.

"Try on the dresses, Rowan. Seren is really excited to help you choose one. Thank you for giving her this experience."

My lungs heave on an exhale, and my inner petulant child makes a reappearance. "You play dirty."

"Nah, sweetheart. I play to win. Have fun."

"Have I ever given you any indication that I would find shopping fun?"

When he doesn't answer, I glare at the phone. The jackass hung up on me. So freaking rude.

Stomping my right foot to shake out all the energy attacking my limbs, I wrench open the door. "Let's do this."

Handing the phone back to Seren, she grins at me as if I've hung the moon. I'd be lying if I said that expression—on this little girl—didn't fill me with more confidence than I've ever had in my life.

"Try the yellow one," Seren pleads. "It's so Kate Hudson from *How to Lose a Guy in Ten Days*."

I lift a brow in her direction. "That movie is older than you are."

"It's a classic," she fires back. "And she's so badass in it."

Tabby doubles over laughing while Stella hides a grin.

A niggling sense of duty tickles my chest as I stare at Seren though. She really can't swear whenever she wants, and that means I have to start being more careful around her too.

Apparently, she and I are in tune because she rolls her eyes, then lowers her voice. "I'll try not to swear anymore."

When she lifts her gaze to mine, I wink. "Okay, let's get

this show on the road. I have maybe ten dresses left in me before I'm handing over the dressing room to someone else, so bring your best."

Stella rushes forward, shoving a hundred-pound Cinderella dress in my face while Tabby comes at me with something in a deep shade of violet draped over her arms that'll show more skin than fabric. I swallow down a groan of annoyance as they place them on hooks in the dressing room.

Seren holds out her hand and we flap our fingers back and forth like fish three times before hooking pinkies, tapping our palms together, touching our pointer fingers, then bumping hips.

It's better than a hug.

"You can do this, Row. You'll be beautiful in them all, but I've got your back. No frogs will be kissed to turn you into a princess."

Affection warms my cheeks. "You're a good kid, Ser."

She shrugs. "I have my moments." I laugh as she walks back to sit on the sofa next to Stella. They both flick me into motion with their hands, and I take a step back, then shut the door and glare at my options.

The Cinderella dress is an immediate no. It's a beautiful dress that would be amazing on Stella, but on me will resemble a mushroom that's gotten so big it's no longer recognizable.

Curse words fly through my mind, causing my lips to twitch as I open the door.

Stella jumps to her feet with her hands clasped in front of her face. "Oh, Rowan. It's gorgeous. I've always thought it would be so fun to be a princess for a day."

And suddenly the dress makes more sense. This is her dream dress. Glancing over my shoulder at the scrap of vibrant purple fabric Tabby handed me, I scowl because that's probably her dream dress as well, but it's so far removed from her day-to-day style it has me questioning everything I've learned about her.

"No," Seren says, boldly standing tall, and a flood of pride washes over me. This little girl is going to grow into a beautifully strong woman. "It makes you look like a cake decoration." When Stella's face falls, Seren is quick to amend her statement. "Ah, maybe you're too tall for it, Row. The waist sits funny. I bet it would be amazing on Stella though."

This kid is twelve going on twenty.

"I think you're right. Sebastian said you needed to find a dress too, Stella. Why don't you try this one on?"

Her brow furrows for half a breath before she's nodding, happiness beaming from her radiant smile.

I've never stripped out of a dress so quickly before. Nor have I ever had so much trouble getting into a dress as the next one I try on.

"I'm stuck," I call through the door. The purple dress Tabby chose has strips of sheer paneling strategically showing skin from my shoulders to my toes. Now that I'm stuck partially in it, I can envision the sex appeal, and as annoyed as I am, I'm also intrigued by the pushy little baker.

What kind of sexy secrets is she hiding?

The door opens, and the three of them stand shoulder to shoulder, staring at me with varying degrees of humor twisting their faces.

"What the hell is wrong with this dress?" I ask, fully aware that they can see my entire ass in the mirror, but I can't get the dress to move up or down at this point and I've lost track of the hidden zipper.

"It has the potential to be sexy as hell," Tabby says with

appreciation coating her words. "Do you have it on backwards?"

I glance over my shoulder, spinning in place, trying to see if she's right.

Seren is the one to reach out, grab my elbow, and stop the manic circling that was about to happen.

"I don't think so," I finally say.

"Upside down?" Stella asks, bending over and looking up at me with her hair dragging on the floor.

"It's not upside down," I say sarcastically, but now I'm not so sure.

"Holy boobs," Seren whispers, and we all stop moving to glance at my chest. Granted, my boobs are generally considered okay, but nothing to stop traffic over. Whatever this dress is doing to them makes them appear porn-film ready, and I quickly cup each one, trying to hide the fact that my nipples are standing at full attention and I'm flashing some major side-boob.

"It's the freaking beading on the dress that's suffocating the girls, that's it."

"This is not the dress," Seren says with wide eyes. "Dad would lose his sh—mind—he would absolutely lose his mind, and isn't this a charity for kids?"

"Uh-huh," Stella says, choking back a laugh.

"I didn't call you in here to give me commentary on the dress, I asked you to help me get the heck out of it. Find the zipper before I hyperventilate."

"How did you lose the zipper?" Tabby asks, running her hands around the fabric.

"I had to zipper it in front because I couldn't reach the top, and then twist the dress around," I grumble.

"Found it," Tabby cheers. Her fingers graze the bottom of

my ass cheeks. Freaking great. "I can't wait to tell Seb I felt you up." She laughs.

"Gross, Miss Tabby. Please don't." Seren gags and is quick to reclaim her seat on the sofa. When she's seated, I wink at her.

Free from the dress, I hold it to my chest and shut the door.

As soon as the silky yellow-and-gold gown glides down my skin, I know Seren has an eye that none of us have. The cut is perfect and hugs every curve and indent of my body, and she's right, it does give off very big Kate Hudson vibes.

Once it's zipped, I spin in the mirror and am mesmerized by how the body of the dress appears to shimmer in the lights. I can't stop staring at myself.

I've never looked this way before.

"Rowan?" Stella asks, gently knocking on the door. "Everything all right in there? You've been quiet for a few minutes."

"C—" My throat is thick and constricting with all the insecurities other people have thrown at me over my life. It's like trying to swallow the spiky edge of a razor. "Can you send Seren in, please?"

A moment later, there's another gentle knock. The door opens and Seren slips in. "Holy crap, Row," she exclaims so loudly the door bursts open again with Tabby and Stella standing in the doorway.

All eyes are on me, and tears dampen my eyelashes.

"That dress was made for you," Tabby gasps.

"Seren, honey. In case you didn't know it, you've found your calling," Stella says in awe.

"Holy hell. Sebastian will shit his pants when you walk out in this." Tabby twirls her finger in the air, and I follow the silent command to spin.

My entire back is on display. The dress dips so low in the back it's almost obscene, but somehow, the cut holds it in place and never exposes anything inappropriate.

"It's perfect." Seren grins. "It's even better than a princess."

"Yeah, kiddo." My gaze meets hers. "I think it is."

27

YOU'RE GONNA LOVE IT HERE

SEBASTIAN

"I'm going to apologize in advance," Leo says as he enters my kitchen through the sliding glass doors that lead to the deck.

"What the hell, Leo? I didn't even know you were here."

He tilts his head to stare at me, but before he can say anything, the glass door opens again, and Beck walks in with his older kids in tow.

"What is this, an intervention? I literally left your house thirty minutes ago."

"So?" Beck shrugs, and Leo's face morphs into a triumphant smile.

"I forgot you've been a city boy your whole life." Leo's grin suggests he's having the time of his life at my expense.

"Oh, that's right," Beck says, untangling himself from the forty different bags he has hanging from his forearms. "Where's Kade?"

My brows reach my hairline. "He's in the bunk room with Miles, getting their swimsuits on."

Beck drops to the floor onto his knees and removes some kind of backpack leash from Ruby. "Listen to me, Ruby. You can go find Kade, but you have to knock on the door and wait for them to let you in. Remember what we said about privacy?"

The little girl is more fidgety than Kade, and I honestly wasn't sure that was possible.

"Yes, Daddy. I can't just go bargin' into people's rooms. It's rude." She extends the U sound to make it a three-syllable word.

"Right. If you don't knock, we'll have to go home."

My two elephants sound on the stairs, and that whole conversation becomes moot.

"I told ya, Miles. I told ya I heard Ruby," Kade says, running down the hallway, wearing a swim shirt and PJ pants, attempting to slide to a stop in his socks, but he crashes into Beck anyway. The three of them topple to the floor, and I'm thankful Beck isn't wearing his baby girl this time.

Leaning over the counter, I scan all the shit he dropped to my floor.

"Beck, where's Cally?"

He sets Kade on his feet, and then lifts Ruby too. "She was being fussy. Lucía and Oliver came over to watch her—they're sort of their adopted grandparents. Stella wouldn't be thrilled about her being passed around to so many people anyway, especially with Emmy just being sick. We need a break from the kiddie funk."

Leo pats the sleeping baby on his chest. "That's why Ryker isn't coming out of this carrier."

Pinching the bridge of my nose, I abandon the picnic dinner I was making for the boys. "What are you talking about?"

"First, I think you need a quick lesson on how small towns work," Leo says, bumping me out of the way with his hip and packing up the sandwich meat I'd pulled out moments before.

Beck waves to someone walking by the side of my house. "Who's that?"

They both ignore me.

"There's really no such thing as privacy in a small town, Seb. Open-door policies will save you a lot of headaches."

"That's why neither of you knocked? Even though Beck had that whole conversation with Ruby?"

Beck scoffs. "Bedrooms are off-limits, but walking into your buddy's home? It would be weird to knock. It's like knocking on the door of your childhood home. It just doesn't happen."

More people walk by my house with giant pieces of wood held over their heads.

"What the hell's going on?" I round the island and cross to the other side of the house. "Why are all these people on my property?"

"Relax, Seb. It's the welcoming committee," Leo says as if that explains it all. "Remember when I walked in, and I said I apologize in advance?"

"Yes," I say, rolling my hands to encourage this conversation along.

"Well, I was at Coastal Comfort, talking to Wanda this morning. She's the owner of the general store," Leo explains.

"We called her Wanda the Weather Witch when we were kids because she has the uncanny ability to predict storms of the human variety," Beck says, nodding his head as if that's a perfectly reasonable explanation. "She knows when shit's about to hit the fan."

"Well, I accidentally said that y'all were planning to stay

here long-term." Leo turns his back on us to put my bread back in the pantry.

"And since it's the middle of summer, they can't exactly have a welcome parade because of all the tourists," Beck says, organizing the snacks he has in his bags while his oldest, Emmy, helps line them up in a row.

"Hey, Emmy," I say, noticing she didn't run off with the other kids.

"Hi, Mr. Seb. You're gonna love it here," she says with a toothy grin. I think she's in between Miles and Kade in age.

"Anyway," Leo says. "Since they can't do the parade in town without jamming up traffic more than it already is, they're bringing the parade to you."

"Who is? And what welcome parade?"

"The Sailport Bay welcoming committee." If Leo shakes his head at me one more time with that *duh* expression on his face, I might toss him out on his ass.

"The welcome parade is the bestest thing ever," Emmy says with stars shining in her eyes. "How else will you know that everyone loves ya if you don't get your parade?"

"Emmy," Miles yells from upstairs. "Are you coming to play?"

The little girl looks at the bags she's sorting, down the hall, then to Beck. He grins and nods toward the stairs. She runs off into the bowels of my home without a backward glance.

My headache sets fire to matches in my skull. "You can't be telling me they do this for every person who buys property here. That's insane."

"Of course not." Beck huffs, taking over whatever Emmy had been doing. "Just those of us who plan to make it home permanently." He pulls out ingredients for s'mores and lines them up on my counter.

A large sign floats by my window, and I do a double take.

Welcome, Rowan is written in giant block letters. More signs follow with all our names on them.

"But I haven't, I mean, Rowan hasn't agreed to stay." Even saying that out loud causes bile to burn the back of my throat.

She has to stay.

"This might be what she needs, then," Beck says more to himself than to me. When he stands upright, something ghosts across his features, but it's gone too quickly for me to recognize. "I'll be honest, it was a little overwhelming for Stella and me too when it happened. That's why Leo and I are here. We got everyone to take it down a notch."

He squares his shoulders as if he's proud of that declaration. "There won't be any carnival rides or taco trucks. They cut it back to a bonfire, some s'mores, and Wanda's punch because she insisted." He frowns and a shadow crosses his face. "Don't drink more than a cup of it though, or it'll knock you on your ass."

"No punch. Got it. You realize that Rowan's going to hate this." I thought I had nerves of steel, but anticipating Rowan's reaction has me pacing in my own home. "I didn't even say for sure that we were staying." My hands land on my hips, and I wait for them to both stop moving.

"You hired movers," Leo reminds me.

"The kids need their stuff here, but I never…"

"Give me a break, Seb." I'm not sure I've ever seen Beck Hayes roll his eyes before, but when he does it now, he appears ten years younger.

I pull out a stool at the island and sit while Leo helps himself to my fridge and pulls out three beers, then proceeds to paw through my drawers, searching for an opener. I don't know why I don't tell him where it is, but I sit frozen as he opens and closes every single drawer in my kitchen before turning to me.

"Where the hell is your bottle opener?"

I'm pretty sure my eyebrows lift to my hairline. Opening the drawer on my side of the island, I pull it out and hand it to him.

"Who organized this kitchen?" Leo grunts, then opens the beers and hands us each one.

"Why are you so prickly?" Beck asks, flopping down into a stool beside me. "You didn't have an issue with this when we had dinner here the other night."

"That just sort of happened," I grouse. "And it wasn't the entire town. All those people out there will freak Rowan out."

"But you had fun at the sand dance," Leo says, doing the baby bounce slide. I spent so many nights doing that with my kids. The bounce, bounce, sway. I used to think it was a mom thing, but I picked it up quickly, while Mya never did.

Leo also has no issues with it now, so perhaps it has more to do with your ability to be a caretaker than your genetic makeup.

The front door slams shut, and Alexei stomps down the hallway.

"What the hell's wrong with you?" I ask.

"I'm guessing it has something to do with why Maria gave her two weeks' notice this morning," Leo mutters.

I spin on Alexei. "You hooked up with the camp director and then she quit?" His blue eyes glow hotter than flames.

"That's not—we knew each other a long time ago." He bypasses me and helps himself to a beer. When he spins around, we're all staring at him. "She was my sister's best friend, okay?" He turns his back and grabs a beer of his own.

"Natalie?" I ask.

He grunts but nods in answer.

Natalie is ten years younger than we are, but Alexei and I have been glued together at the hip since middle school, so I'm surprised Maria's name doesn't sound familiar to me.

"Why is this group so damn incestuous?" Beck grumbles. "First Seb and Rowan, now you and Maria? What kind of cosmic fuckery happens in Sailport Bay?"

"No way, man." Leo stands up, pointing at Beck with his beer bottle. "You can't blame the stars or our town for this. You're the one who brought these two to us." He waves his hand between me and Alexei. "And you recommended Maria. This has Beck Hayes fuckery written all over it—you and your damn one percenters."

"I went to college with Maria's older brother..." Beck cuts off. "Oh, whatever. You know how it is in our circles, and small towns are even worse. Everyone knows or has dated everyone else anyway."

"Guys," I say. The pressure in my head is reaching a boiling point. "We're getting off track here. Alexei, are you sure you didn't do anything to make Maria want to leave?"

His eyes narrow, and he chugs his beer.

"Christ," Leo grumbles, taking a swig of his beer as well.

"What kind of twilight zone have I landed in?" I mutter.

Beck laughs, then music begins to play out on the beach. All four of us walk toward the sliding glass doors.

"There's at least fifty people out there." I groan.

"We told you—we got them to tone it down," Beck says proudly.

"What the hell am I going to tell Rowan?"

"Tell her the truth," Leo says to my left.

"And what's that?" My head throbs in time with my pulse. She's going to freak out.

He looks from me to the ocean, and back again. "That you love her, and you want her to stay."

"That *we* love her, and *we* want her to stay," Beck corrects. "Sometimes being part of something bigger than you've ever experienced before is hard to put into words. Sometimes you just need to experience the love to truly understand it. Let her feel it, Seb. It would probably do you all some good to see what Sailport Bay can do for you."

"Fuck me. You all sound like a horoscope about to go horribly wrong," Alexei grunts.

"Fine, dickhead." Leo chuckles. "You're loved too. Buy a house and we'll give you your own parade, does that make you feel better?"

Alexei shoots daggers from his eyeballs.

"Dad," Seren shouts. "Where are you?"

"In the kitchen." Turning to Beck, my chest rumbles. "If Rowan freaks out over this, I'm holding you responsible. You didn't even give me time to give her a heads-up."

"Small towns, Seb. Get used to it." Leo pats my back, then stands at my side while we wait for the girls to find us.

One by one, they enter the kitchen.

I don't blink until my gaze lands on Row and Seren walking into the kitchen with their heads together.

Right. Rowan is so damn right.

Sensing all eyes on her, Rowan pulls up short. The color high on her cheeks makes my chest ache with longing.

She scans the room with an ease she hasn't had before.

"Dad, no cap, you're going to die, D-I-E when you see Row in this dress." Seren is more animated than I've probably ever seen her.

"No cap?" Beck whispers beside me.

"It means no lie in teen-speak," Stella whispers back, hooking her arm around her husband's middle.

"Seriously, Dad. Next to Row, everyone else will be so mid."

"Basic," Stella says before Beck can interrupt Seren again.

"You found a dress?" I ask. Staring at her, I'm consumed with so much hope and love that it colors my words.

Rowan shrugs. "It was the best of the worst." She chuckles as Tabby scoffs.

"Seren's right," Tabby says, smoothing down the bag in Rowan's hand. "You're going to swallow your dang tongue when she walks out in this dress, Seb. Don't even think about keeping your hands to yourself because the second you release her, there'll be an angry mob lining up to take your place."

Jealously slithers up my tongue, making me hiss. "No one is taking my place."

Seren smirks, and the blush on Rowan's face creeps down her neck.

Before I can say anything else, a loudspeaker crackles to life behind me. "Welcome home, Walkers. Sebastian and Rowan, bring those babies out here, and let's get this party started."

"Welcome home?" Rowan's gaze darts from me to the windows behind me.

"Oh, good grief, Beck." Stella's irritated voice barely registers. "You couldn't put them off a couple more weeks?"

"What is this?" Rowan's frozen to her spot, but Seren walks toward the windows as all the littles come barreling down the stairs.

They run past Rowan on either side, but she stands frozen in place with eyes so wide I see all the way to her darkest fears.

Tabby chatters relentlessly at our side about the

welcoming committee, but it's white noise to my ears and I'm not even sure if Rowan is registering that someone is talking.

A heavy hand lands on my shoulder. "We'll take the kids outside."

Beck.

I nod and move with cautious steps toward Rowan, afraid that any sudden movements will spook her.

She holds up her palm, halting my advance, blinks twice, then mumbles something about putting away her dress.

She's gone before I can open my mouth.

"It's been a long day," Tabby says gently. "But when you talk to her, ask her about the other dress she and Seren picked out together. She might be putting down roots without even realizing it."

The sounds of happiness drift through the salty air like a sensual dance of healing—two steps forward and one step back.

One of these days, hopefully, Rowan will allow me to lead her all the way forward to that happiness she so deserves.

28

HERE WE ARE

ROWAN

I hadn't meant to run, but here I am, sitting on Sebastian's bedroom balcony, overlooking a beach party meant to welcome me home, taking pictures for Instagram that no one will ever see instead of being down there.

Home.

My palms sweat, and I wipe them on the hem of my sweater. The salt air is cool tonight, the breeze strong in its assault, a warning of storms to come.

"Row?"

Angling my head toward the balcony door, I smile at Miles. "Hey, bud."

He holds his arms out wide. "They made us T-shirts."

Sailport Bay's lighthouse is plastered to the center of his shirt and the words *Welcome Home, Walkers* form a circle around it.

"Hey, that's pretty cool."

He nods enthusiastically and sits next to me. "They brought cake too." His big green eyes peer up at me. "I already had two pieces. This one's for you." He shoves the cake with ocean-blue frosting into my hands.

"Are you having fun?" I ask, eyeing the cake suspiciously. It's smashed in a few places—it must have had a hell of a journey up to me. How much of it is all over the floor?

Miles looks from me to the cake and laughs. "Kade was helping me, but then he saw Lucky the cat on the front porch."

Makes sense.

"Are you having fun?" I ask again, pointing to the party down below, fully aware that I'm the party pooper of the evening.

"Yeah, but..." He pauses and scratches his jaw just below his ear. It's so similar to his dad that it steals all the air from my lungs. "Well, I didn't want you to be lonely."

Geez, this kid.

"I'm not lonely," I lie. "I needed a few minutes before I came down."

Both of his little brows raise comically. "You missed dinner, Row."

"There you are." Seren pops her head out onto the balcony, sees the two of us, and plops down on my other side.

"Where are your friends?" I ask.

She points to the bonfire, where three girls sit with their heads together, laughing.

Seren smiles down at them and waves.

"Is everything okay?" I ask her.

"Yeah. Marlo was telling me about the teachers at the middle school. They said the music teacher is actually cool."

"That's amazing, Ser. Then what the heck are you doing up here?"

She shrugs but bumps my shoulder as though I should already know the answer to that.

"For crying out loud," Tabby huffs. "You're impossible to

find when you're hiding." The balcony off Sebastian's bedroom isn't that big, and it's quickly filling up. I'd only meant to come out here for a minute to peek at the party before joining it.

That was an hour ago.

"I'm not hiding. I'm...preparing myself. Did you need something?" I ask Tabby.

She shrugs and slides to the floor beside us.

A loud pop has everyone glancing to the sky as fireworks light up our features. Every face is pointed upward, but my gaze jumps from person to person.

"If I knew this was the place to be, I'd have gotten a contractor out here to make it bigger," Sebastian says, joining us on the balcony. He stands behind me, with one hand on Miles and the other on Seren while he rests his chin on my head.

Down below, I find Beck standing at the edge of the ocean, holding Ruby's hand on his right and Kade's hand on his left. Both kids jump and splash and jump some more while pointing to the sky.

"Surely there's a weight limit out here," Leo grumbles, and doesn't step outside.

"Oh, they're so pretty," Stella says, pushing past Leo and plopping her ass down next to Tabby.

I frown as I place the cake on the small table in front of me.

"What's going on?" I finally ask.

No one tears their gaze away from the fireworks. And if I didn't know better, I'd say they're actively avoiding eye contact.

Tipping my head back dislodges Sebastian's chin from the top of my head. "What's going on?" I whisper, somehow believing that he'll always tell me the truth.

His smile is devastating.

Miles leans into my side, then peers up at me with honesty shining in his eyes. "It's not a welcome home party without you, Row."

The porcupine in my throat tosses out a few more quills.

"He's right." Sebastian's voice is soft yet firm in the conviction of those two little words.

"But..." My voice is rough, like fresh sandpaper on a popcorn ceiling. "Tabby, all your friends are down there."

My hands whip through the air in their manic need to dispel the emotions building within me.

"A lot of them, yes," she says, without ever tearing her gaze away from the sparklers in the sky shooting rainbow-colored stars through the night. "But they don't all need me right now."

"Wh—what do you mean?"

"We gave you space, Row." Stella shifts on the floor to smile up at me prettily. "But we saw you leaning on the balcony railing, staring at everything as though you wanted to be part of it, but something was holding you back."

She's right. I've been sitting up here warring with myself for an hour. Why do I have to be so messed up? It's just a freaking party.

A welcome home party.

"Friendship is about meeting people halfway, Rowan." Leo still hasn't stepped onto the balcony, but his words boom through the night as if he's right beside me. "We're meeting you halfway."

"But the party—it's—everyone's having a good time down there." I'm not making any sense. I don't even know what I mean to say.

"Down there, yes. But one of our lost souls still hasn't

fully entered the orphanage." Stella grins. "So we brought the orphanage to her."

"You brought…" My gaze jumps from person to person. Each expression's filled with more love than the last, and the ache I've lived with since I was twelve years old is suddenly close to exploding.

"Yes." Sebastian's voice is low and even. "Miles was worried about you, so here we are."

Miles was worried about me.

"Can I talk to Rowan alone for a minute?" Sebastian asks.

"Go easy on her, Dad." Seren's tone is serious, but the happiness on her face is kind. "She's had a big day."

As quickly as the balcony filled up, it empties. "I don't understand," I finally admit as Sebastian sits next to me.

His hand finds mine in the dark, and he twines our fingers together.

"We want you here, Rowan. But we're all prepared for you to run, too, and we're prepared to chase you."

I attempt to tug my hand free, but he holds tighter.

"It's what you're used to," he continues. "But there are other ways to live. I love you, Peach, but I don't know how to keep you. The only thing I can do is show you what you have here, regardless of what happens between you and me."

The damn porcupine has found some friends. My throat is raw from the emotional quills hammering away in it.

What does happen if Seb and I don't work out?

"Rowan." He doesn't snap my name, but his command tells me he understands how quickly my mind can spiral.

Turning my chin toward him, he holds me close enough to smell the hops on his breath from whatever beer he drank downstairs. "Whether you ever love me back or not, this place is your home. These people, us, we're your family. So, if you run, we'll keep your heart safe. And when you come home, we'll be here waiting for you, because this is home, Row. It's home for you and me, and it's home for us when you're ready."

My phone rings in my hand, once, twice, three times before he sighs and pulls away. Kissing my forehead, he gives me space, and I do the one thing I know won't cause my pulse to skyrocket so high that I pass out.

I answer the phone. "Single Dad Hotline, I'm your helper, how can I help you?"

"Rowan, I need Lottie's number." He's so loud I have to pull the phone away from my ear.

Thane Wilder has the uncanny ability to ruin a moment. "Thane—"

"Listen. I know she's not going to Paris because she has you to take over Europe now, and I don't even care."

"What the hell are you talking about? How do you—"

"Kara's run away, and I think she's searching for Lottie because she thinks Lottie is heading to Paris. I need her number."

"Ran away? Why would she—"

"For fuck's sake, Rowan. I need the goddamn number." In all my time working with Thane, I've never once heard him emit an ounce of emotion, but now he sounds as though he's drowning in it.

My phone is wrenched from my hands. "Don't fucking talk to her that way."

I jump to my feet and find a very pissed-off Sebastian scrolling through his own phone while growling into mine. In horror, I watch as he recites Lottie's personal cell phone number, then tosses my phone onto the bed behind him.

"Paris?" he asks, the word trembling as it crosses his lips.

I wring my hands together in front of me while the lunch I ate earlier swirls in my belly like shards of glass.

"I told you about Lottie's offer," I say. My voice shakes worse than a category-five earthquake.

"I remember." I can't read his expression, but a fear I've never known creeps up my spine.

It's the fear of losing him, I realize.

"Did you accept the position?" he asks.

I shake my head.

"Did you turn it down?" His tone is a blend of hopefulness and fear that I feel all the way to my bones.

Breaking eye contact, I stare at my wrist while twisting the pretty crystals and shake my head again.

"I see." Two words that convey the hurt in his tone. He steps forward, holds my biceps in his hands, and places a gentle kiss to my forehead. "I meant what I said. This is your home whether you're mine or not. Always."

When he steps back, he doesn't meet my gaze, and that cuts more than my mother's indifference. But this time, the pain that I feel is my own damn fault.

"I'm going to get the kids to bed. It's getting late."

I try to swallow or nod or something, but my mind has lost control of my body and I can't even blink.

He leaves me alone on the balcony. The party down below is filled with people who are trying so hard to include me in their lives, yet I've never felt more alone in my grief and pain.

"Fight for the life you want, not the life you think you deserve."

Pappy's words from my sixteenth birthday come back to haunt me now because I'm beginning to understand that my entire life has been built on fighting for the life I thought I had to have—the one that's a never-ending uphill battle against old wounds.

What if I've been fighting for the wrong thing all this time?

My mind is still in chaotic disarray hours later when my door cracks open and Sebastian slips in.

I hold my breath as he silently closes it behind him before crawling into bed with me. He doesn't wait for me to say anything, he just wraps his arms around my middle and tugs me across the bed to press my back into his front.

We touch from shoulders to toes while he holds my center in a viselike grip, and finally, finally, I feel as though I can breathe.

"I tried to stay away, to give you time to think tonight," he whispers into my hair. "But this, right here, with you is where I belong. I decided it's only fair that if you're fighting to figure out where you belong that I get a chance to fight for you to stay."

The remaining tension that had coiled into my body slowly melts away, taking all the noise in my mind with it.

"Todays and tomorrows." He says it like a prayer, a promise, and an omen.

Together, wrapped as one, I fall asleep, not fighting to get away from my past but fighting for the hope of a future.

29

FEET SWEEPING

SEBASTIAN

"Nick's in New York," Alexei says without looking up from his computer screen.

"We knew he would be." Beck grunts. He too is focused on the screen in front of him.

"What are the chances of him getting into the gala?" My voice is eerily calm for someone discussing the possibility of running into the man who attempted to ruin my life.

"He's not on the guest list," Elijah says. He has two screens going, and his eyes scan from one to the other and back again. "But that doesn't mean he won't be a guest."

"It doesn't matter," I tell this group of men who have become more of a family than I've ever had. "Mya's father won't back him if he doesn't have his own capital, and when I stripped him of the shares of my company, he lost any chance he had. He wasn't born into money the same way we were."

"Speak for yourself," Alexei grumbles. But I know damn well he wasn't destitute growing up.

Nick was. It's what made him dangerous. He has a thirst you can never understand unless you've had to fight for

320

everything you've ever had, but somewhere along the line, he lost the compass that told him right from wrong.

"He's not going to roll over and go away though." Beck taps the end of his pen on the table while staring at the wall behind me.

"No, he won't."

Alexei slams his fist down on the table. "You gave that fucker everything, Seb. You trusted him completely even after I told you not to."

"Don't you think I know that?" The words are quiet but sharp as knives. "You don't think I own the pain he caused my children every goddamn day?"

Remorse flashes across his face. "That's not what I meant. I'm pissed at him, not at you."

"I know."

"That shit won't happen here," Beck says, pointing at each of us. "From here on out, we're family. We have each other's backs."

"Do you want that in a blood oath?" Elijah asks. He smirks while waiting for Beck's response. He loves to get under Beck's skin the same way Alexei does with me.

"Fuck right off," Beck says without looking up. "There's been enough betrayal in our lives. I won't stand for that shit ever again—we won't stand for it."

My phone rings, and the smile their comradery lit is instantly wiped away.

"Fuck," I hiss.

All three faces turn my way as I hit the accept button.

"Mya."

"Seb."

Did she fucking sigh into the phone as though I bring her comfort? I want to destroy this woman.

"What?"

"We need to talk," she whispers.

"Why are you whispering?"

Alexei rounds the conference table and sits next to me. Placing his phone on the table, he hits record at the same time that I put her on speaker.

"I'm not, but we...I need to speak with you. It's important. Please, hear me out, and then you'll never hear from me again." Her speech pattern is off. Alexei and I share a confused glare.

"Are you drunk?"

"No. Just, please. We need to get together so I can speak to you. Does tomorrow work?"

"You're in the country?" I seethe. All this time she's been here and couldn't be bothered to call her kids.

"Yes, but it's...complicated. I'll come by the house—"

"We don't live in Boston anymore, Mya." My body is vibrating with rage. "If you ever fucking called your children, you would know that. You'd also know why returning to Boston isn't an option unless I want my daughter to be destroyed by your actions."

"Our daughter," she says quietly.

"Fuck you, Mya," I roar. "Our daughter, are you fucking kidding me right now?"

Beck stands from the table and shuts the conference room door, then he rounds the table to sit on my other side. The men in this room build an invisible wall around me and my family, keeping us safe within their guard, and it's because of them I'm able to regain a semblance of control.

"Tell me when and where, Sebastian." Her words are barely audible.

I raise a brow to Alexei. Is she high?

Beck scribbles a note on a piece of paper and slides it to

me. It's an address in Manhattan. Under it, he's written Crystal Waters. It's an office building.

"Day after tomorrow, Mya. Be at this address." I recite what Beck wrote down. "You'll have fifteen minutes of my time, but I swear to Christ, if Nick is anywhere near the building, I'll walk right out."

"I'll be there."

That's all she says, and every tear my children have shed over this piece of shit comes flashing back.

"Do you even want to know how the kids are?" I'm vibrating with so many emotions my teeth chatter.

"I—I'll see you in New York, Sebastian."

She hangs up, and my phone screen fades to black.

"She didn't even ask about them," I mumble. "How do I tell them that she called and never once fucking asked about them?"

"You don't," Beck says quietly. "They'll be better off without her."

My phone vibrates and we all look down, expecting something menacing from the viper of a woman I used to call my wife.

Rowan: I called Stella to check on Kade.

Rowan: They're still having fun at the trampoline park.

Rowan: Just thought you'd want to know.

Alexei snorts beside me. "Row isn't even sure she wants to stay, and she's calling to check on kids that aren't hers because she cares about them. Mya's a coldhearted bitch."

I flinch at his words while Elijah smacks him upside the

head. "He's right," I say through a thick ball of emotion. "About them both."

"Rowan is not Mya, Seb. Whatever ghosts haunt Rowan do not make her the same as your ex-wife," Beck says, standing from his chair.

I glance up at him. "But will it matter, for my kids, if she leaves in the end too?"

He drops a heavy hand to my shoulder. "Then you need to decide if she's worth the fight, Seb. If there's one thing I've learned, it's that relationships always have to go through growing pains before you get to the good stuff, but only you can decide how much you're willing to bend."

"Go home, Seb," Alexei says, pulling his laptop closer to him. "We'll get everything ready for the meeting with Coleman and email it to you. You go figure out where you and Rowan stand."

"Maybe I should have gone out and found someone to do my hair and makeup," Rowan says. She's shut herself off in the bathroom, but she's not talking to me.

She's on a video call with Seren and Stella while she gets ready for tonight's gala.

If my head hadn't been so messed up over Mya's phone call, I would have arranged to have stylists meet us at the hotel.

"No way, you've got this." My little girl's voice sounds tinny, but I don't step away. I shouldn't be eavesdropping, but my heart keeps my feet planted where they are.

"Seren's right," Stella says, and I press my ear to the door. "A sleek ponytail is perfect for that dress. Gah, Seb will swallow his tongue when he sees you."

"No, he's—"

The bathroom door swings open, and there's no hiding that I had my ear pressed to it.

I offer her an embarrassed shrug. "I heard Seren's voice."

Rowan flashes a smile that makes me dizzy. She lifts her phone, and my baby girl's face comes into view.

"What do you think, Dad?"

"I think I miss you."

Seren scoffs with an annoyed shake of her head. "No, geez, Dad. What do you think about Row?"

Dragging my gaze away from Rowan's phone, I grip the wall for support as I take her in. "Jesus, Rowan. You're— you're—"

"Perfect, Dad. She's perfect."

Smiling down at my little girl, I nod. "That she is. We'll call you later, kiddo. Be good for Uncle Alex and Pappy, okay?"

"Always." She shrugs and disconnects the call.

My gaze does a slow perusal up Rowan's body. "Peach," I whisper.

"Yeah?" She bites her lip and then starts wringing her bare wrists. I place my hands in hers to stop the motion.

"You're stunning. Literally breathtaking."

Her hair is pulled into a high, sleek ponytail that shows off the long, slender column of her neck.

"Jesus, Peach. I'm not sure I'll survive the night knowing other men will be looking at you."

She rolls her eyes. "I'm thirty-three years old, Seb. That means I've been around long enough to know that no one is looking to sweep me off my feet."

Her words grate, and I move before she can take another step.

"Then I'm glad I can rectify that." With one hand behind

her knees and the other behind her back, I literally sweep her off her feet and into my arms.

She gasps into my chest. "Sebastian. What the hell are you doing?"

With her in my arms, I stalk over to the desk in the corner and set her down on top of it, then grip her face in both of my palms.

"I'm letting it be known that I have, today and tomorrow, swept you off your goddamn feet." Then I take her mouth in a punishing kiss. One that bleeds my emotions and fears. A kiss that dominates and submits. A kiss that breathes life into the only partnership that matters—ours.

I lick a line down her neck, and my fingertips glide over the silky fabric of her dress, slowly inching it higher.

"Seb, you...you're going to wrinkle my dress."

Stepping back, I pull her to standing, spin her around, and gently lower the zipper, then the dress.

"Where the fuck are your panties?" I whisper against the backs of her legs, smiling when goosebumps appear on her skin. She steps out of the dress, then I very carefully lay it down over the edge of the chair.

"The dress was too thin," she whispers. Turning her to face me, I raise a brow as I run one finger through her wet heat.

"You're already so wet for me, Peach."

"We're going to be late," she moans when I circle her clit. I place a palm flat to her belly and push until her hips hit the desk and she sits down again.

With my hands on her upper thighs, I step between her legs, and then kneel. "This won't take long."

I sink my teeth into her hip bone, and she lifts her body into my mouth.

"When everyone else is staring at you tonight, I'm going

to remember that my teeth marks are on you right here," I say, tracing the already fading mark. "I'll be lucky if I don't come in my pants."

"Seb," she whines, and I slide my tongue home. She's right, we really don't have much time, so I attack her clit with vigor. Inserting two fingers, I scissor them in time with the flicks from my tongue, and her hands fly to my hair.

She pulls hard against the strands, and I hope every one of the fuckers at this gala knows it's my face she was grinding on.

"I'm going to, I'm going to..."

"Come, Peach. Give me your sweetness. Only fucking me."

Her body spasms and lifts from the desk. It's a sight to see, but it's the noises that are pulled from her throat that have me memorizing the moment.

She's never been able to be truly free with me. Her sounds have been muffled so we don't disturb others, but here, in this hotel room, she finally lets go, and it's not something I'll ever be able to forget.

Helping her stand, I lift her dress and hold her hand while she steps back into it.

"We're staying the absolute minimum amount of time required."

"What? Why?" she asks, flattening a hand over her stomach. "I thought this was an important event."

"Oh, it is, and we'll get what we're going for. But I'm also not about to waste a second of alone time with you because I can't wait to hear what sounds you'll make when I fill you with my cock. I want you screaming for me, sweetheart."

"Holy crap," she says, then squeezes her thighs.

"I have a love-hate relationship with this dress, Row."

"Why?"

"Because I can see every time you clench your legs together, so I'll know every single time you're turned on."

Her eyes widen in shock.

"I can't wait to fuck you in and out of this dress tonight." Placing my hands on her shoulders, I spin her toward the door. "But now, it's time to go."

Her shaky inhale is like crack for my soul. I can't wait to get another hit of her.

30

SO MANY LIES

ROWAN

"**I**'m nervous," I admit as we walk the red freaking carpet into the event. "I had no idea there would be a red carpet. Don't women practice how to smile and how to walk and all that stuff?" I hiss the last bit from the corner of my mouth.

He tucks me into his chest, then leans down so his mouth is at my ear. The light bulb flashes are intense. This will be the pose that circulates in the press. My hand resting on his chest. His hand covering my own while I press my face into his shoulder.

It'll be a great shot. I only wish it weren't of me.

"Just smile, Peach. We're almost to the door," Seb whispers into my hair.

I force air into my lungs, then turn in his arm as more cameras flash.

"Right this way, Mr. Walker." An attendant finally ushers us to the door.

"Oh my God." I'm panting as though I just sprinted a mile.

"Sorry," he says, taking my hand in his. "I forgot how the

family running this event does things. They go all out to raise the most amount of money for their charities—even if that means exploiting its guests for a few minutes."

"It—it was something."

"Are you okay?" he asks. Concern crinkling the corners of his eyes.

"I'm a nervous pee-er," I blurt, and he takes a step back but doesn't release my hand.

Good lord. What's wrong with me?

"Okay. I'm not sure what that means."

If I weren't running on adrenaline right now, I'd probably laugh at the confusion on his face. "It means my brain tells me I have to pee a hundred times when I'm nervous even though I don't."

"So you need to use the restroom before we find our seats?"

My smile takes over my entire face, and my shoulders relax in relief. "Yes, thank you."

Sebastian's hand falls to my bare back and he aligns our steps as he guides me to the restroom.

"I'm sorry you're nervous, Peach. I promise our second date will be more relaxing."

"Awfully presumptuous, aren't you?"

He smirks down at me. "Sweetheart, I can still taste you on my lips. There will be a second date."

"Gah." I glance around to see if anyone is paying attention to his dirty-talking mouth and make eye contact with a beautiful woman who winks at me. "What's wrong with you?" I ask Seb under my breath, but a giggle slips free too.

"Nothing's wrong with me, Peach. I'm not on dad duty, so I'm taking full advantage of our adult-only time."

We stop outside the red double doors of the women's restroom.

"Here, here." The same woman who winked at me giggles to our left.

She's a gorgeous redhead who stands in an emerald green dress on the arm of an equally gorgeous—but giant and a little scary—CIA-ish looking man.

"Come with me, we can trade dirty-talking stories," she says conspiratorially.

My face must pale because her date groans. "Sloane, not everyone wants to talk about sex all the time."

"Oh." She pauses halfway into the restroom and scans my face before grabbing my arm and tugging me in with her. "Never mind him. He's grumpy because the car ride was too short and we couldn't test out a new scene."

"A scene?" I squeak. "I thought this was a children's charity."

"Oh my God, Sloane. Stop scaring away our donors." Another woman with kind eyes waves at us. "I'm Emory. My husband's family puts on the gala. Ignore my sister. She's a romance author on deadline, and she's fishing for inspiration."

"And no one is off-limits," a third woman with a southern drawl says. "I'm Tilly, by the way. And Ems is right, ignore Sloane. Our inappropriate sister is always fishing for new material."

Sloane turns a cheeky grin my way. "You never know when inspiration will hit."

I nod, unable to speak. This might be the most bizarre bathroom encounter I've ever had, and now I don't even have to pee anymore.

With a sigh, I make my way to the sink and touch up my lipstick that Sebastian smeared in the limo.

"We'll see you out there," Tilly calls over her shoulder as

if we're best friends. Once she leaves, the room falls into blissful silence.

It's just me and one other woman, standing at the mirror fixing her hair. I try not to stare, but she appears to be struggling with a bobby pin that's stuck.

"Do you need some help?" I ask, washing my hands quickly.

The woman glances my way, but her eyes are cold. "No, but thank you. I don't think I'll ever get used to wearing wigs."

She's a beautiful woman, but scanning her face now, I notice she has no lashes or eyebrows either, and my heart pinches for her. I remember the pain of living through cancer.

"Well, if you need a break, come find me. I don't mind hiding out in the bathroom all night." I laugh. "I don't really fit in out there."

The woman stares at me with a strange twinkle in her eyes. "I think you'll fit in everywhere," she says, then exits the restroom.

I grab a hand towel to dry my hands, then follow her. When I reach for the door, a mop in the corner crashes to the floor.

Stupid, stupid superstitions. I'm not having company— not here.

This place is stressing me out and I haven't even entered the gala yet. Forget nervous peeing, I'm not leaving Sebastian's side from now on. Opening the door, I find him leaning against the wall halfway down the hallway, talking to the couple we met on our way in.

When he sees me in the doorway, he waves me over and hands me a cocktail.

"Have you met our hosts?" he asks, nodding at the sisters.

"Oh, we met. Luckily, we grabbed her before Sloane could really dig for information," Tilly says with a grin. She hitches a thumb my way. "I like her."

What? She barely knows me.

"What are the chances of me getting a meeting with your husband?" Seb blurts.

I frown while staring at him. He must be desperate if he's willing to forgo manners and use any connection he has.

"Zero," Tilly says with a chuckle. "He hates people." She turns smiling eyes my way. "But I'll tell you what, if you come back to this hotel tomorrow around one, I'll get a few minutes with him. We live upstairs, and the restaurant has the best brunch in town."

"That's...wow. That would be great. Thank you," Seb says.

"Oh, I'm not doing it for you, Seb. I like Rowan, and I've met some of my best friends in bathrooms, so I have a good feeling about her." She winks at me, and I feel my shoulders relax.

But it's such a random thing to say. Who meets friends in public bathrooms?

"Okay," Sloane interrupts. "Let's get in there so I can get some material for the story I'm working on. People-watching is the best way to get inspiration." She winks in my direction, and I have a feeling what she overheard earlier might be fodder for whatever story she's working on.

Sebastian wraps an arm around my shoulders as we say our goodbyes, then watch them walk away.

His laugh instantly puts me at ease. "I don't know them

well, but both times I've met those women, Sloane has had boundary issues. I'm pretty sure she's harmless though."

I nod, scanning our surroundings while my mind replays the events of the last few minutes.

"Ready?" he asks. When I nod, he leads me through another set of double doors that opens to something straight out of Never Land.

Holy crap. It's beautiful in here. Fairy lights twinkle from above, and delicate rows of ivy scale the walls.

"The sisters are part of the family that puts on the gala," Seb continues, nodding toward an obscenely long table that runs down the center of the room. "They'll all sit there."

"That's a big family."

"You're telling me."

"We're at table twenty-two," he says, ushering me forward.

I almost stumble over my stilettos. Why? What have I done to the number gods this time? The number twenty-two hangs over my head—a flashing neon sign warning of bad omens.

Nothing good happens with the number twenty-two, hasn't anyone else realized this? Someone really needs to ban it like they do the number thirteen on elevators.

"Here we are," Sebastian says, oblivious to the bad omen clinging to me tighter than my dress. He pulls out my chair, and I sink into it with his hand on my shoulder, but when he doesn't slide the chair in, I lean back to peer up at him.

His face is white, and the grip on my shoulder begins to ache. "Sebastian," I whisper, attempting to lower my shoulder from his grasp.

He removes his fingers one at a time as though it's taking him great effort to do so.

"Are you okay?" I place my clutch on the table and

attempt to stand, but he holds me down in my chair. That's when I realize he's not even looking at me.

Following his gaze, I find the woman from the restroom, nervously fidgeting with a napkin next to me, and beside her is a man wearing a sneer so bitter I recoil.

"What did I tell you, Mya?" Sebastian's words slice through the air as menacing as a murderer.

"I didn't know you'd be here," she says. Her hands shake more violently, and then his words hit me.

Mya.

As in his ex-wife?

"You spoke to him?" the man to her left hisses. "You fucking called him?"

Sebastian takes a seat to my right. His right hand is balled into a fist at his side, but he uses his left hand to drag my chair as far away from Mya as he can get it.

The man next to Mya snarls in my direction, but he barely registers as I tilt my gaze back to Sebastian. The muscles around his eyes are tight, and the vein in his throat throbs to an angry rhythm.

"Do you even care that Miles could have died?" Sebastian asks through clenched teeth.

Curiosity has me turning toward Mya, and I register the shock on her face. She didn't know about Miles.

"You won't get Coleman Industries back, no matter what you think you're about to pull off here," the stranger at our table chuckles.

"I'm not here to fucking talk to you, Nick."

My heart flip-flops in my chest. The two people Sebastian trusted above all else. The two people who crushed his trust as if it were nothing sit glaring—Nick at Sebastian, and Mya at the table.

Placing my hand on Sebastian's thigh, I squeeze, then

squeeze again when he doesn't look at me. It takes three more attempts before he registers the contact, and he glances down at me. His gaze softens a touch.

I lean into his chest, and he wraps a protective arm around me. "She's sick," I whisper. "Mya, she's sick."

His gaze snaps to his ex-wife, and I study him as he scans her features. Her cheeks are hollow, her skin tone a little gray, but it's the wig that she didn't bother to finish adjusting that gives her away.

A myriad of emotions play across his features, but he locks them all tightly behind a mask when an older man joins the table and takes the seat next to him.

Threading the fingers of his left hand through mine, he turns to the newcomer. "Mr. Coleman, it's nice to see you again, sir."

Sebastian slips into businessman mode without a backward glance while I'm left sitting mute and suffering the worst case of emotional whiplash known to man.

"You too, Sebastian. You too. Sorry to hear the two of you parted ways though," Mr. Coleman says, waving a hand between Sebastian and Nick. "I can't say I'm overly fond of either of your new partners, but luckily, it's not my decision any longer now that Jacob has finally grown up and taken over."

"Where is Jacob tonight?" Nick asks bluntly, speaking over Mr. Coleman, and even I can tell the guy is out for himself tonight.

The older man barely acknowledges his presence, and it fills me with a smugness I have no right to, but Sebastian is clearly the better man here.

"They'll be along," Mr. Coleman says without sparing Nick a second glance. "That pretty daughter-in-law of mine is a camera magnet. I'm sure they got caught up in the media tent."

An MC takes the stage in a three-piece suit that appears to have been sewn on him, but my mind won't stop focusing on the tension at this table.

My chest aches for Sebastian and the kids. I'm pissed off on Sebastian's behalf that Mya and Nick are even here. There are so many emotions fighting for dominance, I don't notice until halfway through the MC's speech that a new couple has joined us. When I reach for my water glass, I see her, staring at me with the same malice she honed to perfection in our youth.

My hands shake, and water spills over the edge onto Sebastian's pant leg.

He doesn't make a scene when it happens, he simply takes the cup from my hand and tugs me to him. I hear his voice but not his words as my entire world comes crashing into me from all sides. Memories and nightmares clash with the vision in front of me, and all I can do is stare at the smirk I'd hoped I'd never have to see again.

Haley Ford.

My stepsister.

"Sweetheart, are you okay?" Sebastian's words cut through the panic when he places his lips to my ear. With his cheek resting on mine, I close my eyes and allow my body to sync with his for a count of three.

"Sebastian." Mr. Coleman calls our attention to him, but I stare straight ahead. "Let me introduce you to my son, Jacob Coleman, and his wife, Haley."

My entire body trembles. Lie after lie piles up until I'm sure my lungs have reached their bursting point. This can't be happening, it can't. What have I ever done to the universe to deserve this kind of punishment? All of this shitty cosmic karma can fuck right off.

"Coleman?" I whisper and look at Jake.

Haley's manic laugh makes me shiver. She used to laugh that way every time I got in trouble with her father.

"You lied to me *about your name*?"

"Row, it wasn't like that," Jake, or Jacob, or whatever the fuck his name is, says.

"Jacob," the older man hisses, scanning the table as fury ignites in his irises. Was this all a game to them?

"What's going on here?" Sebastian asks. "You know them?" His gaze ping-pongs around the table. "Rowan, how the hell do you know them?"

My internal tremors force their way to the forefront, and my arms tremble no matter how hard I hold myself.

"Oh, grow up, Rowan. You don't belong here anyway. Playing the victim isn't becoming. Didn't my father teach you anything?" Haley's words are laser-sharp and strike just as she intended.

My heart buzzes in my chest. It's no longer attached to my soul, it just flutters there, building up speed until it's ready to deliver the final sting.

"Watch it," Sebastian growls.

"I—I don't belong here," I whisper, no longer able to sit still. "I—I—I'm going to be sick."

Standing abruptly, I hurry in the direction of the restroom, but I only make it to the hallway before a hand on my elbow whirls me around.

"Let me explain," Jake says. How is he here? I don't understand.

"Get your hands off of my girl." Sebastian curses when a server wheels a cart right in front of him. Jake immediately lifts his hands, and he and Sebastian collide.

Chest to chest, they hurl accusations at one another, too blinded by pride and anger to ask questions.

"Sebastian will go bankrupt without that deal," Haley hisses in my ear. "His old partner made sure everything he has is tied into it." She's slithered to my side like the snake that she is. "And I'll make damn sure my husband won't do business with him if he's got a hard-on for you. What does that say about his judgment?" She steps into my space and lowers her voice even more. "Or perhaps I'll take Sebastian to bed too before I watch his empire burn...just because I can."

The buzzing in my ears overwhelms all of my emotions until I stop feeling and can only react.

"You told me your name was Jake Cole for two years," I say, sidestepping Haley and walking between my ex and Sebastian. "We lived together, Jake, and you lied to me about your name for two fucking years? Forget fucking my stepsister. You couldn't even give me your real goddamn name?"

The man I thought I would marry runs a hand through his hair as if he's truly torn, but now I see his actions for the lies that they are.

"We won't work with her." Haley aims her venom at Sebastian. "And I know how much you have riding on this investment." He glares down at her but says nothing. "Get rid of the trash, and then we'll talk. You have one week to decide."

"Who knew you'd make this so damn easy for me, Seb?" Nick stands on the other end of the hallway, but Mya is nowhere to be found.

"Someone had better start explaining. Right. Fucking. Now." Sebastian's face is so red it's nearly purple.

Something inside of me has broken, and I can't hide it this time.

31

TONIGHT

SEBASTIAN

"I hate the number twenty-two," Rowan mutters the second I'm able to pull her into my side.

My heart is breaking as I stare at her, yet I don't even know what the fuck is going on.

"Grow up, Rowan," the angry little gargoyle hisses in Rowan's face again.

"I'm sorry, Rowan. I never got to tell you that," Jacob says from behind me.

"Don't apologize to her," the woman seethes.

"Someone had better tell me what the hell is going on right now," I demand.

Rowan trembles in my arms, and violent storms of rage swirl through my body. A crowd begins to form, and I find more than one member of the gala board standing on the perimeter, so I usher her farther down the hallway, hoping for some semblance of privacy.

"I was engaged to Jake," she says quietly. "Well, he told me his name was Jake. I trusted him with...everything. I—I couldn't stay after him."

If I weren't holding her arms, I'd stumble back a step. Is

she saying this is the fuckwad who broke her trust so badly she never set down roots anywhere?

"We lived together for two years." Her voice grows distant. In slow motion, I'm losing her, right here in my arms. "He told me he didn't have any parents and worked two jobs to go to school. It— Was it all a lie?"

My head whips around to Jacob fucking Coleman.

The fucker actually looks pained, but it's nothing compared to what I'm going to do to him.

"Being with you was the most real thing I've ever had in my life, Row. But..." He waves his hands around the hallway of this luxury hotel as if that's the only explanation she deserves.

"Don't call her that," I bark. He doesn't deserve any piece of her.

She shudders, and her body convulses as if she's about to dry heave.

"I caught him fucking my stepsister, Haley, in my bed." She points to Jacob's wife, who sneers back. "It was the last time I allowed her to hurt me. I moved out of our apartment and finished college living in Junebug...until Pappy came to visit, anyway."

"You're pathetic and got what you deserved." Haley laughs, and Rowan's entire body flinches at the sound.

"Shut the fuck up, Haley." Jacob doesn't raise his voice— he doesn't have to. We all stand silently staring at the woman in my arms.

Someone laughs. It's a cocky one that raises the hair on the back of my neck. I direct my glare at Nick. "What the hell do you have to do with all of this?"

"Unfortunately, not a damn thing. But if I can't take credit for crumbling your empire, I'll take great pleasure in knowing it happened because of your fuckbuddy. Coleman." The prick snaps his fingers. "Our deal is still on the table for twenty-four hours."

"You're done," I promise Nick with lethal venom coating each word. "All of you. I'll make sure of it."

"Remember what I said, Rowan." Jesus, Haley's voice is grating, and I hate the reaction it stirs in Rowan. "It's all up to you how things will play out for him in the end."

I have no idea what she's talking about, but if I don't get out of here soon, I might break something or someone, so I do the only thing I can. I scoop up Rowan and storm out of this fucked-up charity gala—consequences be damned.

The car pulls up quickly, and I usher Rowan out the back of the event hotel. She's quiet on the ride back to where we're staying, and she's pushed herself into the corner, pressed up against the door as if she can't create enough space between us.

She's running, and I don't know how to help her.

In our suite, she excuses herself to the restroom, and moments later, the shower turns on.

Removing my bow tie, I let it hang off my shoulders and text Beck.

Me: We have a problem.

Beck: I saw.

Beck: *(video sent)*

Fuck me.

Someone recorded us in the hallway. From this angle, it appears Rowan is in the middle of a circle with me, Nick, and Coleman surrounding her as she attempts to explain her relationship with Coleman.

Devastation is written all over her face.

I don't bother reading the headlines. It'll all be lies anyway.

Me: How did you get this?

Beck: I have notifications to ping me anytime Coleman is mentioned in the press. Rowan was just caught in the crossfire.

Beck: Alexei's working on damage control, but...

He doesn't have to say it. We both know he's about to rip into me because if we lose Coleman, we're fucked.

The phone rings in my hand.

"Yeah," I answer.

"How is she?" Beck asks with a heavy sigh.

"She's showering. I don't even know what the fuck happened."

"There were rumors," he says. His unease crosses through the phone and into my body.

"What rumors?" My chest heaves with the need for oxygen.

"Jacob never wanted to take over Coleman Enterprises. From what I heard through the grapevine, he went off the grid, completely away from his family for a couple of years. He built a life with someone in upstate New York where he went to college, and then, out of nowhere, he got married to someone else and became a VP in his father's company. He went nose-to-nose with his father for weeks, accusing him of blackmail, but the news died out faster than it started. Before stories could spiral, he was married with a kid, who may or may not be his, and was left stewing in a high-rise office."

The bathroom door opens, and Rowan stands there, wrapped in a towel with steam rushing past her.

I hang up on Beck without so much as a goodbye.

"She told me she was pregnant." Rowan's voice is flat, devoid of any emotion at all, and it hurts me more to see her this way than it did to find my wife with my best friend.

"They'd been having an affair for about four months, but the vendetta Haley had against me began the day she moved into my father's house."

"Come here." Opening my arms, I say a silent prayer that she won't shut me out. But she has to come to me. *Run to me, Rowan, please. Run to me, not away from me.*

She closes the distance and drops her forehead to my chest, and I sag with relief.

"If it hadn't been Jake, it would have been someone else." Her monotone voice cuts me to my core.

Taking her hand in mine, I lead her to the sofa. I sit, and she flops down beside me. My arm drops to her shoulders, and I take a deep breath when she leans into me.

"Haley's father is a horrible man. A financial advisor by day, preacher on Sunday's, and the worst kind of monster behind closed doors."

My heart is beating so hard I'm almost surprised it isn't leaving an imprint on my T-shirt with each crash against my ribs.

"The abuse started as soon as he moved in. He had to *retrain* me because my father had failed. That's what he said. My father had just died, and Tony told me all the ways my father was a failure."

"I'm so sorry. It's inadequate, and nowhere near enough, but I am sorry." We should have saved her.

"It's not your fault," she says quietly. "Haley learned quickly that her punishments were lessened the more I received. We never stood a chance at having a relationship. We were pitted against each other from day one. My mother was indifferent toward me, but she loved Haley. I became the family punching bag. Now, here we are. She spent her childhood learning how to one-up and outdo me, and she figured out early on how to inflict the most amount of pain while doing it."

"Fucking hell."

Rowan smiles up at me, but it's so sad my eyes well up.

"She made sure I caught them having sex. It was March twenty-second—the anniversary of my father's death."

"Jesus Christ."

"I made sure no one would ever be able to hurt me again after that."

My hand slides under her back, and I pull her into my lap.

"That's my story—that's why I'm the way that I am. Now you understand why you need to focus on your family. Mya's sick, Seb. And because of me, you might lose—"

"I'm not losing anything," I interrupt.

"But Mya, the kids. You have to speak to her."

"Tomorrow. Tonight, the only thing I need to do is hold you and know that you're okay."

Her breath catches in her throat, but she nods. "Tonight," she whispers.

We sit in the silence of what she didn't say—she didn't give me her tomorrows—and eventually, she starts to doze off. Then I carry her to bed, once again feeling her slip through my fingertips. I'm not sure if there's anything I can do to make her stay this time.

"ARE you sure you want me to go with you? It already feels a little antagonistic. Don't you think having your hookup sit in on a meeting with your ex-wife will make things even worse?"

We've never put a label on what we are. Rowan utilizes tactics to put space between us, and calling herself a hookup is one of them, but I won't have it. I have a six lane pileup on my hands, but she's the one element I need to untangle all the rest.

The reality is, I need her by my side. Even though she's itching to run, I need her to stay with me through all these tiny battles so we can win the war. I'm stronger with her by my side.

"Don't do that, Peach."

"Don't do what?" She tries to slip her hand from mine as soon as the elevator doors open, but I hold tighter.

"You're not just a hookup and you know it. I love you, Rowan Melody Ellis. I need you here."

She gulps but nods, and I lead her into the restaurant. I changed our meeting location at the last minute to mitigate any more fallout from landing on Beck's doorstep. Mya also won't make a scene in this hotel, so that's a bonus.

I spot Mya as soon as we enter. Every ounce of love I thought I held for this woman evaporated when I found her with Nick. And now I can't even muster an ounce of sympathy.

She spots us as we weave through the tables, her gaze glued to where I clutch Rowan's hand as if I'll never let it go.

Pulling out Rowan's chair, I wait for her to sit, then fold myself into the empty one next to her and clasp my hands together on the table in front of me. Out of the corner of my eye, I catch sight of Tilly. She's facing me while her husband has his back to me, and I throw up a silent prayer of thanks.

Mya doesn't keep us waiting. "He talked about you a lot."

Rowan's head snaps up to meet Mya's gaze.

"That's not what we're here to talk about," I hiss.

Mya shrugs. "It makes sense now, why you could never love me. You never had control of your heart."

I slam my fist onto the table, not caring that all eyes turn to us. "I was a good husband, Mya."

"You were," she says flatly. "You did everything a *good* husband is supposed to do, except love me. I was dying a slow death trying to get you to love me the way you loved Seren, and then Miles, and then Kade."

Rowan stiffens next to me, and her knee starts bouncing. I drop my hand to her thigh, and she settles.

"You're insane, Mya. It will never be a competition between who I love and my children." Shaking my head, I try to organize my wild thoughts. My world is burning down around me, and I have to decide which fire to put out first. "What do you want?"

"I'm dying." She says it so bluntly my mind goes blank. "Have been for a while. I won't say the brain tumor is what made me act out, though the doctors said it's possible, but I'm owning my actions."

"Then what the fuck do you want from me?"

For the first time since we sat down, she shows a glimpse of real emotion. A glimpse of the woman I thought I'd loved. That woman never would've done what she's done. How did we go from what we were to this?

She used to be gentle, kind even. When Seren was born, I'd never seen her so happy. But now, all I see is a vacant shell with no love left to give.

I may never understand her outside of my part in our

downfall. I cared for her as a husband should care for his wife, but if I'm honest, I was never in love with her, and now any positive emotion I felt toward her is gone. I should have known better than to enter an arranged marriage to make my father happy.

"When we divorced," she says quietly, "my father went ballistic because his only hope of keeping his company from collapsing was with a merger between Fitzgerald and Walker, and now that will never happen. Now he's in a rage and partnering with Nick. They'll keep taking aim until they ruin you. I'm telling you as a courtesy, and because I want to say goodbye to the kids."

Rowan sucks in a breath that might have siphoned all the air from the room.

I rub my hand over her thigh, then look back at my ex-wife. "Your father needs a merger because he's a terrible businessman who is in more debt than he can ever crawl out of, and even if we had stayed married, I never would have accepted a deal with him. Nick is a fungus who will feed off the infestation and slowly suffocate himself, so neither of them are a threat. But you? I hate you, Mya. I hate you for everything you've put my children through. I hate you even more now because I know you're going to hurt them all over again. I won't keep you from seeing them, but I will be the one to pick up the pieces you leave behind. Again. And one of these times, they won't be able to forgive you."

She opens her mouth, but I hold up a finger to interrupt her.

"I said I won't stop you from seeing them, but I will insist that a therapist is present at all times because this will break them all over again. You may not care because you didn't stick around to see the fallout of your actions, but now that I know who you are, I will take all steps necessary to protect them, especially from you."

Her gaze darts from me to Rowan, but before she can reply, my phone rings. Removing it from my pocket, I hit silence, then place it on the table, only for it to begin ringing again.

Beck Hayes flashes on the screen.

I hit silence, and once again, it rings.

"What if it's about the kids?" Rowan whispers.

Mya and I look at her. She loves my kids. Her concern wraps around her tone as her eyes plead with me to make sure they're okay.

"You're right." I hit the accept button, but all I hear is Beck shouting. Plugging my free ear, I stand, trying to get better reception. When that doesn't work, I glance between Rowan and Mya. The last thing I want to do is leave them alone, but when Rowan tips her right shoulder up, I nod and move as efficiently as I can toward the door.

I stop in the doorway and glance over my shoulder in time to see Rowan's entire body stiffen.

What the fuck?

"Sebastian?" Beck yells into the phone.

Knowing I have to start somewhere, I exit the room to take Beck's call. I'll deal with fucking Mya and whatever she said to my girl next.

32

HE CHOSE ME

ROWAN

"**I** need you to leave them," Mya says as though she's commenting on the weather.

My skin sizzles as if someone's holding a match to it, and the flame races up my legs to my chest, where the fire grows and rampages through my life.

"Excuse me?" I choke out.

"You love him, which means you probably love my children too." She says the words *my children* like a conqueror declaring war. "So I'm asking you to bow out of their lives so I can say goodbye."

"What will me walking away do?"

She shrugs. "They're not going to forgive me for what I've done."

I don't detect a hint of remorse in anything that she says. Maybe she's a sociopath with no capacity for empathy.

"Again, I'm not sure I understand."

She lifts her glass, and I focus on how her hand shakes.

"If they're sad over losing you, they won't have the energy to hold on to as much anger for me."

Now it's my hands that shake, and I tuck them under my thighs.

"That's not how children work. You're asking me to traumatize them on purpose so you can seek forgiveness you don't deserve?"

"That's exactly what I'm asking."

I sit back in my chair as if she shot me. "Have you lost your mind? Why would I do that?"

"Because if you don't, my father will unleash Nick and give him the power to do whatever underhanded thing he needs to do to ensure Sebastian loses Coleman Industries." She leans forward in her chair, and the evil lurking behind her beautiful blue eyes roars to life. "If that happens, he'll lose everything. He and the kids will have nothing. Is that what you want hanging over your head?"

"Why are you doing this?"

She lifts one bony shoulder. "I'm dying, Rowan. I want my children wiped from my conscience before I go." She lifts her frail wrist and spins the watch on it so she can see the face. "My time is limited, as is your time to make a choice. So what will it be?"

"You expect me to leave? Right now? Without saying goodbye?"

My body launches itself into fight-or-flight mode. It's second nature at this point, but this time, Pappy's words chant in my head.

"Someday, something will come along that's worth fighting for, and it will happen in an instant. You'll have to decide if you can keep running from life or if you're ready and willing to fight for it."

My gaze snaps to Mya's, and it hits me faster than a tsunami.

I'm ready to fight for it.

She's staring at me and playing with the saltshaker. It tips over. My fingers itch to pinch the salt on the table and toss it over my left shoulder, but I don't allow myself to do it.

I'm done chasing good luck. It's time to fight for my destiny. I'm just not sure how I go about doing that.

"Choose, Rowan. If you're still here when he returns, I'll give my father the go-ahead."

As calmly as I can, I stand, toss her a glare I hope will set fire to her wig, and walk away. I'll give her what she's asking for, but on my terms. I can't exit the restaurant without Sebastian seeing me, so instead, I slip into the restroom and peek through the crack I leave in the door. I'll leave as soon as he does.

He's going to hate me, but hopefully, only for a blip in time.

A woman enters the restroom, and I step back to let her in without really looking at her.

"Not that it's any of my business," she says in a voice that feels vaguely familiar. "But that woman's a bitch. You're not seriously going to let her push you away, are you? That man loves you."

My mouth drops open as I stare at my restroom friend from last night.

"Oh, geez. My name's Tilly, and I have an eavesdropping problem. You haven't had an easy couple of days, huh?"

I don't know what overcomes me, but I open my mouth to say *I'm fine* and end up spilling my guts to her. Everything. I tell her every single thing.

My phone is buzzing nonstop by the time I'm finished, and what does this stranger do? She plows into me and wraps me in a hug.

"Two things you should know about me," she says,

wiping away a tear from the corner of her eye. "I really do make the best of friends in restrooms, and I love happily ever afters."

"I—I need to get out of here to handle some stuff, but I can't let Seb see me."

Her kind eyes crinkle at the corners. "Go out there and take what's yours, girl, and email me when you do." She places a card in my hands. "It'll make a great story." I glance down at the card she gave me to see it's for a blog about happily ever afters.

I laugh at the absurdity as she opens the door and peeks out. "Come on, she's gone. I'll help sneak you out. We can use the service exit, and then I'll distract Sebastian by giving him that introduction to my husband he asked for."

"I can't believe your husband owns this hotel." It slips from my lips, and my eyes widen with embarrassment.

She smirks. "He owns a few of them. Now let's get your happily ever after on the road. I'll take care of Sebastian and my husband, so don't worry about that." With a final hug, she uses a keycard to open a side door, and I slip out.

Stepping into the New York sunshine isn't as therapeutic as one would think. It's too damn hot and sticky as hell. Elongating my stride so I don't step on the cracks, I walk toward the sidewalk and freeze.

Step on a crack, break your mother's back.

I've avoided stepping on cracks since I was six years old, and for what? To protect my mother? Turning around, I stomp my feet on one crack, then another and another, until a thin sheen of sweat covers my body.

I'm behaving as though I've lost control of my limbs and smiling like it's an out-of-body experience, but I'm free. Lifting my arm, I wave down a taxi. The little yellow fucker nearly takes me out as it pulls up to the curb, but I slide in, hoping and praying I'm doing the right thing.

"Where to?" the man asks.

"Coleman Industries?" I ask because I have no idea where it is.

The man nods and pulls out into traffic with the speed of a race car driver reentering the track.

My phone is still buzzing, and my entire body aches a little, knowing I've hurt him.

But it's temporary. Hopefully he'll see that when I'm done. I didn't have a choice. I had to allow Mya to believe that she was getting what she wanted so I can do the only thing in my power—take back my life and force Jacob's hand.

Sebastian's name lights up my phone again, and my fingers hover over the keypad. The pain will be temporary, but I no longer am. He's changed me. He's made me want the damn happily ever after and the white picket fence.

Seb: Don't do this.

Seb: What did she say to you?

Seb: Please don't leave this way.

Oh, my heart.

Me: Please trust me. You'll have my tomorrows, but I need my todays.

Seb: I don't understand. What did she say to you? Why did you leave? Where are you?

Me: I'm going to fix things.

Seb: That's not your job. Just come home.

Me: I'll meet you in Sailport Bay.

Me: I promise.

Seb: What the fuck, Row?

Seb: Where are you?

Me: Trust me.

Closing out of his messages, I press Leo's number.

"Row? Where the hell are you? Sebastian's losing his shit."

"I told him not to. Plus, it's only been ten minutes max," I say.

"You left, Rowan. And you have a history of running. What do you think he's going to do? He's losing his—"

"I'm coming back!" I shout to be heard over his spiel.

"Then why are you calling me?"

"Can I stay in cabin twenty-two when I come back? Just for a while." Take that, number twenty-two. I'm taking my power back.

"Why would you..."

"He might hate me for a little while when I come home, but I don't want to be too far away from them."

"Jesus, Row. What are you planning to do?"

"Take control of my life," I say quietly.

"He's going to skin me alive for this," he hisses.

"Is that a yes?"

"It's a yes," he sighs. "What can we do to help?"

"Help?"

"Yes, help, Rowan. That's what families do. How can we help?"

Warmth spreads through my chest. "Just make sure they all remember that I love them."

"Have you told them that?"

The wild thump, thump, thump of my pulse makes it hard to talk. "Not yet, but I will."

"Rowan," he groans.

The taxi pulls up to a tall building. I quickly slide my credit card through the reader and jump out of the car. "I have to go, Leo. I'll be home soon."

"Be smart, okay? Things never work out when one partner goes off half-cocked. You need to communicate with each other."

"Thanks, Leo."

Hanging up, I open the texting app one more time.

Me: Our dresses will arrive tomorrow.

Me: Make sure you hang them up in the closet so they don't wrinkle.

Me: No matter what anyone says, I'll be home for it.

Me: I promise.

Seren: Okay, weirdo. Won't you be back tonight?

Me: No, but no matter what anyone says, I will be back. I just need a couple of days.

My heart splinters knowing she may have to face her mom and I won't be there to help her, but the sooner I can get this stuff handled, the sooner I can get back and fight for the rest of my life.

Seren: I trust you.

Gah. I feel everything she leaves unwritten: I'm trusting you, please don't hurt me. I'm trusting you, please come back. I'm trusting you, please don't make me regret it.

Placing my hands on my hips, I lift my gaze to the top of the building, stretching myself to be as big as I can. It feels like slipping armor on, and if I'm going to face down the battle of my past, I'll need all the protection I can get.

Seb: Please tell me where you are.

Seb: The car will be here to take us to the airport in an hour, should I hold it for you?

Seb: I have to get back. Mya is on her way to Sailport Bay. I can't let her arrive before I do.

Me: I'll be home as soon as I can.

Me: Do what you need to do for the kids, Seb. I'm fine.

Seb: Then why won't you fucking talk to me?

"Can I help you?" the woman at the front desk asks. I'd gone through the motions of entering the building but have no recollection of the journey.

The Walkers have all my focus, just as they have my whole heart.

"Um, what floor is Coleman Industries on?"

"The twenty..." She pauses to check her screen. If she says the twenty-second, I'm going to throw a hissy fit to end all hissy fits. This cosmic bullshit needs to find someone else to pick on. "There it is. They're on the twenty-fourth through the thirtieth floors."

Great. Well. Since he's the boss, I'll assume he's on the top floor. The woman points to a bank of elevators and once the doors close, I suck in air until my lungs burn. How is no one stopping me? They really need to up their security in this building.

Breathe in. Breathe out. Tiny mental freak-out. Breathe in. I have almost thirty floors to get my shit together. This showdown has been a long time coming.

But the elevator doors open on the twenty-fifth floor and my mental freak-out spins out of control.

"Rowan?" Jake holds the elevator open but doesn't enter. "What are you doing here?"

"You owe me," I blurt. Well, crap.

He nods. "Come on. I'd take you up to my office, but Haley and my dad are up there fucking."

My mouth drops open and my nose wrinkles in disgust.

"Yeah, that's my reaction too."

"Then why are you married to her?"

"I'm not. Well, not anymore. It's just for show right now until my father hands over his shares of the company to me."

Jake leads me into an empty conference room. "It's really good to see you, Row."

"This isn't a social call," I snap. "You hurt me."

His face falls in shame. "It was the worst mistake of my

life. I wanted the life I built with you—I swear I did. I loved that life, but my father, well, he isn't a good man, and I paid the price for his shitty decisions. If it's any consolation, I'm still having to deal with her, and that kind of feels worse than hell."

I don't mean to smile, but he's right.

"Why?"

It's the one question I was always too scared to ask.

"She was blackmailing me about my true identity for about six months." Even as he gives me the answers I want —I tune him out. It doesn't matter. Holding up my hand, palm facing him, I wait for him to stop.

"It doesn't matter."

"She wanted to hurt you, Row. But it was never my intention and I'm sorry that I did."

"Don't take this deal away from Sebastian."

"I'm sorry, that's not even an option," he says, leaning against the wall.

"Why not? Because fucking Haley says so?"

He shakes his head, staring at me as if he's never met me before. Well, good. He doesn't deserve to know me.

"No, Row. It's not an option because Sebastian Walker called me this morning and told me to take my company and shove it up my ass. He was choosing you. In fact, his exact words were: he chose you, he'll always choose you, and he doesn't care if his company folds because you're worth more than any deal."

"W—what?"

"He's right to choose you. I'm sorry I wasn't strong enough to do that when we were together, but I—I wish you the best, Row. I really do." His phone chimes, and he glances down. "If you want to hang around the lobby, you might see something that will brighten your day."

Sebastian chose me over his company. He chose me knowing I was still giving him an end date. He chose me.

"Rowan?" Jake calls my name as if he's said it a few times already. "I have to go. Haley and my dad are about to be arrested for insider trading, and I want to be there for it."

"They what?" Karma might become my new best friend.

He grins. "They've been manipulating me since college," he says with a shrug. "It's a long story for another time. I wish you the best, Rowan, I really do, and I'm sorry for everything I've done."

He opens the door to the conference room, and I follow him out. We ride the elevator down in silence. Our door opens just as the one across from us does too.

Haley stands there, screaming at a man in a black suit. Her hands are behind her back, and he holds on to her elbow.

Another elevator chimes, and Mr. Coleman is escorted out in the same way.

"You," Haley screams. "You did this." She's kind of foaming at the mouth while glaring at me.

"This has been the most messed-up day of my life," I say, finally staring at her with all the animosity and loathing I've built up over the years. "And that's saying something, but I had nothing to do with this. This, my dear stepsister, is destiny and karma rolled into one."

She spits in my direction, but I'm too far away for it to reach me.

Jake stands off to the side, not saying a word, and as this all unfolds in front of me, I realize I don't need anything from him to fix the holes in my heart that he left behind.

I can do it all by myself.

Exiting the building, I'm once again smothered in the overwhelming heat of a Manhattan summer. Steam rises from the sidewalk, making them appear wavy, and I don't know which way to go so I spin in a circle.

I had a plan to help Sebastian, but he'd already made his decision.

He chose me, and now it's time I choose him in return.

33

YOU CAN'T FIGHT DESTINY
SEBASTIAN

"What do you mean she didn't come home with you?" Beck asks in a deceptively calm voice. Considering I may have blown up both of our companies, I'm taking it as a win that he hasn't attempted to pummel me yet.

"Exactly what I said," I bark. The boys are in bed, but Seren is still floating around the house somewhere, so we're sitting on my deck because I don't need her hearing this conversation. Not yet anyway. "We met with my ex-wife, I got up to take your fucking call." I point at Beck as if it's his fault she left. "And when I got back, Rowan was gone."

"Did you text her? Call her? Anything?" Alexei asks. He's pacing the length of the deck. I don't know if it's the prospect of losing everything or if he's concerned for Rowan, but the man is as fierce as a caged lion.

"No, I just came home. What do you think, Alex? Of course I tried to call her."

"What did she say?" Leo asks.

Leo, Beck, and I are all leaning forward with our elbows

resting on our knees. I appreciate that they appear as upset by this as I am.

"She said to trust her."

Beck's phone buzzes, and he lifts it from the table. "Shit."

"What?" we ask in unison.

"What the hell is she doing going to Coleman's?" Beck curses again and tosses me his phone.

I click on the link, and Rowan's face fills the screen. First with images from the gala, and then of her standing beside Jacob Coleman in the background as his father is hauled away in handcuffs.

What the fuck?

Betrayal stabs at my eyeballs. This can't be what I'm seeing.

"Don't let your mind run away with you," Leo warns. "You don't know what this means."

"She was engaged to him," I say through clenched teeth.

"And she said to trust her," he reminds me.

I hold the phone high in the air for everyone to see. "Trust her? Trust this? This is…"

"A betrayal she'd never commit," Alexei says, staring straight at me. "You know her, Seb. She'd never do that."

"Fuck. You're right. But what the hell is she doing there?" My vision blurs as I stare at the picture. Alexei takes the phone from my hands and tosses it back to Beck.

"You have to go get her," Leo says, pain lacing his tone. "Don't wait, Seb. It'll only make it worse."

"Leo, this isn't the same," Beck says gently.

"But," Leo says, pulling at the back of his neck, "Rowan's probably feeling overwhelmed and hurt. Pasts have a way of wrecking your future if you don't handle them correctly."

"She needs time," I argue.

"I don't agree," Leo says, slamming his water bottle on the table. "What if your ex said something to her, something truly horrible, and it has her spiraling to a place your relationship can't recover from? Time only makes that shit worse."

"She runs, Leo. This is what she does when she's overwhelmed," I say gently.

"Because she's never had someone choose her before, Seb. Don't you see?"

I shake my head, but apparently Leo is just getting started.

"I married Tabby's sister. Did you know that?" My head snaps up as confusion settles in. "It tore Tabby to fucking bits. It doesn't matter that it was an accident, what matters is that I didn't take accountability and step up to make it right for far too long."

"How do you marry someone accidentally?" Alexei asks.

Leo flops down onto the sofa. "We were young and drunk. I'd moved to Vegas, but I was already missing Tabby. When her sister came to visit with the guy she was seeing, I told her I was going home to marry Tabby. Somehow, we got it in our heads that doing a trial run would ease my nerves. I was worried Tabby would say no because I'd already left her once. I practiced a proposal speech. We met a guy who told us how to get a license, we went to the chapel and talked about how Tabby would walk down the aisle, and then everything gets a little blurry. Her sister went home the next day with the guy she was with, and I thought that was that. It was supposed to be a rehearsal, but somehow, a wedding license showed up at her parents' house a few months later."

"Jesus, Leo," I mutter.

"But my point is, I was too chickenshit to fight for Tabby for too many years. I left her to experience that hurt and betrayal alone. If you don't know what's going through Rowan's mind, then you need to go to her before it festers and rots the foundation you've built. You have to get her back."

"She's coming back." At the sound of my little girl's voice, I jump to standing. I didn't want her hearing this shit, but now she stands in the doorway with Tabby, her chin trembling with uncertainty. "She told me our dresses will arrive tomorrow and to hang them up."

"What dresses?"

"We bought matching dresses for the talent show at camp. We picked them out when we got her gala dress. We're going to do a song together, so she'll be back, but her parents aren't very nice people. I wouldn't want to visit Mom alone, so I don't want Rowan to visit hers by herself either. She needs us, Dad."

My mouth is dry, and there's an uncomfortable tightening in my chest area. She bought a dress for an event that's nearly two months away. She was making plans and putting down roots even if she didn't realize it.

"Wait, how do you know she's going to her parent's house?" Leo asks.

Seren holds up her cell phone. "She posted on Instagram. It took me forever to find her profile, and she literally has no followers, but I found her. She posts a lot of signs and nature pictures. And she just posted one of a sign that says 'Welcome to Dover, New Hampshire,' and she said, 'sometimes going home is the only way to move forward.'"

A set of keys hit my chest, and I look up to see Pappy staring at me. "Looks like we're taking a road trip, son. I'm not sure what's running through our girl's head right now, but she's ours, always has been. I'm not letting those assholes hurt her again, are you?"

"No, we're not," Beck says, standing from his chair before I can even open my mouth and texting feverishly before lifting his head. "We can take my plane."

"Nope. We'll drive," Pappy insists. "I'm not missing out on this—she means too much to me, and there's not a chance in hell I'm getting into a tin box that hurtles through the air. It ain't natural."

I knew he hated to fly, but I never knew he was actually scared to. All my life I thought he wasn't afraid of anything.

"Well, let's go," Alexei says, gesturing wildly toward the stairs.

"We can take my car," Leo says. "It'll be more comfortable."

"It's at least a fifteen-hour drive to New Hampshire," I point out.

"And there's five of us to split the drive," Beck says, tapping away on his phone again. "It'll give you time to work on your grovel speech."

"What am I groveling for?" Suddenly the potential for this night to fall into varying levels of disaster keeps me rooted in place.

All four guys stare at me as if I'm the idiot. Maybe I am.

"For letting her go in the first place," Leo mutters. Followed by a "jackass," under his breath.

"I'll stay with the kids," Tabby says cheerily.

Beck holds up his phone. "Stella will come over in the morning to help."

"What are you waiting for, Seb? Get your ass moving," Pappy calls when he's halfway down the stairs.

"Go, Dad." Seren gives me a gentle nudge. I have a moment's pause knowing that Mya is in the area, but she doesn't know what town we live in, let alone our address, so she can wait one more day.

Wrapping my little girl in my arms, I kiss her head. I hate how mature she is but love the woman she's growing up to be.

"I'll call you when we get there," I tell her, then jog down the stairs to find everyone already crammed into Leo's Suburban.

A road trip is great in theory, not so great in practice. It's just before five in the morning when we finally pull over to get gas. Five grown men in a Suburban in the middle of the night is not my idea of fun.

Pappy insisted on riding shotgun and immediately fell asleep. Alexei bounced his knee next to me for six straight hours. Leo whistled—loudly. And Beck sat hunched over his laptop, trying to find a way out of the mess I've put us all in.

"I should have talked to you about Coleman before I pulled out," I say to Beck at the gas pump.

"You should have," he agrees, but there's no anger in his tone. It's unsettling. "There's a very good possibility of this deal falling through, and we're past all the safeguards that protect us. If this project doesn't move forward, we lose everything we've invested."

"I know that. I won't allow it to happen though. We still have two weeks, and we haven't heard back from Bryer-Blaine yet. I will fix this." Not sure how, but I will.

Beck tucks his hands into his pockets and rocks back on his heels. "It might already be done."

The lever for the pump clicks, and I remove it from the gas tank. "What do you mean? I've run the numbers a hundred times. For a project this size, we need that seventh investor, and I know I'll find one."

He claps me on the back. "Apparently, the shotgun meeting you had with Lochlan Blaine left quite the impression. He's requested a meeting with all of us first thing Friday morning."

My jaw nearly comes unhinged. The Blaine family owns some of the most exclusive resorts in the world, and their empire just keeps growing. A deal with him could literally change everything.

"Rowan must have made one hell of an impression," Beck chuckles. "He said his wife was quite the fan. Now, let's go get your girl so we can cram for this meeting. Who knows what the hell he'll throw at us."

I catch Pappy's eye as he leans out his window. "Destiny, son. Can't fight destiny."

———

"Are we sure this is the address?" Beck asks, staring out at the mile-long dirt driveway.

"They're the only Fords listed in the town census, and the house was previously owned by Jason Ellis. This is it," Alexei says, kicking at a rock in the road.

"This is it, all right," Pappy grumbles. "I'll never forget hauling ass up to that pecker and knocking him out."

Beck and Alexei turn to me for an explanation.

"Pappy beat the shit out of her stepfather when she was a teenager for treating her badly. But we didn't find that out until a few weeks ago."

"He wasn't just treating her badly. He emotionally and probably physically abused her. If she hadn't run away and hid from me, I'd have taken her home with me that day, screw what the police said." Pappy crosses his arms over his chest.

"Well, let's remember, we're here to support Rowan in whatever the hell she's doing, not perform some sort of vigilante justice, okay?" I'm not overly concerned about Alexei or Beck, but Pappy is a loose cannon when it comes to Row.

"How long do you think we'll have to wait?" Beck asks, lifting the binoculars to his face again. We used them when we first arrived to confirm that she hadn't beaten us here. The guy literally packed for a spy mission.

"We probably should have confirmed she was actually coming to her parents' house before we jumped in the car to drag her home." Alexei chuckles. "You fall in love, and we go all caveman."

I grunt, and he laughs harder.

"I tried to call her. Numerous times. Her phone is either dead or turned off."

"We're in the middle of nowhere." Alexei shivers. "Who lives like this? We should've brought snacks. The next time we have a stakeout, someone needs to be in charge of snacks."

"This isn't a stakeout, Alex. We're not kidnapping her."

"Any idea what Mya could've said to spook her?" Beck asks, catching me off guard.

Rubbing a hand over my face, I scrub a few times before looking at him. "I honestly have no idea. Mya told me she wants to say goodbye to the kids, but she could have said anything to Rowan. When I asked her about it, she shrugged as though she had no idea."

"Mya's a real piece of shit," Alexei grumbles.

"She is, but she's my children's mother. I won't keep her from seeing them unless I have to. That doesn't mean I won't burn her world down though."

"You're a better man than me," Beck mutters.

"Try calling her again," Alexei calls from across the dirt road. He's sitting under a giant maple tree in the shade, wearing a suit, and he looks ridiculous. "We've been out here for hours, and not a single car has gone by."

"Welcome to the country, Alex." Beck chucks a pinecone, and it hits Alexei in the head.

Alexei picks it up and whips it back in Beck's direction.

"Boys," Pappy chides, but the smiles on our faces grow.

Alexei's reaching for something else to throw when a low rumble hits our ears, and we all turn to the left, then the right.

"Someone's coming," Beck says, pointing down the road where a plume of dust is kicking up.

The music hits us first, and I know it's my girl. She rolls to a stop in front of her parent's driveway with the sexiness of a pinup girl with windblown hair, rosy cheeks, and sunglasses twice the size of her face.

She's driving a brand new bright yellow Jeep. The paper license plate and her sunshiny smile tell me she's embracing her future.

"What the heck are you all doing here?" She pops the Jeep into park and jumps out. "Is everything okay? What's wrong with the kids? Is it Miles? Is he sick again?"

I reach her with three long strides, grab her face in my palms, and kiss the ever-living hell out of her.

34

THE EASIEST GOODBYE I'LL
EVER HAVE

ROWAN

I'm drowning in a sea of Sebastian. It's the only way to describe this kiss. It's an all-consuming, goosebump-inducing, fear-stealing kiss that leaves me mindless and maybe a little punch-drunk.

When he finally pulls back to rest his forehead against mine, we're both panting hard, and someone is whistling in the background.

"Don't run," he whispers, and my shoulders begin to relax.

"I'm not running." I say it like a vow because it is. I'm done running. "Please tell me that the kids are okay."

"They're fine." He inhales sharply, as if he's hanging onto his sanity by a thread.

"But we couldn't have you running all over the East Coast trying to fix shit either. That's our job as the merry fucking meddlers," Beck says, cracking his first smile of the day.

"I—I tried. I tried to make Coleman stay with you. Why would you tell him to go to hell? Why would you put yourself in jeopardy that way? Jacob would have done what I asked, I'm almost sure of it."

Sebastian growls against my cheek. "That would have only eased his guilty conscience, and I'm not making anything easy for that fucker."

Beck snorts. "Neither is he. I saw this morning he's dismantling his father's company piece by piece. He works fast."

"He's by no means innocent," I say. "But I think Haley did some shitty things that impacted his life too."

"Don't make excuses for that sack of shit," Pappy barks from the front seat, and my stomach crawls into my throat.

"Pappy's here too? What the heck?" I hurry to the front seat and open Pappy's door. He grins and pulls me in for a hug. "Why are you all here?"

"Isn't that obvious to you yet, Row?" Pappy asks softly.

I shake my head, too afraid of the emotions clogging my throat to look at him.

"We're here for you," Seb says.

Pappy pats my back once, and then I pull away from him. Seb takes the opportunity to tug me straight into his arms.

"But...why? I was going up there to get closure, and nothing they say or do can hurt me anymore. I could have done this myself and been home in a couple of days. It wasn't necessary for everyone to come."

"It was," Beck huffs.

"If there weren't kids at home, the girls would be here too," Leo says, shoving his hands into the pockets of his shorts.

More confused than ever before, I try to pull answers from each of their expressions before Seb cups my face in his palms.

"We're aware that you could have faced your past alone, Peach. We're pretty sure you can do anything and everything you set your mind to. The difference is you don't have to do this by yourself anymore. You don't have to do anything alone ever again—unless you want to."

"He's right," Leo says. "You're family, Row. We're not letting you go now."

"The orphanage for lost souls." I giggle, actually freaking giggle.

Without allowing myself to think too much about it, I fling myself at each of the guys and wrap them in a very short hug. Hugs are still not for me—I'd prefer a fist bump, but they're all a bunch of huggers, and today, I want to meet them halfway.

"Thank you." I choke out. "I ah, didn't really have a plan here. I haven't even planned out what I want to say to them."

Beck places a heavy hand on my shoulder. "Sometimes, goodbye is all you need." So many emotions flood his gaze then. What kind of ghosts does he have in his past that makes him able to relate to mine so easily?

Seems we all have some baggage that weighs us down at one point or another.

"You sure you want to do this?" Seb asks, holding my hand and squeezing it as we stand staring at the driveway I never thought I'd set foot on again.

"I'm sure." Turning to face him, I find my future, and it's brighter than I'd ever imagined for myself. "You chose me, Seb." He frowns, then looks over my head at the guys. "You've chosen me day after day, and you chose me over Coleman, not even knowing if I could give you all of my tomorrows. You chose me."

He blinks, and his face softens with understanding. "Sweetheart, I've been choosing you since you were eight years old. If I'd known you were always an option, I never would have let you go." Sebastian kisses my forehead, and all feels right with the world.

"I choose you too, Sebastian. I choose you for today and all my tomorrows." His grin pierces my heart, which syncs to his rhythm for eternity.

"So, how are we going to play this?" Alexei walks up behind us with his arms crossed over his chest. "Should we pretend we're her security and scare the shit out of them?"

"What are you, the mafia?" Beck asks.

Alexei's cheek twitches.

"Are you mafia?" I gasp, staring at each of them in turn.

"No." Sebastian laughs.

"Jesus, Row. Are you reading those mafia romances with Stella? That shit doesn't happen in real life," Beck mutters.

I lift my gaze to Alexei. He doesn't say a word. His eyebrow raises with his shoulder, and he sports a smirk that could get a nun to drop her panties.

Holy shit.

"Stop messing with her, Alex." Sebastian smacks him in the back of the head, and then all eyes are on me again. "It's your call, Peach. What do you want to do?"

I take strength from the hand he keeps at my lower back, then square my shoulders. "Let's go say goodbye to my past so I can move on to my future."

"Atta girl, Row. I knew this day would come. I'm damn proud of you, kid." Pappy's never been shy about showing his emotions, and he doesn't attempt to brush away his tears now.

"Thanks, Pappy." Glancing around, I burst out laughing. "We make quite the sight. All five foot two of me surrounded by giant men. My mother will clutch her pearls."

Alexei waggles his brows. "I'm happy to play up the reverse harem if you really want to stick it to her."

"Jesus, Alex." This time, Leo flicks the back of his head because Seb's too far away.

"One thing before we go up there," Beck says, handing me his phone. "The girls wanted to say hi."

Peering down at the phone, Tabby, Stella, and Seren all cram their faces into the screen. Seren tears up the second I come into view.

"Hey, Ser. I told you I was coming back. Don't cry." My heart starts thwacking at my chest as if it's punishing me for being here and not at home with her, where I belong.

"I know." She nods with exaggerated movements that cause her tears to flow faster. How can love so profound grow in such a short amount of time?

"Hey, Row-Row. See ya tomorrow," Kade yells in the background.

"Yeah, buddy." I swallow my tears. "I'll see you all soon."

Stella, Tabby, and Seren all lean in. "Go kick some history's ass," Tabby says, then whoops. "We'll all be waiting for you when you get home."

And I know they will. For all my todays and tomorrows, these crazy people will be my home.

"Do you want me to knock?" Beck asks on my right. I'm sandwiched between him and Seb, with Leo and Alexei flanking the rear as though I'm the president or something.

I shake my head. Pappy opted to remain in the car because he couldn't promise to keep his hands to himself, and the last thing we need is for him to break a hip or something trying to protect my honor.

"Take a deep breath," Leo says in his calming yogi voice. I follow his instructions and feel Beck and Seb's shoulders rise and fall with the exercise too.

"Ready?" Leo asks, squeezing my shoulder in support.

I nod, and before I can talk myself out of it, I thump the door three times, then jump back and allow Beck and Seb to close the gap, partially hiding me from view.

A few moments later, the door opens, and my entire body goes into lockdown as if I'm ten years old again. White noise fills my ears until Leo places a hand on my shoulder, offering silent support.

My stepfather's face morphs from irritation to excitement when he faces Sebastian.

"Sebastian Walker?" He turns to Beck. "And Becker Hayes? My lord, what a pleasure to have you boys here. Sebastian, I used to work with your father."

"That tracks," Seb growls, but Tony Ford is too enamored by the collective wealth on his front porch to notice.

"This is quite the shock. You two are something of celebrities these days. I was reading the article on you boys in the *Wall Street Journal* just this week. Come in, come in. We weren't expecting company, but my wife can whip something together. Is this about the Westford deal? I thought you boys might want in on that." Tony's still a slimy bastard out to make a buck on the backs of others.

"What a jackass," Leo grumbles behind me.

Seb and Beck move as one, and then I'm face-to-face with Tony. His expression immediately hardens.

"What's this about, Rowan?" The tone of his voice gives away the evil he hides behind careful masks.

When I don't answer, he slips on another mask, this one with a too-charming smile, and says, "If she's done something, it's on her. I'm not claiming responsibility for anything that monster has done. Vicky," he shouts to my mom. "Get me Hayley's number."

Shutting me out of the conversation completely, he turns his venomous grin on Seb. "I'm sorry to hear about your divorce. I really think you'd love my daughter, Haley."

My mouth falls open.

"Are you for real right now?" Alexei asks.

When I peer up at Seb, I find his jaw straining, the muscles in his cheek twitching as if he's grinding his teeth.

"I wouldn't touch your pathetic narcissistic spawn if she were the last woman on earth." Seb growls the words like a rabid dog.

Tony's head is on a swivel, looking from one set of eyes to another. "Are you... What's the meaning of this?"

"Tony? What's..." My mother stops talking when she enters the foyer. "Rowan?" Her hand flies to her mouth, but a second later, she drops it and stands with Stepford-wife precision.

"What are you doing here, Rowan?" Tony shouts, and this time, I meet his angry glare with one of my own.

He's still so much taller than me, but he's older, frailer.

"You know, in my nightmares, you have actual devil horns." His hands twitch the same way they did when I was a child. He wants to backhand me. He might even try before I leave.

Instead, I enter the house. Seb and Beck follow until we're all standing in a circle in my childhood home. The double staircase my father used to chase me up and down is aged and no longer filled with happy memories.

The air is stagnant and stale.

"Rowan, what are you doing?" my mother asks in the monotone voice Tony prefers.

"I used to break myself in half to get one ounce of your love. But you never loved me, did you?" I ask her.

"We're not going down memory lane with you, Rowan. You were a problem child that needed to be dealt with, and obviously, I failed." Spittle settles in the corner of Tony's mouth. He's glaring at me, so blinded by rage he doesn't notice Sebastian step up to him until they're face-to-face.

"Call my wife a problem child again, and we'll see how well you can talk with a missing tongue." Tony's eyes widen at Sebastian's threat.

"Jesus, Seb," Beck mutters.

Wife? What the heck?

"What is it you want, Ellis?" He calls me by my last name. He used to do it when I was a child, too. It was a way of making me stand out from the family, letting me know I never truly belonged here.

"Honestly?" I say, working hard to keep my tone even. "I wanted to face my demons, the monster in preachers' clothing, and tell you that you didn't win. You didn't break me. I'm still my father's daughter." I mention my father to get a reaction out of them, and they don't disappoint. Tony's hands ball into fists, and my mother's armor cracks when tears pool in her eyes. "And you'll never see me again."

I stomp toward the door, fueled by adrenaline, when something catches my attention in the formal living room to our left. I'm standing in front of it before I can speak.

"You—" My voice cracks. "You told me you burned this," I say, holding up the cribbage board.

My mother's face pales, and Tony's flames with anger. "What is she talking about?" he roars.

Clutching it to my chest, I know it'll be coming home with me.

"Get out." My mother's voice barely carries through the small space, but I hear it.

"A mother should never be jealous of a child. You're worse than pathetic, Mother, you're useless."

"*Get out*," she screams.

"Gladly." Before I reach the door, I glare over my shoulder at Tony. "Oh, and Tony? Your precious baby girl was arrested yesterday. She's going to look fabulous in jumpsuit orange."

He steps forward, and my courage gives out. I jump for the door and stomp down the stairs, something that would have earned me a punishment as a child. Then I step on every goddamn crack in their walkway while my family surrounds me and allows me to get my feelings out.

"Row," Seb says eventually, pulling me into his chest. "We should go."

Lifting my head, I suck in gasping lungfuls of air. The guys stand around, protecting me while allowing me the meltdown I needed to have.

Leo chuckles. "My mother was kind of a bitch too." And without saying another word, he stomps on every crack between him and the Suburban.

I take one last look at the house I once called home, and with it, I take all the happy memories with me while laying all the wretched ones at its door.

This time, my goodbye is forever.

35

EASY THERE, KILLER

SEBASTIAN

"She's been in the area for a week. What do you think she's doing?" Alexei asks.

Beck groans and tosses his pen on the table. "I need my own damn office."

Despite his grouchy tone, his comment makes me chuckle. He has an office, multiple in fact, but he insists we work in his home office, and we're all aware that it's so he can be close to the kids and Stella.

"I don't know," I say, answering Alexei's question. "But I'm glad I haven't said anything to the kids. I thought she meant she wanted to see them the day she got here, but I've called twice, and she's had an excuse both times. I'm not chasing her. If she wants to see my kids, she can call me."

"She's always played mind games," Alexei grumbles. He's been particularly pissy this week but says he's fine.

"Hey, I'm here," Elijah says from a screen on the wall. He and Teddy, Crystal Waters' lead counsel, are video conferencing from Raleigh.

"The girls will be here soon," I say as Rowan and Tabby

380

walk through the door. Not a minute later, Stella and her friend Bella walk in.

Beck's home office is as big as a three-car garage, but with all of us in here, it's tight.

"Okay, what's going on?" Leo asks from the corner. He's doing the baby slide while wearing little Ryker.

"A business meeting," I say at the same time Beck says, "A family meeting."

I defer to him—it's been all hands on deck this week and we've each taken over a different area of the project.

"I'm not part of the business," Leo says, grabbing the diaper bag as though he can't wait to escape this meeting.

"No, but you're part of the family, so we need you here. And, whether you accept it or not, you do own shares in Crystal Waters," Beck says. Leo grumbles something unintelligible but goes back to his baby slide in the corner.

"Anyway, things have changed," I say.

"If we accept the deal with Blaine Industries..."

"What do you mean if?" Rowan interrupts. "Don't you have to because of Coleman?"

"No, we don't have to do anything," Beck explains, though there's no hiding how his jaw twitches. "We would take a loss, but not nearly as catastrophic as we would have without the other investors on board. After what happened with Coleman in the press, the other investors have recommitted without restrictions, but Blaine brings us into a whole new arena."

"It's a much larger-scale project than we had anticipated because they'll want to incorporate their hotels," I explain.

"That all sounds like good things to me," Tabby says with a frown.

I stand and walk to the projection on the screen showing

the forecasted growth. "It is, but it means that we'll all be busier than ever."

"We have to decide if that's what we want for our families. It will mean some initial travel, longer hours, and lots of changes for the next year," Beck explains.

Alexei jumps in, "But the long-term benefits would far outweigh the initial sacrifice."

"Says the one man without a family," Beck growls. "We're not going to take on something of this size without everyone on board. That means you all as well." He points to where Rowan, Stella, Tabby, and Bella sit huddled together.

"Well, we have each other to lean on, and a year isn't so bad," Stella says. "If it's good for the long-term sustainability of the merger, then I say go for it." Tabby and Bella nod in agreement.

"Row? What do you think?"

She jumps in her seat. "Oh, I— It's not my— I mean, I'm sure they..."

I stalk her slowly as she stumbles over an explanation. She said she chooses us, but there are still moments that freak her the fuck out and she mentally grabs her running shoes.

Granted, it's only been a week, but she made a commitment, and I'm not letting her go now.

"Your opinion matters too, Rowan, because you're a part of this family."

"Flipping mafia, I swear," she grumbles.

When I cage her in her chair, she sighs. "Fine, yes. I agree with Stella too."

Leaning in, I kiss her forehead. "Was that so hard?"

"Dad?" Seren calls, and the front door slams shut. She's

supposed to be at her friend Marlo's house, so I'm immediately on high alert.

Rowan has already slipped out from under my arms and is hurrying to the doorway.

"We're in Beck's off— Seren, what's wrong?" Rowan's words fill my veins with ice.

"M—Mom," Seren chokes.

Every single person in the room stands and leaves to give us privacy.

"Dad?" She stares up at me with sadness in her over-flowing eyes, then sets her pleading gaze on Rowan. "I saw her. I—she told me to go home. Why? Why is she here if she doesn't want to see us?"

Tugging her into my chest, I hold her tight as she balls up my shirt in her fists.

"Your mom is sick, Ser."

She nods. "I didn't think I wanted to see her." Seren chokes back a sob. "But she's my mom and…she doesn't want to see me. She's going to die, isn't she?"

I hug her tighter. "Yes."

Her nodding continues as if she's processing this information with each bob of her head.

"Are you going to tell the boys?" she asks.

"I—I'm not sure," I answer honestly. "I want to talk to the therapist because there's not a straightforward answer here, Ser."

"If she doesn't want to see us, and if I get a vote, I don't think we should tell them. It just makes it hurt more."

Closing my eyes, I suck in air through my nose until my lungs burn.

"You always get a vote, Seren," Row says quietly.

My soul dies a little. "I wish I could shield you from this heartache, baby girl."

"No," Seren says, swiping angry tears. "It's good that I know so I don't make her out to be something she's not in my head." She glares at Rowan, then her face falls before she glares again.

She has so many emotions she can't process but manages to tell us so many things in that moment with only her eyes.

"I love you, Ser. We all love you." She wrings her wrist in front of her before finally, her shoulders sag. "I know, Daddy. I—I'm going to go to the music room at camp, if that's okay."

"Do you want me to go with you?" I ask.

"No, thanks. I need…"

"I get it," I tell her. And I do, but it doesn't mean I have to like it. "But promise me that you'll talk to us, okay? We can't make the world make sense, but we can love you through the pain of it."

"I will," she promises. She turns to Rowan, and after a moment's hesitation, she buries herself in Rowan's arms.

"Ser, why don't you tell the boys to pack it up, and we'll drive you back to the house. You can head to the music room from there," I say.

Nodding, she pulls out of Rowan's embrace, or tries to anyway. Rowan hasn't quite released her. "Not yet," Rowan whispers.

With a log cutting off my airway, I go help my boys pack up their stuff.

"I'll be right back, okay, bud?"

Miles lifts his face from the puzzle we're doing together. "Sure, Dad."

Patting his arm, I walk toward the deck, where Rowan's pacing with the wind whipping her hair in every direction.

"Peach?"

She stops abruptly.

"Want to talk about it?"

She bites her lips and shakes her head.

"Are you sure? Because you kinda look like you need to talk about some stuff."

"Fine." She throws her hands into the air. "I don't know how to do this." I don't even flinch. A month ago, I would have seized at the words for fear that meant she was leaving, but now, I simply wait for her to work through the emotions she's not used to sharing with other people.

"Just say whatever you're thinking."

"I want to kill her," she blurts. "But I can't say that out loud. And I'm well aware that it's not kind and it's not right. I should probably even be giving her grace because she is, in fact, dying, but I want to wrap my hands around her neck and snuff the life right out of her for hurting Seren again."

Taking her arms in mine, I rub small circles down them until I get to her clenched hands and slowly help her relax them.

"Easy there, killer. You might want to take a break from the mafia romances." It earns me a partial smile, but Seren's pain shines brightly in Rowan's eyes. She's taking it on because she loves Seren more than she loves herself, just as a mom's supposed to love.

"I won't actually kill her," Rowan mutters. "But she can't keep hurting her this way. It's death by a thousand cuts, and it's not fair."

"I was thinking the same thing," I admit. "Well, not the killing part, but that she can't keep hurting them."

"You should go talk to her by yourself," she says. "I don't need to be there for that conversation."

"But I want you to be a part of every conversation, Peach. I want us to be a team." Hopefully she hears the honesty in my words because I'm not sure how else to explain this to her.

"I know," she says. "And it's a lot. I mean, it's good, but it's a lot, and I'm still going to try to flee sometimes, and you're going to have to let me. This is one of those times. I don't have a history with Mya, and everything I've learned about her is clouded by the hurt she's caused. You'll need to come to an agreement with her, and if I'm there I'll be a fiery ball of rage that will get you nowhere. I'm doing this for myself because I hate her, and I'm doing it for your kids because they love her. Make peace with her, Seb, so she can give your children peace."

"I'm keeping you forever." That's not what I had meant to say, but it's what I mean. Shaking my head, I smile. "I meant to say that I love you, and I love that you put us first. And I'm keeping you forever."

At least she laughs instead of runs.

"You should go find her now before Seren gets home."

I press a gentle kiss on her forehead, and I'm almost to the door when she calls out, "Seb?"

"Yeah, Peach?"

"I was twelve years old the last time I told someone that I loved them." My feet carry me back to her. "I told myself I'd never say those words again so I wouldn't ever have to experience that kind of pain when I lost them."

"I get it, and there's no pressure. I know how you feel. I see it in your every action, every touch, and every kiss. I love you."

"That's the thing."

Tilting my head, I study her. "What's the thing?"

"I love you too, and I don't know how to say it."

Game. Set. Match. My heart is forever hers.

"Sweetheart," I groan. "You just did."

Her wide eyes draw me in, and if I never hear those three little words again, I'll still die a happy man simply by this reaction alone.

"I love you?"

I nod, grinning like a damn fool.

"I guess I love you." She laughs, and we finally become whole.

———

I CALLED Mya fifteen times in a row before she finally picked up, and it took fifteen minutes to get her to agree to meet with me.

Now I'm sitting in a hotel bar, waiting for my ex-wife so I can tell her to get the hell out of my life for good.

"Seb," she says, sliding into the booth across from me. Her movements are stilted, and flashes of pain show in her expression.

I say nothing, opting for the silence to draw her gaze to mine.

When she meets my eyes, she huffs. "I didn't mean to hurt her. She wasn't supposed to recognize me."

"You're her goddamn mother," I sneer. "How would she not recognize you?"

"We both know I never earned that title. Parenthood is like preschool where everyone gets a trophy." Her lip curls in disgust. "I wanted to see them, but I never planned for any of them to get close enough to recognize me. And when I saw her, saw how happy she was, I was—I was embarrassed knowing I'd hurt her. I didn't want to cause her any more pain than I had to, so I sent her away."

"What happened to you?" This is not the woman I married. I don't even recognize this person.

"This is what happens when you live a loveless life, Sebastian. My parents never loved me and passed the tradition on to me. Then you, well, we were a good match on paper, but your heart was never in it, and neither was mine."

"Am I supposed to feel sorry for you? My father was a horrible human, who tried to raise me to be just as terrible, but I chose to be different."

"Do you want a medal?" Her words drip with condescension.

What the fuck am I even doing here.

"What's your goal here, Mya? I refuse to allow you to keep hurting them, and when they see you and you turn your back, that fucking hurts them."

She slaps her hand to the table, but she's so weak it hardly makes a noise. "I said that was an accident. She wasn't supposed to see me. She should have been focused on her friends. I didn't mean to hurt her." She sighs, and it appears to take all her energy to keep herself upright.

"How long do you have?" I ask, waiting for a morsel of grief or regret to seep into my consciousness, but it never does.

She shrugs. "I'm going back to Boston tonight. I'll be gone in a month or so."

"You're not going to say goodbye to your children?"

Mya shakes her head. If evil had a picture, she'd be it.

"This is your only chance, Mya." I clench my teeth together to keep my volume from escalating. "Come and talk to your children or don't come back at all. I mean it. If you go back to Boston, don't come back here, don't call, don't text. If you continue to play these games at their expense, I'll make the rest of your days a living hell."

I toss a fifty on the table to pay for the drinks I'd ordered and stand, but she grasps my wrist with more strength than I'd thought she had. "Take care of them," she whispers without looking up.

"I can't even begin to imagine what nightmare is playing in your head, Mya. But if there's even an ounce of love in you, leave and don't come back."

"They may hate you for that request someday."

She's always playing goddamn games.

"That's a risk I'll have to take. If warning you away from them keeps their childhoods happy and safe, then I'll take their wrath as adults when they're able to fully comprehend the actions of a mother who couldn't love anyone but herself."

She nods, and I snap my wrist away from her.

"This will protect you from my father. Consider it a parting gift of goodwill, and take care of our children." Reaching into her bag, she pulls out an envelope and hands it to me. I take it without looking, then walk out of the bar.

It takes all my willpower not to push the limits of my Tesla to get home as quickly as possible.

36

YOU CAN'T FUCK AROUND WITH DESTINY

ROWAN

"He'll be here," I whisper over Seren's head. We're both peeking out from behind the stage in the pavilion at camp—it's become the unofficial gathering place for locals since the summer programs ended.

She tilts her face up to search my eyes.

"He'll be here," I repeat. And even though my pulse is thumping erratically in my ears, I don't cross my fingers or wish on stars.

Sebastian promised he would be here, so he will.

The last two months have gone by in a fever dream.

Sebastian and the guys took on their big project and have taken turns traveling to various places, but they've planned their company around their family, not the other way around. When Seb is traveling, the other families step up to help with carpools or dinners, and we do the same for them.

Alexei returned to Boston full-time but visits at least once a month, and I'm still convinced he's in the mafia, or maybe the Bratva since his last name is Stepanov, but he denies it wholeheartedly.

"I'm nervous, Row. Really freaking nervous. The last time I was on stage I…"

Placing my hands on her shoulders, I squeeze. "I know. But we'll all be here for you."

Sadness flashes in her eyes, but it only lasts a moment. There are times, like this, when she thinks about her mom, and I do my best to be someone she can talk to when she needs me.

We attended Mya's funeral service with the kids but opted out of the wake and reception. They each said goodbye in their own way, and they each struggle with it in their own way, but we've enlisted the help of a fabulous therapist in town. James has been able to make a connection with each child, and I'm grateful for that.

Sebastian and I have made it our mission to be there for them, and I find that every morning I wake up, I want to see their smiling faces more than I want my next adventure.

I never thought I'd find peace in a small town, but it crashed into me like the waves on the shore, and each day is better than the last.

Seren glances down and runs a hand over the shimmery yellow dress she picked out. Mine is the same cut as hers but in midnight blue—night and day, the perfect accompaniment to her song.

A commotion in the crowd has us both looking up, and the nervous flutter in my belly finally settles even if they're behaving like a couple of ten-year-old kids as Sebastian and Beck trip over each other as they try to reach the front row.

"She's my daughter, Beck," Seb whisper-yells.

"Yeah, well, she's my niece, and I have the video camera." Beck holds up a small device in his hand.

"I have a freaking phone."

Tabby leans across Pappy in the front row and hisses, "Guys."

They both stand up straight and snap their mouths closed while the crowd around them snickers.

Sailport Bay has become home for us all.

Lottie sits in the second row. She arrived this morning—with Thane, which surprised me. She's here for an answer about the expansion into Europe, but I've been dragging my feet. Not because I don't think I'll stay with Seb, but because it's a dream job I'm still having a hard time letting go of.

"When we went dress shopping that time," Seren whispers, then pulls away from the curtain to look at me. "When you helped me pick out this dress, I wasn't sure you'd be here to see me wear it."

Guilt makes my ears feel hot. "I'm sorry, Ser. It was a strange time for all of us."

"But you're here. You stayed." Her voice is pitched low, and her lashes flutter against rosy cheeks.

My chin quivers, but I nod. "I did."

I've told Seren a little more about my past over the last month or so in therapy. We go as a—as a family twice a month. In as kid-friendly a way as possible, we explained why I avoided commitments and affection, but that it's something I'm working on and it's okay to work on ourselves for as long as it takes.

"I asked my dad to help me with something." She sounds nervous, which feeds my anxiety. She spins in place and spots her backpack pushed against the wall, then picks it up and retrieves a small black card.

She looks from it to me, then shoves it into my hands. It's a heavy metal card that reminds me of The Single Dad Hotline business cards, but it has a key attached to it.

"What's this?" I ask, turning it over in my hands.

"It's a ticket to anywhere, and a key to come home. So if you need to go, you'll always know where you belong." She glances down at her feet. "Dad said it's for a private plane that will legit take you anywhere." She shrugs. "So that's kinda cool. I just hope you'll take us with you, and if not, that you'll find your way home."

My chest constricts and my hands shake. They gave me the freedom to run and the love to return home.

"Ser, I'm not—"

No one has ever given without taking from me. My fingers trace the tattoo on my wrist and my left earrings. Looking out at the crowd, I know it's Sebastian. He even tugs on his left ear and winks—it's become his silent way of acknowledging that he's thinking about me ever since he learned that the superstition says a ringing left ear means someone is speaking well about you. Some superstitions are just too spot-on to make up, but if Pappy has taught me anything, it's that you can't fuck around with destiny.

"Seren, you're on, kiddo," Leo says, wrapping her in a giant hug.

She smiles, and walks to the stage, wiggling her fingers at me on the way.

Now I do cross my fingers and my toes because sometimes a girl needs all the luck she can get.

Seren takes a seat at the piano, then bows her head. All her new friends are here, but so is half the town. They fill in the pavilion and line the walkways surrounding it all in a show of support for the children with the courage to put themselves on display.

She's so much stronger than I ever was.

Her hands rest above the keys, and she lifts her head, but nothing happens.

Sebastian's gaze cuts from her to me and back again. I

can only see the side of her face from here, but her neck works to swallow, and I fear that stage fright has taken over.

I step forward as Sebastian stands up. It all happens in the span of a moment that feels as though it stretches for an eternity.

He nods for me to go, and I scurry across the stage, taking a seat with her at the piano, the same way her father did for me all those years ago. The difference is that this time no one will stop her. No one will rip her from the stage and irrevocably alter her life.

This is the moment where she can step away from her trauma and forge her own path forward, and I'm the luckiest runaway on the planet because I get to be the one to help her do it.

In a lot of ways, it's helping me too.

"Take a breath, Ser. I'm right here," I whisper, shuffling around sheets of music to create a diversion. "You've got this."

"Yeah, I kind of panicked."

"I'm right here as long as you need me. I'll flip your music sheets for you if you want me to stay."

"That's not my music," she says, staring at the pieces of paper before her.

"I know. But they don't," I say, nodding toward the crowd.

"Okay. Yeah. Thanks." She places her fingers back on her keys and leans toward the microphone. "This song is called 'Stay.' Rowan has spent the last two months helping me write it, but the song has always been about her."

My throat closes up. All this time I thought the song was a plea for her mother to come back, to stay with her.

It's about me?

Tears stream down my face as she sings.

Night and day,

But we got you to stay.

The chorus plays on repeat in my mind long after she's finished, after the crowd gives her a standing ovation, even after the talent show ends and we all find our way to the bonfire.

My life is night and day from what it was a few months ago, and there's nothing I want more than to stay.

Spotting Lottie, I immediately head in her direction, studying the interaction between her and Thane.

I thought it was suspicious when he suddenly stopped calling the hotline, but I've been so caught up in life I didn't pursue it.

They stop talking abruptly when I approach. "Everything okay?" I ask, searching both of their faces. Lottie is obviously annoyed, but Thane's expression is almost—fiery. Observing them now, it could be anger or love that's turning his face an impressive shade of red.

"Fine," Thane grits out, then spins on his heel and marches away.

I lift a brow in Lottie's direction. She shrugs and then collapses into one of the Adirondack chairs.

"It's complicated," she says preemptively.

Leaning back in the chair next to her, I laugh. "Isn't it always?"

Lottie smiles into the firelight.

"I can't take the job, Lottie. I wanted it. I'd love the work, but I've found my home, and I found love here."

She slowly lolls her head side to side. "In all the time I've known you, I've never seen you at peace. Even when you were happy, there was a riot behind your eyes I couldn't reach. All that angst is gone now."

For many years, Lottie was the only friend I had, but I

kept her at such a distance we never got as close as we probably would have otherwise.

"What do you see now?" I ask, no longer fearing answers.

"Love," she says simply.

"I feel loved," I admit.

She reaches out and squeezes my hand. "I'm happy for you, Row. Really, I am." There's a sadness in her tone that she's usually better at masking.

"Are you okay?" I ask.

"I think the hotline is in trouble."

"What?" I jump to my feet, ready to fight by her side. "What do you need me to do?"

"Shh." She tugs me back into my chair. "I don't need you to do anything. It's my own fault. My software and the science behind the questionnaire are so good, competitors are trying to copy, and in some cases, steal it. Lots of people." She hisses the word while glaring over my shoulder. When I tilt my head, I find Thane glaring back. "They think I should adopt a new business model and branch off to create a dating service with it in addition to the hotline. Something about trademarks and other stupid shit."

"You're always searching for a challenge." I bump her shoulder with mine. "And while I don't want to move to Europe right now, I would like to stay on and help you however I can."

She bolts upright, and her eyes flash faster than lightning. "That's it," she says, popping up, wrapping me in a hug, and then sprinting away from me.

"What's it?" I call after her.

She waves her hand without looking back while Thane stomps off behind her. "I'll be in touch," she calls over her shoulder. "And I accept your help. We have plans to make, Row. Big plans."

With a frustrated sigh, I stare up at the stars. I smell Pappy and his old cigar scent before he even sits down. A sense of calm washes over me, and it relaxes my entire body. I love this old man.

"You did good today, kid," he says, patting my knee.

I roll my head in his direction to find his eyes welling with tears.

"I was worried about you for a lot of years, Rowan." His voice cracks, but he holds my gaze.

"I'm sorry, Pappy. I never wanted to worry you."

"Pfft. There's nothing to be sorry about, kiddo. That's part of loving someone—the fear, the happiness, you couldn't have one without fully understanding the other. Now that you know both, make sure you hold on to all the love you deserve with both hands—especially when your mind tells you to run."

My shoulders sag. "I'm done running, Pappy."

He lifts a brow in my direction.

"I am. I never realized how exhausting it was running from my past. Now that I've had this, here, with Sebastian and you and the kids, I'm terrified of losing it."

"You can't lose us, kiddo. That's not how families work."

"Once you're in, you're in?" I joke.

"You know it." He rests his head back and clasps his folded hands over his belly.

We sit in silence until a shooting star lights up the sky.

"Make a wish, Row." He tilts his head to look at me.

"My wish already came true."

He beams at me while nodding. "I told you. It's destiny, kiddo. Plain and simple. You were always meant to be ours."

"Can't fuck with destiny." My entire body shakes with laughter.

"Nope. You can't."

"If this is my destiny, Pappy, I'll gladly take the happily ever after."

He pats my hand. "It's coming, kiddo. You just had to reach out and take it."

Squeezing his hand, I say what I should have said years ago. "I love you, Pappy. I always have and always will."

The old man blubbers and chokes on his words. It takes a full minute before he can compose himself. "I love you too, Row. Always have and always will. Now, I have to go find some damn tissues." He stands, flustered, but his expression is filled with pure joy.

Glancing around the bonfire, I find so many faces of people I'm growing to love.

Never in my lifetime did I think that a lullaby sung twenty-five years ago would lead to late nights and love lines that wrap me up with my entire future.

Late nights and love lines. It kinda sounds like a song.

EPILOGUE

ONLY TIME WILL TELL

SEBASTIAN

Ruby and Kade barrel into the conference room like the little Tasmanian devils they are. I love the friendship they've formed, even if Kade does push all of Beck's buttons by constantly reminding him that he plans to marry Ruby.

My gaze stays glued on the doorway, knowing that at any moment, the woman I said I'd marry when I was ten years old will walk through it.

And she doesn't disappoint. Her hair is as wild as ever, the salt air giving it more volume than she knows what to do with. She's still uncomfortable with the uncontrollable, but I hope her hair is never tamed.

I narrow my gaze when I find her cheeks flushed and her chest heaving.

Stella enters right behind her, holding up an empty bag. "Who's going to give us a jockstrap?"

Beck slams his laptop closed and stands abruptly. "Stella," he mutters. "What the hell are you talking about?"

"We also need a cotton-candy-flavored," Rowan cups her mouth with both hands, then whispers, "condom."

My grin grows. It's been three days since Seren's recital, and there's been a shift in our relationship since. Neither of us has commented on it, but it's there, growing and expanding to catch up with the love that hangs in the air all around us.

Even when Seren introduced her as my girlfriend to her new teacher, Rowan didn't run.

She's got twitchy fingers, and her toes tap every time she considers pulling away, but she's stayed, she's fought, and I love her all the more for it.

"I need a holey sock, a skipping stone, and a mouse," Seren says, holding up a sheet of paper.

"What's going on?" Teddy asks. He's technically Beck's general counsel, but as our companies become one, he's slowly making the transition to Meridian Waters. It's a lot more work, but he's handled it seamlessly. He's the only one Beck trusted enough to handle the Bryer-Blaine account, and as I spend more time with him, I can see why. The man doesn't have a disloyal bone in his body.

Kade pushes himself between Beck and Stella, then jumps up and down in front of him. "I need a grasshopper and a lollipop."

"Leo has the entire town in a tizzy over this scavenger hunt the camp's hosting," Stella explains. "Each age group has a different list, and everyone in town is in on it. You should see Main Street right now."

Across the room, Leo shrugs with a mischievous grin on his face. "I'm only sponsoring it. Wanda put the list together at her store. I haven't even seen them yet."

"What's the prize?" Teddy asks with his face buried in his computer screen.

Every head in the room turns to him.

"Besides bragging rights?" Beck says with a scoff, as though bragging rights are the only reason to do it. "The adult winner also gets to choose the theme for the fall send-off."

"Marlo said it's the biggest party of the year," Seren says, practically bouncing on her toes. "It's a send-off for the tourists, and the town celebrates another great summer season."

"You guys sure do love your parties around here," Teddy says with a grin. According to Beck, he's still adjusting to small-town life.

"You have no idea." Elijah smirks. Though he lives in Raleigh, he's been staying in Sailport Bay while we sort through this merger with Bryer-Blaine, and he understands how this town works.

"But the send-off is really just the lead-up to the *Sailport Games*," Beck explains, then begins pacing behind his chair. "It's Sailport Bay versus Sailport, South Carolina, and having the ability to pick the theme is crucial. The winner from Sailport Bay then faces off against the winner of Sailport in the winter games, and Sailport has been trying to cheat their way into a win since I was a kid."

Teddy groans. "Are you telling me we're putting another workday on hold to finish a scavenger hunt? I love this town, don't get me wrong, but we have a tight turnaround time here, Beck."

"No, we're not putting the workday on hold." Beck grunts. "We're going to kick ass at this scavenger hunt during the day and then work all night if we have to. The hunt changes daily for one week."

I lift my brows at him.

"What?" he grumbles. "We can't let Sailport win. They're a bunch of cheaters."

"Yeah, Dad. Come on. We have to win." Seren grins and tugs on my arm.

I hold up my hands in surrender. "Rowan and I are leaving for New York this afternoon. The scavenger hunt is all you guys."

Leo shakes his head, mumbling about shit to do, but then Kade pushes into his lap. "It's okay if you're not a winner, Uncle Leo. We'll still love you."

And just like that, the switch is flipped on my friend. "I know how to win, Kade," Leo chuckles. "And since I'm on kid duty while your dad's in New York, looks as though we're going to have to win one for the team."

Beck scoffs. "You're not going to win."

"Why not?"

The tension in the room builds as we watch a silent war break out between Leo and Beck, then, without warning, Beck slides his hand across the conference room table, sending papers and pens flying before he sprints from the room.

"Because I'm going to win the whole freaking thing this time," he calls over his shoulder.

"I..." Stella snaps her mouth shut. "That's the least Beck Hayes thing I've ever seen my husband do."

"Give me your list, Row." Leo snatches it from her hand and follows Beck outside with my kids in tow.

"What the heck was that?" Rowan asks, her shoulders shaking with laughter.

"I guess we still have a lot to learn about our new hometown." I kiss her forehead before she can reply. "Let's go talk to Lottie before we have to head to New York, Peach."

"You're sure Leo can handle the kids?"

"I know he can," I say easily. "And if he can't, Beck, Stella, and Tabby will be right there to back him up."

Rowan's eyes light up. "I love it here, Seb. It's overwhelming and chaotic, but so full of love and happiness I never thought would be part of my life."

"Peach." My tone carries a thick thread of emotion. "The love and chaos are here for you today and all of your tomorrows."

She buries her head in my chest, so I wrap my arms around her and hold her close.

"We should get back to the house," I say, checking my watch. "Lottie will be there any minute."

"I still don't know what her plan is."

Taking her hand in mine, I lead her from Beck and Stella's house. "There's only one way to find out."

––––––––

ROWAN

I STARE at my friend sitting across from me at the kitchen table, still trying to process what she's telling me.

"You're the only one I trust to take over The Single Dad Hotline. You understand the process and can make the matches," Lottie says again.

"Yeah, I got that part," I mutter. "I'm still trying to wrap my head around that thing you keep trying to gloss over. Someone is trying to steal your intellectual property. Are you sure?"

"Everyone wants it," Thane says in his monotone voice that's even more unsettling face-to-face.

"Even you?" I challenge.

"Especially me." When I frown, he leans closer to the table, studying my face. "You're upset by that answer."

"Yeah, I'm upset. You just admitted that you're no better than whoever is trying to steal from my friend and yet, here you are, sitting at her side."

"Row." Lottie gentles her voice while Thane seems to literally memorize every inch of my face. "Thane doesn't—um..."

"I don't process feelings the same way that you do." He throws it out there as if he's commenting on the weather. "I want her data and the science behind her matchmaking test because I want to study it, make it available to other people who may not...view the world the same way everyone else does. But I'm not trying to steal it away from her."

His little speech might be compelling if it didn't sound as though he were reading numbers on the stock exchange.

"You want Rowan to take over your position at the hotline, and then what? What's your next step?" Sebastian asks.

"I've worked too hard to have some middle-aged assholes steal my ideas simply because they have the means to do so. That's how my father operates, and I'm not standing for it anymore. If I can entrust the hotline to Rowan, then I'll go to war against everyone in the tech industry who believes they can simply take from people with no repercussions." Lottie's face is red and splotchy by the time she's done speaking.

"But how do you plan to do that?" Seb asks again.

"By rolling out my product to the masses and staying ahead of the slimeballs currently attempting to replicate my data. Honestly, I don't have all the details worked out yet. I know I'll need to invest in the actual technology, but I have to raise that capital first. Elijah said—"

"I told you I'd front the money," Thane says while brushing his hands across the table. He scrunches up his face when his hand comes away covered in crumbs from Kade's breakfast.

Lottie turns to face him, and I brace for the impact of her words. I've known her long enough to know what's coming. "Listen very carefully, Thane. And watch my face so you fully understand my meaning. If you ever attempt to throw money at my problems again, I will physically remove you from this conversation myself."

It's interesting how he scans her face as she speaks. It's as though he truly is missing a connection between the words and the feelings behind them.

"That would be a physical impossibility. I outweigh you by at least eighty pounds, and I have over twelve inches on you." His words are so...factual and straightforward. I almost expect Lottie to lose her shit, but she blows out a harsh breath while her nostrils flare.

"It was a figure of speech, Thane," she says, but I can tell the effort it took to keep her tone even.

"Not to interrupt whatever is happening here," Sebastian says with a smirk.

"She's said something you find amusing?" Thane asks.

Lottie pinches the bridge of her nose. What the heck is going on between these two? I've never seen her exercise this much patience with anyone before.

Sebastian ignores Thane's commentary. "Your plan is to invest in a technology company, one that's not owned by Thane." He raises his brow, and when Lottie nods, he continues. "But Thane will be involved in...some way?"

"Unfortunately, he understands the technological aspects in a way I don't. Not yet anyway. But I built this company. It's important to me that it stays mine regardless of how I utilize what I've created."

Sebastian taps his fingers against the table, drawing my attention away from my friend and her odd new relationship.

"I may have a solution," Seb says. "It sounds as though you're willing to partner, at least in some way, with Rowan, correct?"

"She's the only one I trust besides my brother," Lottie grumbles.

"I've said that you can trust me." Thane furrows his brows as he stares at her.

"You also bought the house next door to me in an attempt to gain my trust. And I told you, that's fucking weird," she hisses.

Now Thane looks thoroughly confused. "I was under the impression we'd moved on from that."

Lottie drops her forehead to the table with a dull thud.

"Ah, as I was saying," Sebastian interrupts again. "If you're willing to partner with Rowan, and if that's what she wants, I'll make a deal with you that will, I believe, allow you to move forward as you wish to."

My friend slowly lifts her head to stare at my amazing boyfriend. A little shiver works through my body every time the word boyfriend crosses my mind. Sebastian Walker is my boyfriend.

What is this life I'm living?

"What's your deal?" Thane asks, pulling out his laptop from the bag at his feet. His gaze lifts to mine. "I need to take notes. I see things in black and white, and this helps me process."

I nod and smile at him. For so many weeks I was annoyed with this man, and perhaps I'd been unfair to him.

But there's something about the way that he looks at Lottie that lets me know he's pushing himself beyond his realm of comfort to be here, with her, and that makes him okay in my book.

Well, I might need to look into this little house-stalking issue of his, but otherwise, he might be good for her.

"That's fine, Thane," I say with a smile.

"My ex-wife." Sebastian still can't say her name without growling. He clears his throat and tries again. "She made a last-ditch effort to save her soul, or maybe she was trying to protect my kids. Anyway, when I married her, I purchased five percent stock in her father's company. Each of my children inherited ten percent when they were born. Mya has always owned twenty percent, but in her last few months, managed to acquire another ten percent without her father knowing."

This isn't news to me. He'd told me as soon as he'd opened the envelope she'd given him, explaining that even though her behavior was vile, she wanted to be sure they'd always be taken care of. He's sure it was a way to ease her guilty conscience, but I'm choosing to see it as her loving her kids the only way she knew how. But even knowing what Mya did, I don't know where he's going with this any more than Lottie does.

"Her father never changed the terms of my children's inheritance. I assume that was because it never occurred to him that Mya wouldn't will her shares and executive powers of my children's shares back to him when she passed. But she didn't. She willed it all to me. I now control sixty-five percent and am the majority stakeholder of The Fitzgerald Group."

"That's perfect. Perfect," Thane mumbles while poking away at his keyboard with his two pointer fingers.

"I'm not sure I follow," Lottie says. I nod in agreement.

"The Fitzgerald Group is, or was, in the top ten tech companies in the United States. It's been mismanaged," Thane says robotically. "But the company has the infrastructure that you require, and with the right people behind it, could be wildly successful."

"What exactly are you suggesting, Seb?" I ask.

"I want nothing to do with that company, but I don't want it to sink either—my children may feel differently about their mother's inheritance someday. So what I'm proposing is selling my shares, at a deeply discounted rate, to Lottie. With the understanding that I'll vote on behalf of my children's shares however she needs, as long as Thane has a hand in bringing that company back from the brink of foreclosure. And that we oust Fitzgerald and his lackey Nick, of course."

"Brilliant. That's a brilliant plan." Thane's nodding excessively. I think it might be the most expressive I've ever seen the man.

"Why would you do that, though?" Lottie asks, crossing her arms over her chest. It's a defensive move I rarely see her make.

Sebastian smiles. "Because I love Rowan, and she loves you. And because I've been sitting on this company for months now with no ideas for how to move forward. This kills two birds with one stone. It gives Rowan a career she loves, it's a giant fuck you to the two people left in my life who think they can screw me over and come out on top, and because if the rumors are true, whatever it is that Thane's working on will carry over to every project he touches, and that will ensure a very secure future for my children."

He lifts his brow in her direction. "Is that reason enough?" he asks gently.

"Yes," Thane grumbles. "A simple 'because I want to' would have covered it."

Lottie rolls her eyes, then the weight she's been carrying on her shoulders appears to lift with the twitch of her lips.

"It looks like we're going into business together then."

She holds out her hand, but I run around the table and hug her tightly.

"This is going to be amazing," I whisper. "Thank you for trusting me with your baby."

"Thank you for being my friend," she whispers back through a cloud of emotion. "It's going to be a ton of work."

"We can handle it," Thane says.

Lifting my gaze to his, I find him watching our interaction with something close to longing sheltered behind his eyes. I almost feel sorry for him. And when Lottie turns and wraps her arms around his middle, I know there's more than business brewing between my friend and the elusive tech billionaire, Thane Wilder.

Only time will tell how it all plays out.

Looking for more single-parent romances?

Check out the following:

Cross My Heart—a single dad, small-town romance.

Your Last First Kiss—a single mom, found family romance.

Love Notes & Lifelines—Beck and Stella's story.

BONUS SCENE
A HAPPILY EVER AFTER

SEBASTIAN

"She's going to be here any minute now, Dad." Seren stands behind a frame that's been painted to look like a broken mirror while the merry meddlers put the finishing touches on all of the ladders we've borrowed.

We may be tempting fate with the theme of this year's festival, but no one was willing to take the chance and actually break all the mirrors we have hanging throughout the town square.

"I know. I'm almost ready."

Tabby ties some sort of sash across my chest. When I told everyone that my plan was to propose to Rowan tonight, amidst all her superstitions, Tabby was the one to insist that I dress as Prince Charming.

"It'll offset all the bad luck you're tempting."

Her response still makes me chuckle. What Tabby didn't understand was that we'd already outrun all the bad luck. The only thing in store for Rowan and me was a long happily ever after.

"What would you have done if I hadn't let you confiscate my scavenger hunt prize and pick this year's theme?" Beck asks with a chuckle. "You know, my idea of *The Wizard of Oz* would have made a great theme too."

Leo groans. "We tied, Beck. You and I tied, so you wouldn't have been choosing anything. Let Sebastian have his day."

"We did not tie. I was very clearly over the finish line first. You shouldn't have even been participating because you're the one who sponsored the entire event."

"Guys," Bella interrupts. "Stella will be here with Rowan in five minutes. Is everyone ready?"

My found family scatters before I can say a word. They all get into position while the townspeople mill about. They're all in on it today. Everyone has a role to play, and by the time Rowan has made it through the maze of omens, I'll be waiting on bended knee. She's the only good luck charm I'll ever need again.

Now I just have to get her to say yes.

———

ROWAN

"I thought you hated that cat," Stella says from the doorway to the family room.

I stand in a huff. The truth is, I didn't want to like the little fucker, but if ever there was an animal who captured my spirit, it would be Lucky.

Lucky, the black freaking cat, is me in feline form. Go figure.

"He's made it abundantly clear that he isn't going

anywhere, so I figured we should at least make him comfortable," I mutter.

Stepping back from the new cat tree I assembled, I can sort of see why she'd think I've softened toward the beast. Lucky currently has six cat beds in our house, and now there's a basket of toys that rivals Kade's in the kitchen.

"And you like him," Stella teases. "It's okay, your secret is safe with me."

Lucky rubs himself along the insides of my ankles.

"Fine, I like the little jerk."

"Has Sebastian seen your costume yet?" she asks, giving me a once-over.

I hadn't intended on being a sexy witch, but that's what arrived in the mail this afternoon, and if I'm being honest, a witch is fitting after spending so many years surviving by adopting every superstition known to man.

"Not yet," I say with a grin.

"He's going to love it as much as he hates it, but there's no going back now. We have to leave, or we'll be late."

Stella is dressed as Morticia Addams, and everything about it is wrong. Stella is literal sunshine, and seeing her in head-to-toe black, complete with black lipstick, is just too much.

"You should have dressed up as a Care Bear or something," I tell her. "I'm not sure how to handle sour Stella."

She laughs, and it's so at odds with her costume I can't help but join her.

"Beck wanted a specific theme for today, so we're all dressed as the Addams family."

I peer down at my costume and say a silent prayer that a nipple doesn't pop out. It's supposed to be a family affair, after all.

"I wonder why Seb didn't want to do a family costume, and why is everyone else helping at the festival and we were told to come late? Is there something going on I should know about?"

Stella's lashes flutter wildly as she looks everywhere but directly at me.

"Stella?"

"Please, please don't make me lie to you. They've been working on this all week. Can we just go, and you can see for yourself?"

My chest expands sharply, but it's restricted by the corset top I'm wearing. "Should I be nervous?"

"No. Everyone loves you," she says, dragging me by my arm out the door.

"Is that a...Stella. Why is there a freaking horse and carriage in my driveway?"

"Sebastian wanted it to be special. So please don't tell me you're allergic to horses or something."

Biting my lip to keep my chin from trembling, I follow her to the carriage, where a local teen I recognize from the grocery store waits for us.

"Good evening, Miss Stella, Miss Rowan."

Taking his hand, I step into the open carriage and sit next to Stella while she makes small talk with the kid.

What the hell is Sebastian up to?

My mind creates story after story for the five-minute ride into town, but nothing could have prepared me for what I find waiting at the town center.

"What the hell?" I ask, jumping out of the carriage, not even waiting for assistance.

The town is centered around a small park that's usually well-lit, but right now it's completely dark—except for one lamppost. Seren stands at the park entrance, dressed as a genie, or maybe a fortune-teller. Behind her, the entire entrance is blocked by open ladders.

"What's going on, Ser?"

It takes a few more seconds for Stella to catch up to me, but she just gives me a hug, ducks under one of the ladders, and disappears into the darkness while my heart freaking stops.

"Here you go," Seren says, handing me a card. Glancing down, I'm shocked to find a tarot card with a ladder on it. Below the picture, it says: *Stepping through the past.*

"Go on. Follow the trail. You'll know what to do."

"You want me to willingly walk under a ladder? Do you know how much bad luck that causes?"

"My dad thought you'd say that." She leans forward and turns the card over in my hands.

On the back of the card, it says: *We make our own luck, Peach. Step into our future with me.*

Well, shit.

"If I do this and end up in the gallows, I'll never forgive your father. You tell him that for me, okay? I'll come back and haunt every second of his life."

Seren gives me a gentle nudge. Squeezing my eyes shut tightly, I run underneath the stupid green ladder. I don't stop until I'm a good twenty feet on the other side of it.

"You did it. Keep going, Row." Seren's face breaks out into the most sunshiny smile I've ever seen on the kid. "Follow the path. And make sure you step on every crack."

My brow furrows when she turns and walks away, leaving me alone in the park. Where the heck is everyone?

Following the path that crisscrosses the park, another lamppost flickers to life. Below it is a sign with black balloons tied to it. As I get closer, I see the sign says: *Pick up your cards, they'll show you your future.*

"Seb?" I call out and am met with silence. A shiver runs through my body, a mix of fear and excitement, so I continue walking, and within seconds I find the first card laid carefully across a crack.

Picking it up, I smile at the next tarot card. This one has a photo of me and Seren at her recital in the center of it, and my eyes tear up. There's another lying on the path up ahead, so I hurry to it.

"Don't forget to step on the cracks," someone yells from the shadows.

Backing up, I step on the crack, then hurry to the next card. The second card has a photo of me and Miles with our new metal detectors. The third is of me and Kade wearing mud masks. I don't feel the tears sliding down my cheeks until I hiccup—the emotions of the night fighting to escape.

Up ahead, another lamppost illuminates. "You did it, Row-Row."

Lifting my head from the cards in my hands, I find Kade standing up ahead, dressed as a pirate.

"I did what, Kade?"

"You found me, silly. Here you go." He hands me another tarot card. This one contains a broken mirror, with me on one side of the crack, and Sebastian on the other. "Keep going, Row-Row. Miles is waiting for you."

I'm slightly lightheaded as I bend down to press a kiss on his little head. "You're a great pirate, Kade."

His grin shines from ear to ear. "Thanks. Love ya." He spins on his heel and runs ahead of me while I follow the path, clutching the cards to my chest.

I freeze in place when I round the next corner as another lamppost lights up. Thousands of mirrors hang from trees, light posts, and benches, but a full belly laugh nearly doubles me over when I notice that some of them have glass clings that make them appear cracked, and some of them have been painted.

"No one wanted to actually break the mirrors?" I call out.

"No way," Miles says quietly, stepping out from the shadows. "Daddy said that was going too far."

He runs to me with open arms, and I brace myself for impact. It's only recently that he's started showing affection the way his little brother does, and every time he does it, my heart grows too big for my chest.

When Miles pulls away, he hands me another card. "I love you, Rowan."

Those dang tears start fresh. "I love you too, buddy. Your Secret Service costume came out amazing! Auntie Stella did an incredible job."

He touches his fake earpiece with a nod. "I've secured the package," he says with a grin before excitedly poking the card in my hand.

This one has a broken clock in the center, and I frown while studying it. I'm not sure what this one means.

"It was 12:28 when Daddy saw you again at Uncle Leo's camp."

A lump forms in my throat. The clock on the card is stopped at 12:28. When I don't speak, Miles hugs my leg. "Daddy said he knows it because his Apple Watch set off a heart rate warning when you got out of your Jeep."

A sob escapes from deep in my throat.

"It's okay, Rowan. James said it's okay to cry happy tears and sad tears. Are these happy tears?"

Freaking James, the child psychologist, has been a lifesaver.

"They're such happy tears, buddy. I've never been so happy in all my life."

The worry that was pulling at his face eases into a beautiful smile. "Okay, good." He gives me a gentle nudge forward. "Keep going then, Row. You're almost to the party."

"I love you, Miles. So very much."

"I know," he laughs. "You're the best Rowan in the entire world."

"And you're the very best Miles I've ever met."

One more gentle shove, and he takes off into the dark. I have no doubt that our found family is lurking in the shadows, pulling all the strings to make this happen…whatever this ends up being.

Suddenly the entire park is lit up with lampposts flickering on and fairy lights strung through the trees and bushes. Straight ahead, Sebastian stands, looking as though he stepped straight out of a children's book of fairytales.

I walk toward him only to be stopped by Pappy emerging from my left.

"Seems like a lifetime of bad luck has finally led you home, sweetheart."

Meeting him halfway, I wrap my arms around him and allow my tears to flow freely.

"You're free, Rowan. There's not a superstition or a bad omen in the world that can keep you from your happily ever after. You just have to make the decision to take it." Stepping back from my embrace, Pappy hands me two more cards.

The first is a photo of myself I've never seen before. I'm probably ten or eleven, and I'm clearly crying. But it's the little boy sitting next to me that has my attention. Little Sebastian has the same expression on his face that he did when he found me sitting on his porch at the welcome home party. He looks like he'll burn the world to the ground if he can only stop my tears.

The second card is a photo of the Walkers surrounding me on the sofa while we watched *Inside Out* as a family for the first time. I remember being struck by how often I felt called out by that movie. In the photo, I'm staring down at the boys, who are both cuddled up on my right. Seren sits to my left with Sebastian next to her, but he's staring straight at me with the same expression he had from the other card.

Sebastian Walker has loved me for three-quarters of my life.

Beck must have taken this from his perch on the chair across the room from us.

"And now," Pappy says, drawing my attention back to him. "Now you choose."

A final lamppost lights up, and Sebastian steps back until it illuminates his entire face. Then he falls to one knee, and I burst out laughing when I finally notice that he's planted himself underneath hundreds of upside-down horseshoes.

Sebastian curls one finger in a come-hither motion, and I'm helpless but to follow.

When I'm close enough to read his eyes, the ground nearly drops out from beneath me as he pulls a ring box out of his pocket.

"Rowan Ellis, we don't need good luck. We don't have to heed every superstition. In fact, we don't have to play by anyone's rules but our own. From this day forward, we make our own luck with the love and trust we have for one another. You, my beautiful Peach, are the only person I see my future with, and it would make me the happiest man on earth if you would give me all of your tomorrows...as my wife. Will you marry me, Rowan? Will you be my partner, my wife, for the rest of our days?"

I sway on my feet, and he leaps to his. I'm in his arms before I've even blinked.

"I love you, Peach. I love you today, and I'll love you

tomorrow. I'll spend every day of my life showing you where you belong because that's our destiny. You were always meant to be mine, just as I was fated to be yours. Marry me. Give me your todays and tomorrows, and I'll promise to give you a lifetime of love and trust and friendship."

"Did she say yes?" Kade squeals, breaking free of Beck's hold and charging toward us. It causes a chain reaction, and the rest of our family steps forward while the town fills in the gaps around us. "Well, did ya? Did ya, Row-Row?"

My gaze darts from Kade to Pappy. Then to Miles and Seren before finally falling back to Sebastian. I can barely see any of them through my tears.

Sebastian uses his thumbs to clear the tear tracks, but it's a useless endeavor. The floodgates have opened a path to happiness, and I clutch it with both hands.

"Yes. I say yes. I promise to give you all my todays and all my tomorrows for the rest of my life."

Sebastian slams his lips down on mine in a punishing kiss that tastes like home and still manages to slide a ring I haven't even looked at onto my ring finger.

He kisses me once, twice, three more times before resting his forehead against mine.

"I love you," he whispers. "So damn much. You've just made me the happiest man on earth."

I swallow hard, and open my mouth to respond, but he subtly shakes his head. I watch as he carefully folds up the sleeve on his right arm, then peels back a bandage and turns his wrist over to me.

There, on his skin, is the mirror image of my peach tattoo.

Sebastian takes my hand and entwines our fingers together. That's when I realize that when he holds my hand, the tattoo on my left wrist lines up perfectly with its twin on his right wrist.

"You are my Peach, for today and all my tomorrows." He lifts our joined hands and shouts into the crowd, "She said yes!"

Everyone moves in a blur of colors. We're embraced on all sides by the people who love us most and I finally, finally understand what it means to belong because here, with these people, and by Sebastian's side, I choose happiness. Now and forever.

Maybe I had to go through all the heartache and pain of life to fully appreciate the gift of love. It's a gift I'll never take for granted, and it's one I'll cling to for all my days.

The love lines I spent a lifetime avoiding have finally become the lifeline that guided me home.

———

Are you curious about those gala sisters, Sloane, Tilly, and Emory? You're in luck because they each have a story of their own!

Tilly: Without a Hitch
Emory: Saving His Heart
Sloane: Romancing His Heart

ACKNOWLEDGMENTS

My family: I wouldn't be here without them. Thank you for putting up with my chaotic schedules and for loving me even when I feel unlovable. It's been a tough year for us, but like Pappy said in this story, you can't fuck with destiny...ours is just still being written.

My publishing team at TWSS: I'm forever thankful you took a chance on me and continue to help me grow as an author and as a businesswoman. Me and my three-year plans appreciate you.

Team Avery: Thank you for being the solid foundation of all things Avery Maxwell. I'll never be able to be a one-woman show, and I appreciate you sticking with me through all my ups and downs.

My support system: You know who you are, and I make it through the tough days of authoring because of your support, your kindness, and your ability to kick my ass into gear when all I want to do is wallow. Your friendship means the world to me.

My readers: My dear readers! None of this would be possible without you. From the Luvables in my reader group, to the readers who respond to my newsletter week after week, I appreciate you. Your confidence in me as a person and as an author and your unwavering support is what keeps me going. Thank you for being the very best part of authoring.

Jessica Snyder and her team at HEA Author Services: You make me a better author. From coaching calls, middle of the night DMs, mastermind meetings, and everything in between, thank you for pushing me, encouraging me, and supporting me in my effort to level up.

Kari March Designs: Kari, you bring my books to life in picture form, and you knock it out of the park every time. Thank you for being so easy to work with and for being the very best at what you do.

GET TO KNOW AVERY!

Hello, Luvs!

Want to hang out with me? I'm in The Luv Club every day sharing my chaos, my mess, my life. Pop in to say hi, meet the other luvables, and stay a while. It's the happiest, kindest, messiest, most inclusive group on the internet and I'd LUV to see you there!

https://geni.us/AverysLUVclub

ALSO BY AVERY MAXWELL

Standalone Romance:

Without A Hitch

Your Last First Kiss

Falling Into Forever

The Westbrooks Series:

Book 1 - Cross My Heart

Book 2 - The Beat of My Heart

Book 3 - Saving His Heart

Book 4 - Romancing His Heart

Book 5 - One Little Heartbreak - A Westbrook Novella

Book 6 - One Little Mistake

Book 7 - One Little Lie

Book 8 - One Little Kiss

Book 9 - One Little Secret

Single Dad Hotline Series:

Book 1 - Love Notes & Lifelines

Book 2 - Late Nights & Love Lines